PRAISE

MW01110374

"One of the most ⟨
stories ever written. . . . ~~The deciphering of Stern's past~~
which reveals him to have been an incurable idealist,
plunges the reader into a hall-of-mirrors world. . . . By a
wave of his storyteller's wand Whittemore turns the
whole operation into an exploration of the options for
good and evil thrown up in terrifying times."
Publishers Weekly

PRAISE FOR THE JERUSALEM QUARTET

"Whittemore's colorful characters wrestle fitfully with
meaninglessness, time, and the grim realities of war.
Sinai Tapestry ends with a portrait of the Turks' 1922
genocidal assault on Smyrna that sobers up the reader
like a jackboot at a sock-hop. As the Quartet progresses,
the novels become less playful, their earlier flights of fantasy increasingly tempered by failure and pain into a
resigned yet mystic melancholy . . . . Though the geopol-
itics of the Middle East always loom in the background,
Whittemore is constantly probing for the gaps and loops
in time. As in Gabriel Garcia Marquez's *One Hundred
Years of Solitude*, characters return in name and shape
through their progeny, while people, events, and certain
phrases are regularly reintroduced, giving you the feeling that you are wandering through a labyrinth of memory. The Jerusalem Quartet is rich with homegrown the-
ology, and leaves you with a mystic taste for the empty
network of all things: 'All lives are secret tapestries that
swirl and sweep through the years with souls and strivings as the colors, the threads. And there may be little
knots of tangled meaning everywhere beneath the surface, tying the colors and threads together, but the little
knots aren't important finally, only the sweep itself, the
tapestry as a whole.' "
The Voice Literary Supplement

NILE SHADOWS

BY EDWARD WHITTEMORE

Quin's Shanghai Circus (1974)
Sinai Tapestry (1977)
Jerusalem Poker (1978)
Nile Shadows (1983)
Jericho Mosaic (1987)

NILE

SHADOWS

by Edward Whittemore

Introduction by Ben Gibberd

With a Foreword by Tom Wallace
and an Afterword by Judy Karasik

OLD EARTH BOOKS
Baltimore, Maryland
2002

NILE SHADOWS

ACKNOWLEDGEMENTS

The essay, "An Editorial Relationship" also appeared in AGNI 55, Spring 2002

Published by
Old Earth Books
Post Office Box 19951
Baltimore, Maryland 21211
www.oldearthbooks.com

Original Interior Book Design by A. Christopher Simon

Book Production: Old Earth Books Edition
Garcia Publishing Services
Post Office Box 1059
Woodstock, Illinois 60098
www.american-fantasy.com

10 9 8 7 6 5 4 3 2 1

ISBN: 1-882968-24-7

PRINTED IN THE UNITED STATES OF AMERICA
By Thomson-Shore
Dexter, Michigan

FOR JANE

Contents

Foreword: "Edward Whittemore (1933-1995)"   xv
by Tom Wallace

"Nile Shadows: *The Improbable Art*   xxix
of Edward Whittemore" by Ben Gibberd

PART ONE

1 An Australian Hand Grenade   3
2 The Purple Seven Armenian   8
3 Hopi Mesa Kiva   35

PART TWO

4 Vivian   61
5 Liffy   81
6 Sphinx   98
7 Monastery   110
8 Maud   136
9 Menelik   144
10 Ahmad   154
11 Trombone   176
12 Beggar   200

PART THREE

13 Cohen   215
14 Bletchley   240
15 The Sisters   247
16 Two Candles   297
17 Mementos   310
18 Crypt/Mirror   321

PART FOUR

19 *A Golden Bell and a Pomegranate*   365
20 *A Gift of Faces, a Gift of Tongues*   372
21 *Purple Seven Moonlight*   389
22 *Bernini's Bag*   417
23 *Nile Echoes*   431

Afterword: 461
"An Editorial Relationship" by Judy Karasik

Photo: Musa Farhi

Edward Whittemore (1933-1995)

"Some twenty years after the end of the war with Japan a freighter arrived in Brooklyn with the largest collection of Japanese pornography ever assembled in a Western tongue. The owner of the collection, a huge, smiling fat man named Geraty, presented a passport to customs officials that showed that he was a native-born American about as old as the century, an exile who had left the United States four decades before." Thus begins *Quin's Shanghai Circus*; it ends with the largest funeral procession held in Asia since the thirteenth century.

The year was 1974, the author Edward Whittemore, a forty-one year-old former American intelligence agent; he and I had been undergraduates at Yale back in the 1950s, but then we had gone our separate ways, he to the CIA and I to a career in book publishing in New York City. Needless to say, I was pleased that my old Yale friend had brought his novel to me and the publishing house of Holt, Rinehart and Winston where I was editor-in-chief of the Trade Department. I was even more delighted when the reviews, mostly favorable, started coming in, capped by Jerome Charyn in *The New York Times Book Review*: "*Quin* was a profoundly nutty book full of mysteries, truths, untruths, idiot savants, necrophiliacs, magicians, dwarfs, circus masters, secret agents . . . a marvelous recasting of history in our century."

In the next fifteen years Whittemore went on to write four more wildly imaginative novels, his Jerusalem Quartet: *Sinai Tapestry, Jerusalem Poker, Nile Shadows,* and *Jericho Mosaic.*

Reviewers and critics compared his work to the novels of Carlos Fuentes, Thomas Pynchon, and Kurt Vonnegut. *Publishers Weekly* called him "our best unknown novelist." Jim Hougan, writing in *Harper's Magazine*, said Whittemore was "one of the last, best arguments against television.... He is an author of extraordinary talents. . . . The milieu is one in which readers of espionage novels may think themselves familiar, and yet it is totally transformed by the writer's wild humor, his mystical bent, and his bicameral perception of time and history."

Edward Whittemore died from prostate cancer in the summer of 1995 at the age of sixty-two, not much better known than when he began his short, astonishing.writing career in the early 1970s. His novels never sold more than 5000 copies in hard covers, three were briefly available in mass market paperback editions. But the Quartet was published in Great Britain, Holland, and Germany where Whittemore was described on its jacket as the "master American storyteller." The jacket on the Polish edition of *Quin's Shanghai Circus* was a marvelous example of Japanese erotica.

*

Whittemore graduated from Deering High School, Portland, Maine in June 1951 and entered Yale that fall, a member of the Class of 1955. Another Yale classmate, the novelist Ric Frede, labeled Yale undergraduates of the 1950s "members of the Silent Generation." The Fifties were also the "Eisenhower Years" that comfortable period between the Second World War and the radicalism and the campus unrest of the 1960s. Ivy League universities were still dominated by the graduates of New England prep schools. Sons of the East Coast "establishment," they were closer to the Princeton of F. Scott Fitzgerald and the Harvard of John P. Marquand then the worlds of Jack Kerouac and Allen Ginsberg. They were "gentlemen" and athletes but not necessarily scholars. Often after receiving "gentlemanly C's" at Yale and the other Ivys, they went on to careers on Wall Street or in Washington; to the practice of law medicine or journalism. They entertained their families and friends on the playing fields of Yale as well as at Mory's. They ran *The Yale Daily News*, WYBC (the campus radio station), *The Yale Record* (the humor magazine), *The Yale Banner* (the year book), and sang in various Yale music groups. They were usually members of a fraternity and were "tapped" by one of the six secret Senior Societies.

By the Yale standards of the day, Whittemore was a great success, a "high school boy" who made it. Affable, good-looking and trim, he presented a quizzical smile to the world. He casually wore the uniform that was "in": herringbone tweed jacket, preferably with patches at the elbow, rep tie, chinos and scruffy white buck shoes. In a word, he was "shoe" (short for "white shoe," a term of social approval). He was not much of an athlete, but he was a member of Zeta Psi, a fraternity of hard-drinking, socially well-connected undergraduates. At the end of Junior year he was tapped for Scroll and Key.

But his real distinction was that he was the Managing Editor of the 1955 *Yale News* Board at a time when *News* chairmen and managing editors were as popular as football team captains and the leading scholar of the class. During the immediate postwar years and the 1950s the *Yale News* produced such prominent writer-journalists as William F. Buckley, James Claude Thomson, Richard Valeriani, David McCullough, Roger Stone, M. Stanton Evans, Henry S.F. Cooper, Calvin Trillin, Gerald Jonas, Harold Gulliver, Scott Sullivan, and Robert Semple. They would make their mark at *The New York Times*, *The New Yorker*, *Time*, *Newsweek*, *The National Review*, *Harper's*, and the television networks, and go on to write many books.

*

I met Ted early in the spring of Freshman year. We were both "heeling" the first *News* "comp," and as was usually the case with survivors of that fierce "competition" to make the *News*, we remained friends throughout our years at Yale. It was assumed by many of us on the *News* that Ted would head for Wall Street and Brown Brothers Harriman, a blue-chip investment firm where Old Blues from Scroll and Key were more than welcome and where Ted's older brother later worked. Or at the very least, he would get on the journalistic fast-track somewhere in the *Time-Life* empire founded by an earlier *News* worthy, Henry Luce.

But we were wrong. Whittemore, after a tour of duty as an officer in the Marines in Japan, was approached there by the CIA, given a crash course in Japanese, and spent more than a decade working for the Agency in the Far East, Europe and the Middle East.

During those years Whittemore would periodically return to New York. "What are you up to?" one would ask. For a while he was running a newspaper in Greece. Then there was the shoe company in Italy and some sort of think-tank in Jerusalem. Even a stint with the New York City drug administration when John Lindsay was mayor. Later, there were rumors that he had a drinking "problem" and that he was taking drugs.

He married and divorced twice while he was with the Marines and the Agency. He and his first wife had two daughters, but under the terms of the divorce agreement he was not permitted to see them. And then there were the women he lived with after the second divorce. There were many; they all seemed to be talented—painters, photographers, sculptors, and dancers, but never writers.

There were more rumors. He had left the Agency, he was living on Crete, he had no money, he was writing. Then silence. Clearly, the "fair-haired" undergraduate had not gone on to fame and glory.

*

It was not until 1972 or 1973 that Ted surfaced in my life. He was back in New York on a visit. On the surface he appeared to be the old Ted. He was a little rumpled, but the wit, the humor, the boyish charm were still there. Yet he seemed more thoughtful, more reflective, and there was Carol, a woman with whom Ted had become involved while in Crete and with whom he seemed to be living. He was more secretive now. And he had the manuscript of a novel he wanted me to read. I thought the novel was wonderful, full of fabulous and exotic characters, brimming with life, history, and the mysteries of the Orient. The novel that came to be called *Quin's Shanghai Circus* went through three more drafts before we published it in 1974. Set in Japan and China before and during the Second World War, two drafts even began in the South Bronx in the 1920s and involved three young Irish brothers named Quin. By the time the novel came out only one Quin remained and the Bronx interlude had shrunk from eighty pages to a couple of paragraphs.

As mentioned, *Quin* was a bigger success with the critics than it was in the bookstores. Readers loved the novel, even though there were not nearly enough of them. But Whittemore was not deterred. Less than two years later he appeared in my office with an even more ambitious novel, *Sinai Tapestry*, the first volume of his Jerusalem Quartet. Set in the heyday of the British Empire, it takes place in Palestine during the middle of the nineteenth century. Foremost among the larger-than-life characters were a tall English aristocrat, the greatest swordsman, botanist, and explorer of Victorian England; a fanatical trappist monk who found the original Sinai Bible, which "denies every religious truth every held by anyone;" and an Irish radical who had fled to Palestine disguised as a nun. My favorite was (and still is) Haj Harun, born three thousand years earlier, an ethereal wanderer through history: now an antiquities dealer dressed in a faded yellow cloak and sporting a Crusaders' rusty helmut while pursuing his mission as defender of the Holy City. He had several previous incarnations: as a stone carver of winged lions during the Assyrian occupation, proprietor of an all-night grocery store under the Greeks, a waiter when the Romans were in power, and a distributor of hashish and goats for the Turks. Before I first went to Israel in 1977, Whittemore, who was then writing in New York, gave me the names of several people in Jerusalem. One was named Mohammed, the owner of an antiquities gallery. When I finally tracked him down in the Old City I saw before me a fey character who, if he had been wearing a faded yellow cloak and a rusty helmet, would have been a dead ringer for Haj Harun.

Clearly Ted had been caught up in a new life in Jerusalem. The immediately preceding years in Crete where he had been living on a modest pension in the early 70s were behind him. He had been sharing a house with friends in Khania, the second largest city on Crete. In its long history it had been occupied by the Romans, conquered by the Arabs, Byzantines,and Venetians before becoming part of the Ottoman Empire in the seventeenth century. Now it was a sprawling Greek City. Athens without the Parthenon, but with an even richer history. In other words, a perfect place for a former intelligence agent to take stock and decide what history was all about, to re-examine what he had learned as a Yale undergraduate.

*

While in Japan in the 1960s Whittemore had written two unpublished novels, one about the Japanese game of Go, the other about a young American expatriate living in Tokyo. In Crete he began to write again, slowly, awkwardly, experimenting with voice, style,and subject matter, distilling his experience in the Agency into that sweeping raucous epic, *Quin's Shanghai Circus.* By the time he embarked on the Quartet, he was more assured, he was becoming a writer, and he had found a subject that was to engage him for the rest of his life: Jerusalem and the world of Christians, Arabs and Jews; faith and belief; mysticism and religious (and political) fanaticism; nineteenth century; European imperialism, twentieth century wars and terrorism. But above all Jerusalem, the City on the Hill, the Holy City. The novels would still be full of outrageous characters, the humor was still often grotesque and macabre, and there was violence aplenty. But there was also a new understanding of the mysteries of life.

The new novel, finally published in 1979, was *Jerusalem Poker*, the second volume of the Quartet. It involves a twelve-year poker game begun in the last days of December 1921 when three men sit down to play. The stakes were nothing less than the Holy City itself. Where else could a game for the control of Jerusalem be played but in the antiquities shop of

Haj Harun? Actually, Ted did not come to live permanently (that is "permanently" according to his ways) in Jerusalem until he was well into writing the Quartet. His knowledge of Jerusalem was based initially on books, but later on he wandered endlessly through the crowded, teeming streets and Quarters of the Old City. Merchants of every kind, butchers, tanners, glass blowers, jewelers, silversmiths,and even iron mongers spoke nearly every known language and dressed in the vibrant and exotic costumes of the Middle East. I once remarked to Ted while we were making our way along a narrow passage in the Arab Quarter, that I fully expected we would run into Sinbad the Sailor coming the other way.

The next time I visited Jerusalem, Ted had settled down with Helen, an American painter, in a spacious apartment in a large, nineteenth-century stone building in the Ethiopian Church compound. The apartment overlooked a courtyard full of flowers and lemon trees. Over one wall there loomed a Cistercian convent, and around the corner there was a synagogue full of Orthodox rabbinical students praying twenty-four hours a-day, or so it seemed to me. And standing or quietly reading in the courtyard were the Ethiopian monks. One morning I woke at six in my sunlit room and heard the Cistercian nuns singing a cappella. They sounded like birds and I thought for a moment I was in heaven.

After a midday nap we usually headed for the Old City, invariably ending up in the same cafe, a pretentious name for what was little more than an outdoor tea garden where hot tea and sticky buns were served. The proprietor sat at one table interminably fingering worry beads and talking to friends, an ever-changing group of local merchants, money changers, students, and some unsavory hard-looking types. They all seemed to have a nodding acquaintance with Ted, who knew as much, if not more, about the Old City as its inhabitants.

*

By 1981, Whittemore was living much of the year in the apartment in the Ethiopian compound, but in the years ahead he also rented a series of rooms in New York, a walk-up on Lexington Avenue, a studio apartment on Third. And he was writing steadily. I had left Holt earlier that spring for another publishing house and Judy Karasik took over the editorial work on Whittemore's new novel, *Nile Shadows.* She has written the epilogue to this book, a eulogy which she should have but didn't give at Whittemore's funeral twelve years after *Nile Shadows* appeared.

Nile Shadows is set in Egypt, it is 1942 and Rommel's powerful Afrika Corps is threatening to overrun Egypt and seize control of the entire Middle East. A group of characters, some old, some new, hold the fate of the world in their hands. At the very beginning of the novel, Stern, an idealistic visionary in *Sinai Tapestry* turned gun-runner a half century later, is killed by a grenade thrown into the doorway of a backstreet bar. Violence as well as mysticism dominates Whittemore's novels. Elsewhere he had described with horrible abandon the "rape" of Nanking and the sack of Smyrna in 1922 when the Turks butchered ten of thousands of Greek men, women, and children. A *Publishers Weekly* reviewer said: "One of the most complex and ambitious espionage stories ever written." And a critic in *The Nation* said: "Whittemore is a deceptively lucid stylist. Were his syntax as cluttered as Pynchon's or as conspicuously grand as Nabokov's or Fuentes', his virtually ignored novels might have received the attention they deserved."

But sales still hadn't caught up with the critics. By the spring of 1985, Ted was finishing the novel that was to be called *Jericho Mosaic,* the fourth of the Jerusalem Quartet. I was in Israel for the biennial Jerusalem International Book Fair. Afterwards, Ted suggested we drive down to Jericho, that oasis to the southeast of Jerusalem from which most of the caravans of Biblical times set out for the Levant, Asia Minor, and Africa. On the way we visited several Greek Orthodox monasteries in the Judean wilderness. Since they were built into solid rock at the bottom of isolated ravines reachable only on narrow paths, we had to leave the car up on the road and scramble down hillsides more suitable for mountain goats than a novelist and a New York editor. However, once we made it safely to the bottom, the monks proved to be extremely hospitable. Whittemore was a frequent visitor and the monks seemed to enjoy his company.

After being shown around the rocky quarters, not much more than elaborate caves, and consuming some dreadful retsina (the monks didn't drink it themselves) we continued to Jericho and a typical lunch of dried figs, a bread-like pastry and melon and hot fragrant tea. Then we made our way to the Negev. Over the years Ted had befriended some of the local Bedouins and we were greeted like old friends at several encampments. We spent one night at an Israeli meteorological center/desert inn near a Nabatean ruin. There seemed to be antennae and electric sensors everywhere, and as we used to say in those days, gray men in London, Washington, Moscow, and Beijing could probably hear every sparrow-fart in the desert. In retrospect, I sometimes wonder if Ted had ever really retired? Was he still, in this case, visiting his "controller," and using me as his "cover?"

Several months later, when Ted sent me a post card urging me to save a spot on an upcoming list for his next novel, the design on the card was a Byzantine mosaic of "the Tree of Life" Ted and I had seen on the stone floor of a ruin in Jericho. I took it to the art director at Norton where I was then a senior editor. He agreed with me that it would make an excellent design for a book jacket. All we needed was a manuscript.

*

Jericho Mosaic arrived before the end of the year, a fitting culmination to Whittemore's marvelous Quartet. In my opinion, *Jericho Mosaic* is the most breathtakingly original espionage story ever written. The novel is based on events that actually took place before the Six Day War and Whittemore demonstrates his total knowledge of the craft of intelligence and its practitioners, his passion for the Middle East, his devotion to the Holy City, and his commitment to peace and understanding among, Arabs, Jews, and Christians. The novel and the novelist maintain we can overcome religious, philosophical, and political differences if we are ready to commit ourselves to true understanding for all people and all ideas.

This humanistic message is imbedded in a true story involving Eli Cohen, a Syrian Jew who sacrificed his life (he managed to turn over to Mossad the Syrian plans and maps for the defense of the Golan Heights) in order that Israel might survive. In the novel Whittemore tells the story of Halim (who is clearly based on Eli Cohen) a Syrian businessman who returns to his homeland from Buenos Aires to help forward the Arab revolution. Halim becomes an outspoken advocate for Palestinian rights, he is the conscience of the Arab cause, "the incorruptible one." But Halim is a Jew, an agent for the Mossad; his codename is "the Runner," his assignment to penetrate the heart of the Syrian military establishment. At the same time the novel is a profound meditation on the nature of faith in which an Arab holy man, a Christian mystic, and a former British intelligence officer sit in a garden in Jericho exploring religion and humanity's relation to its various faces.

There were fewer reviews of *Jericho Mosaic* and even fewer sales than before. Arabs and Jews were involved in a bloody confrontation on the West Bank, there were lurid photographs in the newspapers and magazines and on television every day, and even more horrific stories. The times were not propitious for novelists defending the eternal verities, no matter how well they wrote. One critic did, however, proclaim Whittemore's Quartet "the best metaphor for the intelligence business in recent American fiction."

Shortly after *Jericho Mosaic* was published Whittemore left Jerusalem, the Ethiopian compound, and the American painter. He was back in New York living during the winter with Ann, a woman he had met years before when she and her then husband befriended Ted and his first wife. In the summers he would take over the sprawling, white, Victorian family home in Dorset, Vermont. The windows had green shutters, an an acre of lawn in front of the house was bounded by immense stately evergreen trees. Twenty or so rooms were distributed around the house in some arbitrary New

England Victorian design, and the furniture dated back to his grandparents, if not great-grandparents. Ted's brothers and sisters by now had their own houses and so Ted was pretty much its sole occupant. It was not winterized and could only be inhabited from May through October. But for Ted it was a haven to which he could retreat and write

*

In the spring of 1987 I became a literary agent and Ted joined me as a client. American book publishing was gradually being taken over by international conglomerates with corporate offices in Germany and Great Britain. They were proving to be more enamored of commerce than literature and it seemed to me I could do more for writers by representing them to any of a dozen publishers rather than just working for one.

I regularly visited Ted in the fall in Dorset. "The foliage season," late September, early October, is a very special time of year in New England: crisp clear days, wonderfully cool moonlit nights. We walked the woods and fields of southern Vermont by day, sat in front of the house after dinner on solid green Adirondack chairs, drink in hand and smoking. Actually I was the one drinking (usually brandy) because Ted had stopped years ago (his "habit" had become so serious that he had joined Alcoholics Anonymous); while we talked I would smoke a cigar or two, Ted would merely smoke one evil-looking cheroot. Comfortably ensconced on the lawn near the United Church, where his great-grandfather had been a minister, within sight of the Village Green and the Dorset Inn, our talk would turn to books and writing, family and friends. To his family, Ted must have been the "black sheep," the Yalie who had gone off to the CIA, had, so to speak, burned out, had come home via Crete, Jerusalem, and New York as a peripatetic novelist whose books received glowing reviews that resulted in less than glowing sales. But they, and "his women," supported him and continued to believe in him.

It was during these early fall visits that I discovered that his Prentiss great-grandfather had been a Presbyterian minister who had made his way up the Hudson River by boat from New York to Troy and then over to Vermont by train and wagon in the 1860s. In the library of the white, rambling Victorian house in Dorset there were shelves of fading leather-bound volumes of popular romances written by his great-grandmother for shop girls, informing them how to improve themselves, dress, and find suitable husbands. I gathered she was the Danielle Steele of her day, and the family's modest wealth was due to her literary efforts and not the generosity of the church's congregation.

We talked about the new novel. It was to be called *Sister Sally and Billy the Kid* and it was to be Ted's first American novel. It was about an Italian in his twenties from the Chicago of the roaring Twenties. His older brother, a gangster, had helped him buy a flower shop. But there was a shoot-out, the older brother was dead, and Billy has to flee to the West Coast where he meets a faith healer not unlike Aimee Semple McPherson. The real-life McPherson disappeared for a month in 1926, and when she returned claimed she had been kidnapped. The stone house in which Billy and his faith healer spend their month of love (from the beginning it is clear that the idyll must be limited to one month) has a walled garden behind it full of lemon trees and singing birds. Although that house is in southern California, the garden bears a close resemblance to another garden in the Ethiopian compound in Jerusalem with a synagogue on one side and a Cistercian convent on the other.

Then one day in early spring 1995, Ted called me. Could he come by the office that morning? I assumed it was to deliver the long-awaited manuscript. There had been two false starts after *Jericho Mosaic*. Instead Ted told me he was dying. Would I be his literary executor? A year or so earlier Ted had been diagnosed as having prostate cancer. It was too far along for an operation. His doctor had prescribed hormones and other medication and the cancer had gone into remission. But now it had spread. Less than six months later he was dead. They were terrible months for him. However, during those last weeks and days while he slipped in and out of consciousness, he was looked after by "his women," one of whom,

Carol, had returned to his life after a nearly two-decade separation.

There was a hushed memorial service in the United Church in Dorset that August. Afterwards, a reception was held on the large lawn in front of the family house. It was there that the disparate parts of Ted's world came together, perhaps for the first time; there was his family, his two sisters and two brothers and their spouses, nieces, and nephews with their own families (but not Ted's wives or the two daughters who had flown to New York to say "good-bye" to the father they hardly knew); there were neighbors, Yale friends, and a couple of colleagues from the Lindsay years. Were there any "spooks" in attendance? One really can't say, but there were eight "spooks" of a different sort from Yale, members of the 1955 Scroll and Key delegation. Ann and Carol, who had become allies while watching over Ted during those last, bitter days, were, of course, there.

Jerusalem and Dorset. The beautiful Holy City on the rocky cliffs overlooking the parched gray-brown desert. A city marked by thousands of years of history, turbulent struggles between great empires and three of the most enduring, vital religions given by God to mankind. And the summergreen valley in Vermont (covered by snow in the winter and by mud in the spring) where Dorset nestled between the ridges of the softly rolling Green Mountains. Once one of the cradles of the American Revolution and American democracy, and later a thriving farming and small manufacturing community, it was a place where time stood still since the beginning of the twentieth century. One was the subject of Whittemore's dreams and books; the other the peaceful retreat in which he dreamt and wrote the last twenty summers of his life.

Ted had finally come home to New England. It had been a long journey: Portland, New Haven, Japan, Italy, New York, Jerusalem, Greece, Crete, Jerusalem, New York, and now Dorset. Along the way he had many friends and companions, he was not a particularly good husband or father and disappointed many. But gradually he had found his voice, written his novels, and fallen in love with Jerusalem. I would like to think that Ted died dreaming of his Holy City. In a sense he was at one with that stone-cutter turned medieval knight, turned antiquities dealer, Haj Harun. For Whittemore was the eternal knight-errant who "made it" at Yale in the 1950s, "lost it" in the CIA in the 1960s, and then made himself into a wonderful novelist with the voice of a mystic. The voice of a mystic who had absorbed the best of Judaism, Christianity, and Islam. His great-grandfather the minister and his great-grandmother the writer would have been equally proud of him. His spirit rests peacefully in Dorset, Vermont.

Tom Wallace
New York City, 2002

Nile Shadows:
The Improbable Art of Edward Whittemore

What to make of a book like *Nile Shadows*, or an author like Edward Whittemore? No matter how determinedly catholic we like to think our literary tastes, there are some works that leave our inner critic feeling uncomfortably at a loss when it first encounters them. *"Yes, but is it any good?"*, it keeps asking with tireless persistence as the rest of us answer that question by happily turning page after page. Like many authors belonging to that large and unfortunate caste, "the unjustly neglected", Whittemore suffers from being an embarrassingly good read. He also suffers from a bigger crime, in that he is almost impossible to pigeonhole. Reviewers' comparisons bounce from Pynchon to Nabokov, Greene to Calvino and Fuentes to Vonnegut, only to hastily assert that he is, of course, very much his own man. Reading Whittemore, I found myself adding my own — a touch of Hesse here, I thought, a dash of Robertson Davies there, yet without what could be termed a debt to either of them. Each new reader will inevitably supply more.

So what is it that makes *Nile Shadows*, and the rest of Whittemore's works, so infinitely flexible? Are they simply baggy monsters into which one can throw whatever one wants? In a sense they are, and it's not a criticism to say that Whittemore is probably one of the baggiest writers this century — his books represent that most vain of ambitions and the downfall of more than one literary great: a complete explanation of everything. Nothing less than a unified theory of human history is what Whittemore is after, and it's a sign of his mettle that he realizes such an ambition is doomed from the start, yet undertakes it anyway. *Nile Shadows* is set in an anxious Cairo of 1942, awaiting the arrival at any moment of Rommel and his Panzer divisions from out of the desert. The distant rumble of gun fire and armored vehicles is the rumble of history itself, bearing down on Whittemore's characters as they engage in their desperate machinations to avoid defeat. And yet what do those characters do in the face of such pressure? They talk, is what they do, and they talk and talk and *talk*. Each conversation leading on to something else, which in turn leads to something else, and suddenly a new character is introduced – a thumbnail sketch surely, a literary prop, no more – but no, suddenly he starts growing in front of our eyes, acquiring a languorous history stretching out over pages and pages while we think, Quick! Do something! The enemy is coming!

At times there is something outright perverse about this compunction to hold forth. When Joe O'Sullivan, the novel's protagonist, encounters the mysterious Ahmad, undoubted possessor of vital information about the man he has been sent to uncover, we get the following:

> Well now, so you've come from America, have you?
>
> Yes, murmured Joe, his eyes drifting around the room in a trance.
>
> Well now, isn't that a strange coincidence? The world is really very small. It just so happens I once was given a complete edition of the collected letters of George Washington, some thirty-odd volumes in all, and they certainly added up to some fascinating reading.
>
> They did?
>
> Oh very. Let's see now. Did you know, for example, that Washington's false teeth were made from hippopotamus teeth? He also used teeth made from walrus tusks and elephant ivory and even cow teeth, but he always preferred Hippo. He claimed it gave

him a superior bite and chew. With Hippo, he said, even peanuts and gumdrops were possible.

Even peanuts and gumdrops? murmured Joe. President Washington?

So he stayed with Hippo whenever he could.

And this sixteen pages into a conversation that has already touched on Ethiopian nationalism, the history of Cairo's sex trade, the Ahmadmobile (Ahmad's failed fish and chip enterprise) and Ahmad's even greater failure as a poet.

The conversation can be serious, too, taking on the form of a grave philosophical discourse as the characters take turns to expound their views of life. When Joe finally comes face to face with his elusive prey, Stern, the chit chat gives way to pure oratory:

> Revolution, said Stern. We can't even comprehend what it is, not what it means or what it suggests. We pretend it means total change but it's much more than that, so vastly more complex, and yes, so much simpler too. It's not just the total change from night to day as our earth spins in its revolutions around a minor star. It's also our little star revolving around its own unknowable center and so with all the stars in their billions, and so with the galaxies and the universe itself. Change revolves and truly there is nothing but revolution. All movement is revolution and so is time, and although those laws are impossibly complex and beyond us, their result is simple. For us, very simple.

And yet, this is where Whittemore's great strength comes in: just as we are beginning to accept that this is more a philosophical treatise than a spy story, a pleasant meta-fiction, Whittemore suddenly pulls the strings taut with a dramatic piece of action worthy of Le Carré (more comparisons). When Joe first arrives at the dubious Hotel Babylon, for example, there is this description:

The door burst open under his hand and Joe went flying across the room, hurling his valise at the screen in the window. The screen and the valise disappeared and he dived after them, landing with a roll on the soft earth behind the hotel as a dull thud went off in the room above him. He was on his feet at once, in a crouch, but there was nothing to see. He was standing in a small courtyard strewn with debris. A door behind him led back into the hotel. Another door faced him from the far side of the small courtyard. Joe picked up his valise and crossed to the door in the far wall. He tried the handle and the door opened. Stairs led down to the basement.

This heady mixture of the philosophical and the dramatic runs throughout the book, the one underlying the other, and the result, unlikely though it may be, is a seamless unity rather than an awkward tugging of opposites. Life is talk, after all, lots of it — crude, bawdy, serious, occasionally transcendent — and that's what Whittemore gives us. It's also a world of action and of unthinkable violence — in this century particularly like no other — and Whittemore gives us that, too. Because of the stream of conversations, memories, theories and thoughts that make up so much of the book, it's easy to overlook the significant amount of violence contained within it. The book begins with an act of extreme violence, in fact, a hand grenade casually tossed into a bar that instantly kills one of the main characters, setting off a chain of events linked in almost unimaginable ways to this moment. Then there's Stern, the elusive agent O'Sullivan is sent out to hunt down, who may or may not be giving secrets away to the enemy. Stern, a Christ-like figure who seems to have taken all the woes of humanity upon his shoulders (he even has a stigmata of sorts), is haunted in particular by the memory of his having once slit a dying girl's throat as an act of mercy, a grisly scene that reemerges repeatedly throughout the book, bubbling up from Stern's tormented mind, as fresh for him each time as it is for us.

Something else apart from this heady fusion draws us in to *Nile Shadows*, though, and that's a certain compulsive quality that, as in all great novels, appears to be beyond the author's control. On the one hand Whittemore is the master story teller, weaving his tale of good and evil with its great cast of characters over its great span of time, while on the other he is also telling a much simpler story, a story about himself, one feels, and telling it again and again. If every fictional character is unavoidably a portrait of its author, then Whittemore seems to have taken this to a pathological extreme. Young or old, good or bad, male or female, they're all flat-out Whittemores on the page, unabashed author substitutes. You don't need to be aware of all the biographical details of the author's life (there are plenty in the prologue and epilogue of this new edition) to realize that something is afoot here. This is a book in which every character, literally or metaphorically or both, is a secret agent, presenting one face to the world and another to themselves. There's Joe and Stern, who between them in their lifetime have disguised themselves as endless apparitions, from gun runners to beggars, antiques·dealers to morphine addicts, and more besides. There's Liffey, the jovial chameleon, not coincidentally named after Dublin's famous river, and like that other great Everyman, Bloom, also a Jew. And there's the mysterious Bletchley, his face hideously disfigured by a bullet during the First World War, who's every facial expression is a grotesque inversion of his true feelings. "It's all a matter of man seeking his true home . . ." as Joe says.

Once again, Whittemore escapes what might be a fatal mistake in another author. Far from the funhouse hall of mirrors one might expect from such endless fracturing, the compulsive replication of this same idea only intensifies the book, turning it into a single mirror and magnifying the image. What is the true nature of man? How close can one ever come to it? Is there something worthy and strong enough inside that will outlast our more barbaric impulses? The repetition of these themes by so many voices exerts a hypnotic sense in the end, like listening to an endless choral chant. It might almost be called "the poetry of self-exile", if that didn't strike too pretty a note for a book that for all its abstract bent is so firmly planted on the ground of historical fact and place.

And here we come to the deepest concerns of Whittemore's mind, for historical fact and place are as much his obsession as his loftier flights of imagination, indeed they are inextricably linked to them. The real protagonists of the *Quartet* are surely the parched and beautiful deserts of the biblical lands, with their oases and ruins, and above all the Holy City of Jerusalem itself. Whittemore is profoundly in love with these, and it's a love that shines forth in all the books. Much of the "talky" nature of the book comes not just from his characters endless speculations and declarations, but from their loving memories of past nights spent idling by the Nile, or the magnificence of the pyramids at dawn, or the smell of a scented garden during some long-ago secret assignation. What you come to realize as you read, unconsciously at first, and then with growing awareness, is that these are not really digressions at all, but rather the very meat of the book. The land speaking to the people, and the people speaking to each other in an endless cycle is the closest definition of what it's all "about", if one needs to pursue its meaning into some final corner. The book, and the whole *Quartet*, is a monument to digression, to the necessity of the circuitous and the round-about as the only way to truth. Certainty of vision, unquestioned clarity of purpose, leads only to oppression – as the ruthless and single minded Nazi presence hovering in the background serves to remind us.

What this amounts to, and what makes the critic with his nose for genre and structure so nervous, is that by all accounts this shouldn't be a good book at all, should in fact be a really terrible book, and the *Quartet* a rambling, self-indulgent mess. It's too clogged up with words to be straight forward action adventure, it's too in love with the power of old-fashioned story telling to be a safe member of any experimental literary camp, it's too bawdy to be a tastefully controlled work of the intellect (what other work about the primacy of Man's soul contains a sizable section on the history and art of prostitution?), and it's combination of travel and digression, action and introspection, while they remind one in flashes (those comparisons again) of writers like Chatwin and Theroux, are too loose, too much under the sway of Whittemore's pack-rat, all-encompassing, constantly changing focus of attention. In the end, against all odds, the book works because something binds together its lofty ambitions and disparate parts and makes it, if not a whole, then at least the tantalizing shape of something about to come into being at any moment. That something is the force of Whittemore's integrity of vision.

Ben Gibberd
New York City, 2002

Ben Gibberd is a freelance writer and editor who lives in New York City. He is currently working on a book about Manhattan's shoreline with the photographer Randy Duchaine.

PART ONE

1

An Australian Hand Grenade

On a clear night in 1942 a hand grenade exploded in a Cairo slum, killing one man instantly.

The explosion shattered the mirror in the half-light of a poor Arab bar, a bare room where laborers went to sip arak into oblivion. The hand grenade had come flying in through a shabby curtain separating the bar from an alley, thrown from a group of Australian soldiers who were out drinking and brawling and victoriously celebrating life, recent survivors of the disastrous battle for Crete.

Other than the dead man, no one in the bar received more than superficial injuries. And in the confusion following the explosion, amidst the shouts and screams and drunken cries of *bloody wogs*, the young Australian soldiers had fled into the shadowy byways of Old Cairo and disappeared, never to be officially identified in life, some never to be identified in death as well.

Such violent incidents were far from uncommon in wartime Cairo. The fierce campaigns in the Western Desert still raged uncertainly, as Rommel's powerful Afrika Korps threatened to overrun Egypt and the Suez Canal. From there the Middle East and much more would be open to the invading Germans, so soldiers in the British forces were apt to play desperately with time and darkness before going into the desert to meet the advancing panzers.

In such a situation, one stray death in a Cairo slum could be of little significance, and an Egyptian policeman quickly concluded his routine investigation.

From documents found on the dead man he was identified as a minor criminal and morphine addict, a petty gunrunner sometimes known as Stern, a vagrant with no visible means of support who had moved erratically from one poor lodging to another in various Cairo slums over the last few years.

Stern's criminal record further stated that his name was to be found in the files of a number of police departments in the Middle East, and although he didn't appear to be of Egyptian origin, his dialect was said to be flawless. It was therefore assumed that he was probably a genuine Levantine by birth, whose sordid pursuits in the 1930s had caused him to spend at least as much time in Egypt as elsewhere.

The history of Stern's criminal activities was unimpressive. In the years leading up to the Second World War he had smuggled arms to many groups in the Middle East, with perhaps more emphasis on Palestine. Yet he had never been clever enough to make any money from these operations, for his record also showed that he had lived in unrelieved poverty. On several occasions he had been apprehended and sentenced to brief prison terms on secondary charges.

Stern, in short, had lived an obscure and meaningless life, a marginal existence that had come to nothing.

Only one brief entry in Stern's file tended to contradict this uneventful account, a daring escape he had made from a Damascus prison in the summer of 1939. From the nature of the escape it was apparent it had been unplanned, and what made it inexplicable was the fact that Stern had been due for release from the prison within twenty-four hours. But then a few weeks later Hitler's armored divisions had crossed the Polish border to begin the war, so the matter had soon been forgotten, a strange and isolated episode in Stern's otherwise purposeless career.

Stern's nationality was listed on the death certificate as *Unknown*, lost long ago in the maze of counterfeit documents he had used throughout his life. So numerous were the aliases in his record, in fact, there was no way to know whether *Stern* was the dead man's true name.

In addition, so contradictory were the disguises of his background, it could not even be determined whether he was a Moslem or a Christian or a Jew.

There were also no associates to question. Stern, or whoever he was, had not only worked obscurely but lived his life alone, without family or friends, without acquaintances or neighbors to remember him. To all appearances, without anyone at all. Yet when the time came to dispose of the body, done quickly in Cairo because of over-crowding among the dead, a shabbily dressed woman turned up at police headquarters saying she wished to make arrangements for a burial. The woman carried a Greek passport and the story she told seemed plausible.

She had first met the dead man about a year earlier, she said, in a small neighborhood restaurant where she sometimes took her evening meals. Subsequently they had fallen into the habit of eating there together on an irregular basis, never more than once a week and often no more than once every two or three weeks. It had been company of a sort for both of them. She had known the dead man only as Stern, and he had called her by her Christian name, Maud. Although she was an American by birth, she had lived in the Eastern Mediterranean for years.

Since Stern had never known more than a day in advance when he might be able to come to the restaurant, he had left notes there saying when he would show up. She had gone to the restaurant every day to check for these notes, even when she wasn't planning to eat there in the evening. She didn't know where he had lived or what he had done. It was wartime and people came and went. Explanations were pointless, reasons meaningless. She had assumed he held some kind of minor clerk's job, as she did.

Why do you say that? asked the policeman behind the desk.

Because of the way he dressed.

How was that?

Like me. Trying to make ends meet.

Did you speak Arabic together?

No, you can hear I don't speak it well. We spoke in Greek or in English.

French?

Sometimes.

The policeman switched to French, which he was studying in the evenings to promote his career.

Did he ever talk about the past? What he used to do?

The woman was trying hard to control herself. She looked down at her worn shoes and suddenly clenched her fists in despair.

No. I just assumed he was from somewhere and had done something once. Isn't everybody from somewhere? Hasn't everybody done something once? We never talked about the past. Can't you understand?

5

The woman broke down and quietly began to cry, and of course the policeman did understand. The Balkans had been overrun and Greece had fallen and there were refugees everywhere in Cairo, people who didn't want to remember what they had lost.

So he saw no need to go into the matter further. If this woman wanted to bear the expense of burying a man she had hardly known, out of whatever personal reasons might be involved, that was her affair. Nothing would be served by telling her that Stern had been a petty criminal, a minor gunrunner and morphine addict. Obviously she wanted to bury someone, and it was no concern of his how she went about wasting the little money she had.

I'll just be a minute, he said, and went to make a telephone call to her office to prove that she was the person she claimed to be. The connection was made, to some obscure British department having to do with the Irrigation Works, and it took surprisingly little time. He returned and filled out the release papers, copying down the entries from her passport and marking her *A friend of the deceased.* He took the forms to be signed and told the woman where to obtain the body. She thanked him and left.

Whereupon the case was closed so far as the Egyptian authorities were concerned.

The policeman who had arrived at the Arab bar after the explosion had remained there for about half an hour, but most of that time he had spent helping himself to drinks. Another ten minutes or so had been spent by his superior at headquarters, the following morning, glancing through the dead man's file. And not much more time than that had been required for the interview with the woman that morning, to release what was left of the body.

In all, then, no more than twelve hours had passed since Stern had been killed at midnight. In just such a brief period of time were the formalities of his death concluded, his life forgotten. But there was one minor curiosity that seemed to have been overlooked.

How did it happen that this casual acquaintance of Stern, this shabbily dressed woman of American birth, had come to police headquarters in the first place?

Why had she turned up so suddenly when she was only accustomed to receiving notes from Stern once a week, or every two or three weeks, in a small neighborhood restaurant?

How, indeed, had she even known that Stern was dead?

For there had been no mention of the event in the newspapers, nor would there be. Such incidents occurred and it was generally known that they did. But the British censors still had no wish to see displayed in print the fact that Allied soldiers, drunk on occasion and facing possible death themselves, relieved their tensions by tossing hand grenades into Arab bars.

Yet these questions concerning the American woman, as it turned out, were of little importance. Elsewhere, the real enigma behind the killing was already being studied by intelligence experts, and for them even the simplest facts involved in Stern's mysterious death, and his equally mysterious life, had begun to suggest a vastly disturbing puzzle that might decide the outcome of the entire war in the Middle East, and perhaps beyond.

2

The Purple Seven Armenian

The names of four witnesses appeared in the brief report drawn up by the Cairo policeman who had investigated the hand-grenade incident, the other customers having fled the bar immediately after the explosion at midnight. Of the four, one was the Arab owner of the bar and two others were glassy-eyed Arab laborers who had heard nothing of the world since sundown, due to the effects of opium.

The fourth witness had produced a passport that showed he was a naturalized Lebanese citizen *in transit*, an itinerant dealer in Coptic artifacts. The name of this fourth witness was unmistakably Armenian. And although the policeman at the scene had carefully noted that the Armenian's status was *in transit*, he had failed to determine where the Armenian was in transit to, or from.

Teams of British enlisted men routinely checked every name that appeared in any Egyptian police report, no matter how insignificant the case might be. They checked these names against master lists, which gave no indication whether the name listed was that of a deserter or an alleged informer, a male or female prostitute suspected of infecting lost battalions of soldiers on leave, or belonged to any of the other categories of people that might be having an adverse effect on the war.

The Armenian's name appeared on such a list. The facts were duly forwarded to Special Branch, where a further check was made against names listed in various color codes. The Armenian's name was found

under the highly sensitive Purple Code, which required that the in
formation be sent at once to Military Intelligence.

There, the significance of the name was accurately defined by lo-
cating it on the select list known as *Purple Seven*, the briefest of all
the lists and also the only one of the many secret color codes to merit
the ultimate British classification for speedy handling in the Levant.

> Most Most Urgent:
>
> Here we go again, old boy.
> Let's forego tea and keep
> the Hun on the run.

At once, a goggled officer courier signed for the packet of information and climbed into the sidecar of a powerful dispatch motorcycle,
driven by an expert heavy-diesel mechanic who was fluent in Malay,
also goggled and armed with a Sten gun, two automatics, three
throwing knives and a hidden derringer. The courier's destination
was a drab building housing the Third Circle of the Irrigation Works,
an obscure civilian department that happened to be under the direct
control of the British commander-in-chief, Middle East Forces,
seemingly due to the strategic value of water. But actually the drab
Third Circle was the headquarters of a secret British intelligence
unit colloquially referred to by specialists as *the Waterboys*.

And thus by noon that day a sickly-looking British agent, a Cairo
pimp and blackmarketeer with a bad liver and a certain low-level
reputation along the riverfront, was flashing his stained teeth as he
strolled through a filthy slum of the city, his jaundiced grin meant to
welcome anyone who might be in need of illicit services of any kind.

To fortify himself against the swindles ahead, the yellowish blackmarketeer decided to stop off for a glass of cheap Arab cognac. And
the café he chose, by chance, happened to be only a few doors away
from the bar that had been damaged the previous night by a hand
grenade.

Gently the pimp eased his swollen liver under a table. He rubbed
his eyes and casually turned his attention to the next table, where
the owner of the damaged Arab bar, a neighborhood celebrity for the
moment, was dramatically recounting for the hundredth time his
experiences from the previous night. The bar owner had been doing
so since sunup, speaking breathlessly to anyone who would listen,

9

but more especially to anyone who would buy him a drink in exchange for the whole truth about the war and the world and history.

By now the Arab bar owner was thoroughly drunk and his account had taken on the proportions of a major battle in the ongoing struggle for Egyptian independence. Like many of his countrymen, he viewed the British as colonial oppressors and was more than ready to welcome the Germans into Cairo as liberators.

In fact it was precisely because of his well-known patriotism, he said, that the cowardly British had sent an elite platoon of masked commandos to attack his bar under cover of darkness. But he had valiantly repulsed the assault and was to receive a medal from Rommel when the invincible panzers entered the city.

By the weekend, he said, his eyes glittering from the noontime rush of gin in his veins. By the weekend, according to the secret information he was privy to.

There was no need to boast, he went on, but there was also no need to hide the truth any longer. Not now, after the British had showed how much they feared him by mounting a regimental assault at night with their very best antitank weapons.

He lowered his voice and adopted the manner of a dedicated revolutionary. Awesome nationalist victories and the great personal sacrifices that led to them, he noted, deserved the deepest respect.

The *whole* truth? he whispered. The whole truth is that Rommel no longer writes to me through intermediaries. Now when he asks for my advice he does so in his very own hand, on Afrika Korps stationery.

Sighs and shrewd nods passed through his audience. At that moment his unemployed listeners undeniably had the hard knowing eyes of determined men. From the next table, the yellowish black-marketeer leaned sideways toward the bar owner.

How's his Arabic? he whispered.

Whose?

Rommel's.

Excellent, of course. The Germans aren't stupid like the British.

I never doubted it. But next weekend, you say? Rommel is going to be here as soon as that?

He told me so himself, answered the bar owner.

The blackmarketeer looked suddenly pained. He eased his fingers down over the right side of his abdomen and tried to prop up his liver.

Then I'm in trouble, he whispered. The Germans drink beer, strictly beer.

They do?

Of course, and here I am with this left on my hands. I thought it was going to make my fortune, but now it's turned out to be useless.

Your liver? whispered the bar owner.

The blackmarketeer shook his head and reached down for the valise he had with him, opening it just enough for the bar owner to peek inside. What he saw was a new bottle of Irish whiskey, its seal unbroken. The valise was quickly snapped shut again.

Direct from Shepheard's Hotel, whispered the blackmarketeer. Stolen at great risk and at the cost of many bribes. But now I'm doomed by God's will.

How much? whispered the bar owner suspiciously.

Cheap. Absurdly so, in view of God's will and Rommel's arrival.

God speaks in mysterious ways, countered the bar owner.

Assuredly, He does. And only those who are deserving hear His voice. Now as one revolutionary patriot to another, I suggest we retire to your damaged premises to inspect this despicable destruction wrought by a division of cowardly British paratroopers hurtling down from the heavens under cover of darkness.

It was more like the whole Eighth Army, said the bar owner. Tanks, huge cannons, minefields, massive formations of lumbering bombers, everything.

I never doubted it.

And they were led by Churchill himself.

Who was probably raving drunk as usual. But you fought back with all your strength and Rommel will be personally toasting you this weekend. While in the meantime, a little privacy perhaps?

The bar owner rose and dismissed his audience with a haughty gesture, almost losing his balance as he did so. But the yellowish blackmarketeer was quickly by the bar owner's side, his sickly eyes darting to and fro as he tendered his support, and in another moment he had the bar owner in an upright position and was steering him down the alley, the two of them hand in hand with their bodies rubbing together in the traditional Levantine manner of whole-hearted cooperation.

Early that evening, then, a British Major returned to the Irrigation Works after debriefing his agent, the unhealthy-looking pimp. The Major laid aside his pith helmet and went in to report to his Colonel, the man in charge of the Waterboys.

It's about the Purple Seven alert that came in this morning, said the Major. It took some time to look into because the bar owner needed sobering up.

The Colonel nodded. Let's call this Purple Seven *the Armenian,* he said. Go ahead.

He's described as a small dark man of European origin, closely clipped beard, deep lines around the eyes, probably a drinker. Thin, wiry, getting on toward forty. A reddish hue to his hair, or at least that was the impression in the poor lighting of the bar. Nothing particular about the way he dressed except that it was definitely on the shabby side. Collarless shirt, rumpled and none too clean. An old suit that might have been secondhand, rather too big for him as if he had lost some weight recently, or perhaps just seen better days in general. Shabby overall, but otherwise ordinary in appearance.

Or experienced, said the Colonel. Go on.

He entered the bar shortly after Stern did, sometime around ten maybe. The bar owner's pretty useless when it comes to time, he doesn't own a watch and there's no clock in the bar. Stern and the Armenian sat together at the counter. The two of them were speaking English and the bar owner only understands a little. They drank the local cheap brandy. Stern had a couple, the Armenian rather more. Stern did the ordering and also the looking about.

How?

They were sitting sideways facing one another, each with an elbow on the counter, Stern positioned so that he had a full view of most of the room and also the entrance, which he could see over the Armenian's shoulder without moving his head. A curtain hung in the open doorway, separating the room from the alley. They smoked cigarettes while they talked, Stern's cigarettes, a cheap Arab brand. It was a quiet conversation at first, low tones, some gesturing. The Armenian was doing most of the talking at that point. But then Stern did some talking and the situation grew more heated, as if there were some kind of disagreement. The Armenian seemed to be the one who was disagreeing, while Stern's manner was more one of self-confidence or relief. But that might be a bit too strong. It's only based on an impression of an impression.

Relief over something he'd learned from the Armenian? Why that impression?

Stern began smiling at that point. Or smiling occasionally. We're on unsure ground here.

Go on.

The Armenian's reaction to Stern's relief or self-confidence or whatever it was, suggested puzzlement, not anger. He didn't seem to understand whatever it was Stern was feeling, or else he understood it but was reluctant to accept it. Something along those lines. It was at that point that the discussion became heated and the disagreement developed. Stern seemed to be trying to explain himself, or justify himself or whatever, and the Armenian was refusing to go along with it.

I see.

Stern would speak quietly, forcefully, for a minute or two while the Armenian listened, trying to understand what Stern was saying. Then the Armenian would shake his head *no* and gesture and argue again. Both men seemed tired, *weary* is a better word. Perhaps the disagreement was an old one, something they'd been through before. It went on like that until midnight and the explosion. Physically, Stern seemed exhausted, but also exhilarated. Again, that's only an impression of an impression. And that's all we have prior to the hand grenade.

The Colonel nodded. Let's stay with that for a moment, he said.

He rose and began pacing awkwardly back and forth, as if he wasn't quite used to walking on his false leg. There were no windows in the room. He filled his pipe and absentmindedly left it on a table.

Stern seemed exhausted but happy or relieved, said the Colonel. What about the Armenian? He'd be a good ten years younger than Stern, maybe more. Exhausted too, physically?

Impossible to say. Apparently he couldn't be read so easily.

Why not?

The way he moved or held himself. Tended to give less of himself away. More contained perhaps?

Unlikely. But experienced, I'd say, definitely. No one ever gave less of himself away than Stern, although one never had that impression of course. Quite the opposite. Naturally your man wouldn't have known that. Whom did you send?

Jameson.

Excellent taste, observed the Colonel. I'd tend to trust his impression of impressions, so yes, we do have a few things here.

The Colonel looked around for his pipe. The Major had his own questions to ask but the time for that would come later. He waited.

Let's go on to the hand grenade, said the Colonel. How did it start?

There were shouts outside in English and the sounds of scuffling getting louder, a brawl working its way down the alley. The owner was nervous and so were some of the others in the bar. The Armenian, whose back was to the curtain, turned around to look several times but Stern went on talking, appearing to take no notice. Of course he could see the curtain without moving his head, so he might have been taking an interest without showing it. In any case, Stern went on talking and the shouting grew louder. Then the curtain flew back and something came lobbing into the room. The owner saw it all right but he didn't know what it was. Nobody knew what it was except Stern.

The Colonel frowned, looking down at the floor, a sad expression.

Yes, he said softly. I can imagine.

Stern hit the Armenian in the chest and sent him flying, continued the Major. The owner was standing near them at that moment, behind the counter, and he saw the Armenian's face when Stern hit him. The Armenian was astonished. Obviously he had no idea what was going on. At that point the owner went down, threw himself on the floor behind the counter. It was an instinctive reaction to Stern hitting the Armenian, a dive for cover. Not away from the grenade, which he didn't recognize, but away from Stern. The roar went off and that's all we have from the owner until the glass stopped showering down.

Mirror behind the counter?

Yes.

The Colonel found his pipe. He went over and sat down on the sofa, using his hands to move his false leg into a straight position.

Stern?

The grenade must have been coming directly at him. He had time to hit the Armenian and knock him clear, and that was that. Full in the chest probably. Nothing much left above the waist.

The Colonel struck a match. Ever been close to that? he asked. Had it happen right next to you?

No.

It's the worst sound in the world. Does something to your brain. For an instant you're no longer human. It's another existence, primeval, black. You see something inside yourself. Go on.

There was the roar and the shattering glass and smoke and confusion, said the Major. When the owner showed his face, men were screaming and pushing out the door. Bits and pieces everywhere, and blood. The Armenian was still sprawled in the corner where Stern's blow had sent him. Besides the two Arabs who were unconscious from opium on the far side, the Armenian was the only other man left in the room. He lay there on the floor in the smoke, staring up at the spot where he and Stern had been sitting. Slowly he got to his feet, dreamlike, and just stood there staring. The owner was dazed and he did the same thing, just stood there staring. But the owner was watching the Armenian.

Yes, said the Colonel, the fascination is incredibly intense. You don't know whether you're alive or dead and you're not in your own body at all. In fact you have no body. It's strange . . . a kind of sudden sense of pure consciousness. Your mind looks around and the first thing with any sign of life utterly captivates you. At that moment the merest flicker of an eye contains all the mystery of the universe. Go on.

The Armenian still didn't move, he just stood there staring. After a bit the owner came to his senses and began screaming himself. People shouted and stuck their heads in, and there was nothing really after that until the policeman arrived.

What kind of man?

Average, unfortunately. The confusion and damage got to him but not much else, except for one curiosity. When he first came in, something about the Armenian struck him as peculiar. But only vaguely, he can't recall it exactly. It happened when he first glanced around the place and he might have only imagined it, or it could have been a trick of peripheral vision. Anyway, it was a sensation of something unusual, in the sense of inappropriate or out of place. At least that's my interpretation of it. The policeman isn't able to describe it with any degree of accuracy, apparently it only flashed through his mind. But what it amounts to is, he had the sensation the Armenian was smiling. Staring and smiling. And that's all we have on the incident itself.

The Colonel nodded.

But there's one other very curious fact, added the Major. The owner says the Armenian came to the bar yesterday morning, very early. There was nobody else there and he'd just started his cleanup when all of a sudden the Armenian came rushing in with a wild man.

A what?

That's how the owner describes him. A ghostlike figure in rags, an Arab, thin and small and caked with dust and dirt, hair matted and eyes bulging out of his head. According to the owner, he looked like a desert hermit who'd been off in a cave somewhere for years. He seemed deranged. He was clawing at the air and making strange sounds as if he couldn't breathe. The Armenian came rushing in with this wild man and ordered coffee and the two of them collapsed in a corner. Then the wild man began to sob and a moment later they were rushing out again, the Armenian in the lead, the wild man running after him.

Nothing more specific on this other man?

The owner kept mentioning his eyes, frantic bulging eyes. Frightening, wild. He was convinced the man was insane. That was the only time the owner has ever seen this other man, and it was the only other time he has ever seen the Armenian.

And lastly there's this, said the Major, placing a small length of worn curved metal in the Colonel's hand. The bar owner found it on the floor after the policeman left. It was lying at the foot of the counter where Stern and the Armenian had been sitting. So far as I can see it's exactly what it appears to be, an old Morse-code key. From the last century, probably.

The Colonel turned the small piece of worn metal between his fingers. The key was highly polished from innumerable handlings.

Stern used to carry that, murmured the Colonel. It was a kind of good-luck charm. He was never without it.

The Colonel frowned. He took a bottle of whiskey from a cupboard and poured into two glasses. The Major sipped his whiskey, waiting. The room was in the heart of the building and few sounds reached it. The Colonel worked on his pipe in silence. Finally he picked up the other glass.

Are you and Maud friendly these days?

Yes. Should I speak to her?

The Colonel shook his head.

No. You see, I think we've stumbled upon an operation that belongs to somebody else, and the reason we found out about it is because something went wrong in that bar. I'm sure the Armenian's name was never supposed to turn up in a police report. No, certainly not. As for Maud, it's not possible that she has anything to do with the operation, because if she did, I would have to have been told.

But she knew Stern had been killed, said the Major, and someone had to tell her. A Purple Seven alert comes directly to us. So we were the first to know of Stern's death, and we're still the only ones who do know. Unless, of course, you've already passed the information along.

I haven't, said the Colonel. I will tonight. But as for us being the first to know of Stern's death, that's not quite true, is it?

The first to know inside, I meant. The Armenian knew, of course.

Yes, our Purple Seven knew. Our man with the Armenian name who's conveniently in transit while dealing in Coptic artifacts. Our small shabby European who wears a secondhand suit and likes to have his morning coffee in a Cairo slum with some wild Arab hermit from the desert, and who has all the signs of being an experienced professional. He knew.

And told Maud?

That's right, said the Colonel. But what I meant before is that she can't have anything to do with the operation itself, as such. It's obvious she must have a good deal to do with some of the people involved in it. From a personal point of view.

Wasn't her connection with Stern known from the beginning?

Oh yes. Stern was the one who recommended her to us, and he was right on target as usual. She's been a fine addition. But tell me, what do you know about Stern?

Only what comes through from the files, replied the Major. That he seemed to be able to find out almost anything.

Ever wonder why that was so?

Excellent contacts, I assume.

Yes, the best. The French and the Germans and the Italians, Turks and Greeks and Arabs and Jews—he had them all. And why was that, do you suppose?

Because he must have made it his business to have them, said the Major. Because that was what he did. His life.

Yes, what he did. But I'm beginning to wonder about that . . . what Stern really did. Stern gave information as well as took it, but the real reason people trusted him was because they always felt, deep down, that he was working just for them. In the end, just for them. We believed that, didn't we?

In answer, the Major frowned. In the short time he had worked for the Colonel, there had been some extremely sensitive operations set in motion almost entirely on the basis of information supplied by Stern. And there must have been many other such operations in the past, so he found it difficult to follow what the Colonel now seemed to be suggesting about Stern.

That's not to say he wasn't working for us, continued the Colonel. It's just that ultimately . . .

The Colonel broke off, trying to order his thoughts. For some reason he had suddenly recalled an obscure incident from before the war, Stern's escape from a Damascus prison in the summer of 1939. The episode had never made any sense to the Colonel, because Stern had been due for release from the prison within twenty-four hours.

Yet Stern had risked his life to escape. Why?

Later he had talked about it with Stern and Stern had turned the whole affair into a joke, moving around in his chair in his awkward way and belittling any courage it might have shown on his part, claiming simply that he had felt more useless than usual and had decided on a sudden whim to try to prove his superiority over his Syrian guards. Stern had even showed the Colonel the scars left by the thumbnail he had ripped away during the escape, clawing his way through some masonry, deep ugly scars slashing up the back of his thumb. The Colonel remembered how painful they had looked at the time, but Stern had dismissed them with a shrug.

It's nothing, Stern had said, laughing. Really painful wounds never bother with the body, do they? They cut deeper and the scars they leave are elsewhere.

And then they had gone on to talk of other things. But now the incident in Damascus troubled the Colonel and he began hunting through Stern's file. He seemed to recall that Stern had said he had gone to Haifa after the prison escape, and had hidden in Haifa until the war had broken out a few weeks later, turning everyone's attention elsewhere.

The Colonel stopped at a page in the file. He had found the corroborating evidence taken from the reports of other contacts that Stern had been in Haifa in August 1939. But when the Colonel looked at the evidence now, he realized that all the scattered bits and pieces of information had been provided by contacts who were known or suspected Zionist activists, involved with illegal immigration into Palestine.

The Colonel turned more pages in the file. Stern's unlikely adventure had also brought Poland to mind. Why the association? Simply because the German invasion of Poland had followed so soon after Stern's escape?

No. There was a connection and he found it. A short paragraph from an informer's report to the Turkish police in Istanbul. To the effect that the informer had seen Stern in Istanbul shortly after his escape from Damascus. That Stern had been carrying a forged Polish passport and had been frantically arranging a secret trip to Poland. To the Pyry forest near Warsaw, on a mysterious mission of great importance.

Or so the informer had speculated, offering a personal opinion without a trace of evidence to back up his claim.

Under normal circumstances the Colonel would have smiled at these cobwebs of conjecture. The Turkish police were wildly inaccurate about everything, and Istanbul was notorious for its legions of aspiring informers who would gladly claim anything in exchange for a minor official favor. And in this case not even the informer's identity had been included in the report. Even the fact that the informer had subsequently been found dead floating in the Bosporus meant nothing, given the situation in Istanbul in that last summer before the war.

Pure invention from some desperate refugee. Ridiculous rumors whispered across a café table and set adrift in the clouded brain of a Turkish policeman lazily puffing hashish, dimly trying to focus his eyes on the crotch of a serving-boy across the way.

And yet?

The Colonel closed the file. He frowned.

Perhaps he had made a serious mistake in accepting Stern's explanation of what he had been doing in those last few days before the war began. Perhaps Stern had actually made a secret trip to Poland without telling anyone about it.

Why? wondered the Colonel. What did it mean and what had he been hiding? Why had he lied and taken such care to make sure his lie had been covered?

Stern had been unusually experienced and clever. He had been dedicated to a cause that was probably too idealistic ever to be realized, but the cause had still been straightforward and comprehensible, as splendid in its simplicity as Stern's ideals had been.

Or rather, as they had appeared to be. For it was obvious now that someone else had stumbled upon Stern's Polish adventure and had decided to look into it more deeply, and in so doing had caught a glimpse of something unexpected. A suggestion of some enigma, some profound truth, that must have subsequently been uncovered by the Armenian.

Who had then told Stern what he had discovered. Just before a hand grenade had come flying in through the door of a dingy Arab bar in a Cairo slum, and Stern had been killed saving the Armenian's life.

Where were we? asked the Colonel, looking up.

I'm not sure, replied the Major. You were talking about the important work Stern did for us, and then you seemed to have some doubts about something.

Yes, well, it's just that the situation isn't as clear in my mind now as it was. Because that seems to be the very nature of this operation. Somewhere a doubt arose, as I see it, a doubt with very serious implications. So a man who knew Stern from somewhere, an outsider, was recruited to come in and find out what he could about Stern.

That would be our Purple Seven, said the Major.

Yes, the Armenian. A professional who might have been a friend of Stern's once, or who might have worked with him at some point in the past. Possibly in Stern's gunrunning activities, without knowing they were just a cover for his role in intelligence. Well the Armenian went about his business and my guess is he was successful. Either he

20

discovered the truth about Stern or he came close enough for it not to make any difference.

The Colonel leaned back. There was admiration and even a touch of awe in his voice.

My God, you just can't appreciate the enormity of that task without having known Stern. The layers to the man, the subtleties. He grew up in these parts and knew every language and dialect, every nuance, every corner and what lay around it. There was simply no competing with him out here. He could go anywhere and be anyone, and at one time or another he did seem to go everywhere and be just about everyone. As he wanted, as it served his purposes. Describe a tiny corner of the desert and he knew it. Mention a shop hidden away in a bazaar in any of ten dozen towns and he'd been there, knew the owner. An extraordinary experience, dealing with a man like Stern. And he was modest. You didn't even begin to sense the depths to the man until he happened to mention some unexpected thing in an offhand way.

The Colonel grimaced. He reached down and moved his false leg.

Anyway, the Armenian must have done whatever he did and then gone to Stern with what he'd learned, which is strange in itself. You'd think he would have gone first to the people who'd hired him, but obviously he didn't. Because if he had, those same people would now know that Stern is dead, and they don't. Not yet, because I haven't told them.

So the Armenian went directly to Stern, continued the Colonel, and that was the meeting in the Arab bar. The Armenian got in touch with Stern and set up a meeting, and then he sat down in that bar and told Stern what he'd discovered, and it was the full truth or close to it. Which was what caused Stern to begin smiling halfway through their conversation. Because at last, after all these years of subterfuge, someone had uncovered the truth about him.

Stern's reaction to that would be to smile? asked the Major. Why not just the opposite?

I have no idea. It might have to do with who the Armenian is. The Armenian confronted Stern with the facts, in any case, and Stern's reaction was to smile with relief. That was the expression you used.

Jameson used, corrected the Major.

Yes, Jameson, our alter ego in this case. So we have Stern smiling and the Armenian not liking it at all, and that's when the conversation grew heated. The Armenian didn't agree with what Stern was doing, couldn't agree, and he argued about it. But Stern was confident. He was convinced of his rightness and he went on to justify himself. Your words again, or Jameson's rather. And that was where matters stood when the grenade came sailing in the door and Stern saved the Armenian's life.

The Colonel paused.

Important, that. I don't know why, but it has to be. It was Stern's last act and there's a meaning to it. Something to do with the discovery the Armenian had made, or perhaps going further back, to the whole relationship between the two of them. Which was profound, I'd say. Something quite special to both of them.

You know, concluded the Colonel, the curious part in all this is that we seem to have some of the answers without knowing the questions. More whiskey for you?

The Major poured for them both. A clock ticked on the wall. When it appeared the Colonel had nothing more to say, the Major decided to ask his own questions.

Whose operation do you think it is? The Monastery's?

Yes, no doubt. It's much too deep and roundabout to be anyone else's. And it's bizarre and wildly improbable, not what anyone would expect. All the characteristics of a Monastery operation.

What about the Armenian?

I've been thinking about him but no one comes to mind. Frankly, I haven't the least idea. Of course I know who originally used that Purple Seven identity, in fact I helped put it together for him. But that was three or four years ago, in Palestine in connection with the Arab revolt, and somehow it all seems irrelevant now.

Who was that? The man who used the identity then?

A fellow from the ranks. Sergeant O'Sullivan was his name.

Sergeant O'Sullivan, murmured the Major, a faraway look coming into his eyes. You're not referring to *the* Sergeant O'Sullivan?

Oh yes, the same. It rather slipped my mind how famous he used to be. I suppose you must have heard of him, even though you were very young at the time.

Yes, replied the Major, leaning back in his chair to reflect upon this astonishing piece of information from the past.

During the First World War, at least in the early part of the war, the exploits of Sergeant Columbkille O'Sullivan had been gloriously famous in every household in Britain, after he had been awarded two Victoria Crosses for extraordinary heroism in the gruesome slaughter known as the First Battle of Champagne, the only man of any rank to be so honored in the Great War. Then he had been referred to everywhere as *the* Sergeant O'Sullivan, or with even greater affection as simply *Our Colly of Champagne.*

But the celebrated little sergeant's reputation had mysteriously begun to deteriorate after his Irish compatriots raised their Easter Rebellion in 1916. By the summer of that year a rumor was rife in London that *Our Colly* was drinking to excess, and by the time autumn blew around it was generally known throughout England that *Their Colly's* reckless bravado in combat had always been due to drink and drink alone.

Further, while stationed in France and slyly acquiring Victoria Crosses through gross misrepresentation at the First Battle of Champagne, *Their Colly*, according to updated reports, had had the absurd arrogance to pretend that drinking anything less than vintage champagne was beneath him, even though when he was home again and on tour as a hero, he had reverted to his natural ways by gleefully swilling down anything alcoholic that passed through his trembling hands.

Thus the once renowned *the* Sergeant O'Sullivan had been entirely forgotten by the end of the Great War. The Major himself, in the course of his professional army career, could not recall ever having heard the famous name in any context, historical or otherwise. Yet to him, as to tens of thousands of British schoolboys, *Our Colly of Champagne* had been a unique folk hero when they were growing up.

My God, exclaimed the Major. Whatever *did* happen to *Our Colly?*

Oh he reenlisted again after the war, replied the Colonel.

He did? *Our Colly?*

Yes. And because of all that notoriety he'd received at such a young age, he wanted to get away from England, so he joined the Imperial Camel Corps out here. He even reenlisted under another name, just plain Private So-and-So. He'd developed an absolute passion for anonymity.

The Camel Corps? *Our Colly* on camelback?

Exactly. But before long he'd been promoted to sergeant again, and of course it was impossible for Colly's extraordinary talents to go unnoticed anywhere, even if he happened to be just loping around the deserts on a camel. So he was invited into this end of the business, and once with us Colly couldn't help but carry on with his usual flair. Anonymously, of course, undercover. In fact you could say it was just what he'd always been looking for. And all that talk in the last war about his drinking was utter nonsense. Colly enjoyed a glass as much as the next man, but he was careful never to take a drink on duty. Drank only water when he was on assignment, made a point of it. Wouldn't even touch a cup of tea. And there are stories that anyone would find hard to believe. Some remarkable episodes in Abyssinia against the Italians, and then later in Palestine when we had to deal with the Arab revolt.

Palestine? murmured the Major. I was in and out of there during the Arab revolt. Where was *Our Colly* working then?

Up around Galilee. He was using several covers at the time. One was as the Armenian dealer in Coptic artifacts and another was as a captain in the King's Own Scottish Regiment. Every few weeks he'd slip into Haifa and transform himself. Something of a trickster, Colly was. He enjoyed that sort of thing.

Our Colly, murmured the Major. What was he doing at Galilee?

Oh he had several assignments going on at once, as he usually did, but probably the most important one then was helping the Jewish settlers organize their Special Night Squads, the first real mobile strike force they had. Colly was the man who trained those squads and set them up. He did that in his cover as the Scottish captain, and the methods he developed soon became one of the important operating principles of the Palmach.

The Colonel smiled.

The fellow had dash, damn it, it just came natural to him. I remember talking later to one of the young Haganah men Colly had taken on as a deputy, fellow by the name of Dayan, and he told me how astonished they all were the first time they met Colly. The Arab revolt was in full swing and Dayan and Allon and these others had gone up to defend a settlement near the Lebanese border. Well one moonlit night they were manning the pickets when up drove a taxi with its headlights off and its taillights on the front of the car to confuse the enemy, and out of the taxi stepped this lean small figure carrying two rifles and a Bible and a drum, an English-Hebrew dictionary and five gallons of New England rum.

Our Colly?

None other. His daring at coming up there alone at night, Dayan said, made a tremendous impression on everyone. They'd never met a military man like that before and it affected their thinking a good deal. The idea that warfare, irregular warfare at any rate, could be based on something other than parade-ground drill.

Amazing, murmured the Major.

Yes. Colly often worked for me in the most difficult of situations, and more than once I tried to convince him to accept a commission. But Colly always adamantly refused, saying he preferred to keep his standing as *the* Sergeant O'Sullivan. Even though his rating was secret of course, and no one knew he had any standing at all. He was quite a man, no question about it. And as for the role he played in the Spanish Civil War, that still has to be kept close to the chest.

Why's that? asked the Major, his head spinning with these revelations about the hero of his childhood.

Because Colly was fighting on the Republican side, don't you see. Officially he was on a leave of absence, and unofficially he was doing a number of things for us, but still, a regular army man and all. It just wouldn't do. Not then, not even now.

The Major was more astounded than ever.

Our Colly? he repeated dreamily, gazing down at the papers in his hand. Then something caught his eye and he laughed abruptly.

Did you choose this name, sir?

Which name?

The cover name for Colly's Purple Seven identity. *A. O. Gulbenkian.*

The Colonel smiled.

Oh no, that was Colly's doing. As a matter of fact, it was the name he used when he reenlisted and went into the Imperial Camel Corps after the last war. Says something about his sense of humor, I suppose. He thought it would be amusing to skulk around the Middle East on a camel, using the last name of a famous Armenian oil millionaire.

Bizarre, murmured the Major. Gulbenkian does seem to be an odd name to come across here. But what were the initials A.O. supposed to stand for?

The Colonel laughed.

Alpha and Omega, probably. Colly's sense of humor again.

Our Colly of Champagne, murmured the Major. Extraordinary.

Yes, the same. And he was small and dark all right, and thin and wiry and every bit a professional. So I admit the description you brought back had me disturbed for a moment.

The Major was even more confused.

Why? Couldn't he be our Purple Seven, working out of the Monastery? You said the identity was issued to him originally.

It was, and it's also true that he was working out of the Monastery the last time around. But those Monks in the desert have been up to something since then. Do you recall the facts concerning the kidnapping of the German commandant of Crete?

Certainly. Did *Our Colly* have something to do with that?

His show from the beginning. Thought it up and worked out the details and then went along to see that it went smoothly. Well it did go smoothly, as an operation. They grabbed the commandant and walked him across the island to the south coast, and the submarine was where it was supposed to be on the night of the pickup. But that night Colly's luck ran out. He'd been defying the law of averages for just too long.

What happened?

He and his group crossed tracks with a German patrol. Colly made a racket and headed up into the mountains to lead the patrol off the scent. He was shot and wounded in the darkness but he managed to keep on going, until he had to look for a place to hide toward dawn. That section of the mountains is as bare as a lunar landscape, and the only place where he could get out of sight was inside one of the underground stone cisterns the Cretan goatherds use up there, to gather the runoff in the spring when the snow melts.

The Colonel scowled.

On their way by, the Germans left one of their men at the cistern because he was having an attack of dysentery and couldn't keep up, but Colly didn't know that. Colly waited long enough for the patrol to move on across the mountain, then stuck his head out of the cistern to take a look. Shivering, numb, barely able·to move. He'd been standing up to his nose in the mountain-cold water of that cistern for an hour by then. And as chance would have it, the lone German happened to be squatting on a knoll right behind Colly.

The Colonel grimaced.

A freak accident really, I don't like to recall it. The startled German tossed a hand grenade and death was instantaneous for Colly. Decapitation.

What? *Our Colly?*

So the only way he could be part of these new events is if he'd been resurrected, which would certainly explain the enigmatic smile on the Armenian's face after the explosion in the bar. If O'Sullivan had been resurrected, he'd certainly be one to smile about it.

What?

No, he's dead all right. This Purple Seven isn't Colly. There's another Gulbenkian out there somewhere now.

The Major recovered and thought for a moment.

As I remember, there wasn't any mention of a British sergeant in connection with the kidnapping in Crete.

That's right, said the Colonel.

It was described by us as the work of some British officers.

There were a couple along, yes. And we broadcast that so the Germans would stop rounding up Cretan villagers and shooting them in retaliation. Since it was army to army, we said we'd shoot German POWs if they did that, and they stopped.

But why didn't they mention the fact that they'd killed O'Sullivan?

Because they didn't know who the dead man was, said the Colonel. Colly was disguised as a Cretan mountaineer and the Germans decided to keep us guessing about whether that mountaineer was alive or not, just in case he happened to be someone who was important to us. And also, so we could never be sure what he might have told them. Is telling them, for that matter.

The Major nodded. It was obvious to him that since the Colonel knew exactly how O'Sullivan had died, he must have a source in Crete who had reported the truth to him. Most likely a partisan, he thought, who had been following the German patrol and had witnessed the incident at the cistern from afar. But Crete was outside the Major's area of concern, so he said nothing more on the subject.

The Colonel, meanwhile, was pursuing a new chain of thought that struck him as curious. In fact he did have a special source in Crete who had reported the circumstances of O'Sullivan's death, as the Major suspected, but the agent was far more valuable than a partisan in the mountains. And it was in order to protect this agent's highly sensitive position as an apparent collaborator with the Germans, a dangerous role to attempt in a place like Crete, that the Colonel had decided not to reveal to anyone the fact that he knew for certain Sergeant O'Sullivan was dead.

Until now, when these nostalgic reminiscences concerning *Our Colly* had caused him to forget himself in front of the Major.

But before this moment he had told no one. Not even the elite intelligence unit for which O'Sullivan had been working when he went to Crete, the obscure command in the desert often referred to by the Colonel and others, in private and with some disdain, as *the Monastery.*

Thus a question had suddenly occurred to the Colonel.

How did the Monastery know O'Sullivan was dead?

For they certainly had to know. Otherwise they would never have assigned his Purple Seven identity to another man. And yet the Monastery was unaware of the Colonel's special source in Crete. Was there someone else, then, who could have been in touch with the Colonel's special source without the Colonel knowing about it? One of the agents, perhaps, who had been landed in Crete by submarine since the time of Colly's death?

The Colonel reached for another file, then stopped and nodded to himself. There was no need to look up any names. Who, after all, had provided the Colonel with this valuable source in Crete in the first place?

Who indeed? *Stern,* of course. Stern had recruited the woman soon after Crete had fallen to the Germans. She had been an acquaintance of Stern's from somewhere over the years, and it had been Stern who had gone to her and convinced her to undertake the role of a collaborator, with all the danger and humiliation that entailed. And then not long after Colly had disappeared in Crete, Stern had managed to get himself sent there on another assignment altogether. But obviously his real purpose in going had been to find out about Colly.

Stern must have known Colly, the Colonel now realized, from the time when Colly had been in Palestine. Perhaps they had even become close friends then, for they were the kind of men who would have been naturally attracted to one another. Colly with his resourcefulness and his many idiosyncrasies, an eccentric dreamer who was more religious than rational, who was a firm believer in the Bible and who had become an ardent Zionist while working in Palestine fired with a mystical sense of the special mission of the Jews.

Yes. Colly would have appealed to Stern and they had probably become close friends, unknown to the Colonel and even to the Monastery. So when Colly hadn't returned from Crete, Stern had worked out a way to get himself sent there, to find out what had happened to his friend.

It fit, the Colonel was sure of it. It was exactly the kind of thing Stern would have done. And once in Crete, Stern must have left the safety of the mountains and taken the risk of going down into town, disguised as a Cretan mountaineer, and looked up the woman he had previously recruited for the Colonel, to learn for himself what Colly's fate had been. And later mentioned the fact of Colly's death to the Monastery, disguising his source.

It fit, and it troubled the Colonel. It was a little bit terrifying sometimes to think of the chances Stern had taken. This one, for example, strictly on his own. Thinking up a plausible assignment in Crete and getting himself sent there, simply to find out about a friend. To the Colonel, there was something disturbing about that. Something profoundly puzzling and suggestive of Stern's whole character.

But for the moment the Colonel put aside these intriguing considerations. Before he did anything else, he had to set matters straight in his own office.

I'm afraid I might have given you the wrong impression just now, he said, when I implied O'Sullivan had been killed. The truth is, we don't know whether he's dead or not. *Our Colly* might well be still alive in the mountains of Crete, which are extensive and rugged, after all.

I understand, answered the Major.

I'm sure you do. Undoubtedly you heard a lot about him as a boy, and you know there was no stopping him ever. Absolutely astonishing when you think of it. *The* Sergeant O'Sullivan. *The* noncommissioned officer of the Empire. I mean our very own, yours and mine and everyone's *Our Colly of Champagne*, right? So all we can say about it now, here, is that Colly can't be the Purple Seven who was in that Arab bar last night with Stern. And that's *all* we can say in respect to Colly.

I understand fully, said the Major.

The Colonel paused. Another thought had come to him. He went back to the report drawn up by the Egyptian policeman, to the information that had been copied down from the Armenian's passport after the explosion. The physical characteristics given for the Armenian were the same as Colly's had been. The Monastery hadn't even bothered to change any of the entries in the passport, although they certainly would have, if there had been any reason to. Did that mean the Armenian not only resembled Colly, but resembled him exactly?

The Major must have already noticed this coincidence of physical details.

Did *Our Colly* have a brother? he asked.

The Colonel groaned.

Please. There's no way we can get into that.

Sir?

There were an enormous number of brothers, all of them older, as I recall. Colly used to claim the reason he had so many brothers was because his father ate so many potatoes. Some kind of local superstition where he grew up. Anyway, most of the brothers emigrated to America at an early age, to someplace called the Bronx, where they became roofers or drunkards or both.

Roofers?

Reaching for the stars in the New World, was the way Colly used to put it. And becoming drunkards, sadly, when the stars still proved to be out of reach, even over there. But no matter. It's an intriguing idea but it can't lead anywhere. The Bronx is simply too far away. Even Jameson couldn't penetrate such an exotic place.

The Colonel shook his head.

Stern, he muttered. *The Armenian.* That bar in a slum. One way or another, I don't think they're going to be very happy at the Monastery when I tell them about this.

One way or another? asked the Major.

Yes. If the hand grenade was their doing, it has to mean they intended to kill both of them. And if it really was a sordid accident, at the very least it tells them the Armenian went to Stern with what he'd learned, rather than to them. And now that Stern's gone, the

Armenian's word is all the Monastery has about anything and everything concerning this operation of theirs against Stern. . . . No, I'm
afraid there's no way out of it for the Armenian. Whatever the situation, he's in trouble.

Perhaps we could look into it further?

On our own, you mean. Yes, we could try to do that. But it's still
the Monastery's operation, so I can't wait any longer to tell them
about Stern's death and all the rest of it. Even a little thing like our
sending Jameson over for a look is going to make them furious.

What about Maud? She might be able to pass on a message to her
friend, the current Gulbenkian.

Oh that's not important. He doesn't need to be told where he
stands. But I did intend to speak to her anyway, she's waiting now.

The Colonel looked down at the floor. He sighed.

The point is, you know as well as I do that when the Monastery's
running an agent as a Purple Seven in this kind of case, against a man
who was probably our most valuable agent and perhaps their most
valuable agent as well, then that Purple Seven can't help but have a
very short life expectancy, considering what must have been at stake.
What is at stake? If he won he loses, if he lost he loses. And he's
going to have to be a very wily Armenian now to live even a day or
two with the Monks after him. I only hope he's half as clever as his
predecessor in that identity was.

From what you've said about O'Sullivan, that seems unlikely.

I know it does. You just don't come across a man like O'Sullivan
very often. You can't expect to and you don't.

Once more the Colonel shifted his false leg. The Major rose to
leave.

Sir?

Hm.

I'll look into this as quietly as possible, but do you think you could
give me any suggestions? There are so many names and dates and
events in Stern's file, I could spend a year just trying to sort them
out. Do you have any idea at all what the Armenian might have been
looking for?

It's just a guess, said the Colonel, but my inclination would be to
start with Poland.

The Major looked completely bewildered.

Poland? Here in Cairo? . . . The war started with Poland, he added
blankly

And so it did, said the Colonel. Oddly enough, and so it did. But the war only ostensibly started there. Its origins have to lie more deeply in the past, as origins always do. By the time something becomes apparent, well, it's already traveled some distance, hasn't it? It's already been on its course for years and decades and it has a history to it. So although I'd start with Poland if I were you, I'd also keep in mind that's only a beginning. We have to go back, *back*, to find the Armenian. Because that's exactly what he did to find Stern. Does it sound complicated to you?

Frankly it does, said the Major.

But it's not really. It can't be. Stern was a man and the Armenian's a man and Poland's a place. And the Armenian managed to do it working alone, while we have enormous resources at our disposal.

Why do you say he was working alone? Surely he had the resources of the Monastery behind him?

No, I'm quite sure he didn't, not in any substantial way. The Monastery would never share anything of consequence with an outsider, that's not the way they operate. There's a reason why they have the name they have, as with most names in this world. So my guess is the Armenian was as alone before as he is now, and he's certainly alone now if the Monks are after him.

The Colonel gazed off into the distance. It must be an extremely important case, he mused.

Sir?

Just on the face of it, from what little we know. Stern and Colly's successor supposedly working against each other? Yet at the same time, not working against each other in some strange way? My God, if you had ever wanted two men to do something for you out here, it goes without saying you would have picked Stern and Colly.

And Colly's successor?

The Colonel shook his head.

Yes I know. It's a mystery, and a pity.

Sir?

Oh it's just that I always had such great affection for Colly, and I suppose I must be inadvertently transferring some of those feelings to his successor, this new Purple Seven.

The Colonel smiled, almost shyly.

Odd, how we do that. I haven't the least idea who this Purple Seven is. He's just a man without a name whom we call the Armenian for convenience. Yet I can't help but feel sad when I think about him. Where he is now and what he knows and what it's come down to for him, just all of it. Of course there's no rational explanation for my feelings, but all the same, a man who could uncover the truth about Stern . . .

The Colonel sighed.

Well I guess we'll just have to see, that's all.

At a remote site in the desert, deep within an ancient fortresslike structure, a monk in a hooded cassock moved quickly down a narrow subterranean corridor lit at rare intervals by torches fixed to the walls. The corridor disappeared in the gloom and the only sound was the muffled swish of the monk's robes as he padded quietly down the worn stones in the half-light.

The monk was a powerful stocky man with an unkempt beard, which only partially covered the piece of his jaw that was missing. He stopped at a low iron door cut into the rock, pausing before he flung it open, a shattering noise in the underground stillness.

The monk was facing a tiny cell. At the far end a man with only one arm knelt in front of a plain wooden cross, his back to the door, heavy chains twisting away from his ankles to a rusty iron ring in the wall. When the door slammed open the man's wasted body jerked forward, flinching away from the crashing noise. But he didn't turn around nor did he lower his hand, which remained in front of him in an attitude of supplication.

The man looked like a desert hermit. His hair was matted and his bare feet were black with dirt. Apparently he had been praying in absolute darkness, for the cell lacked even a candle, only a little light reaching it now from the flickering torches in the corridor. The face of the hooded monk was invisible in the blackness.

For a time neither man moved in the shadowy silence, the two of them somber and stationary in the separate poses of their separate worlds, the powerful stocky monk framed in the low iron doorway, the shackled man facing the crumbling wall as he trembled, waiting. And then all at once the distant opening chords of Bach's Mass in B Minor could be heard booming forth from somewhere high above them in the ancient fortresslike structure.

The monk crossed himself and removed a coiled whip from under his cassock, a long thick scourge of braided leather. He let the whip unwind until it dangled down to the floor, an ugly many-tongued lash. The shackled man jerked slightly, his head sinking lower. It was cold in the cell, yet drops of sweat had broken out around the lips of the monk. He licked the sweat away and spoke in a hard contemptuous voice.

The Armenian survived the hand grenade, he said.

The stark words rang in the stillness and a sudden spasm gripped the shackled man, an unmistakable shudder of eagerness, an almost sensual expression of loathing. Frantically he began clawing at the rags on his shoulders, stripping them back to reveal his wasted flesh, deathly white skin crossed with dark uneven scars. In another moment the kneeling man had bared himself to the waist and buried his face in his single hand, rigid again, waiting.

The monk stood with his feet wide apart. He whipped the scourge into the air and brought it down with all his strength on the pale back of the kneeling man. The ugly leather tongues hissed and whined against the flesh, snapping up again. After the third brutal lashing the monk tossed the bloodied scourge into a corner. He licked his lips and stared. The shackled man had been driven to the floor by the force of the blows, and it was only with a great effort that he managed to raise himself to his knees.

He was breathing heavily, fighting to keep from falling back on his face. Again he raised his one thin hand to the cross on the wall in an attitude of supplication, the palm of his open hand now wet with tears. His body shook violently as he tried to control himself.

The Armenian's a dead man, muttered the tortured figure. He's dead but he doesn't know it yet. *Kill him.*

But he has eluded us, murmured the monk with great deference. We don't know where he is, Your Grace.

In that case, whispered the shackled man, find him and then kill him.

Yes, Your Grace.

The monk lingered a few moments to see if there were to be any further instructions. But the shackled man in rags seemed oblivious to his presence now, so the monk backed slowly away into the corridor and closed the heavy iron door on the tiny cell, leaving his scourged superior alone once more in the blackness with his ripped flesh and his simple cross, alone and bleeding . . . praying.

3

Hopi Mesa Kiva

Some months before the obscure gunrunner Stern was killed in Cairo, a large black automobile sped silently down a remote secondary road deep in the arid wastelands of the American southwest.

In the rear of the automobile sat three distinguished gray-haired men wearing rumpled white linen suits and broad Panama hats, their faces creased by the long journey from Washington in a military aircraft. In addition to having been youthful heroes for their respective nations in the First World War, the three shared reputations for unorthodox brilliance in their different professions. And now with a new war sweeping over the earth, they had become men of vast secret powers in innumerable corners of the world.

Of the three, only the Britisher was completely unknown to his countrymen at large. An old Etonian and a member of two London clubs, he was a professional military officer who had been a colonel in the Life Guards before being anonymously seconded, years earlier, to an anonymous post requiring strictly anonymous secret duties, in keeping with traditional British anonymity in matters of intelligence.

At the moment he was knitting.

The Canadian was small and slight with hooded eyes that watched everything. Originally famous as an air ace in a Sopwith Camel, then as the world lightweight boxing champion and the man who had perfected the method of sending photographs by radio, he had gone on to become a millionaire industrialist with worldwide business interests.

The Canadian was stirring a mixture over ice in a chemist's beaker.

While the large Irish-American contented himself with gazing out

35

the window at the dwindling light of that late desert afternoon. A law-school classmate of the American president and the former commander of the famed New York regiment known as the Fighting Sixty-ninth, he was a self-made success who had become a Wall Street lawyer with international dealings.

The Britisher was known to the other two men as *Ming*, from the first syllable of his surname, which wasn't spelled that way at all. He was the first to break the silence in the backseat.

Let's see how this is for length, he said, the knitting needles in his hands running through a final flurry of clicks.

He raised the black knitted material from his lap, held the end of a tape measure to one of its corners and reached across the rear seat. The American took the other ends and pulled them taut, while the small Canadian in the middle, his view suddenly blocked by the screen of black material in front of him, slid down in his seat and peeked beneath the knitting in order to keep his beaker in view.

Still a little short? suggested the American.

Although commonly known as Wild Bill, the American was referred to as *Big Bill* on the various joint committees run by the subordinates of the three men, to distinguish him from the Canadian, who was half his size and had the same first name, and who was consequently known as *Little Bill*. The small Canadian, in his quiet intrepid way, being considered as wild as anyone.

Rumpled white linen suits and dented Panama hats eccentrically cocked at odd angles.

Big Bill. Little Bill. Ming.

And in Washington and Ottawa and London, mysterious identical memos in the hands of their staffs stating cryptically that *the chief* would be in the company of the other two chiefs for the next forty hours or so, strictly out of touch on a secret mission of great importance, destination and purpose unknown.

Apparently Ming agreed with Big Bill about the length of his knitted material. He nodded without expression and went back to work with his knitting needles. Little Bill removed a chilled long-stemmed glass from an ice bucket, gave a last stir to the contents of his beaker and poured. He added a twist of lemon peel, then sipped judiciously.

Delicious, he murmured, immediately taking a much deeper drink so that none of the martini would spill.

For some minutes the three men sat once more in silence as the automobile sped across the barren wastelands, the stillness inside touched only by the hum of the automobile engine and the rhythmic clicking of Ming's knitting needles. Again it was Ming who interrupted their musings. Briefly he laid aside his handiwork and fitted a Turkish cigarette of strong black tobacco into a cigarette holder Without lighting the cigarette he sucked vigorously on the mouthpiece of the holder three or four times, then stuffed the still-new cigarette into an ashtray on his armrest. Sitting very erect, he looked out the window to his right and surveyed the empty lunar landscape. They were now not far from the secret destination that had caused so much speculation in their respective capitals, a tiny Indian pueblo, or village, where they would meet the chief medicine man of the Hopi tribe.

What really might make him do it? asked Ming, as much to himself as to anyone else. Surely not patriotism, our cause isn't his. And not these illegalities we have on him, they're not enough of an inducement. Why would a man leave this peace and quiet to go halfway around the world and face the possibility of being killed? The war seems so far away here, it's almost as if it didn't exist.

Adventure? murmured Little Bill, sipping from his glass. From what your people in Cairo imply, he seems to be the kind of man who might be finding life in these deserted parts a bit too quiet by now, a bit too peaceful. After all, it's been about seven years since he came out here.

There's that certainly, agreed Big Bill. As for his illegal status and the dealings he had when he first entered the country, you're right that they amount to nothing, not even an opening card. A man like that could disappear whenever he wanted, just about anyplace he wanted, and no one would be able to trace him. Those are commonplace skills to him. No, if he does agree to go, I think it will be out of curiosity.

But not over Rommel, said Ming. That kind of concern, I suspect, would have no meaning to him at all. Is the file handy?

Here, said Little Bill, retrieving a folder from the stack of confidential reading material they had brought with them to pass the hours on the flight from Washington. On the tab of the file the real name of the Hopi medicine man was typed in purple letters.

O'SULLIVAN BEARE, J.E.C.K.K.B.

(JUNIOR, BUT NEVER SO KNOWN)

Little Bill opened the file on his lap. He sipped his martini and peered at the first page.

What was it you wanted to review?

Nothing in particular. Just run through some of the basic facts, if you would.

Little Bill began to read.

Joseph Enda Columbkille Kieran Kevin Brendan O'SULLIVAN BEARE.

Subject was born in the Aran Islands and is commonly known as Joe. No formal education. His Christian names all represent saints who were originally from his island, which is tiny and windswept and rainy and has produced more saints and drunkards, per capita, than any other area in Christendom.

Subject grew up speaking Gaelic and worked as a boy on his father's fishing boat. He is the youngest of a large brood of brothers, only one of whom is ever known to have distinguished himself, the next to the last and the closest in age to the Subject. This brother dropped the appendage Beare and was known simply as Columbkille O'Sullivan, or occasionally as Their Colly in the vulgar press, where he attained a brief notoriety as a loutish drunken layabout during the First Battle of Champagne, the Great War, 1914–1918.

Now there's a name from our salad days, mused Little Bill. Although in my unit, we always called him *Our Colly* then.

And in mine, added Big Bill. Your archivist, he said to Ming, would seem to have some kind of historical bent.

Ming said nothing, his knitting needles clicking methodically. Little Bill smiled and read on.

Subject joined the Easter Rebellion in 1916, at the age of sixteen, and managed to escape from the Dublin post office when it fell. Went into hiding and fought alone until trapped, when he managed to escape again, this time disguised as a Poor Clare nun on a pilgrimage to the Holy Land.

In Jerusalem, through a ruse and another disguise, the Subject took up residence in the Home for Crimean War Heroes, a local British charity. There, on behalf of a grateful nation, he was awarded the standard prize of honor for all heroes who survived the Crimean War—a used khaki blanket. The Subject has carried this blanket with him ever since as a kind of memento.

Little Bill smiled.
A kind of memento? he murmured.
Big Bill cleared his throat as Ming's knitting needles clicked quietly. Little Bill sipped from his class and read on.

Soon after arriving in Jerusalem, the Subject met Stern and went to work for him, running guns into Palestine.

Another initial acquaintance in Jerusalem was an American woman, Maud. The Subject lived with her for some months and a son was born of the union in Jericho, while the Subject was away on one of his frequent trips for Stern. The American woman subsequently left Palestine with the baby, abandoning the Subject, who broke with Stern thereafter, blaming Stern for what had happened.

The Subject then took part in founding what came to be known as the Great Jerusalem Poker Game, a blasphemous game of chance that lasted for a full twelve years, or until 1933, when President Roosevelt announced a New Deal for the common man in the United States. The Subject then left Jerusalem and the Middle East but not before there was a complete reconciliation with Stern, initiated by Stern and welcomed by the Subject.

Since that time the Subject is known to have kept in touch with Stern, at least on an irregular basis. There is also evidence that he has sent money to Stern over the years, probably an arrangement whereby the Subject could provide funds to the American woman, Maud, without her being aware of their true source.

In 1934, the Subject crossed into the United States from Canada, in disguise once again, using forged papers. After spending a brief period of time in Brooklyn, organizing an illegal business, he traveled west and ended up on the Hopi reservation, where he became chief medicine man of the tribe. When entranced by firelight he is said to mutter in Gaelic, which his untutored parishioners take to be some mysterious tongue of the Great Spirit.

What kind of illegal business in Brooklyn? asked Ming.

Garbage, replied Little Bill. At least that's what it says here, but what's it supposed to mean?

Sometimes, explained Big Bill, the garbage or carting businesses in New York are controlled by mobsters.

Ming looked mystified.

You mean to say there's money in garbage in Brooklyn?

It's possible.

Money in dustbins, mused Ming. How very odd indeed. Even though you Americans are our cousins, it does seem you've been strangely affected by these wild dreams of the promise to be found in the New World.

Well that brings us up to date, said Big Bill. What do you think?

Good man to have in a scrape, commented Little Bill. Resourceful, independent, capable of thinking on his feet. And above all, experienced. The disguises and so forth. I like that.

Knows his own mind, added Ming. But with no use for politics, left that behind long ago. Twelve years playing poker in Jerusalem, only to give it all up because Roosevelt happens to announce a New Deal on the other side of the world? A romantic, an idealist. Yet right after that there's this dustbin episode in Brooklyn. Mobsters, you say. So a romantic with a twist, an idealist with a touch of cynicism. There are contradictions here, conflicts in the man's makeup. And then after that we have seven years out in this desert as a recluse, a hermit totally cut off from his own kind. But what is his own kind? That's the point. On the face of it, there's no way to know.

Strictly his own man though, concluded Ming, and I like that. I'm just not sure how we can appeal to him.

Nor am I, said Big Bill. But I do think our important card, perhaps our only card, is his feeling for this man Stern. The curiosity he may have about Stern, what has happened to Stern and why. It's not that Stern might be secretly working for the Germans when he appears to be working for us. We know Stern deals with everybody, that's his value. And our Hopi medicine man may no longer care about our side and their side, but I think he may care about Stern's dozen sides. *Why* Stern is doing whatever it is he's really doing. I suspect an unusual bond still exists between the two of them, a unique bond even, despite the years that have passed since they've seen one another. And that might cause him to go, for his own reasons. We'll just have to explore it when we sit down with him. Get him to talk about Stern and see where it leads.

And let's not forget the American woman, added Little Bill. I've found it's best never to overlook the woman in a case.

Big Bill tipped his head.

Is that so?

Little Bill smiled.

Quite. Now let's just peruse the facts. Our man on the Hopi mesa that lies ahead was quite a remarkable revolutionary once, and although the romanticism may have worn a bit thin since then, or become a mite twisted as you call it, we have to consider what the Middle East must have meant to him once. A young Irish lad suddenly cast into the Holy Land and living in mythical places with names like Jericho and Jerusalem? It must have been pure magic for him after growing up on a deathly poor little rainy island in the Atlantic. The sun and the desert and Maud? Love in the Holy City? A son born in Jericho? Dreams come from the likes of that.

Ming, intent on his knitting, glanced sideways at the ice-cold martini perched on his friend's knee, the delicate stem of the glass lightly held between Little Bill's thumb and forefinger.

You're a romantic yourself, he said dryly. With a twist, of course.

Of course, agreed Little Bill, smiling. Then too, there's the fact that our Joe is still in the desert. Or once more in the desert, which should tell us something.

But what? murmured Ming, as much to himself as to anyone else.

So when you put it all together, continued Little Bill, it wouldn't surprise me if our Hopi medicine man turned out to be willing to leave the safety of his kiva for a journey halfway around the world. There's Maud and there's also his mysterious friend, the enigmatic Stern . . . A journey into his own past, perhaps?

He was a mere youth when he gave up on war and revolution, said Ming. That was twenty years ago and it's been almost that long since he's seen the woman. Men change their ways with time.

Or grow in their ways? said Little Bill. Just possibly his romanticism is incurable, despite two decades of this or that. Who's to know what to expect from an Irish-Hopi?

Ming nodded and held up his knitting. The three men stretched the black shawl across the rear seat. Big Bill read the tape measure.

Just right, he said. I'm told the Hopi take ceremonies very seriously.

Ming put his knitting needles away and Little Bill busied himself clipping the loose ends off the shawl with a small pair of scissors. On the horizon ahead several puffs of smoke had appeared. Ming pointed.

The Hopi signal corps announcing our arrival?

He fitted another strong Turkish cigarette into his holder and inhaled deeply three or four times, then crushed the unlit cigarette in the ashtray that was already full.

But this is *preposterous*, he suddenly roared. An utterly absurd situation. Leaving our three services to dither among themselves while we fly all the way out here for *this*?

Big Bill laughed.

Mostly it was an excuse to get you away and give you a feeling for the size and scope of our continent, your new ally.

Large, muttered Ming. But all the same, you two should be much too busy for this sort of thing.

We are, replied Big Bill. Still, it seemed only appropriate that the three of us, just once, should have the opportunity to recruit an agent together. Just once, as a matter of ritual.

A unique moment in the history of the great democracies, murmured Little Bill. If the Germans should win, it will all be over, all of it, because there's a streak in man that simply can't abide what freedom requires. So it does seem appropriate for the three of us to mark the moment in our little way. . . . And to hope.

Ming turned and gazed at the two of them.

All of that's true, I daresay, and I'd be the last man to say there's no meaning in rituals. But what could *anyone* make of this, when you look at it? The chiefs of our three secret intelligence services, at a moment like this in the history of the West, contemplating Hopi smoke signals at sundown? It's a ritual all right, but it's also a piece of secret intelligence I don't intend to report to anyone at home, and certainly not to Winston.

Little Bill smiled.

Then I will, he said at once. He'd love it.

Ming looked out the window and lapsed into silence.

Yes, he murmured after a time, that's true, Winston *would* love it. And that may be one of the quieter differences between our side and theirs.

Darkness was rising from the wastelands by the time the automobile left the road and slowly began to climb a stretch of hard-baked desert, heading now toward a huge lone mesa that soared above them in the twilight, the pink and purple hues of its lower reaches giving way to sheer golden cliffs in the sky. At last the automobile glided to a stop and the driver switched the headlights off and on three times. The three men stepped outside and gazed up at the awesome cliffs of gold.

Sunset and the myth of the Seven Lost Cities of Cibola, murmured Little Bill. The conquistadores must have kept their eyes on the ground. No wonder they were never able to sort out the dreams and realities of the New World.

Big Bill cleared his throat. No more than ten yards away a silent Indian was standing on one leg, his other leg drawn up beneath him in the timeless pose of a watchman in the wilds, his somber presence as immutable as the vast monoliths soaring majestically above the wastes. The Indian showed no sign of recognition, no sign of even being aware of their presence. He seemed to be as alone out there as he had always been, mysteriously rooted to some secret spot of sand and stone assigned to him at the very dawn of creation. He stood like that for some moments and then his eyes abruptly flickered and he raised his head toward the mesa, as if hearing a whisper descending from the massive walls of gold. The three men followed his gaze upward but heard nothing, not even a touch of wind that might have been caressing the towering dream above them.

The Indian turned and walked away. They followed him a short distance and came upon three burros standing behind a boulder, the creatures as immobile in their solitude as the Indian had been before them.

Preposterous, muttered Ming.

The three of them mounted the burros and the ascent began up a path cut into the face of the cliff, led by the Indian on foot. Higher and higher they climbed, the twisting ledge often no more than a few feet wide, the drop to the side falling off hundreds of feet to the desert below. As they worked their way upward the golden sheen of the rocks receded and the dark vistas beneath them spread out with ever greater mystery, until by the time they reached the summit of the mesa the faint glow on the horizon, the last of the dying sun, had left but a shadowy dimness to the air.

They slid to the ground amidst low adobe shapes built one on top of another, in what appeared to be the central courtyard of the pueblo. While they were dusting themselves off and straightening their clothes, their Indian guide drifted away with the burros. There was no sign of life anywhere in the village.

Not exactly what you'd call being piped aboard, whispered Ming. Is it possible we've come several hundred years too late?

They may all be at vespers, whispered Little Bill. In a setting such as this, a huggermugger at sundown would definitely seem to be in order.

But why are we all whispering? whispered Big Bill.

He squinted through the darkness and pointed.

Isn't that the kiva over there?

In the center of the courtyard a mound of fitted stones rose four or five feet above the surface of the ground, what appeared to be the roof of an underground chamber. Protruding from an opening in the top of the mound was the end of a ladder. They climbed up to the ladder and lowered themselves, one by one, down through the opening into the interior of the mound.

The underground vault they had entered was round and spacious with smooth walls of stone. In the middle of the chamber stood a low unadorned altar, and in front of the altar a lone Indian sat crosslegged on the ground, cloaked in a blanket. The chamber was roughly divided in half, the semicircle where the Indian sat having a lower floor level than the side where they had descended and now found themselves standing awkwardly, their disheveled linen suits filthy from the climb up the face of the cliff, their Panama hats bashed and askew. Here and there torches hissed on the walls, casting uneasy shadows.

The Indian watched them impassively, his dark skin deeply etched with lines. His hair was long and greasy, what little of it showed beneath a thick wool hat squashed down to his ears, a hat that might have been bright red once but was now badly faded by time and the elements. Although crudely woven by hand, the hat didn't seem to be of local manufacture. Instead it gave every appearance of being the product of some hovel-industry in the Old World, the meager handiwork of an aging peasant laboring in perpetual rain and twilight. In Ireland, perhaps.

The impression given by the hat was vaguely disquieting to the three visitors. Peaked front and back and pulled down over the Indian's head at a raffish angle, it suggested nothing so much as the shoddy costume of an itinerant frontier trickster eager to unload worthless bottles of some all-purpose health tonic, fortified with gin and laudanum, in exchange for valuable furs.

As for the Indian's outer garment, the threadbare khaki blanket covering him from neck to ankle, it was so worn and tattered it looked like a campaign relic from another century, and indeed, a legend stamped on its edge stated that it had originally been issued for use among Her Majesty's forces in the Crimea, 1854. Of course the blanket was immediately recognizable to the three men, having been prominently mentioned in their intelligence files as a souvenir from the Home for Crimean War Heroes in Jerusalem.

As soon as they were off the ladder and standing together, the Indian made a gesture commanding silence. Another gesture and the three of them were sitting in a row facing him and the altar, higher than he was both because he was such a small man and because of the lower level of the floor on his side of the chamber. They watched him as he reached under his blanket and brought out something in a closed fist. Solemnly the Indian thrust his fist in the air and muttered a guttural incantation, then dropped his fist and moved it sideways with a tossing motion.

From up to down. From left to right. The Indian was throwing cornmeal at them, sprinkling them with cornmeal. And as he did so, strangely, he seemed to be making the sign of the cross in the air.

His face still stern, the Indian reached under his blanket again and this time brought out a flat papery corn husk, together with a handful of rough homegrown tobacco. Deftly he rolled a thick cigarette, struck a wooden match on the sole of his bare foot and put the flame to the end of the cigarette, which flared briefly. The Indian puffed several times and handed the loose cigarette over to his three visitors, who drew on it in turn, coughing and sputtering. The Indian nodded and took the cigarette back. Abruptly he smiled, speaking in a soft Irish voice.

. . . takes getting used to, I guess, like life and a lot of things. And that business you've probably heard about Indians using peacepipes by way of welcome, well, it's strictly that. The business. The Hopi have always smoked their tobacco in what we'd call cigarettes. And speaking of myths, the Hopi view of creation is that the first thing ever said by anyone in the universe was simply this. *Why am I here?*

The Indian laughed.

. . . makes sense, you say? Well you're right about that, questions generally do. They have just a lovely way of being straightforward and to the point, I know it. It's only when we try to come up with answers that we lose our way and wander, like the stars overhead. For the stars do that, don't they? Forgetting what we've been told, I mean, isn't that surely the way the heavens look? Astray and incomprehensible?

. . . astray, muttered the Indian, and that's the truth of it. Well according to the Hopi myth of creation, those were the very first words ever spoken in the universe. *Why am I here?* And just maybe the longer we live, the more we feel the sense of them

Nor do I need to tell you that this first and most basic query was spoken by a woman, *the* ancestress, don't you know. For the Hopi believe the first life in the void was a woman's, which also makes sense. No strutting males for them in the beginning, because no life ever comes from us, only the living and the observing of it. Descent among the Hopi remains traditional and matrilineal, as I'm told it does in some other old societies.

Whereas my bare feet aren't poking out this way because I'm a savage, but only to show humility. The same reason I'm expected to sit in the lower half of the circle of life down here in the kiva. Among the Hopi, the more powerful you are the more humble. But I guess that's always the true way anywhere.

So to bring you rapidly up to date then, still following the Hopi view of the matter, this ancestress went on to create twins as the next step, males this time for balance, and what do you suppose were the very first words that popped into the heads of those two fellows?

That's right, just what you'd expect, the same as hers but with that added yearning for identity so common to our sex. *Why are we here,* certainly, but quickly right on top of that the other card in the main male riddle, the question that's always there worrying us to the grave, *Who are we anyway?*

So the basic human enigmas seem to dip well back in time and a sound answer on the spot has always been tricky stuff, which brings me around to us. That advance party of yours that climbed up here a couple of weeks ago didn't really say much about who you'd be when you turned up, and moreover, why you'd be turning up in the first place. So I wonder if one of you might have some thoughts on the matter? Why we're here together, I mean?

The Indian reached under his blanket and scratched himself.

Feel free to consult among yourselves, he said. I'll just retire inside my head and you can give me a whoop whenever you're ready.

The Indian closed his eyes and began to snore. His three visitors exchanged glances and one of them cleared his throat. Instantly the Indian's eyes flew open.

How's that? What did you say?

We weren't sure how to address you, answered one of the men.

Oh is that all. Well as the wind carries you, is the answer. The Hopi are great believers in echoes. The way they hear it, everything in the universe is a sound coursing through everything else. So much so that most of my job as the resident shaman here is listening, no more. Straining to hear those echoes, don't you know. But as for me, well . . . why don't you call me Joe?

Fine, said one of the men.

The Indian nodded, smiling.

Yes, simple but fine. And you needn't bother to run out those cover names you must have packed along for yourselves, Gaspar and Balthazar and Melchior, or whatever strange ring the exotic names may have. Since we're way out here in a desert of the West, I'll just put you down as the Three Wise Men from the East, traditional figures that a man can comprehend and sense, if not know. So tell me, have you turned up bearing those merry gifts of gold and frank-incense and myrrh, as you are said to do in the traditional tales?

We can provide gold, answered one of the men.

And I'm sure that's so, but unfortunately I don't have any use for it. What a medicine man needs is medicine, the kind that helps the soul. Now then, with everybody's credentials established, suppose we get down to the particulars of this era. You've made a long journey way out here because you must want me to do something for you. Where, I wonder?

In the Middle East.

Ah yes, I've heard of it. Said to be as dry as here but better-known to history. Where in the Middle East, I wonder?

Cairo.

Ah yes, I've heard of that too. It's in the ancient land of the pharaohs, said to be a place for pyramids and mummies and lost secrets in general. Known far and wide for its great river of life, and also for those steamy fleshpots that always seem to pop up along any river of life. But *I* don't know Cairo at all. *I've* never even been there. And that has to mean you need an outsider to poke around and look for something, either in the fleshpots or in a pyramid or two. But look for what, I wonder? A lost secret perhaps? A wandering pharaoh? A mummy who refuses to take you to his leader? . . . Just what might it be you want me to find, directly?

A person. A man.

Joe reached under his blanket and scratched. His face was thoughtful.

The one of you is American, another British, and the third speaks somewhere in between. Canadian?

Yes.

Then it's pretty much of a high-level international delegation I'm facing, which isn't my level at all, and that means one of two things. Either I know this man and you don't, or you know him and I don't. Which is it?

You know him. We're only acquainted with him through the files, and through others.

Joe stroked his chin.

I could grow a beard again. Indians don't do with beards and it hurts to pluck out your whiskers one at a time. But there's another angle. Did any of you know that Hopi means *peace*? Well it does, and although there aren't many of us left, that's what we are, the

People of Peace. Our religion forbids us to harm anyone, to molest anyone, to kill anyone. We just can't do it and that's the shape of our sky, and also why we're so few. The Navajo are fierce and all around us and they've been plucking us off for years. So what do you say to that?

We wouldn't ask you to do anything that's against your beliefs, said one of the men.

I know it, no one ever does. It's just that others have a way of shifting your beliefs around a bit to make themselves more comfortable with them.

Joe pushed a forefinger into the earth at his feet.

Well I think it's time we had a name here. Who is it you're looking for?

Stern.

Joe's face grew serious. For several long minutes he gazed at his finger in the earth and said nothing. When he finally looked up there was a deep sadness in his eyes.

I knew that would be it. The moment those men arrived here a couple of weeks ago, all secrecy and mystery, I knew it was the beginning of something that would lead to Stern. All they said was that I was going to have some important government visitors, but I knew. He's not missing, though, is he? That isn't what you meant by finding him?

No.

No, I didn't think so. Your problem is that Stern knows a thing or two, and you're not sure what.

Something like that.

Well what exactly? He's working for you, I'd imagine, and he's also working for the other side. But you always thought he was really working for you in the end, and now all at once you're not so sure. Is that it?

Yes.

And naturally it's important that you know. How important?

Very. It's crucial.

Crucial? Stern? You're not exaggerating?

No, not at all. We can't emphasize it strongly enough.

Joe looked from one face to another and the three men somberly returned his gaze.

I see, said Joe. *Crucial,* then. And yet Stern used to be known as a petty gunrunner with a morphine habit, so how could it be that such a nobody as him is suddenly upsetting the war in the Middle East? Or should I remind myself that almost everyone who has ever been important in history was nobody to begin with, and that maybe the most important ones of all always stay that way? . . . Invisible, don't you know. Like a voice speaking the truth.

Joe's gaze drifted off into the distance. He stirred, scratched the side of his face.

Of course anyone who knows Stern at all would never think of him as a petty gunrunner with a morphine habit. That's just the way he might appear from a distance. Up close there's a whole secret world to Stern and one way or another he's always been in my life, just there, a big shambling bear of a man with a mysterious smile and an awkward way of moving sometimes, a bit of clumsiness about him from all the batterings through the years, and maybe even no shape to him you might say . . . or *all* shapes to him. That's another way to put it. But just substantial and bulky and *there* with his soft voice and his kind touch and that gentle way he has with people. *Helping* them, that's what he does. Stern has this quiet way of helping people when they don't even know it, when they don't even suspect what he's doing, and he never says a word about it himself. Years can go by and maybe just by chance you happen to come across something he did once. Changed a life. Saved someone's life. Sure. . . . And as often as not a stranger's.

I remember an incident like that from years ago. Somebody else told me about it, not him of course, not the woman involved either. It was a dreadful rainy afternoon by the Bosporus and the light was dying and a desperate woman was standing by a railing getting ready to die herself, to throw herself in the water, and along came this big awkward man shuffling out of the rain, a stranger, Stern, and he went up and stood beside the woman at the railing and gazed down at the dark swirling currents with her, and he began to talk in that honest halting way he has, just *nothing* but the truth, and some time went by and pretty soon he'd talked her right back into life. . . . One little incident a long time ago. Just one that I happen to know about.

Yes. And I know there's no knowledge without memory, and certainly I remember every twist and turn of my times with Stern as clearly now as when they happened. It was right after the First World War when we met, in Jerusalem naturally, Stern's beloved myth of a Jerusalem. And I didn't know much of anything then, and Stern took me in and taught me things and I loved him dearly in the beginning, loved him with all my heart. . . . He can have that effect on you easily enough. His ideals, don't you know.

And then some things happened and I came to hate him with all the passion of a young man who feels betrayed. Because he can have that effect on you too. Those impossible ideals of his again. They can cut you to the heart and shame you maybe.

Stern's ideals. No wonder you're not sure whether he's working for you or not, in the end. *Complex*, that's what they are. . . . Unravel them and you just might learn a very great deal.

Well, so some more time passed and my feelings for him changed again as feelings can do with time, as the years and the loss of them weather a man's heart in the same way as the wind and the sun weather his face. And I understood it better by then. The trouble I'd always had with Stern was the trouble I'd always had with myself, and it's just awful how we do that. We're a damnably self-centered bunch, the curse of the race, it is. It's just so hard to learn to feel others even a little bit. To let them stand there in front of you and see them as themselves, rather than as some part of you that you happen to be liking or disliking at the moment. . . . It was with Stern and through Stern, you see, that I was first exposed to the truly harsh and pitiless winds of life. With him that I first heard the roaring oblivion of the universe in all its terrifying silence.

Joe poked at the earth.

Yes. So what it comes down to is, I've never been able to get Stern out of my life. I've spent years trying to forget him, and I even came halfway around the world to this little corner of peace and nowhere, thinking I was getting away from Stern and all the rest of it. But no matter, no matter at all. He's still right there in front of me as much as he ever was, a shuffling wreck of humanity who's never done anything but lose, just lose is all, one thing after another year after year. . . . Has none of you ever met him?

No, none of us has.

Makes sense of course, no reason why you should have. You're successful and powerful and it's never been that way for Stern, nor will it be, not like that. But I can tell you your files don't begin to catch the feeling of the man, especially that gentleness of his. I used to think he was out of place in what he was doing, but maybe not and who's to say where people belong. As Stern himself used to put it, our souls are always our own to make of what we will. . . . What's that?

Excuse me? said one of the men.

No, pay no mind. It's someone back in the pueblo, I'll see to it later.

Joe shook his head.

So it's Stern again, is it? Twenty years later and here I am still looking into the mirror and trying to make out the shadows, trying to decipher those whispers in the wind. Trying, something with a little clarity to it, something at least. . . . *Stern.* Sure.

Once more there was silence in the kiva as Joe gazed at the earth, lost in thought. His three visitors waited. Before he spoke again he reached under his blanket and scattered cornmeal in front of them.

The last time I saw him was just before I left Jerusalem, right at the end of my twelve years of poker. Winter it was and snowing, and Stern was wearing those dreadful old shoes of his that I've never been able to forget, the ones he had on in Smyrna when we were there during the massacres in '22. How many hundreds of miles had he walked in those shoes to get to that hell of fires and screams and death in Smyrna? How many years and how many stumblings to get to *that*, God help us?

Well it was more than a decade later when I saw him the last time, and it was in Jerusalem. He got in touch with me and we met in a filthy Arab coffee house where we used to go in the old days, in the Old City it was. A cold and empty place, bare and cheerless, a barren little cave where the two of us used to huddle over a candle late at night, talking and drinking wretched Arab cognac. And it was snowing when he came shuffling in that night, a stumbling ruin of a man even worse off than I'd remembered. And he smiled that mysterious smile of his and said how good it was to see me again, and I took one look at him and I wanted to scream, that's all, just scream those questions that have the sad sad answers. . . . How does it happen, Stern? How does a man get to look like you? What kind of a hell does he live in? And for what? *What?*

But I didn't scream, not then I didn't. Instead I pulled out a roll of money because I happened to have money then, and I put it down on the table next to his hand. That's always the easiest way to deal with people. I mean there he was in front of me after all those years when I hadn't seen him, since Smyrna really, just there in his shuffling beaten way with all he owned on his back, still wearing those same Godawful shoes, a lifetime of devotion with nothing to show for it but still trying to smile in a way that would break your heart, poor as the night is long and still trying, and with what going for him, I ask you? *What,* for God's sake?

The same as always. Dreams is all. He still had those and I suppose we all did once. I know I did.

But the thing about Stern was, you always knew he'd never stop dreaming. No matter how futile it was, no matter how it destroyed him, he'd go right on with his hopeless dreams. Just hopeless, there was no reasoning with him at all.

A great peaceful new nation in the Middle East? Moslems and Christians and Jews all living together in a great new nation with Jerusalem as its capital? All these pathetic specimens of a mad race living in peace in Stern's belóved myth of a Jerusalem? *Everybody's Holy City?*

No hope in that. No hope ever. No hope in Jerusalem for Stern's dream, no hope there or anywhere under the sun. But Stern went on believing despite what people are, and he knows what they are, more than most of us, he knows. Yet he insists on staggering along, shooting a little morphine into his blood at dawn to get himself through another coming of the light, as he used to call it.

So yes, we had times together, Stern and I did, and they were some of the best and the worst I've ever known. Because when you dream the way Stern does, when you look that high, it also means you have to look the other way, right down into the blackest of the black. And sometimes you slip, it has to happen sometimes. And when you begin to fall it's as deep as forever and there's no end to the darkness at all, by God. . . .

Joe broke off. He pointed to a small shallow pit in the earth beside the altar.

See that? Here in the kiva it represents the exit from the previous world the Hopi lived in. And the ladder-opening up there represents the entrance to the world yet to come. For the Hopi, there's only one entrance and one exit in this sacred chamber they call a kiva, which is to say in life. Or as they put it in one of their sayings, there's light in the world because the sun completes its circular journey at night, traveling from west to east through the underworld.

Joe frowned.

It's sad to say, but it seems we can't have light without darkness. It seems we can't stretch our souls in the sun without first being lost in the night and knowing terrible anguish. And I suppose it may have to do with that circular journey of the sun and with the nature of the sun wheel, which has always been our symbol for life and hope, the most ancient one of all. And a good symbol it is and a true one, but a wheel does go round and it does have spokes, and spokes on a sun wheel make crosses. And what with sun wheels today in their ancient form as swastikas, that cross spinning in the deep becomes as complex and contradictory as man himself. Death and life in the very same symbol, and one no less real than the other.

Joe rubbed the earth in front of him, feeling it, stroking it.

Will you do it, then? asked one of the men.

Do what?

Go to Cairo. Accept the Stern assignment.

Joe looked up. He smiled.

I would prefer not to, as a scribbling man once said.

Abruptly, then, Joe's smile was gone and his mood changed. A haunting somberness came over him and his voice was suddenly very quiet, very soft in the stillness.

Ah, but is that all you're asking? Just for a moment sitting up here in the sky as we are, underground as we are, I thought you might have had something difficult in mind. But now I see all you want is the truth about Stern and his strange doings in the bazaars and deserts of that mythical place he calls his home, that sandy stretch of crossroads and history where man has been dreaming and killing himself since ever he was around. . . . Just there in the desert sea is all, the truth about Stern and the tides.

A shudder passed through Joe's thin shoulders and he wrapped his arms around himself, under the blanket, trying to control it.

But Stern sits inside the Sphinx, he whispered, didn't you know that? His life is made up of the ancient enigmas of those ancient places, and he peers out from the Sphinx across the nighttide deserts of life, and what he sees is what the rest of us don't want to see. So you have to be careful when you look into Stern's eyes. You have to be careful because there are fearful things to be seen there . . . the world and yourself and a kind of madness, a kind of utterly futile hope without end.

Joe stared at the earth in front of him.

Stern, you say. A man as unjustified and lonely as other men, a man who has never known the secret adventures of order. And all you want is for me to look into his eyes and tell you what's there.

Sadly, Joe smiled.

Fancy. . . . *Only* that.

Another evening, another sunset, and Joe sat alone at the edge of a cliff on top of the mesa, watching the light die. He had spent the last days visiting each of the homes in the pueblo, and that night there was to be a special ceremony in the underground kiva, a solemn gathering of the elders of the various clans to honor his departure.

Of course I don't have to go, he thought, and as scared as I am, why should I? The New World's big and I could just go anywhere and nobody would ever have to know.

And who wants the eternal grief that's over there anyway? Who wants *that* desert? They dream and they make up our religions and they spin our tales of a *Thousand and One Nights,* and that's all just fine and lovely so long as you keep your distance from the madness and don't walk in those dreams and live in those tales and get yourself lost forever.

Oh the three of them were clever all right, passing themselves off as the Three Fates and getting me to go on and on about Stern, trying to get me to persuade myself I ought to go back there. And Maudie even, hinting at that too. The Three Fates just coming to call as clever as could be.

But I know what I'd run into over there. They've always been at each other's throats and always will be. Bloody Greeks and Persians and Jews and Arabs and Turks and Crusaders, there's no end to it. And the odd bloated Mameluke floating down the Nile and the odd mad Mongolian whipping his horse into a frenzy, barbarians on their way in as usual to mix it up with assorted Assyrian charioteers and crazed Babylonians intent on the stars, while all the while the Chaldeans are sweeping in on the flanks and the Medes are sweeping out, and the Phoenicians are counting their money and the Egyptians are counting their gods, maybe the high priests of both of them getting together every millennium or so, to compare notes and see if either of them has come up with more of one than the other.

Talk about echoes. Talk about confusion and chaos. If there have been forty thousand prophets since the beginning of time, as rumored, surely most of them have spent their lives careening through those very wastes, shaking their fists and screeching their truths and clamoring on to their very last breaths right there.

Here it is, they shout. The one true God and the one true path at last, and just by chance that one true path happens to be the path where *I've* always been walking. So just listen to me, for God's sake. *Me.* Listen.

Oh help. Why bother with it at all? Confusion and chaos raising a Tower of Babel, that's what *He* spotted over there a long time ago. The tower to *me*, not to anybody else. The tower everybody's always been trying to raise, everybody who's a man anyway. Dreadfully proud of our erections, we are.

Mythical spot all right. The birthplace of religions and man's first heavenly erections, and an eternal torment to the rest of us. Must have a lot to do with the desert, I suppose. Nothing like forty days or forty years tramping around in a desert sun to jumble your brains. Water hard to come by and feverish chills shaking you all night, and nothing to eat in the morning but a handful of locusts left over from last night's supper. Do that for a while and how can you help but begin to see things and hear things?

War again over there, I'm told? Most amazing piece of news since the last report that barbarians were scaling the heights of Jerusalem.

War in the beautiful wilderness?

Astonishing news, that's what. Or as Stern used to say, *Good morning.*

Joe tugged his faded red wool hat down over his ears and pulled his new black shawl, a gift from his three visitors, more tightly around his thin shoulders. It was cold with the sun setting, cold with the coming of the night in the desert.

A small girl was standing some yards away, watching him. Joe made a sign and she came over and stood beside him, so young she had never known another medicine man in the pueblo. He wrapped his shawl around her against the cold and took her tiny hand and held it.

The little girl said nothing and neither did Joe. When the sun had sunk below the horizon she slipped away, still wearing the shawl, a gift he had made to her. Joe gazed after her as she disappeared in the shadows. He didn't think she had seen them but there were tears in his eyes. He didn't know why.

Ah well, he thought, we do what we can. It makes little difference but we have to do it anyway.

Stern's words, he suddenly realized. Stern's very own words spoken to him long ago, whispered now in the shadows in another time and place altogether.

Strange, he thought. Time is.

. . . and just as suddenly he was with Stern and it was a night twenty years ago in a city once called Smyrna, *once* long ago in the century before the age of genocide, before the monstrous massacres had come swirling out of Asia Minor to descend on Symrna while Stern and Joe were there . . . the massacres ignored then by most of the world but not by everyone, and not by Hitler, who had triumphantly recalled them only days before his armies invaded Poland to begin the Second World War. . . . *Who after all speaks today of the annihilation of the Armenians? The world believes in success alone.*

. . . a night, once, in a hell of smoke and fires and screams, Joe lying wounded on a quay and Stern standing over him and everywhere the dead and the dying huddling together, heaped near the sea while the city burned . . . while beside Joe, moaning softly, an abandoned little Armenian girl lay ripped and torn and dying in unspeakable pain.

. . . Joe unable to touch the knife by his hand and shrieking at Stern in his anger, his pain . . . yelling that Stern just wasn't as much in charge as he wanted people to believe, that he could do his own butchering if he wanted to play the great visionary who knew all the answers, the great hero dedicated to a cause of a kingdom come.

. . . Stern staring down with eyes that burned in blackness, Stern wild with anguish and violently shaking as he clutched the knife and buried his hand in the little girl's hair and pulled back her head, the tiny throat so white and bare.

. . . the wet knife clattering on the cobblestones and Joe not daring to look up then, not wanting to see Stern's eyes then . . . a night twenty years ago and forever and but a prelude to the century, but a shadow of the far deeper descent into darkness that was yet to come. . . .

Joe shuddered. He passed his hand in front of his eyes.

And who will be Stern's witness now? he asked himself. . . . Who will do that for him, who will look into *his* eyes? A man with a dream that was just hopeless from the very beginning. A good dream and hopeless, with nothing coming from it ever. . . .

Joe got to his feet. Of course he already knew how it would end over there, how it would have to end for Stern. And he wasn't going because he felt he owed Stern something, because he didn't feel that way. But after all these years of Stern trying and failing, someone somewhere did. And now when Stern was going to die, the gift had to be repaid.

Silently the greatly revered shaman of the Hopi walked up the path to the pueblo on top of the mesa, to the underground vault where the elders of the tiny nation sat repeating their guttural chants and birdlike whispers, those mysterious sounds of life and death they had heard since the beginning of time, echoing through all things in the universe.

PART TWO

4

Vivian

The sky was cloudless above Cairo airport, unmarred at that early hour by even the softest haze from the sun still low over Sinai. The cargo plane swung around and came to rest, bringing into view a pack of military men marching in twos and threes across the runway toward the plane. The men wore wide starched walking shorts and the different shirts and caps of uniforms from several corners of the British Empire.

Brisk and crisp and most of the colors of the species, thought Joe, watching the men. You'd have to know what you were up to, or think you knew, to march around the world looking like that every morning.

The military men advanced rapidly, intent and in step, their right arms swinging high, their left arms cradling clipboards tightly clasped at the ready. Some of them were already pushing on board when Joe reached the door of the plane and started down the stairs. He had only taken a few steps when he caught sight of a bizarre figure in white who seemed to be staring at him. Immediately the man nodded to himself with conviction, barking a silent order as he did so. Then he snapped to attention with parade-drill gusto and marched forward.

Jesus, thought Joe. What *is* that?

And indeed, the man cut an astonishing figure.

An elegant white shirt, open to the waist and displaying the insignias of a subaltern. White walking shorts and high white socks and snowy white tennis shoes. A regimental leopardskin casually draped over one shoulder, a glittering gold pendant bouncing on the man's chest. And looming above it all an enormous broad-brimmed white hat, one side attached to the crown in the Australian manner.

Christ, thought Joe, as he reached the bottom of the stairs and found his way blocked. The man in white came to attention no more than a foot away and slammed his foot into the runway, saluting.

Sah, he bellowed. I say, pleasant flight and all that?

A blast of early morning fumes struck Joe full in the face. Unable to speak, he nodded instead.

Right, bawled the subaltern, blasting him anew. Two massive rows of perfect white teeth suddenly flashed in the man's face. Without thinking, Joe ducked.

Right, shrieked the subaltern. Right? Right. But I say, sir, is it true you Yanks are coming over to win the war for us? Hands across the ocean again?

Joe swallowed.

I'm not American, he said.

What's that, sir? *Not* American? All the way from that barren wasteland, what do you chaps call the place, Arizona? All the way from a bloody colony like that and you're not even American?

Heads turned. Eyes stared. The subaltern was still screaming, blocking the stairs.

Sorry to hear that, sir, rum show actually. Just dropped in out there for a buffalo shoot, did you? Show the flag and let the wogs know who's in charge?

Joe pushed forward to move around the man, a gesture the subaltern misinterpreted as a sign of friendliness.

Or something else altogether, sir? A quiet foray among the little maidens in buckskin? New pelts for the library and a well-earned notch or two for the old blunderbuss?

At last Joe was around the man and heading in the direction of the terminal buildings. The subaltern dropped his salute and fell in briskly beside him.

No offense, sir, screeched the subaltern. About my taking you for a Yank, I mean. Some of my best friends are Yanks. Be glad to give you the name of my tailor here.

Joe walked straight ahead. The man had quick-stepped several times when he fell in beside Joe, trying to adjust his stride, but he didn't seem to be able to get it right and was now doing a permanent dance at Joe's elbow, prancing forward and falling behind a pace, quick-stepping again.

Different drummers, shrieked the subaltern. We're a race of individuals, after all. And please veer to the left, sir, as the Bolshies say. The clandestine war wagon's to the left.

Joe veered to the left without breaking stride. They were moving away from the groups of milling staring men. Joe spoke in a quiet voice.

Will you kindly tell me what the meaning of this is?

The subaltern caught the forceful tone in Joe's voice but apparently without hearing the words. In order to get closer he quick-stepped in, misjudging the distance and crashing into Joe with the power of a body-block. Joe pitched forward and landed on the runway on his hands, the subaltern coming to rest sprawled across his back. The subaltern peered upward, scanning the sky.

Spot something, sir? Jerry up there for an early morning go, is he? Shows good reflexes, that dive of yours.

Jesus Christ almighty, muttered Joe.

Can't spot the blighter, murmured the subaltern into Joe's ear, still scanning the sky intently. Blasted clever, the Hun.

Get off my back, muttered Joe. The subaltern, his face only inches away, peered sideways at Joe.

What's that, sir? You only *thought* you saw a Stuka coming in out of the sun?

Off my back. Now.

The subaltern grinned nervously and began to untangle himself.

Yes, sir. Sorry about that, sir. It's just that you can never be too careful when the Hun's around. War *is* hell, after all.

The subaltern climbed off Joe, grinding his knee into Joe's back. Joe struggled to his feet.

Listen, you bastard, you tell me right now what the meaning of that was supposed to be.

Meaning, sir? *Meaning?* Pardon me, sir, but in a world at war you're actually looking for *meaning?*

Stop it. That performance you put on back at the plane. And this ridiculous costume you're wearing. What the hell?

Oh, my uniform. Well you see, sir, since secret intelligence work requires a high degree of initiative, we're encouraged to express our individualism in our dress of the day. And as for the manner in which

I hailed you when you debarked, we've found that the direct approach is the best one. When matters are secretly at their murkiest, in other words, we try to keep outward appearances as natural as possible. It's by far the most effective cover.

I wasn't aware, said Joe, that tennis whites and a leopardskin would look natural at Cairo airport in wartime.

Oh yes, sir, if the whites are modified a bit. You may be a little rusty now, been out of touch and that sort of thing, it could happen to any retiree from Arizona attempting a comeback. But the naked truth of the matter today, sir, is that we don't carry on the way they did in the old films.

I see.

Precisely, sir, that's it in a nutshell. This is definitely espionage in the 1940s that we practice here and the old films are definitely out of date, irrelevant to say the least. And then too, we're in the plain old sandy sunny Middle East, not lounging around in a shadowy parlor car on the Orient Express as it goes weaving into Bulgaria, while you and I lunge at our glasses between hoots. The servant problem, sir. Lackeys just aren't what they used to be, neither as nations nor individuals. Take the Balkans, for example.

What?

Exactly, sir, especially the Balkans. They're not at *all* what they used to be. In fact it would probably be wise to put aside your secret hopes of outwitting some sneaky little Dimitri in the sewers of Sophia, despite his many masks, in order to obtain the truth about the Bulgarian submarine force. This just isn't the place for vague notions about honor and fair play and all that rot. Times change, sir, what?

Joe groaned.

. . . can't straighten at all, he muttered.

No? Well don't be discouraged, sir. People pretty much expect a spy to look like Quasimodo loping around in his belfry with a demented leer on his twisted face. The important thing is to keep abreast of the latest technical developments, that's the name of this game. In intelligence, you're modern or you're nothing. Can you just imagine how it would look if the two of us were to skulk around Cairo airport first thing in the morning in trench coats with a cigarette or two dangling out of the corners of our mouths? Looking over our shoulders to see if Peter Lorre has caught up with us yet? Or possibly even the fat man?

Oh.

Precisely, sir, the locals. They may be no more dark-skinned than they were in the epics of yesteryear, but they're just *not* as predictable as extras used to be.

As he rambled on, the subaltern was keenly observing Joe. After several painful attempts, Joe managed to straighten. The subaltern grinned, nodding.

Very good, sir. I see we're making a stunning comeback. So the point is, we have this slovenly lot of blithering wogs hanging about with time on their hands, just waiting to catch a glimpse of something they can pass on to Jerry. Such as a suspicious little foreigner arriving at Cairo airport early one morning? A wiry little fellow in some dreadful secondhand suit that's much too big for him? Suspiciously sporting a scruffy growth of whiskers on his face as if he were trying to *look* like the anonymous spy of tradition? Could it be that you're growing a beard, sir?

I am.

Very good, sir. Although given the sand in the air around here, most of our fighting men seem to prefer a moustache when it comes to providing that distinguishing touch. When a show of hair is wanted, sir, to emphasize brute masculinity.

Quietly, the subaltern guffawed. He himself wore an enormous walrus moustache, its waxed ends nearly reaching to the tops of his ears.

Hair aside, said Joe, I was told to expect a different reception.

Were you, sir? Could we be referring to the recognition signals, so called, which veteran spies use to spot one another when among the common herds in the trenches?

The subaltern immediately slammed his tennis shoes together, coming to attention. He saluted and narrowed his eyes.

Please assume we are in the airport terminal, sir, and you are having your papers examined by some barely literate enlisted swine. As you dither around, a handsome subaltern sweeps up and shrewdly engages you in amiable conversation, in the course of which he chances to use two key words. *Brooklyn* and *garbage*. At that point the subaltern suavely removes a key ring from his pocket and jangles the keys in the air, as if bored.

Still holding his salute, the subaltern reached into his pocket with his left hand and brought out a key ring. He squinted intently at Joe, rattling the keys in front of his face.

Right, sir, and so far so good. Now stuffed into the left pocket of your shabby jacket is a rolled-up edition of a popular London illustrated weekly. You remove this rag with your right hand, the old cross-draw, and hold it up in the air as if curious about which way the wind is blowing. The formidable subaltern is satisfied as to your credentials and takes it from there. Well, sir, on the mark, are we?

Joe handed him the magazine.

It's a little old. I stole it from a library in London to save money. Chamberlain's on the cover announcing peace in our time.

Excellent, sir, we could all use a little of that. Now then, the trusty clandestine steed is right over here.

The subaltern opened the door of a small old-fashioned delivery van and stood proudly beside it, waiting. The van was a civilian model, cream-colored and ancient, dented in a number of places. Bright green lettering, obviously new, was splashed across the side of the van.

GREASY FISH

AHMAD'S   &

LEVANTINE CHIPS

The subaltern followed Joe's gaze. He snorted.

Clever, what? Known secretly in undercover circles as the impregnable *Ahmadmobile*, and out here it's worth a regiment of tanks any day, I can tell you. Confuses the enemy and makes the wogs think we're in the delivery business, which in a way we are. But the fact is, you can never be too careful when you're serving a sentence in the spy trade. Not only a keen lookout at all times, but the keener the lookout the better the times, that's my motto. Are we right then, sir?

As soon as they had climbed into the cab of the small van, the subaltern made a show of carefully locking both doors. He then reached over and fumbled around in Joe's lap, groping for Joe's hand, pumping it enthusiastically when he found it.

Vivian's the name, sir, and despite appearances I'm not a regular army man. Actually I'm an archeologist in real life. I don't have to tell you how these intelligence types get carried away by men with

66

unusual backgrounds. Their eyes positively light up. Well I did some digs over here before the war, and that's how I happened to get into this end of the show. Know the underground terrain, so to speak.

Oh. I see, yes.

Right, sir, the pharaohs that be don't miss a trick. Well briefly, it came about like this. When Jerry figured out another generation had gone by and it was time to give it another go, *war*, damn it, I naturally presented myself to the authorities in London straightaway. Vivian here, I said, and went on to explain that I'd be more than happy to carry a rifle in whatever trench was weak. But they took one look at my digging experience and packed me off to one of those unnumbered rooms you know about near Queen Anne's Gate. See here, old horse, said the unnumbered general in mufti, we can't have you oozing around in the mud of Flanders like some common uneducated lout, you're much too valuable for that. We simply have to have you in the secret show, what those on the outside call intelligence. Now what do you say to that?

Vivian wiggled his eyebrows.

Well needless to say, sir, what I said to that was, *Top drawer*. Just point me in the general direction of Mata Hari, I said, and I'm off to make do in the gloom. Whereupon the general in mufti gave me a hearty shake of the hand and mumbled, Good show, old fruit. And now that you're officially a secret agent, Viv old horse, Vivvy my boy, old Viv dear fellow, now that you're a mysterious spy like the rest of us, added the general in mufti, the first thing you have to do is trundle yourself out back and see C.

And do what? asked Joe.

Vivian chuckled.

Very good, sir. Well I went out the back door, as instructed, and strolled down the appropriate alley to another unnumbered address, and climbed more stairs to another unnumbered room, and all at once right there in front of me was the very secret chief of the Secret Service, C as we secretly call him, sitting in his very own chair but turned around and facing the wall, keeping his secret identity secret. *Well.* Here was a devilishly clever fellow, our good old secret C, I knew that from the beginning. So I flashed the old smile at his back and said, Viv here, secret agent of the Empire, ready and willing. Whereupon good old C said, his back to the world, See here, Viv, C here.

Vivian guffawed.

Or perhaps our secret chief said, *C* here, Viv, *C* here. Or he might have said, See here, Viv, see here. Or in other words, who in God's name has any idea *what* he said? No doubt a secret *C* has to be unknowable by nature, a regular Delphic oracle when it comes to garbled meanings and ambiguous messages.

Vivian nodded eagerly.

You're beginning to smile, sir, so it's obvious we agree as to the essentials. Now then, to continue.

Viv? muttered *C*, addressing the wall, please listen carefully because I can only say this once. The Suez Canal is in danger, the very lifeline of the Empire, and we need a reliable man down there to keep an eye on the locks. So just pick up that black pill on the desk behind me, that thing that looks like a jelly bean, regulation potassium cyanide in case life ever seems as black as all that, and head for the Nile and may the best team win.

And there you have it, sir, and all the time while *C* had his back to me, he seemed to be knitting.

Knitting? asked Joe.

Vivian chuckled.

Right, sir. The knitting needles of fate, I suppose. Then after that I was given intensive training in silence and exile and cunning, and a quick course in forgery with emphasis on forging the uncreated conscience of the race, and here I am. *Vivian of Arabia.* . . . Now then.

Vivian hummed a music-hall tune and started the engine. A thunderous roar crashed around them. Vivian grinned, shouting to be heard above the deafening noise.

Sorry about that, sir. Hole in the exhaust somewhere, only happened yesterday. Haven't had time to let the maintenance apes get their paws on it.

I see.

What?

It's a nice day, shouted Joe, leaning into Vivian in order to be heard. When Joe sat back again he seemed more at ease. He reached under his jacket, apparently to scratch himself somewhere, but actually to tuck away Vivian's wallet, newly stolen, in an inside pocket.

68

That's better, shouted Joe. Carry on.

Very good, sir. Off we go then.

There was a fierce grinding noise and the small delivery van went careening away down the runway at full speed, the heavy tread of its soft desert tires screeching wildly. Vivian laughed and swerved back and forth, assuming a racing position. Joe stared. The impressive walrus moustache had come loose in the wind, revealing a cloth backing to it and a thin line of glue above Vivian's upper lip. One end of the waxed moustache had climbed up his face, giving him a permanently crooked smile. And when he bared his teeth at a spot of grease on the runway and careened around it, snarling as he whipped the wheel to and fro, the expression on his face seemed dangerously close to delirium.

A gate with a sentry box came into view. Vivian began to slow down.

Security check coming up, he yelled. Just play dumb, sir. I'll handle these sun-crazed dolts.

They stopped. Several military policemen were standing around in front of the sentry box, metal cups in their hands. When one of them came over to the van, Vivian leaned out and sniffed at the man's cup.

Tea, he yelled to Joe, and turned back to the military policeman.

This shabbily dressed fellow, he screamed, is a Yank who's come over to win the war for us. But see here, lance corporal or battle-ax corporal or whatever you are, you look like you could use a stiff one this morning, right?

Vivian guffawed.

Am I right? *Right?*

The military policeman studied the card Vivian had given him.

What's this? he asked in wonder.

What's what, my dear fellow?

The military policeman read out loud.

This coupon good for all the bearer can drink at the Kit Kat Kabaret. Just say Ahmad sent you and you'll never be sorry. But remember, AHMAD SENT ME. *Those are always the magic words in the ancient land of the pyramids.*

(And Ahmad also has other coupons, if you are interested. See him today and make your dreams come true. Mummies available by special appointment.)

The military policeman stared down at Vivian, who laughed happily.

Wrong pocket, what? Have to keep a tight rein on before breakfast. But look here, my dear fellow, why don't you keep that bit of cheer as a gift from the management? Now then, this is what we're looking for when there's a war on.

Vivian fumbled in another pocket and came up with a pass. The military policeman waved them through. They left the airport and worked their way into a long line of military traffic moving in the direction of the city. Before they had gone very far Vivian began screaming again.

Now I know what you're dying to ask me, sir. What about the locals, is that it? The other fellows can loll over their gin and beer when they're not giving it a go in their tanks, but a spy has to move through the desert the way a fish swims through water, right? As the old saying goes?

So what *about* the locals, you say, sir? Well as history tells us, the casts of thousands who built the pyramids were fed exclusively on onions and garlic and radishes.

Vivian belched noisily.

Got the picture, sir? *Stink*'s the word I had in mind. No doubt onions and garlic and radishes must have fired up those extras who built the pyramids, but the truth is, five thousand years of history haven't made your average Gippo's breath any sweeter. Brings us up to date, does it?

They turned off the highway and drove through crowded streets. Vivian was continually honking the horn and waving and smiling at the masses of people.

Bloody wogs, he shrieked out of the corner of his mouth. They look a fruitless bunch but they're cunning, *cunning*'s the word.

Joe's eyes widened. They had been inching along more and more slowly through the crowds until they had to stop altogether. While Vivian was turned toward Joe, the gaunt solemn face of an Arab had suddenly appeared in the window right behind Vivian. At first the Arab didn't seem to be begging, merely curious. He studied the interior of the van, a piece of chalk between his teeth. Then he stared hard at the back of Vivian's head, pulled his own head out of the window and took the chalk from between his teeth. He seemed to be writing something, and sure enough, a small blackboard appeared outside the window a moment later.

I AM A MARXIST MOSLEM MUTE.
GIVE ME ONE LARGE FREE ORDER OF GREASY
CHIPS BUT PLEASE HOLD THE SALT. I'M
ON A SALT-FREE DIET BECAUSE IT IS WRITTEN,
LIKE DESTINY AND HISTORY.
PRAISE BE TO ALLAH AND MARX, ALL POWER
TO MOHAMMED AND STALIN.
THANKS. HAVE A NICE DAY.

A *slatternly* people, screamed Vivian, unaware of the blackboard wagging a few inches behind his head.

Just plain *slack*, he shrieked. Fingers always on the move, sir, never forget that for a moment.

The blackboard disappeared. A hard wipe of the Arab's arm across the slate and he was writing again. The blackboard bobbed up.

ARE YOU REFUSING TO SERVE ME BECAUSE
I'M DARK-SKINNED?

I've said it before and I'll say it again, screamed Vivian. You can never be too careful when you're rubbing shoulders out here.

The Arab looked murderous. Down went the blackboard, up it came again.

BUGGER YOUR CHIPS, YOU GREASY
CAPITALIST FISH.

Vivian stared hard at Joe.

In other words, *watch out for wogs.* Got it, sir?

They drove awhile longer and finally pulled up on a quiet back street with the engine off. Joe sat entranced, listening to the squeals and cries of the city.

Here we are, sir.

Fine, Viv. Where?

A time-dishonored area, sir, well known to romantic travelers be-

71

fore the war as the Coptic Quarter and also as Old Cairo, but known to its residents, now as then, as simply a slum. Once infamous, now merely famous. This alley you will be going to is legally called the rue Lepsius, but popularly remembered as the rue Clapsius. It's said that a good part of nineteenth-century Cairo acquired an incurable dose of nostalgia in these shadowy byways, and certainly the byways do give that impression. So if I do say so myself, sir, it seems an appropriate setting for your poetic Irish reveries between passes at the bottle.

Well thanks for the lift, Viv.

And thank you, sir, for your charming company this morning. War *is* hell, after all, and we frontline fellows would do well to live life fully when we're not knee-deep in mud in the trenches.

Vivian vaguely pumped his hand in the air in a philosophical manner, a gesture apparently meant to end with a thoughtful fingering of his false moustache. But instead Vivian found his moustache halfway up the side of his face. He pressed it back into position and grinned.

The spy trade, sir, a queer and deadly game. Now if you meander forward and turn down the next alley, you'll come to what must have been one of the last of the bawdy houses in this quaint decaying neighborhood, an excessively unseemly place, and that is where you will find your lodgings. Look for a dirty nondescript structure called the Hotel Babylon, formerly a tenth-class hovel used by failed commercial agents and poor clerks in search of romance during their siesta hours, a place of broken dreams and dreams that could never be.

But that was formerly, sir. For some time now the Hotel Babylon has been under the clandestine supervision of HM's Secret Service, serving as an all-purpose hideaway for wandering spies in transit, a discreetly sordid haven amidst the turmoil for just such errant seekers as yourself.

Let's move right along, Viv.

Indeed, sir, now then. Immediately within the half-light that pervades this rotting structure, you will come across the local hermit-in-residence, the keeper of the keys to this odd kingdom, a large Egyptian who will be reading a newspaper and wearing a distinctive flat straw hat, of the kind referred to in civilian circles as a boater. You can call him *Ahmad* if you like, and all you have to do is tell him Mr Bletchley sent you.

72

Bletchley, you say?

That's it exactly, sir. The Bletch is our local groundskeeper, ancillary services and so forth, the man who sprinkles the potted palms in the background and arranges for the billeting of transients such as yourself. A cipher, sadly, our Bletch. But you'll see for yourself.

That it, Viv?

For now, sir. But after you've had time to soak in a first-rate Babylonian bath and pop into your town outfit and burn those rags from your journey, one of our fellow spies will be coming around to collect you.

When?

This evening, I should imagine. All set, sir?

Joe asked a few more questions and then started down the street. Before he reached the corner of the rue Lepsius, or Clapsius, the van had thundered off in the opposite direction. At the corner Joe paused to light a cigarette and get his bearings. He also spent a little time apparently scratching himself under his jacket, actually looking through Vivian's wallet. A telephone number caught his eye.

The Viv, he thought. What a way to begin.

The Hotel Babylon was a narrow structure of four or five stories. The paint on the façade was peeling and the front door was open. The hotel lacked a lobby. Instead there was a counter built into one side of the narrow corridor on the ground floor. Farther on toward the back of the corridor an ancient pianola stood in the dusty gloom.

A large man was perched on a high stool behind the counter, peering at a newspaper through enormous horn-rimmed glasses. He was wearing a flat straw hat and he obviously heard Joe's footsteps in the corridor, but he didn't bother to look up from his newspaper.

Mr Bletchley sent me, said Joe.

The Egyptian reached up on the wall behind him, still without raising his eyes, and took down one of the keys.

Top floor rear, he said. It's the quietest room and also the largest. There's a tattered silk cord near the door meant for summoning the maid, but don't bother to pull it. There's been no maid here since the First World War.

I see. Mr Bletchley also said you might be able to send out for something for me.

The large Egyptian known as Ahmad looked vaguely annoyed.

Well I can try, but it's still rather early in the day, you know. Generally speaking, those sorts of people are just getting to bed about now.

I meant a bottle of whiskey and breakfast.

Oh. An English breakfast?

If you can, yes.

It will take about half an hour. There's a retired belly dancer up the street who understands that kind of thing. As for the whiskey, I can get that up to you in a few minutes.

That's about what I had in mind.

I'll see to it. Three knocks for the whiskey, two for breakfast.

Joe turned toward the stairs and stopped, as if a thought had just come to him.

Oh by the way, would you happen to have something on the first floor up? Heights bother me.

The large Egyptian reached for another key.

First floor rear. Smaller, but just as quiet really.

Joe climbed the stairs and found his room at the back of the building, away from the street. He looked around and then dropped lightly to his knees to peek through the keyhole. He could see the end of a narrow bed, a chair, a table. On the far side of the room was a window with a screen in it. He unlocked the door carefully and dropped the key into his pocket. Then he picked up his valise and held it to his chest. He turned the handle.

The door burst open under his hand and Joe went flying across the room, hurling his valise at the screen in the window. The screen and the valise disappeared and he dived after them, landing with a roll on the soft earth behind the hotel as a dull thud went off in the room above him. He was on his feet at once, in a crouch, but there was nothing to see. He was standing in a small courtyard strewn with debris. A door behind him led back into the hotel. Another door faced him from the far side of the small courtyard. Joe picked up his valise and crossed to the door in the far wall. He tried the handle and the door opened. Stairs led down to a basement.

At the bottom of the stairs was another door. Joe opened it and found himself in a narrow cellar with a low ceiling. A man was sitting at a table, mostly obscured by the newspaper he was reading. A single naked light bulb burned overhead, a string hanging from it. An electrical cord spiraled down from the fixture to an electric ring at the man's elbow. A kettle was steaming and there was also a chipped teapot and several battered metal cups. Joe dropped into a chair and brushed off the dirt he had picked up in the courtyard.

Bletchley?

The man continued to read his newspaper, hidden behind it.

That's right.

What went off up there?

Oh, just a popper. Of course it could have been a bomb.

Of course. But is that your standard welcoming procedure?

You might call it that.

Why the game?

It's not a game, they just like to know whether you're on your toes or not. There's no room for amateurs out here.

On my toes, is it? And what did they expect after sending that crazed item to pick me up at the airport?

The man known as Bletchley peered over his newspaper at Joe, only one of his eyes showing. There seemed to be tears in his eye and there was something wrong with his expression, something very wrong. But his head disappeared again and Joe didn't have time to make out what it was.

Is he crying? wondered Joe. Why is he hiding like that?

Vivian must have been in an expansive mood this morning, said the man known as Bletchley. He's an old music-hall trooper, an actor by profession, and he can put on quite a show when he has a mind to. Perhaps you caught his fancy, or perhaps he's just bored these days. Cup of tea for you?

Thanks.

The teapot disappeared behind the raised newspaper.

How many sugars?

None.

It *is* just sugar.

I'm sure, but I don't take any.

Get your share through the drink, do you?

Something like that.

A metal cup, a hand pushing it, appeared from around the side of the newspaper. The hand was that of an old man, which the voice wasn't. A withered hand, trembling slightly. Joe reached for the cup and sipped, burning his lips on the metal. He held the cup away and blew on it.

Did you have all the rooms up there wired?

No, just two. The rear rooms on the first two floors. If you'd jumped out the front of the hotel on the first two floors you'd have taken a chance of breaking a bone on the cobblestones in the alley, and if you'd jumped from higher up, front or back, you almost certainly would have broken a bone, quite possibly your neck. But I didn't imagine you'd want to do that, so I didn't imagine you'd be anywhere but where you were.

Well that makes sense, said Joe.

Yes it does. Now I assume you'll want to get some sleep after your trip. These stairs in front of you will let you out in another alley. Follow your nose around to the left and you'll be back at the corner where you started. You didn't hurt yourself, did you?

No.

That's good. They wouldn't want that to happen before you even got started.

And that makes sense too. Tell me, is this cellar your regular office or just one of your forward supply depots in the field?

The newspaper rustled but the man's head didn't appear. For a moment there was silence at the table.

Unfriendly innkeeper, thought Joe.

Listen, said the voice from behind the newspaper. There's no reason for you to take this personally, but you might as well know from the beginning that you're nothing special to me. I don't know who you are or what your assignment is, and I don't care. That's not my job. I do what's required of me and the Monastery expects you to do the same. If my orders include wiring a door, I wire it. And if you're looking for fellowship, you can try your luck on the streets like anybody else. With me, business is business. Understood?

Fair enough, said Joe.

Good. I'll meet you here at nine o'clock this evening.

Joe tried his tea again but the metal cup was still too hot. He stood.

Know a man named Stern by any chance, Bletchley?

Not personally, all of that's much too high-level for me. I just chair the Monastery's arrival and departure committee. Pleasant dreams.

Joe started toward the stairs. When he was halfway up he turned and looked back at the raised newspaper.

Oh by the way, could you see that this wallet is returned to Vivian? There's not much of interest in it but he may be wanting it back all the same. And who might Cynthia be?

One of Bletchley's eyes appeared above the newspaper.

Who might what be?

This little lovely by the name of Cynthia. There's a slip of paper hidden in the lining of the wallet with her name and telephone number on it.

Who cares?

I don't know, I thought you might. The telephone number is almost the same as one I was given for emergency contact. I mean it wouldn't do, would it, to have one of your music-hall performers dallying with one of your secretaries, without you knowing about it. Of course it's all in the committee family, but I would imagine Papa would like to know what's going on in his family by way of a little incest. Insofar as it affects Monastery business, I mean, no other reason. I'll just leave the evidence on the step here so you can take a look when you're finished with the personal columns.

The man known as Bletchley said nothing. His withered hand trembled slightly and his single eye, rapidly blinking back tears, continued to glare over the top of the newspaper as Joe leapt up the last few steps and closed the cellar door behind him.

Once outside, Joe walked a short distance and stopped in a patch of morning sunlight. He leaned against a wall and closed his eyes, taking deep breaths.

From the Viv to the Bletch, he thought, heaven help us. But at least things ought to get better. Have to, you'd think, after starting out like this.

By the time Joe was walking back through the front door of the hotel he was whistling happily. An unusual occurrence in the Hotel Babylon, perhaps, for Ahmad immediately looked up from his newspaper.

Beautiful morning, said Joe.

Ahmad stared at him, an astonished expression on his face.

You people are amazing, he murmured.

Joe smiled.

We are? Why do you say that?

Because of your disguises. I could have sworn your exact double just walked in here.

Joe's smile broadened.

This double of mine, he headed upstairs, did he?

First floor rear. No more than five or ten minutes ago.

Badly in need of some whiskey, was he, when last seen passing in front of your counter?

Ahmad held up a bottle.

Here it is. I was just going to take it up.

Well there's no need for both of us to make the trip, said Joe. I'll see that he gets it all right. He and I have some talking to do.

Joe took the bottle as Ahmad studied him, perplexed.

Wait a minute, said Ahmad. Are you really that other one's double, or are you the same man?

That depends, replied Joe. We both happen to occupy the same head but that doesn't mean we think alike all the time, or even most of the time. That one upstairs tends to listen a lot and keep his thoughts to himself, while me, I'm not like that at all.

Slowly, a shy smile spread across Ahmad's somber features.

Oh I see. Well I ordered the breakfast, that's why the whiskey wasn't up sooner.

Lovely. And isn't it a beautiful morning here in the land of the Nile?

Ahmad looked confused.

You keep saying that but what are you referring to? The weather? Yes.

But the weather's always the same here. It never changes.

And that may well be, but *I'm* not always the same.

And what does *that* mean?

Just that I like the desert and I like the sun, said Joe. And I think I'm going to like the Coptic Quarter, also known as Old Cairo. And probably this seedy place you call the Hotel Babylon, and probably Vivian too. Not Bletchley, I wouldn't imagine. But then, everything can't be perfect.

Ahmad stirred, gazing at Joe.

I know Bletchley of course, but who's Vivian?

78

Joe described him. Ahmad shook his head.

I've never seen anyone like that around here.

You haven't?

No. And I've never heard of anyone called Vivian, either.

I see. Well is this the only Hotel Babylon in the neighborhood?

Fortunately for all of us, it's the only one in Egypt.

And your name *is* Ahmad, isn't it?

Ahmad smiled. There's no doubting that, he said. I live with it and I know.

Well there. That's a start at least and more than enough for now by way of facts, I'd say. Too many facts at one time can only be confusing. So then. Beautiful morning, and good-night now.

Joe laughed and made for the stairs with the bottle of whiskey in his hand.

Breakfast? Ahmad called out.

Whenever it gets here. Two knocks, I'm waiting.

Joe went whistling up the stairs. Ahmad watched him until he was out of sight, then got down on his hands and knees again behind the counter, where he had been when Joe had come bursting into the lobby the second time. He didn't think Joe had noticed him down there, but all the same he decided he would have to be more careful now that there was a guest, at last, staying in the Hotel Babylon.

A mysterious smile played on Ahmad's face as he silently opened the secret panel in the wall behind the counter.

High in the ancient fortresslike structure in the desert known as the Monastery, an orderly climbed the last steep steps of a spiraling tunnel stairway and knocked on the wooden door at the top. He waited, slowly counting to twelve, then pressed down on the thick iron handle to the door.

The tower room he had entered might have served once as a lookout for the ancient place, for it was small and round with tall narrow slits cut through the thick masonry at regular intervals, giving a view of the desert in every direction. Tiny shafts of brilliant sunshine pierced the heavy shadows of the little room, which was still gloomy at that early hour despite the blinding light outside.

79

A man with only one arm, immaculately dressed in starched khakis, stood close to one of the slits in the far wall. His back was turned but he appeared to be studying the desert to the west, the direction of the advancing Germans. The man held himself rigidly erect at parade rest, his one hand tucked stiffly into the small of his back. The orderly waited. After a moment a dim strain of organ music rose from somewhere below in the ancient fortress. The man with one arm swung around to face the orderly.

Oh it's you. What is it?

The orderly held out a sheet of paper to his superior, who read the message at a glance and turned to gaze out again at the desert.

Well well, he murmured. So our new Purple Seven is finally in place and ready to begin. . . .

He smiled, his face hidden from the orderly.

Who met the Armenian at the airport?

The actor, sir. The man called Liffy. He knows nothing. He met the plane and took the Armenian directly to the Hotel Babylon.

The man with one arm laughed.

For the Armenian, a bizarre introduction to Cairo, no doubt. And also perhaps a trifle misleading. . . . Well he has much to learn but not much time to do it in. Are the maps laid out for the briefing?

Yes, sir.

I'll be down in ten minutes. Have the shutters closed and everything ready.

Yes, sir.

That's all.

Yes, sir.

The orderly clicked his heels and left, quietly closing the door behind him. From the depths of the Monastery the organ music soared and swelled more loudly, filling the small tower room with its booming echoes.

Stern, muttered the man with one arm, his face hard. And now we'll finally be done with this traitor and Rommel won't know our every move before we make it. . . . But we must be meticulous, without a mistake.

Without a mistake, he repeated, his eyes narrow as he sensuously stroked the thick medieval masonry protecting him from the merciless glare of the desert sun.

80

5

Liffy

Several nights later Joe was sitting alone in his tiny hotel room, perched on the windowsill gazing out at the darkness, when all at once a light rapping fell on the door, so soft he almost didn't hear it.

Two knocks for food and three for drink, although he hadn't asked Ahmad for anything. With one hand in his pocket, Joe crossed to the door and opened it.

A slight man faced him from the middle of the corridor, a non-descript figure neither young nor old, his nationality impossible to place. The man's eyes darted back and forth and he kept moving his lips, a twitch here and a nibble there, his face abruptly smiling and somber and uneasy by turns.

Joe stared in wonder.

Most amazing mouth I've ever seen, he thought. Just never stops at all.

A wild gleam suddenly flashed in the stranger's eyes, an eerie play of colors and lusters and depths. He shuffled his feet and shifted his weight, his height shooting up and down as he did so. Then his gaze cast about in panic and he retreated even farther away down the corridor, never once looking at Joe, staring down at the floor in defeat.

Bundle of nerves all right, thought Joe.

The stranger sputtered and grinned, shaking his head as if some overwhelming doubt had seized him. Even his size seemed to expand and contract as Joe watched him moving back and forth in the corridor, now large and looming as he worked his elbows and thrust his head forward, then small and shrinking as he subsided back into himself, not a part of him ever still, his entire presence constantly changing.

To and fro, thought Joe, like a wee boat tossing on the shadowy nighttides of the Nile. But what's it supposed to mean and who is he anyway?

The stranger's arms were heaped with shopping bags, which he was having trouble holding together. He took a step forward and attempted what might have been meant as a smile, but the smile abruptly faded and a gargling sound rose in his throat, an effort to speak gone wrong.

Arghh?

Graaa. . . .

Joe was reminded of a shy lion cub fitfully rolling its head and muttering to itself.

Can I help you? asked Joe, reaching for the bags before they fell. He scooped up several and carried them back inside the room. The stranger still stood in the hallway, nervously shifting his weight back and forth.

Don't you want to come in?

Two if for food and three if for drink, muttered the stranger. Paul Revere said that.

The stranger reluctantly shuffled forward, avoiding Joe's eyes. There was a wistful sadness in his voice.

The hell with Paul Revere, who cares about him. You don't recognize me, do you?

I don't think so, said Joe. Should I?

I suppose not. I suppose there's no reason why anybody should ever recognize me. That's my problem.

Excuse me?

Being recognized as myself, when I'm myself. Nobody ever does. Wouldn't you find that a problem too?

Joe had to resist an urge to wrap his arms around the stranger, so forlorn did he seem. Instead he eased the last paper bag out of the man's arms and put it safely down on the table.

They're heavy. What's in them?

The stranger shuffled his feet in embarrassment and said nothing. Joe touched the man's arm.

Who are you?

The stranger stole a timid glance at Joe and lowered his eyes.

I'm the official tourist guide for this street, he whispered, although frankly business has been terrible since the war started. The last war, that is, not this one. But nonetheless . . .

Yes?

The stranger took a deep breath.

. . . but nonetheless, the rue Clapsius was once world-famous among those who knew the secret of life. In fact this little rue used to be considered the ultimate oasis of the soul by many, many philosophers. There was even a popular saying acknowledging the fact. *See the rue Clapsius and leave the world humming.* And do you know why this little rue used to be considered more significant, finally, than the Sphinx and the pyramids and even the Nile?

Why?

Because of its hum-jobs. History is really very simple, isn't it?

Joe's eyes widened. He stared at the stranger, who continued to move nervously back and forth, his mouth working all the while, never still.

Hum-jobs, you say?

That's right, muttered the stranger, and I'm talking now about the ultimate in good vibrations. The whores on this little rue, you see, were once spectacularly clever at humming off their customers. So much so that it wasn't at all unusual to find philosophers from every corner of the globe, strong men, determined men, simply curled up and gurgling on the cobblestones at all hours of the day and night, unable even to drool, not even a hint of a syllogism in their heads, mere husks of their former selves. . . . But what do I mean? I mean *drained.*

The stranger flashed a smile, which immediately faded.

I'm talking about the best, he muttered. Europeans like to think hum-jobs were discovered in Bologna around the beginning of the Renaissance, what really got the Renaissance going, so to speak. But they go much further back in time than is generally suspected, like most things having to do with people. In fact the hum-job tradition on this street goes back to what Europeans call the Dark Ages, when things weren't nearly as dark in the East as in the West. In the East scholars were still studying the *Thousand and One Nights* and passing on nibbles of their erudite findings to selected acquaintances. . . . Are you familiar, perhaps, with this classical piece of literature?

Joe gazed at the man, dumbfounded. At last he found his tongue.

I believe I've heard of it, yes.

The stranger flashed another smile, apparently less nervous than before.

Good. Then you probably know the Arabs borrowed the *Nights* a long time ago from the Persians, who in turn borrowed them much earlier than that from India. . . . But it's intriguing, isn't it, this notion of an enlightened East with the primitive buzz of hum-jobs echoing up through the mists of ancient India? Frankly, before I knew the truth, the very idea of all those strange tongues down there in the subcontinent of our souls always used to exhaust me. But now that I know better, I can see what a truly brilliant innovation it was on the part of the Indians to connect hum-jobs with the civilizing impulse. . . . Fakirs indeed. Fiendish really. . . .

The stranger tossed his head and snorted, a kind of depraved mysticism creeping across his face.

But admit it, he suddenly roared in excitement. Didn't you always think *Om* was the important sound out of India? Didn't they fool you with that one too? And doesn't this new information mean, then, that the *Hum* and the *Om* may be far more closely entwined than anyone has ever suspected? That to chant the one is secretly to chant the other? That the Indian sages, in their wisdom, may long ago have discovered this astounding way to sound the bells of the soul and the flesh simultaneously? That the soul and the body, therefore, contrary to Western thought, are not only on secret speaking terms with one another, but are actually one and the same thing beneath it all? That the entire human story can thus be summed up in one profound phrase? That it's all a matter of man seeking his true home? From *hummmm* to *ommmm*, in other words, and so to *home?* And so at last to *hommmme.* . . .

Joe stared. The humming sound went on and on as the stranger shifted his weight back and forth, all the while vigorously nodding his head in encouragement, a shy maniacal grin on his face. Finally Joe was able to shake himself out of the trance he had fallen into.

But this is *extraordinary,* he murmured.

Is it? asked the stranger eagerly. You mean wonders never cease? Not even in an alley as shabby as the rue Clapsius?

Joe laughed.

What did you say your name was?

The man's smile instantly disappeared. All at once he was gazing at Joe with an immensely grave expression Solemnly, he cleared his throat.

Didn't say, did I. But my name's Vivian and I drove you in from the airport and I'm sorry about everything. *Sorry.*

Vivian blushed, his arms swinging in agitation. Joe laughed and warmly shook his hand, once more resisting the urge to embrace him.

Viv? It's really you without the wigs and tennis whites and leopardskins? Good to see you again.

Vivian shrank back a little, looking even more doubtful than he had when he first entered the room.

Is it? I know who you are, they told me a little about you. Not much, just a little. You're not angry with me?

No, of course not. Why should I be?

Because of my rank behavior at the airport. But I'm sorry, it was a part, a role. When picking up someone new I'm expected to play some kind of exotic role. . . . I think . . . and sometimes I just lose hold and go blasting off in every direction. It's the madness of the times that does it to me.

Forget it, Viv. Anyway, you should be the one who's upset.

Vivian looked bewildered.

Me? What on earth for?

That business about Cynthia. I hope you realize it had nothing to do with you. It was Bletchley who was bothering me.

Vivian sighed.

Oh yes, the Bletch, none other. I understood that right away. Our local supply sergeant can be very unpleasant sometimes, especially when he adopts that business-is-business attitude of his. Don't take it personally, the Bletch likes to say, but what nonsense. Of *course* I'm going to take it personally. This is my life that's being tossed around out here in this Bletchedly dry business known as the Western Desert, and would you mind if I sat down immediately? My feet hurt.

Of course, Viv, take the chair or the bed. It's not much of a room.

Vivian pulled off his shoes and slumped down on the bed with grunts and sighs. When not playing a role he seemed to wheeze heavily. He moved the pillow down to the bottom of the bed, covered it with his jacket and lay down with his feet up. Briefly he gazed at the paint peeling off the ceiling, then closed his eyes.

Flaky, he murmured. But even so, when meeting someone in real life I always try to raise my feet above my head in order to increase the trickle of blood to my brain. Quite frankly, there's seldom a time when my brain couldn't use a little more oxygen. It's my asthma that slows me down and the odd thing is I never had it until I came to Egypt, can you imagine that? A desert climate is supposed to cure such things, not cause them, but there we are. Another performance of the blues.

Vivian smiled weakly from the bed.

Yes, the blues. For some reason life has always struck me as pretty much of a raffish rendition of the blues. Rhythmic intensity, a stressing of weak beats, riffs.

Vivian groaned. He felt his throat.

Oh this *body*, he muttered. This wheezing jazz band of the soul.

He opened his eyes and laughed.

Flaky, your ceiling, no question about it. But life as music aside, let me tell you straight off this visit has nothing to do with business. I'm here to apologize and I'm just me now, nothing more. Are you hungry at all?

Famished, Viv. I was just getting ready to go out when you knocked.

Good. I've brought some roast chicken along, and also some wine and loquats, to try to help you forget my body-block at the airport the other morning. The chicken's usually quite tasty, I get it from a retired belly dancer up the street whom Ahmad knows from another era. She's also the one who told me about the local hum-job tradition. And the wine should be good, if you can make do with German wine. One of our Long Range Desert Groups plucked it out of Rommel's personal supply van no more than a week ago.

Vivian frowned.

But perhaps you'd like to save the wine for a more important occasion. You wouldn't be hurting my feelings if you did. I'm used to slaps and kicks and punches.

Hold on, Viv, this is the important occasion. Just let me get to it.

Vivian smiled in relief and began singing a popular tune. Joe went to work opening one of the bottles.

Oh by the way, Viv, is your name really Vivian? I ask only because Ahmad chanced to mention he'd never seen or heard of a Vivian around here.

Vivian scowled. He groaned.

Oh he did, did he? Ahmad actually said that?

Yes.

Vivian rolled sideways and gazed sadly at Joe, his mouth nibbling and chewing, never still.

That's a heavy blow, he sighed. Why on earth would you ask me that?

Well I don't know, Viv, the thought just came drifting by. But no offense meant, let's forget it.

Forget it? My name? Please study me carefully and tell me the truth. Don't I *look* like a Vivian?

The cork popped out of the bottle.

Well maybe not, said Joe. Can't say you do, really.

Did I before? Coming in from the airport?

Yes, maybe so. I guess you did.

But I don't now?

No, maybe not.

Not even a little bit? Isn't there anything in this world but slaps and kicks and punches?

Wait, said Joe, I think I'm beginning to see it. Vivian, you say? *Vivian?* Of course, it's unmistakable. There's a startling resemblance, Viv.

There is?

Oh yes, simply stunning. The only reason I missed it at first was because I'm not used to seeing a Vivian. You don't come across one every day on an Indian reservation in Arizona.

I can imagine, muttered Vivian gloomily. And how about a Vivian McBastion, then?

A what? Is that true?

Yes.

Well now, I like it, said Joe. It has the tang of an aristocratic Scottish fortress hunkering down in the cool mists and repulsing every assault.

On his back, Vivian cast a bleak smile at the ceiling.

Don't leap to conclusions. There's an enormous amount of confusion in the world and I'm afraid I play a part in it. I'm afraid that's only the beginning of my persona. There's more to my mask, much more. Are you ready to hear all of it?

Of course, why not?

You'll see. Brace yourself then. My full name is *Vivian McBastion Noël Liffingsford-Ivy.*

Jesus, Viv, is that the truth?

Vivian scowled and his voice was gloomier than ever.

Furthermore, I'll tell you why I don't look like a Vivian, let alone all the rest of it. I'm not.

Well *there*, cried Joe with relief.

I mean that's my legal name, but it's not really me. My father's name was Lifschitz. When my parents came over to England from Germany they wanted something that sounded less foreign, so they did a potter around in a hunt for common syllables and *Liffingsford* is what emerged, like a new Tory leader in Parliament. The *Ivy* was an afterthought, meant to add a comfy appearance of having been around awhile. I'm not sure how well they understood English at the time.

I know how that is, said Joe. I didn't understand it myself until I was fifteen or sixteen.

They bought a little shop when they came to England, a cozy thatched-roof affair in the heart of London. They thought it was the only decent thing to do. Fair play, England my England, a nation of shopkeepers and so forth. Then when I came along they did a hunt through the Sunday tabloids to find a name for me, and that odd lot is what they came up with. Later I disappointed them though. I didn't become a dentist.

I see.

But everybody has always called me *Liffy*, with the exception of my mother and father and Bletchley. . . . Blasted authority figures, they always get everything wrong. But Ahmad knows me as Liffy, and everybody else around here does.

Fine, Liffy, that's what I'm going to call you then. And I like the name, because it just happens to recall a river I know.

I suspected it might, said Liffy, and it's always pleasant to remind someone of a river. But I never became a dentist, I have to tell you that right now. I became a clown, a sad clown. That's my problem.

Have some wine, Liffy?

Thanks, I will. My liver hurts.

Maybe you ought to ease up then?

No, it can't have anything to do with drinking, I almost never drink. My liver often hurts at night, and I think the reason it does is because the liver was considered the seat of the passions in the classical world, back before barbarians destroyed the classical world and the passions were transferred to the heart. But somehow in my case the transfer never seems to have been made. In other words, Joe, I'm a throwback.

To what?

I'm not sure, that's my problem. But I have an uneasy feeling I may be the Wandering Jew from antiquity. Everything seems to suggest it.

Have you wandered a lot then?

Oh yes, that's all I did before the war. I wandered around Europe as an itinerant entertainer, making people laugh after dinner. Then I sat in empty railway waiting rooms late at night, feeling hungry and waiting for a milk train to nowhere. The restaurants were always closed by the time I finished work in the evening, and when I arrived in a new place the following morning I'd take a nap in the railway waiting room to save expenses, until it was time to appear in a show that night. So I almost never slept in a bed and I didn't see much daylight either. In those days I lived almost entirely on milk and it made me quite pale. All told, it was a ghostly experience.

Were you really a professional clown, Liffy?

Well it was that general aspect of life. I worked as a clown or a mime or an actor, a juggler or an acrobat or a song-and-dance man, the fat drunken companion of a Shakespearean king of merrie olde England or a not so merry Shakespearean moneylender in gloomy old Venice, sometimes in blackface and sometimes in white, but far more frequently in gray. And more often than not in the end, after giving my all, done in. It seems that in every human drama there has to be someone who loses, and for some mysterious reason that role became my specialty. Occasionally I had to be taken seriously, but in general I was the absurd chameleon of the species, the ludicrous jester and buffo, the all-purpose fool. Making people laugh was my profession. It's a sad way to make a living.

I believe it, said Joe. And what about your work here, Liffy? What do you do?

Little things. Play a role for an hour or two or a day. Anything that might require a disguise and some makeup and a language or two. I'm just a prop really. I do a turn as an Italian general or a Syrian merchant or a Czech peasant, whatever's wanted. When they need a prop they trundle me out and I rage and swagger or skulk and cringe, bending my knees and shifting my weight and detesting kulaks or Jews, Jerries or Tommies, as the case may be. I'm the local illusionist, that's all. A sad clown.

Why sad, Liffy?

Because the world's sad

Why a clown then?

Because the world's so sad we have to laugh, otherwise it would be an even more dangerous place than it already is.

Liffy smiled shyly.

But there. Like everybody else, I like to pretend there's some lofty explanation for my private quirks. The truth is I'm probably sad because I spent so much time in empty railway waiting rooms before the war, at night. Have you ever noticed that people who live at night seem to have no bones? Perhaps it's the bad lighting.

And why did you become a clown, Liffy?

Why? Well I don't think I did in the beginning. I started out as a child imitating grown-ups, as every child does, and before long I discovered my imitations could make people laugh, and making people laugh brought me a sweet or two. So I went on doing what I'd grown accustomed to doing, the thing that brought in a sweet or two, and thus a career and a life in the usual manner.

But you're not like most people, Liffy.

No, I'm sure I'm not. I've been drifting around the world too long for that.

Liffy smiled.

How long, you say? Do I really qualify as the Wandering Jew from antiquity? Well sometimes it does seem as if these wanderings of mine have gone on for a full twenty-five hundred years, more or less. Sometimes it does seem that long when I'm alone at night and afraid.

Liffy sadly lowered his eyes.

And I am often afraid, he whispered. But then too, there's another reason why I may be different. In order to imitate people you have to understand them, and that's my problem, I do. You have to be angry to get ahead in this world, or if you really want to get ahead, you have to hate people. But how can I hate anyone when I know what people are feeling?

Liffy sighed.

Sometimes I wish I'd become a dentist. A spot of black turns up and you grind it away, just like that, and slap some shiny gold in its place. It's easy, it's satisfying, people wait in line to see you and call you Herr Professor Doktor or Panzergroupcommander. But to get ahead like that you have to think of people as teeth, the way the Nazis do.

Liffy gasped and stopped for breath. An asthmatic rattle wheezed up his throat.

Although it's not just hate in general that lets you get ahead. Mostly it has to do with yourself, like all strong feelings, so I guess you'd have to call it self-disgust. Have you ever noticed that people seem to hate us, Jews, according to how much they're secretly disgusted with themselves? Not that there aren't innumerable reasons why people choose Jews to hate, rather than themselves. After all, who wants to hate himself? Who wouldn't rather hate somebody else?

You've seen a lot of hate, Liffy.

Naturally, I'm a Jew. When I'm not the king of merrie olde England, that is. Or a buffoon. Or the Holy Ghost in some timeless tale of life and death and resurrection.

And you speak in a very crowded way, Liffy.

That's only because I've wandered so much, and been so many people in so many places, that I can't pretend to separate the sounds of the world easily. Or fool myself into thinking they're simple, rather than mysterious and complex. . . . Hate a Jew? What could be simpler than that? It's as simple as hating a tree or the wind or the sunrise.

Liffy raised his eyes and gazed at Joe, a soft expression. All at once he seemed very small and fragile.

But I can also hear simple sounds, Joe. You may think from what I've said that I'm a bitter man who sees only the harsh things in life, and that's not true at all. It's the good things, the kindly side of people, that interests me and concerns me. It's just that sometimes now, with the war and the Nazis. . . .

I understand, Liffy.

Do you? *Do* you? Can I tell you how I really feel, then?

Liffy smiled shyly.

Do you know what I really feel life is, deep down? A golden bell and a pomegranate.

Liffy smiled even more shyly.

Isn't that a beautiful way to describe it? Long ago I heard that and I've never forgotten it. And when life does seem bitter and cruel to me, I take those words into my heart and whisper them over and over, until I can manage again.

It is beautiful, said Joe. And who might have spoken such words, I wonder?

Liffy's eyes shone.

Who? Who else but the good voice within us. God.

He laughed.

Yes. God speaking to Moses in the desert, describing the robe that the priests of life are to wear.

> *And beneath upon the hem of it thou shalt make pomegranates of blue and of purple and of scarlet, round about the hem thereof, and bells of gold between them round about. A golden bell and a pomegranate, a golden bell and a pomegranate, upon the hem of the robe round about.*

Liffy smiled.

And it has a special meaning for me that gives me hope so I can go on no matter how dark the way.

Can you share that special meaning, Liffy? Can you tell me what a golden bell is in this world? And a pomegranate?

Liffy lowered his eyes.

I am, he whispered. I'm both of them at once. And you are, and every human being is. For we are strange and wonderful creations and the sounds within our souls are as clear and haunting as the ring of a golden bell. And yet the taste on our tongues is always of the dusty earth, the sweet dusty taste of the pomegranate rich with seeds in the hot sun.

Liffy looked up. He smiled.

So you see, I haven't really wandered too much, nor have I played too many roles. Life is an awesome blessing and the more we know of it the richer we are. The more we know of its dust, no less than the golden toll of its bell. The two of them always together, inseparable upon our hearts.

92

Suddenly Liffy sat up and laughed, flashing two perfect rows of brilliant white teeth. Then his fingers flickered in front of his mouth and his shoulders sagged and all at once he was a shrunken little man, toothless and decrepit. He held up the two dental plates he had removed from his mouth and gazed at them, moving one and then the other in the manner of a puppeteer.

Up went the upper plate. Laughter.

Down went the lower plate. Tragedy.

He slipped the plates back into his mouth and stared at Joe.

Teeth, he said. They're false. Some time ago I formulated a theorem to cover my situation, which I've always referred to privately as *Liffy's First Law*. To wit, *Good teeth suggest mindlessness*. Do a little surreptitious checking around and you'll see I'm right, although it's also true we try very hard to justify ourselves. Naturally, since we can never escape the fact we're somebody's child. Even the wisest old man in the world, in his thoughts at least, is still a little boy to someone. But none of that's my problem. I'm neither wise nor old and my problem is a bad lower back.

You're practical, Liffy.

No not really, as you'll find out soon enough. I understand practicality but it has never appealed to me. In fact when I examine myself, I come to the conclusion that fantasy has meant more to me than positive knowledge. And all of that's a quote. Do you know who said it?

Some dreamer?

Yes, Einstein. And do you also know Cynthia won't sleep with me these nights? She's upset because I got her into trouble with Bletchley.

I'm sorry to hear that.

Oh she'll get over it. Her only trouble seems to be she thinks the Middle East is romantic, so she always wants me to be someone different when I come to call. One evening I have to be a long thin Bombay Lancer charging the Khyber Pass, a randy brown fellow who never takes off his boots. Then the next night I have to be a short slimy sheik rolling around on the rug, obsessed with my greyhound.

Liffy frowned, his mood changing.

Romanticism? Imagination? But hasn't it always been *the* human enigma? Has anything ever been so circular and contradictory, right from the beginning? It spins from sublime to harmless, from Einstein to Cynthia, and so around the circle to the horrors that Zarathustra also spake, sadly for all of us.

Liffy groaned.

That's right. I'm talking about the lowest of the low now, German supermen. Before the war the Germans used to get very excited over the idea of a mud pit filled with muscular naked blond women, viciously wrestling with each other. After the regular evening entertainments were over in the provinces, that was often the special show put on backstage for an extra fee. A discreet side entrance for couples, single ladies invited free of charge. The mud flying and the slime oozing and naked grunting women sinking in primordial muck to the accompaniment of Bach and Mozart, the phonograph blaring, with a dramatic switch to Wagner and on-the-spot promotions to Panzergroupcommander for those who grunted the loudest, after one of the hulking combatants had managed to squash all the other heads under the mud. . . . Bliss and more. Yes.

Liffy choked and sputtered for air, wheezing painfully.

The truth always takes a little bit out of me, he rasped. And have you noticed that when Rommel is wearing civilian clothes, he looks like some small-time hoodlum? Surly little Swabian fellow with a snarl on his face and his felt hat mashed down on his head? And he's supposed to be the *good* German general. Well if he's so good, how did he get to be the commandant of Hitler's personal headquarters before the war? Must have ingratiated himself, wouldn't you say? And Hitler must have liked what he saw, which says a good deal more about our Desert Fox than any amount of racing around in an African desert ever will. . . . Hitler likes him? That's *good?*

Liffy gripped his throat. For a moment he seemed unable to breathe.

And I also imagine that to someone from the New World, I may seem unduly sensitive to the loping images I find in that simple Germanic term, *Panzergroupcommander.* Well I can only say that it's much worse than you think. Much worse. Frankly, it's a howling nightmare of a word to me and you might as well scream *COSSACK* in my ear. The one conjures up the same primeval blackness as the other. . . .

Liffy shuddered, as if shaking off a mood.

More of Rommel's wine was opened as the night deepened and the talk swirled in the little room in the Hotel Babylon, as Liffy learned more about Joe and his interest in Stern, and Joe learned more about Ahmad and Bletchley and the British intelligence units known as the Monks and the Waterboys, the one with its headquarters in the desert, the other in the Irrigation Works in Cairo itself.

Of course Liffy knew Joe had been brought to Cairo by the Monks, since Bletchley was a Monk. And he was also friendly with Stern, as it turned out, although he had no professional connection with Stern and knew almost nothing about what Stern did.

We met through work, said Liffy, but that's not how we're friends and we never talk about work. With a war on, who'd want to? Mostly we just sit in one dim Arab bar or another and talk.

What do you talk about? asked Joe.

Oh, empty railway stations, living at night, Europe before the war. Stern was a student in Europe when he was young and he likes my imitations. They make him laugh, or at least they used to. Nothing much makes him laugh these days.

Have you met any of his other friends then?

Well there's the American woman, Maud, who works for the Waterboys. Translations, I think, not operations. I've met her with him once or twice. And of course there's Ahmad, they used to be friends. But you know how it is out here these days, Joe. People tend to keep the different parts of their lives separate, very much so.

Joe nodded.

But what about these Monks and Waterboys, Liffy? What can you tell me about them?

Liffy's mouth worked silently, nibbling and chewing over his thoughts.

Well they have their different areas of interest, naturally, but the areas don't seem to have anything to do with geography. It's more a matter of the kinds of intelligence involved, or the levels, I guess you could say. The things the Monks do always seem more obscure, and they're fanatical about keeping their affairs to themselves. They take things from the Waterboys all right, information and support and so forth, but it never works the other way. The Monks are always careful to keep an outsider on the periphery of things.

Do the two groups compete with each other then?

Liffy shook his head.

You couldn't say that really. I suppose there's some overlap in their operations sometimes, there'd have to be. But in the end their goals are different, their levels of interest again. The deeper you go, the more likely you are to find it's the Monks who are involved, not the Waterboys. The more regular aspects of the business, that's what concerns the Waterboys. And the Monks . . . well something more, but I couldn't begin to define it exactly. . . . By the way, just out of curiosity I checked to see if the Waterboys know anything about you, and they don't. They've never even heard of you.

No? But why would the Waterboys tell you something like that, one way or the other?

Liffy smiled.

Oh they wouldn't, so I didn't bother to ask them. There's a file clerk on the graveyard shift who's a friend of mine, and . . . well, and so forth.

I see. And Stern? Which group is he with?

Liffy hesitated. He frowned.

Stern's an exception in many ways, isn't he? He seems to have done a lot of work for both the Monks and the Waterboys, which is so dangerous I don't even like to think about it. . . . But look here, Joe, I'm sure you realize by now how little I understand these things. I'm just a prop out here as I told you, and I only work on the fringes, and who knows, anyway, what to make of people called Monks and Waterboys? These days intelligence groups seem to pop up out here the way religions once did. In fact it's enough to make you wonder sometimes whether it's not our modern way of doing things, although God knows I'd certainly prefer to believe the Monastery is some kind of wartime aberration out there in the desert, rather than a permanent anything.

You speak of the Monks in a curious way, Liffy.

Well they're a curious bunch, and Bletchley with his grim business-is-business attitude is just the beginning of it. One of the more bizarre assignments I've had with the Monks is being taken on drives at night out to the pyramids, Bletchley acting as a silent chauffeur in front while some stranger sits in back with me talking inscrutably, while I fiddle around with a cigarette holder and occasionally toss off a prearranged question I don't understand. . . . Come on, Joe. A businesslike Cyclops who simply enjoys a nighttime spin at the wheel and a glimpse of the Sphinx by moonlight? Is this the spy trade, then, or some convention of myths, or both? . . . But if you think Bletchley's odd, just wait until you meet Whatley.

Who's he?

The end of the line. The man in charge out at that parched and pitiless center of nowhere. The abbot, I guess you'd have to call him. Or simply, Your Grace. He seems to like that. And he's really peculiar. I know it's human nature to prefer to fight the last war, yesterday being easier to understand than today, but Whatley seems to overdo it. Excessive in his obsessions, you know. So much so that sometimes I wonder if he's aware what century he's in. Of course everybody's born at the wrong time in the wrong era, and it's also true that madness doesn't age, that it's simply ageless. But all the same, you see some strange things in the inner cells of the Monastery, cancerous things perhaps. Life living and growing, but living and growing the wrong way and coming out deformed somehow, destructive somehow. . . .

Liffy's voice drifted off.

Or so it seemed to Joe as he sat listening to Liffy's darkly shifting visions of the Monastery. Joe's mind blurring then and slowly sinking in the uneasy shadows of a restless sleep.

6

Sphinx

It was late when Joe looked at his watch, no more than an hour or two before dawn. He realized he must have dozed off in the chair beside the table, but he had no idea how long he had been asleep. Liffy was still stretched out on Joe's narrow cot, wheezing softly. Joe glanced at the table littered with empty wine bottles and chicken bones and frowned. Liffy was watching him with concern.

Awake again? And are you all right? Do you feel feverish at all? You seemed to be doing battle with yourself last night while I was briefly recounting the history of the world.

As a matter of fact I don't feel too well, said Joe, easing himself forward and holding his head in his hands.

Perfectly understandable, murmured Liffy. A concise history of the world would have that effect on anyone. There's nothing more disquieting than memory. And I know exactly how you must feel this morning because I know exactly how *I* felt the first time I awoke in this world. When I was born, I mean. Not many people can remember that far back, but I can.

Joe moaned, holding his head more tightly.

And how did I feel at that moment? asked Liffy. Outraged. Appalled. Utterly stunned by what lay ahead of me now that I had been expelled from my tropical sealike Eden, that warm and fluid and rhythmic womb where I'd been happy and safe. And I was only seconds old, mind you, a mere tiny red-raw bundle of quivering impressions. And then all at once this huge figure in white, who was wearing a mask, naturally, snatched me up high into the air and *viciously* slapped me on the back. *Slap*, just like that. And I screamed my way into the world then, just *screamed*, Joe. And I understood it all at that moment, just everything, and I said to myself,

Oh shit, you're in for it now.

Suddenly Liffy sat up on the bed, intensely alert.

Well? I was right about that, wasn't I? It was one of those rare cases of a man being right from the very beginning. The *very* beginning.

Liffy laughed, then frowned.

But are *you* all right this morning, Joe? Our bodies are but shoddy armor for the soul, after all. . . . And why are you wearing that hat?

What hat?

That faded red wool thing. Your Irish disguise. You look like some sort of sickly elf in need of a handout.

I told you I'm not feeling too well, muttered Joe.

Then we must get out of here immediately, said Liffy, rising. Dawn is about to break over Egypt, so why wouldn't a glimpse of the pyramids at sunrise be just the thing? Come on, Joe, why not? Fresh air at least, and aren't we a race of fearless hunters when all's said and done? Daring adventurers fated with the need to know and to seek?

Joe cleared his sticky lungs, his mind still a blur. Liffy snorted.

Of course we are, Joe, don't argue. Adventure is everything to men like us. It's in our very blood, along with chicken fat and the sour residue of Rommel's wine. Just consider my clandestine orders, the real secret orders I was given in London when I was being sent out here as a spy. Didn't I tell you what they said?

No, muttered Joe. What?

Head east, my child, ever east.

They did?

Precisely. And after that general introduction, they got down to specifics.

A. *Yes, my child, a leisurely journey is what we have in mind for you, so stop look and listen.*

B. *Mingle, eat the local mush.*

C. *Tarry in caves and open spaces and mark well the local aphorisms.*

D. *Even graze a goat or two, if there's time.*

E.   But above all head ever east, for these are your orders in life, my child. For now anyway.
F.   Good luck.
G.   Have a nice trip.

Liffy laughed.

A trifle vague perhaps, but no more so than most things having to do with intelligence. In fact it wouldn't surprise me if your orders were secretly the same, so come along then. Come.

Liffy helped Joe to his feet and removed his hat. Gently he steered Joe toward the door, murmuring in a soothing voice all the while.

Fresh air, yes, I know how you feel . . . you need to escape from this room and from the Hotel Babylon in general, which unfortunately has changed very little from the time when a detachment of Napoleon's camel corps was bivouacked here. . . . Ahmad tells the story. Apparently there used to be a plaque in the lobby commemorating the event. . . . *Napoleon's camels slept here. With their eyes open*   . . Of course, Joe, it's that kind of place. Come along now. .

Liffy locked the door behind them.

Easy does it, he whispered. In this quarter the darkness has ears, and as spies, we must lurk without a sound.

They tiptoed down the stairs and the pianola on the ground floor came into view. Ahmad was asleep at the counter, sitting on his high stool with his head resting on an open newspaper. Next to his elbow were several large round sesame wafers, apparently left over from a midnight snack. Liffy scooped them up.

Survival rations for the dawn patrol, he whispered. The home front has all the luck. But have you ever noticed that all the spies in Cairo always read newspapers while waiting for their next clandestine strike?

While he whispered, Liffy was making a show of leaning over the counter to hang up Joe's key. But at one point he suddenly reached under the counter and grabbed for something, which he then hid behind his back. And a none too skillful maneuver at that, thought Joe.

They tiptoed toward the door.

I thought everybody in Cairo always did nothing but read newspapers? whispered Joe.

That's true, they do, but that's only because everybody in Cairo is a spy. Out here a man has no choice. Spy and be spied upon—it's the real secret of the pyramids.

They tiptoed through the open door into the darkness and made their way up the rue Clapsius.

What we obviously need this morning, whispered Liffy, is a dramatic breakthrough. Now I'm going to fetch the van while you turn left at the next corner and follow your nose to a little square where there's a fragment of a Roman fountain, a pained marble face with an alarmed mouth spouting water. You can't miss it and it's also a chance for a quick wash-up. I'll meet you there.

Liffy trotted off, a long cylindrical leather case and a bundle of what looked like laundry tucked under his arm.

He must have left those things under Ahmad's counter when he arrived last night, thought Joe, wondering why Liffy had bothered to hide them behind his back in such a halfhearted way.

In an upstairs window at the end of the alley, in the dilapidated building owned by the former belly dancer who now roasted chickens for a living, a young man laid aside his newspaper and dialed a telephone number.

They've left the hotel, he whispered. Just the two of them.

Most of the young man's fingers were missing. He listened care fully.

All right, he whispered. Yes . . . I'll be here.

He hung up the phone and smiled.

And now for a real old-fashioned English breakfast, he thought, banging twice on the floor so the woman downstairs would hear him.

Joe found the little square and washed his face and hands, still unable to shake off the blurred feeling in his mind. He was standing in front of the small Roman fountain, gazing numbly down at the worn marble face and wondering what could be keeping Liffy, when suddenly a chilling shriek exploded behind him. He whirled.

A huge horse and pale rider were wildly thundering out of the shadows and bearing down on the little square, the rider a fierce bedouin straight from the interminable depths of the desert, his great sword of Allah raised high as he charged headlong through the dim alley toward Joe. The hooded bedouin crouched low as the animal leapt and smashed its hooves into the cobblestones, rearing out of control in the half-light, enormous and fiery beneath the crackling robes of the horseman.

God help us, thought Joe, huddling in the little square and not daring to take his eyes off the monstrous vision, lest he be trampled or cut in half by the demon's slashing sword. The beast reared and charged anew, plunging recklessly back and forth as the bedouin whipped his mount into an ever greater frenzy, hair streaming and sparks flying, horse and rider hurtling skyward and filling the air with a stench of cold sweat.

Joe threw himself to the side as a blast of damp breath shot by his head. He slipped and went crashing down on one knee, catching himself at the last moment and spinning toward a wall, limping and stumbling, running, the awful vision of the horseman's face towering over him.

. . . gaunt stony features and a ghastly pallor in the eerie light. A hawk's beak and sunken glittering eyes and cruel twisted lips. A crazed primitive face from some lost wilderness.

Death, thought Joe, the image flashing through his mind despite himself.

Death's the rider and there's no escape.

He was pressed against a wall and moving sideways, frantically groping for a doorway, shelter, anything. He felt a cavity in the wall and slipped into it, shrinking backward, pushing against the stone with all his strength.

But as soon as Joe had slipped into the safety of the doorway, he began to notice things.

For one, the huge sleek stallion seemed to have curiously knobby knees. And its stomach sagged and it was swaybacked, and there were thick clumps of matted hair spreading down over its hooves.

For another, the huge beast wore a heavy wooden halter of the kind used to weigh down common workhorses. And there were strands of old rope trailing from the halter that looked as if they might have been attached to a wagon not too long ago.

Joe stared.

Instead of the fierce bedouin who had come thundering out of the shadows, he now saw a frightened figure desperately hanging on to his tired mount as best he could, a man who was all elbows and knees and terrified squeals as he crashed around on top of the old horse, his perch so precarious he was clinging to the horse's head and squashing an old rag over the poor animal's nostrils.

Even the long powerful sword was no longer what it had appeared to be. In fact it wasn't a sword at all but a long cylinder of dull metal thrashing harmlessly this way and that, obviously wielded more for balance than anything else.

In any case the spectacle was abruptly over, the strange illusion gone as quickly as it had come in the shadows of the little square. With a groan the exhausted workhorse heaved itself into the air a final time and came tumbling down on the cobblestones, its bones cracking ponderously in the stillness and its legs nearly buckling under the impact, the old creature shuddering once before becoming instantly immobile, its head hanging, a vision of worn-out flesh weary beyond belief.

Just before the horse landed, Liffy jumped free. He pushed back his hood and grinned.

Double-time, he whispered. This way.

In another moment they were running down an alley. As Liffy pulled him along, Joe looked back and saw the huge old workhorse standing alone in the little square, its belly sagging and its tail swishing, its nose nestled against the alarmed marble face of the small Roman fountain. Liffy wheezed happily.

We needed that to get the day started, he whispered. Quick, this way.

Why are we running? asked Joe.

Liffy slowed to a trot.

No reason really. It's just more dramatic.

But what was all that about?

Liffy sneezed. He smiled.

Drama, he whispered. The inescapable drama of life. I decided we needed a bracing event to get ourselves going this morning.

Bracing? You scared me half to death.

Liffy laughed.

I did, didn't I, I could see it in your face. For just a moment you must have thought fate had come riding in from the desert to pay you a call.

Joe tugged on Liffy's arm, slowing him to a walk.

And not just fate either, Liffy.

No?

Liffy stopped, suddenly serious. He stared at Joe.

And I looked, he murmured, and behold a pale horse, and his name that sat on him was Death.

Liffy touched Joe's chest.

But you just see how it is? You must be careful, Joe. The desert is never far away here, and even Old Cairo can be a dangerous place. And perhaps even the Hotel Babylon, if you're its only guest.

Joe looked at him.

Is that true? There's no one else staying there but me?

No one, said Liffy. And what's more, no one has stayed there in several months. You can ask Ahmad.

But why?

Who knows, Joe? Perhaps it was condemned or forgotten by certain sinister secret forces . . . until you arrived on the scene. Perhaps there's even far more to Bletchley's potted palms than we suspect.

Liffy nodded. He smiled.

But we've had enough of the Hotel Babylon for now. The point is the classical world still lives and the trick works. It took me awhile to find an old horse unattended, that's what kept me. There he was just roped to his wagon in a dreary back alley with the prospect of another dreary day ahead, old and tired and thinking he'd seen it all, when suddenly he shed the bonds of a lifetime and the two of us went flying away like the wind. Like *the wind*, Joe, I could feel it. Will wonders never cease?

Joe smiled.

I don't think they could if they wanted to, Liffy, not when you're around. But what did you do to that old workhorse to make him move like that?

I merely reminded him of the joy of life, answered Liffy.

How?

By recalling a day in the life of Alexander the Great.

What?

Yes. That rag I had pressed to the old gent's nostrils is actually a footnote from history. You find a mare in heat and acquire her scent, then when the magic is applied to the nose of a stallion, even a decrepit old jade as tired as that one, his blood wildly surges and all at once he's a bounding prancing colt again, deliriously out of control. Can't help himself, you see, not when you put it right under his nose. Sex, it's called.

Alexander the Great did that with a horse? asked Joe.

It was either him or one of his lackeys, and there you see how well it works. The scent seems to be good for several days, as well it might be. Clever, these ancients. Had their wits about them on occasion and discovered a thing or two about the meat of the matter. Including the fact that it's all in the mind, as we've often suspected. Sex, I mean.

Liffy hummed, whistled, sneezed.

Do you think Cynthia would be shocked if I told her about this? My guess is she'd pretend to be shocked while secretly relishing the whole idea. And who knows what it might lead to later in the evening, for who knows what lechery lurks in the minds of women? Or who knows what lurks in anyone's mind? Or . . .

Joe smiled. Liffy threw back his head and studied the sky.

Now where did I leave that secret van? Our wholly inconspicuous Ahmadmobile?

He laughed and they started off again.

Oh I remember, it's just that it's like everything else in this world. We're not there yet, but we're getting there.

After twisting and turning through more alleys, they finally arrived at the small delivery van, its side panels boldly advertising AHMAD'S greasy fish & levantine chips. Before they climbed in Liffy zipped up his former sword, a long collapsible spyglass, in its leather case.

Ahmad's, he said. He always keeps it handy under his counter, for those times when he feels the need to take an especially penetrating look at the past. I couldn't tell him I was taking it without waking him, but he won't mind. He only uses it at night . . . Saturday nights, I believe.

Liffy gazed at the bundle of clothing under his arm. He smiled.

The bedouin cloak goes with me for another day, but I think I just might play God this morning by leaving this magical rag, heavenly scented, right here on a windowsill. And should a weary workhorse chance to pass this way today, and should the sagging old jade chance to raise his weary head at the right moment and catch a whiff of this Alexandrian rag, he'll be rewarded by music far beyond his wildest dreams. For the old jade's blood will suddenly surge as he abandons himself to the passionate dances of his youth, and his owner will be astounded and everybody will be astounded and the whole neighborhood will gather *to behold,* as they used to say.

Solemnly, then, Liffy drew himself up and gazed at Joe, his hand held high.

And behold it was written, the neighbors will say one unto another, a gleam and a twinkle in every eye and the glory of divine grace full upon them. For if a broken-down old workhorse can suddenly become a prancing playful colt, dare we imagine what this must mean for the rest of us?

And behold it was written, they will say. And the word will go forth from this place and be good news throughout the land, bringing great joy to all who hear it, as from a golden bell. For there are miracles in this world, they will say, that surpasseth all understanding. And these miracles come to those who raise their eyes from the cobblestones and look to the heavens, to search in their hearts for the darkness and the light. . . .

Liffy smiled shyly. He dropped his hand and nodded.

And I *know* that must be written, Joe, because miracles happen all the time, *they do.* It's just that we have to raise our eyes to look for them. And mostly we don't because we're weak and afraid, but when we do . . .

Liffy went on smiling, nodding.

Well, an interlude then on the dawn patrol. But wouldn't it be wonderful if we could witness a small miracle this morning? Especially a miracle involving someone who deserves it? Someone like Stern? . . .

The engine of the delivery van started with a quiet purr.

Less noise than when we drove in from the airport, said Joe.

That was the muffler cutout, replied Liffy, sometimes useful when the traffic's clogged. Just a flip of a switch and our Egyptian friends think Rommel's panzers have broken through the Eighth Army and are thundering into Cairo. Instantly the traffic clears and I go roaring through with waves and cheers on every side. It sets you up a bit until you remember why they're cheering. Off we go now.

They drove through the narrow streets of the Coptic Quarter, past horse-drawn carts and men bent double under loads of sacks and vegetables. The air was fresh and cool. Here and there a café was opening.

Best moment of the day really, said Liffy. The heat and corruption haven't settled in yet, and the mind hasn't had time to be horrified by what lies ahead. Do you need coffee or can you wait?

I can wait. Where are we going?

It's a surprise, a secret destination.

Liffy hummed a music-hall tune, a habit he apparently shared with Vivian. Joe gazed out the window, once more bothered by the blurred sensation in his mind. They seemed to be driving out of Cairo toward the desert, where a gathering of light lay on the horizon. The road turned and Joe caught a glimpse of the pyramids against the dim sky.

You weren't joking? We're going to the pyramids?

The dawn patrol, murmured Liffy. We're heading toward the dawn of Egyptian civilization, and although five thousand years have passed since the pyramids were built, we still may be in for a surprise. At least I hope so. If we're lucky. . . .

They lay on a rise of sand, the pyramids and the Sphinx in full view in front of them, a deep red glow above the desert to the east. Liffy handed the long spyglass to Joe.

Now adjust the spyglass to the Sphinx, said Liffy Have him yet?

Almost.

Beautiful?

Exquisite. The light.

Yes. Now look at the right eye of the Sphinx and concentrate on that. What do you see?

Shadows, Liffy.

Fine, keep looking. Shadows assume unexpected shapes and that can be intriguing.

But what am I supposed to see?

Who knows for sure. That odd-looking mythical creature with his human head and his animal body has always been a riddle, unlike the rest of us. Just keep looking.

Joe did so, feeling the cool sand against his chest and smelling the freshness of the desert, his thoughts far from any war.

Nothing yet? asked Liffy.

More light.

Good. We could all use a little more of that. Just keep looking.

Joe strained to see through the spyglass. For a moment he thought he saw something moving in the right eye of the Sphinx. A flicker, shadows, he couldn't be sure. Perhaps the sun rising toward the horizon was causing shadows to play on the worn ancient stones.

Beside him Liffy began to whisper.

Last night, remember? You talked a lot about Stern and what he means to you, and why you came here. You also said you'd heard about that friend of Stern's, old Menelik Ziwar, who was an Egyptologist in the last century. You said you'd heard stories about him when you were living in Jerusalem. But did you also know old Menelik had found time to do some serious poking around inside the Sphinx? Did anyone ever mention that to you?

No, whispered Joe, staring intently through the spyglass, trying harder and harder to see, not believing what seemed to be happening out there.

Well he did, whispered Liffy. Old Menelik decided he wanted to do a potter of sorts inside the Sphinx in the last century, lovable old mole that he was, and so he had a small tunnel dug from the outside, right into the Sphinx. The entrance to the tunnel is hidden as it has always been, and it leads to a tiny lookout old Menelik fashioned for himself right inside the riddle itself. . . . . What do you see?

Something moving, whispered Joe.

In the right eye?

Yes.

A stone being removed?

It could be.

And now?

It looks like a face, a head, appearing.

Where?

Right in the middle of the eye.

On his back on the sand beside Joe, gazing straight up at the sky, Liffy sighed happily.

In the pupil of the eye, you mean?

Yes.

It looks like a face, you say, a head? And it's becoming the pupil of the right eye of the Sphinx? Still shadowy?

Yes.

Do the shadows have a shape you can recognize?

No, it's too far away. Too small and indistinct.

Of course, the Sphinx's a riddle. Look harder.

Joe did so. He leaned forward on his elbows, holding his breath, straining to see through the spyglass. All at once he whistled softly.

Impossible.

Beside him, Liffy closed his eyes, a blissful smile on his face.

But it *is* real, whispered Joe, I can recognize him. Oh my God, it's *Stern. Stern.* . . .

Ah, murmured Liffy, he wasn't away after all. He's there watching the sunrise from his favorite perch. You can't always count on it anymore, Ahmad says, not the way things are these days. Just once in a great while can you find him at it. . . . But it's a sight, isn't it, Joe? Something worth looking for and waiting for and hoping will happen, our very own Stern gazing out through the eye of the Sphinx at dawn . . . and it doesn't happen much these days, according to Ahmad, so we were lucky to catch Stern at it . . . very lucky. Unless Stern knew you were arriving in Cairo. Could he have known that?

No, I didn't tell him.

And Bletchley wouldn't have said anything to him?

Oh no.

Are you sure?

Yes, positive.

Liffy hummed. He smiled.

Lovely then. It's chance, pure chance, and I was the one who was able to show it to you. . . . Ahhh, the wonders of life, the miracles. Sometimes I feel as light as a dove on the dawn. *Ahhh.* . . .

7

Monastery

Liffy was surprised when Joe told him he had a daytime meeting coming up with Bletchley. According to Liffy, the Monks were notorious for always conducting their briefings and meetings at night.

Strictly at night, said Liffy. Darkness is the sea they swim in. Do you realize that in all my time here, I've never once been to the Monastery except at night? But if Bletchley's really taking you into the desert to be briefed by Whatley, in broad daylight, at least you may not have to watch those awful films they show out there.

Films? asked Joe, pouring himself more gin. The two of them were sitting in the small crumbling courtyard behind the Hotel Babylon, a narrow enclosure strewn with rubble and old newspapers and piles of ancient debris.

On the dangers of venereal disease, said Liffy. Those same films they show back in England to young army recruits before they're sent overseas. Noses missing . . . no eyes . . . holes in heads going nowhere. Just terrible. When you arrive at the Monastery at night you have to sit through a couple of those films in the cloisters first, before you're allowed inside. Ugliness by starlight, in other words, to put you in the appropriate frame of mind before you enter the black bowels of the place. It's a kind of ritual they have out there, and not the only one from what I hear. . . . Just blackness everywhere. *Disgusting.*

Joe sipped his gin, thinking how the mere mention of the Monastery always disturbed Liffy so profoundly, in a way Liffy himself seemed unable to explain.

But what is it that bothers you so much about the Monastery? asked Joe.

Liffy shuddered and clasped his hands together, twisting his fingers around themselves. For a moment he stared at his fingers in horror, as if their slithering movements reflected his feelings.

But that's just it, Joe, I don't know, I don't *know*. When you first arrive out there everything seems normal enough. You look around you and it *seems* to be just an old fortress or an old monastery or whatever it was, that an intelligence unit has made its headquarters. Just a secret place where agents come and go in the darkness, carrying out the commonplace horrors of wartime. But somehow there's more to it than that, a sickness of the soul, and after a while you begin to sense it.

Well can you give me an example, Liffy? Something specific that makes you feel that way?

Liffy waved his hands in the air.

Take the maps, for instance, those copies of maps from the fourth century. Whatley has them all over the walls in one of the cells, along with contemporary maps showing the German-occupied areas of Europe and North Africa. And there's a copy of the Athanasian Creed, prominently displayed, with symbols in the margins that correspond to symbols on the maps, both the ancient ones and the modern ones, as if there were some sort of connection between the two. . . .

Liffy suddenly began to wheeze, struggling to breathe, the same trouble he had as when he talked about the Nazis or Germany.

What do you mean, Liffy? A connection between what and what? I think you've lost me.

Between the German armies and the Athanasian Creed.

I've heard of the Creed, Liffy, but what does it have to do with the maps? What's the connection?

Exactly. That's what's so strange about it all. And frankly, I've always avoided thinking about those maps, just as I've always avoided the implications of those disgusting films they show out there. But would you like me to try to make some sense out of it for you?

Joe nodded. Although Liffy had made it clear more than once that he hated to talk about the Monastery, he began to do so now in a kind of monotone, slipping into what was almost a trance.

Well first of all, murmured Liffy, the Creed grew out of the Arian controversy, didn't it, a great crisis in the early days of Christianity. The Arians took their name from Arius, the Libyan theologian who taught that Christ couldn't be both human and divine. Instead they claimed that Christ was human only, and it took some time before the Church was able to overcome the heresy, stating its position in the Creed. Arianism was pagan to the core and the Germanic tribes embraced it especially, so there were great wars as a result. The Roman Emperor Justinian had to destroy the Vandal armies in North Africa and the Ostrogoths in Italy, and campaign against the Visigothic kingdom in Spain, because they continued to adhere to the heretical view. And who, by chance, was the Church father in faraway Egypt who was so influential in helping to overcome the heresy?

St Anthony, said Joe despite himself, his head beginning to whirl.

St Anthony, repeated Liffy in his trance. The same St Anthony who'd gone into the Egyptian desert and become the founder of monasticism. And didn't all of that occur in the fourth century after Christ? And what, pray, is Whatley doing out there in the desert today, connecting Hitler's armies with the Arian controversy? Doesn't the Nazi madness have to do with A-r-y-a-n-s? And isn't this the twentieth century, not the fourth century? And don't fifteen hundred years count for anything in human history? Or is the answer to that merely a shrug and the sad whisper, *Not always, my child.*

Joe was stunned. For a long time he sat gazing at Liffy, his thoughts tumbling and racing.

But what are you implying? he finally asked. What does any of it mean?

I can't imagine what it means in its entirety, said Liffy, but I should add that Whatley can be a very charming man when he wants to be. A trifle erudite and also rather preoccupied with his own concerns, unlike the rest of us. But charming. . . . So the straightforward facts concerning the Monastery seem to be these. St Anthony and Whatley are out there in the desert with their secret armies of monks and Monks, and they appear to be mounting campaigns against heresies traditionally adhered to by the Germanic tribes, while all the while the Vandals and the Ostrogoths and the Visigoths maraud in the fourth century, and the Nazis viciously replay the ancient barbaric performance in the twentieth century.

Whatley, said Joe. Could you put your imagination to work on him for a moment?

You want conjecture, you mean? Not facts?

Yes.

Well if I had to try to understand what Whatley is truly up to out there in the desert, I think I might ask myself if it's a case of Whatley believing the Germans are denying the divine part of our natures? And if Whatley thus sees these new barbarians, the Nazis, as simply the old barbarians dressed up in snappier uniforms, with black and leather and death's-heads everywhere, who embrace the heretical Arian doctrine in the same way as the Germanic tribes did fifteen hundred years ago? And whether Whatley assumes, therefore, that he's some kind of latter-day St Anthony doing righteous battle against the evil Germanic heresiarchs?

Liffy sputtered and coughed, struggling for breath.

And if so, why? Because Whatley's a religious fanatic? A fanatic of history? A fanatic for the cause of moral uplift? . . . And I don't need to add that these Christian metaphors are merely that, merely metaphors. Christianity is only incidental to the matter, only the form of moral uplift that happens to have been the most obvious one in the West over the last two thousand years. The matter goes much deeper than any specific religion or philosophy, for what the Germanic streak in human nature really can't bear is change. Any kind of change. It prefers what was, in our case the animal state. Very deep is the well of the past, says Mann. May we not call it bottomless? says Mann. And thus that seductive whisper oozing out of the blackness, the Germanic whisper in all of us. . . . Where you were is where you are, my child. So gaze backward and downward, my child. Forever. . . .

Liffy gasped for breath.

Which translates in modern times into a mindless loping around on the savanna, *killing*, to the accompaniment of Bach.

Liffy choked.

I'm sorry, Joe, I just can't talk about this anymore. I hate to think about the Nazis and their black and their leather and their death's-heads. It's a gigantic pyramid of skulls they're after and it's monstrous.

Joe stood up and sat down again. This *Whatley*, he muttered.

Liffy nodded.

I know it. It's a regular Whatley, what? *What?* And there always does seem to be a Whatley out there somewhere, morbidly flagellating his flesh because he wishes he didn't have any, because purity would then be possible. But the Whatley factor exists and there's no use denying it simply because we don't like it. A part of us always *does* yearn for purity, clarity, absolutes. Yearns for it, alas, even though living matter and clarity are opposites, as Einstein said.

And he was right as usual, said Joe. But we human beings seem to be far more confused than any other living thing, and why is that?

Because we think. And there's nothing more ruinous to clarity of purpose.

Ah, said Joe, now that has a ring to it for sure. Is it yours or are you quoting again?

Mine, said Liffy softly, no more than mine. It just came to me here in these ancient ruins of a courtyard, a kind of local aphorism to be contemplated on the journey east. In fact we just might codify it as *Liffy's Second Law.* To wit. *If you want to be sure you know what you're doing, never think. . . .* But this whole conversation leads me to suspect that much lies ahead of you, if the truth is ever to come out.

And which truth is that? asked Joe.

Liffy nodded. He smiled.

The truth about Stern, of course. But is it really possible to learn the truth about someone else? *Is it?* . . . I've often wondered about that. It was one of those unanswerable questions that used to plague this ancient child of a soul of mine, late at night, back in empty railway waiting rooms before the war.

Liffy smiled gently.

A Wandering Jew does wonder about such things, after all, because in the end that's what his wandering is all about and that's the whole point of his destiny. The mystery of other faces and other tongues—*wonder* in all its guises. . . . *To behold,* as they used to say.

They left the courtyard soon after that, Liffy to keep an appointment and Joe to lie down in his room until it was time for his meeting with Bletchley. The blurred feeling had begun to come over

Joe again while they were sitting in the courtyard that morning, just as it had the last time when he and Liffy had talked about the Monastery. An uneasy feeling on Joe's part, a shadowy warning from somewhere within him.

Meanwhile, on a roof not far away, an observer lay on his stomach peering down into the narrow courtyard of the Hotel Babylon, his binoculars resting in front of him. Having been deaf for some years, the observer could read lips with ease. Yet he found he was having difficulty that morning with the man called Liffy, because of the way his lips moved continually whether he was speaking or not. Nibbling and chewing, that mouth never seemed to rest for a moment.

The other man, the one called Joe, was no problem at all. But unfortunately it was the constantly nibbling Liffy who had done most of the talking in the courtyard.

They won't like it at all, thought the observer, crawling backward with his binoculars.

Damn that bastard Liffy and his lips that never stop. . . .

Later, when Joe tried the door on the far side of the courtyard, he found it locked. He used a key Ahmad had given him and groped his way down the stairs in the darkness to the second door at the bottom.

The cellar was just as he remembered it. A cool oblong room with a ceiling so low he had to stoop. A table with a single naked light bulb overhead, a cord leading down from the fixture to an electric ring where a kettle was steaming. A teapot and a raised newspaper.

But Bletchley seemed to be in a better mood that day, even though Joe was late for their meeting. As soon as Joe walked in Bletchley put aside his newspaper and rose to shake hands, putting out his hand that wasn't crippled.

Now there's a first, thought Joe. He began to apologize for being late but Bletchley waved the apology aside.

No matter, he said, I was just having a second cup of tea. Care to join me?

Joe thanked him and Bletchley reached for the teapot, an ugly expression flashing across his face.

Jesus, thought Joe, he's trying to smile. That piece of ugliness is his way of smiling.

Bletchley was wearing an old set of khakis that day, which gave him quite a different appearance. In a business suit, at night anyway, he looked both elegant and efficient despite his bulky black eye patch. But in baggy cotton trousers and a wrinkled open shirt, both badly worn and faded, there was a shabbier quality to the man. His belt was too big for him, gathering his trousers in clumsy folds around his waist, and his shoes were old and scuffed. One of his shirtsleeves was rolled up while the other flapped around without a button. There were even some roughly mended spots down the front of his shirt, rips repaired at home, it appeared. In all he was a much less impressive man than Joe remembered. Certainly not overbearing in any way, rather frail in fact. A slight weary figure with an attentive air about him.

For a moment Joe had the impression of a lonely recluse puttering around in a garden that wasn't his own, embarrassed at being out of place, painfully uncomfortable among plants and flowers he didn't recognize.

Bletchley poured tea.

I dropped in to say hello to Ahmad this morning, he said, and he mentioned that you must have gone out early for a walk. I'm an early riser myself, always have been. Of course I don't sleep much these days anyway. Still no sugar?

Right, thanks. Anything of interest in the newspapers today?

Mostly Rommel as usual, said Bletchley. He's only forty miles from Tobruk and nothing seems to be going right. It's almost as if Rommel knew beforehand every move we're going to make. Damn it, but that's exactly how it is.

Joe blew on the tea in the metal cup. And what if that were true about Rommel? he wondered. What if he did know every British move beforehand? Could anyone have intelligence sources as good as that?

Well what about the personal columns? he asked. Any better news there?

Not really. One man heard from, one not. It's odd but business aside, I've always been intrigued by the personal columns in local newspapers. They give you such a strangely intimate view of a place and people's lives in that place, or at least an illusion of it. Oh by the way, you haven't tried to get in touch with Maud yet, have you?

No. I'm following instructions.

Advice, murmured Bletchley. I'm sure they're not trying to control your every move. I'm sure they want you to go about it in your own way. But it's my impression they feel the more looking around you can do before Stern finds out you're here, the better off you'll be. Yes, that's it. Stern's going to find out soon enough anyway, once you begin moving around.

And when will that be, do you suppose?

Soon. Right away. They've gone slowly with you because of something to do with Stern's schedule, Stern's activities, but now I've been told Stern's leaving tonight on an assignment that will keep him out of Cairo for several weeks. Two weeks at the very least, that's it. So now you should have time for a good headstart.

He won't be in contact with anyone in Cairo?

Not with anyone who could tell him about you. I assume it was arranged that way.

Fair enough, said Joe, picking up his teacup and hesitating, not wanting to burn his lips again as he had the first time he came to the cellar. And he was also trying to decide what to say, because he felt it was important to try to move closer to Bletchley. He looked up now and made a gesture toward the black bulky patch over Bletchley's right eye. Most of the scars seemed old, although some of them, curiously, not that old.

Catch that trouble in the last war, did you?

Yes, replied Bletchley, surprised by the directness of the question.

How'd it happen? asked Joe, gazing over the rim of his cup.

Abruptly Bletchley dropped his stare and went perfectly still. For a long silent moment he looked down at the table, his single eye round and blank and uncomprehending. But when he spoke at last his voice was matter-of-fact, without emotion.

It was fairly early in the last war. I was using a spyglass when a bullet struck the thing and shattered the casing, driving metal and glass fragments into my eye and severing some muscles in my hand. A friend tried to pull out the metal bits in my eye but he couldn't manage it. Then he was killed and I had to lie there for five or six hours until help came. Later they were able to reconstruct the bridge of my nose and fix up the hand a little, but removing the fragments from the eye socket turned out to be a drawn-out process. Months, years, it just went on and on, that's it. For a long time I felt useless.

Joe shook his head sadly. Bletchley was still staring down at the table, his eye wide, uncomprehending.

The worst part about it, then, was that I'd been in the regular army, and of course there was no future in that. When you're young, it's hard to accept the fact that you're never going to have the chance to do what you want in life. Most people may end up that way, but at least the disillusionment takes place over time. It's not like knowing from the start that you don't have a chance.

Joe nodded.

Headaches too, I imagine.

Sometimes, but generally it's just an ugly itching sensation, something gnawing at your brain that's always there, that just won't go away.

Yes.

They sat some moments in silence. Bletchley still hadn't looked up at Joe. He was staring blankly down at the table, a frail figure in worn-out mended khakis. Then all at once he began blinking rapidly and covered his eye patch with a handkerchief, dabbing at something.

There are effusions from the socket, he said. I wanted to have a glass eye put in but the bones around the socket are shattered and there's nothing to hold one. They tried several times but it didn't work. It looked like a glass bead stuck in the corner of my face at an angle. Finally there was nothing more to be done, so I had to settle for a patch.

It covers most of it, said Joe.

Bletchley went on wiping with his handkerchief.

I hate the way it frightens children, especially in this part of the world where they believe in the evil eye. Children can't stand it. One look and they begin to scream. It makes me feel like a monster.

Have you been out here long?

Not so long here, mostly in India. I grew up in India, we were an army family. After I'd gotten back on my feet I was offered this kind of work, and it seemed the closest I'd ever come to the army so I took it, that's it.

No, he added, I haven't been in the Middle East very long, only since the war started. India is what I know.

I've never been there, said Joe. I'd like to go someday.

118

At last Bletchley raised his eye from the table and looked at Joe.

Oh yes, it's a beautiful country, the land and the people, all of it. I know the desert appeals to some, but I'll never feel that way about it. To me, India is home and always will be. There's just no other place like it in the world.

Bletchley's face lighted up and he smiled at the thought of his homeland and the memories of his early years there.

At least it was meant to be a smile, but because of the missing bones and the severed muscles in his face, it came out differently. His good eye widened and stared grotesquely in what appeared to be a harsh cold expression, arrogant and disdainful.

The agony it must cause him, thought Joe. He tries to be friendly and his own face mocks him. It's no wonder children scream and run away. He looks cruel and it's not his fault, and they think he's sneering at them and it's not their fault.

But Bletchley's thoughts were far away in his beloved India at that moment, and he was smiling and pushing back his chair and getting to his feet, humming to himself, happy with his beautiful memories of a homeland that he probably already knew would never be his home again.

Well then, said Bletchley, shall we be on our way?

Right, to the Monastery at last, said Joe. And you have to admit that *is* a curious name for an intelligence unit, even one hidden away in the Egyptian desert. Rather human, isn't it, how we like to make things sound mysterious. . . . *And when you finally get to the Monastery in the desert, my child.* . . .

Bletchley laughed.

I know, he said. No matter how dull reality is, we do try hard to make it sound exotic. A natural inclination, I suppose, to add a touch of grandeur to our drab little lives. A romantic tendency in all of us, that's it.

So it seems, said Joe. And whether it's to be called romantic or not, I wouldn't know, but surely we do have to dream. If we didn't, where would we be? That much is evident just on the face of things. But of course there are all kinds of dreams, which is what can confuse a man.

When he looked back on it, Joe realized he should have known something was wrong with him long before he and Bletchley left the cellar. As they climbed the stairs, Joe missed a step and nearly lost his balance. He might have fallen if Bletchley hadn't rushed up to catch him from behind.

Are you all right?

I'm not sure. I feel a little out of touch.

They stepped into the bright sunlight. Joe's legs were heavy and he didn't seem to have any command over them. As they walked up the alley Joe sneaked a glance at his own hand, mildly curious about its shape, not quite sure it was the way he remembered it.

It may be exhaustion left over from the trip, he said. It's a long way from Arizona to Cairo and I don't know that I've caught up yet.

Your stopovers were short? asked Bletchley.

Yes, after the training camp near Toronto. I crawled into the ball turret of a bomber and crawled out again in Scotland. . . . Fetal position. I don't know how those gunners can manage for any length of time. Then London was just one briefing after another and it was straight over here.

That's it, said Bletchley, a delayed reaction to all your time in the air.

And that ball turret was terrible, muttered Joe. . . . I just can't seem to get ahold of anything today.

Joe's sense of unreality grew more profound as they drove out of Cairo. He sat in a daze, a dream, gazing out the open side of the small desert car, watching the city drop away. Several times he noticed Bletchley sneaking glances at him.

What's worrying him? he wondered.

He wasn't sure whether he'd spoken since the drive started, or even how long they'd been on the road. He knew he could check his watch but somehow it didn't seem important. They'd left the city behind and now everything was the same, sand and more sand and the hot sun and the glare, Bletchley shifting gears as they drove more deeply into the desert, Bletchley's good eye flickering toward him every so often.

Ever east, my child, thought Joe. *Stop look and listen. Mingle.*

Ought to mingle and say something, he thought, and was immediately surprised to hear his own voice asking Bletchley a question.

Do you have a family?

Bletchley shifted gears.

What do you mean? A wife and children?

Yes.

No, I don't. I've never been married. I was too young before we went to war the last time, and after that there were those years spent getting patched up. By then I was too accustomed to living alone to be of much use to anyone.

You weren't though.

Weren't what?

Too old to get married.

When?

After you'd been patched up. When was that, a couple of years after the last war? You must have still been in your early twenties.

Chronologically, but in other ways I didn't feel that young. Nothing very chronological about life, after all, it doesn't always follow a logical sequence the way we like to pretend. Some people stop growing in their early twenties. Just stop, say that's enough for me, and get off and sit down beside the road for the duration.

Ever east, my child, thought Joe. *And when you finally reach. . . .*

Besides, continued Bletchley, I still had hopes. I was trying to have a glass eye put in and when they couldn't do it in one place, I'd try another. Paris, Johannesburg, Zurich, I kept making the rounds. The last operation wasn't that long ago.

Oh.

Just three years ago, in fact. They'd done all the rebuilding they could by then, and the glass bead stuck in at an angle was the result.

The glass bead game, thought Joe. That has to be one of the worst.

So I finally gave it up and accepted the fact that I'd have to be a monster.

Children don't understand things, said Joe. You can't expect them to.

No that's true, you can't. But what about mature men and women? What can you expect from them?

Joe gazed at the desert. The glare off the sand hurt his eyes and he pressed them shut. Bletchley was shifting gears, not waiting for an answer to his question because there was no answer.

On the mesa in Arizona there had been an old woman with a badly deformed face, born that way, so severely deformed she had been hidden away since she was a baby. Throughout her entire life she had never been known to leave the little room where she had come into the world. Many nights Joe had sat up with her in her little room, listening to her sing in the most beautiful voice he had ever heard, a startling voice filled with wonder for all the things she had never seen or known. She sang for hours and when she ended they would sit together in silence for a time, then the old woman would turn her back and Joe would get up and leave without a word. To have said anything would have been cruel beyond belief, for her singing was all she had of the world, her song the flight of her soul.

Hungry? asked Bletchley. I brought some things. I thought we might stop for a bite along the way.

They sat on the sand, squeezed into the shade beside the small desert car, Joe with his back against one of the warm tires. Bletchley opened some tins of marmalade and biscuits. There was also a thermos and two battered cups.

Joe took a few bites and all the food tasted exactly the same, a harsh metallic flavor. He fumbled with a cup and finally let Bletchley fill it for him. The liquid, cold tea or whatever it was, also had a harsh metallic flavor. Dully he watched Bletchley spreading marmalade on a biscuit, an action that seemed to go on forever.

What's the matter? asked Bletchley.

I was going to ask you the same thing. You seem to be moving very slowly today.

Bletchley put his hand on Joe's forehead.

You're running a bad fever, he said. I wouldn't be surprised if it was the change in the water. It happens fairly frequently.

Time and change and the water, thought Joe. Not exactly the trouble you'd expect to find out here where there is no water, but it's best never to rely on appearances. And sand and more sand and utter desolation, just as Liffy said. So it's not all green hillsides on the journey to the East, ah no. *There are wastelands to cross, my child, before you sleep. Wastelands, bright and deep . . .*

They were driving again, Bletchley shifting gears, the glare off the sand intense. And for Joe, sinking more deeply into his fever, the sky and the desert had lost whatever boundaries they might once have had.

I've known men who've followed the desert, Bletchley was saying, adventurers who see it as a primeval force, like the sea. But there are dangers in the desert that a seagoing man doesn't have to face. The sea, with its overall evenness, tends to moderate men by suggesting an essential balance to all things. But the desert, with its harsh extremes, can have just the opposite effect by making things seem clearer than they are, so you always have to beware the temptation of idealism. God knows human affairs are murky enough, but out here there's the danger of forgetting that, because everything is so stark, so much itself. *Appears* to be, that is.

Bletchley shifted gears. They left the paved road for a rougher track.

The fact is, he continued, we're apt to romanticize things we don't understand, what we were talking about earlier. Take that old expression, *to follow the desert*. It gives an impression of adventure and makes one sound like a wanderer, but the bedouin aren't really wanderers. They always have their home with them, their tent, and their country is always with them, the desert. An outsider, a northern European, will view it differently. But that's because a northern European is accustomed to seeing his home and his country in a different light. *Less of it.*

Joe nodded. Puffs of smoke had appeared on the horizon, followed by a spatter of dull muffled booms. In another moment they had rounded a dune and Joe could make out a battery of British howitzers parked off in the wastes, raising great clouds of sand as they methodically fired into the desert. The front lines, he knew, were many miles away.

What are they doing?

Bletchley turned his head to get his eye on the battery.

Shelling the desert, he yelled above the booming salvos

The empty desert?

Looks that way.

But why?

Who knows, maybe they thought they saw the enemy. It's impossible of course, but they might have thought they saw something.

Just *thought* they did? wondered Joe. Well why not. It could be a case of right you are if you think you are, the desert as you like it.

But as they drove along above the camouflaged battery, Joe sensed there was something even more out of place than the vast stretches of barren desert separating the howitzers from the nearest German units. He concentrated as best he could and at last it came to him.

They're facing east, he shouted. Isn't that the wrong way for them to be fighting the war? The Germans are to the west.

Bletchley snorted, yelled.

The wrong way? But how can there be a *right* way to slaughter people? And anyway, mirages are common enough in the desert. I don't have to tell you that.

Correct, thought Joe, you don't. But all the same it still seemed strange to him as he gazed down on the howitzers, watching them fire and recoil, fire and recoil. The cannon crews were moving quickly, hurrying back and forth as if they had a certain number of rounds to fire off that day.

What do you think? he shouted. Are they working against a quota of rounds they're supposed to expend?

Very likely, yelled Bletchley. Supplies have to be regulated for maximum effect in wartime, so naturally quotas and rationing are the order of the day.

Joe nodded, still groping in his mind for a rational explanation to this furious and relentless artillery barrage, aimed at nothing.

But aren't they wasting a lot of valuable ammunition? he shouted. Just firing off into the empty desert like that?

So it seems, yelled Bletchley, but no one has ever claimed war is a force for conservation. It spends and consumes and destroys, that's all. The only reason we seem to have it around is because there's a streak in man that finds it exhilarating. Or more accurately, the *idea* of it. Not one of our nobler streaks, but there you are. And I think it would also be safe to say the nature of that exhilaration won't bear very close scrutiny.

Agreed, thought Joe. It won't and doesn't. Because that streak is the killing of people and the exhilaration in that is just plain unspeakable, a blackness at the bottom of the soul. Very deep is the blackness, may we not call it bottomless?

Better try again, thought Joe, put it some other way to Bletchley. There has to be some explanation for behavior, even when it's idiotic. It may be human nature to want to bombard an empty desert, but someone as smart as Bletchley would have to have some kind of reasonable reason for it. The greater good? The grand design? The missing link and the unknowable universe?

Listen, shouted Joe. If you feel that way about it, the uselessness of war and so forth, why did you want to make the army a career? Family tradition aside.

I suppose because the army provides a form and a structure, yelled Bletchley. A regulation for everything. Not a reason for doing something, but a clear order that it's to be done. As human beings, we like that. Gods provide the orders for some people, political systems for others. But without orders and commands and regulations, the chaos of being is simply that. Chaotic. And that tends to be too hot a situation for most people to handle.

Too hot to handle, hummed Joe, recalling a bawdy line from one of Liffy's music-hall tunes, watching the artillerymen slam home shells and slam closed breechblocks as the howitzers puffed and recoiled, the air crackling and the dust billowing in the unending cannonade.

Hold on, yelled Bletchley. There's rough going here.

Joe lurched forward and grabbed hold of the handle in front of him. *Rough going here,* he hummed, recalling another line from one of Liffy's bawdy tunes. Off in the desert ahead he spied what appeared to be a railway boxcar coming into view. The boxcar was undersized and lying on its back, its wheels in the air with no railway tracks in sight.

How did that get out here? he shouted.

Bletchley was staring straight ahead, concentrating on the driving, unable to take his eye off the rough roadbed.

What is it? One of those old Forty and Eights?

Looks like it, shouted Joe, remembering the term that had been used in the last war for a small French freight car, so named because it had been able to carry forty men or eight horses to the slaughter at the front. But of course the French hadn't been fighting in the Egyptian desert then, they'd been dying back home in muddy trenches. Joe hummed, *It's a long way to Tipperary.*

Wouldn't it have been more logical to call those boxcars Forty *or* Eights? he shouted. After all, that's what they were.

Nothing very logical about war, Bletchley grimly yelled back.

All true, thought Joe. No arguing with that one.

In fact when you look back at the last war, yelled Bletchley, the whole thing seems utterly senseless.

Joe nodded and looked back at the endless barren wastelands. The overturned French boxcar had dropped out of sight, but now there was an overturned chariot standing on the horizon. It was of a heavy primitive design, its huge wooden wheels capped with iron that had rusted very little in the dry desert air.

I've seen one of those before, thought Joe. In pictures anyway. The Assyrians used them back at the beginning of the Iron Age when they were a-thundering out of the north, taking their turn as the much a-feared barbarians of the day.

Which last war were you referring to? he shouted.

How's that? yelled Bletchley.

I said, *which* last war? Whose? The one you said was utterly sense-less when we look back on it?

Oh, well anybody's. What difference does it make? Don't all last wars look pretty much the same when you look back at them? Mur-der and mutilation and wreckage, and all for what?

For what? thought Joe. *What?* It's a regular Whatley, that's what.

Bletchley glanced at him sideways.

Are you all right? he yelled.

Not particularly, shouted Joe, but listen. What are you really afraid of, Bletchley? Can you tell me that?

What do you mean? In what context?

Personal context. Deep down, right there where you are in this world. What are you really afraid of?

The Germans winning the war, yelled Bletchley. I'd do *anything* to keep that from happening.

And that's surely reasonable, thought Joe, surely sound and sane and then some. The man doesn't want to let the Mongols in. Of course that *anything* of his is a warning to me in regard to Stern, but who would argue with keeping out these mechanized barbarians who go by the name of Nazis?

Bletchley? he shouted. Have you ever wondered why the Germans make so much out of defending the Eastern Front against the barbarians? National destiny, holy assignment, racial mission and so forth? Why is it the Mongols of this world always tell us they're defending us against the Mongols?

Human nature, yelled Bletchley. Men always justify wars by claiming they're fighting the barbarians. What they don't bother to add is that the reason wars are continuous in history is because the barbarians are inside us. Have you ever been in a crowd when it's transforming itself into a mob? There's a Genghis Khan on every side of you. Give any one of them a horde of men on horseback and you'd see the thirteenth century in flames again.

And that's the truth, thought Joe. And Bletchley is just plain *sound* today, his thinking as clear as a bell.

Soon they were passing other strange relics cast off in the wastes.

An abandoned battery of Napoleonic muzzle loaders loomed up beside them, facing south toward the heart of the Dark Continent, stubby three-pounders mired in the sand, the debris of another civilizing adventure in Africa. But apparently the muzzle loaders had been no match in their day for Lord Nelson's swift barkentines, one of which had brilliantly outmaneuvered Napoleon's cannons and was now resting comfortably on its side behind them, clearly commanding a superior field of fire.

A barkentine way out here in the desert, thought Joe. Extraordinary when you think of it, even though the winds of the Mediterranean have always been known for their treachery. But what can match man's, and I wonder what the local bedouin make of the sight? Probably they think Europeans are a little daft.

A single arch from an ancient Roman aqueduct came into view, a magnificent arch fully one hundred feet high and leading east or west as the case might be, barren desert stretching off in both directions. While not far away the solid surface of a well-engineered Roman road emerged from a sand dune and traveled at least ten feet before being swallowed up in another sand dune. There were also whole fleets of glittering sunspots on the sand, although they didn't seem to be going anywhere either.

Lord Nelson also had one eye, thought Joe.

But by far the most awesome spectacle Joe saw was an enormous siege machine bristling with fire buckets and catapults and battering rams, covered with animal skins in receding tiers so that it had roughly the shape of a pyramid, an eagle's nest at the top, a superb lookout for a mad tyrant to look down upon the nonexistent city he was about to destroy in the desert. Or a superb lookout for looking down upon all nonexistent cities in the world for a thousand years, why not. The thousand-year Third Reich in the wastes of nowhere . . . in all its stunning glory.

Leaders are a wondrous invention, thought Joe. What would we ever do without them? How would we ever get the slaughter done?

Bletchley shifted gears. As they rattled along Joe's thoughts kept returning to the primitive siege machine they had passed, that huge deathly apparition all by itself in the desert, waiting to lay siege. The image of it haunted him and he couldn't get it out of his mind. Was it because there had been a suggestion the machine was made of human skulls? A pyramid of skulls? The Nazis' final solution to life, as Liffy had said? Or was it simply because of all the monuments reared by man in those desolate sun-blasted wastes, it was the only one that didn't look abandoned and out of place?

Joe shivered.

It's ghastly, he thought. Ghastly.

The air snapped. Bletchley was shifting gears.

How are you feeling? It's not much farther.

Good, I couldn't go much farther. It's exhausting out here, frightening too.

Bletchley slowed.

Because it's all bleached bones and illusions, thought Joe.

They stopped. The engine died.

Call of nature, said Bletchley quietly. I'll only be a moment.

They started off again. Joe drifted around in his seat, occasionally humming one of Liffy's tunes.

Was the Monastery ever actually a monastery? he shouted at some point.

You mean before we took it over? yelled Bletchley. Well St Anthony is known to have spent time in this part of the desert, but since St Anthony had visions, I don't think anyone could say with any certainty where he was abusing his flesh all the time. It might be that one of his caves is down in the bowels of the Monastery somewhere, but who knows? St Anthony's chains were of the invisible kind.

The water got to him, thought Joe. Bad water or no water or even a change of water can bring on an advanced case of hallucinations out here. Or visions, as saints raving in the wilderness used to call them.

Joe drifted off. A moment later his head snapped back. The track was climbing, Bletchley shifting gears.

What's that up ahead?

We're there, yelled Bletchley. That's the gate to the back entrance. Most of the Monastery is up above, you can't really see it very well from down here.

They drew up in a small paved courtyard where other military vehicles were parked. High walls of rough masonry reared above them, narrow slits cut into them. The walls overhead receded away from the courtyard, so that it was impossible to guess how far up they went.

Not all that far, whispered Bletchley, it's not really that big a place. It just looks big because it was built around the top of a small mountain, a hill really.

Round hill?

Yes.

Probably shaped like a head, thought Joe. Bowels and intestines and other internal organs in hiding down below, along with St Anthony's memories and Whatley's maps.

This way, whispered Bletchley.

Bletchley unlocked a wooden door and they passed through a short tunnel into another courtyard, this one larger and unpaved, with cloisters running along its sides. Men with long staves in their hands appeared languidly from amongst the shadows under the colonnades, strolling up to take a look at Joe and then retiring out of sight somewhere, while still others went on milling around the courtyard rather like pilgrims who had arrived unexpectedly at some way station on their journey, ahead of schedule, and were unsure what to do next. The pilgrims seemed to be wearing every conceivable kind of costume, both uniforms and civilian clothes, some dressed as lawyers and businessmen and bankers and professors, others as commandos or balloonists or even bedouin. But all of them without exception, the moment they caught sight of Bletchley, turned away and withdrew slightly, showing only their backs.

The multitude of tall staves carried by the pilgrims was particularly striking to Joe. Gently the staves waved to and fro as stalks of grain might toss in the wind, protected and enclosed, touched only by the mildest breezes.

It must be about time for the refectory to open for early tea, whispered Bletchley. Otherwise you'd never see such a large idle gathering of agents milling around out here.

Abruptly Bletchley seized a startled pilgrim at random, grabbing the man by the arm, spinning him around. The pilgrim looked so frightened he was ready to deny anything.

What's for tea? demanded Bletchley.

Three kinds of sand . . . sand . . . sandwiches, stammered the man. Including cucumber. They said we could choose the kind we like, so long as we don't all choose the same one.

And which are you going to choose? demanded Bletchley.

I was hoping for cucumber, whispered the pilgrim, but I'll gladly eat anything.

Bletchley released the nervous man, who immediately faded back into the milling crowd. From somewhere high above, the opening chords of Bach's Mass in B Minor came booming down over the courtyard.

That man seemed afraid of you, said Joe. Why is that?

Bletchley smiled.

We'll just step this way, he whispered.

Bletchley unlocked another door and Joe followed him down one dimly lit corridor after another. All the chambers in the Monastery seemed to be kept in perpetual near-darkness, which was cool and soothing after the strong sunlight outside. As they padded along, the distant strains of organ music faded and lapsed, only to surge anew from some unexpected quarter. They descended stairs and more stairs and finally entered a small cell lit by a single candle. There was a folding camp table with a huge swivel chair behind it, sumptuously padded in dark leather. Bletchley pointed at the comfortable leather chair.

Just sit down and make yourself at home, he said. I'll let Whatley's aides know we've arrived.

Joe collapsed in the swivel chair and swung slowly back and forth. In a corner stood an apparatus on wheels which he knew he should be able to recognize, but in his fever he couldn't quite place it. The apparatus consisted of several tank cylinders and various hoses and gauges. Bletchley, meanwhile, turned the crank of a military telephone and whispered into the mouthpiece.

Whatley's on his way down, he announced. Now then. . . .

Bletchley wheeled the apparatus over to a position behind the huge leather chair. He leaned down and studied it, testing a valve or two. Joe had swung around to face him.

What is it? asked Joe.

Nitrous oxide. Laughing gas.

What's it for?

For your interview with Whatley.

Bletchley went on tinkering with valves. There was a long low hiss and he smiled.

Nothing to be alarmed about, he murmured, spinning dials. It's just laughing gas. Dentists use it all the time.

I know they do, but what's the point of using it on me?

Standard Monastery procedure, that's all.

But why?

Wartime, murmured Bletchley. Ours not to reason why and so forth. But look at it another way. Wouldn't you rather face what's coming with a comforting cloud of nitrous oxide inside you? Wouldn't *any* man at war? Just to make matters *seem* a little more reasonable? Not *quite* so idiotic as they actually are?

Bletchley laughed.

To be honest, there's not an agent up there in the cloisters who wouldn't love to be on nitrous oxide at this very moment. Of course they wouldn't want to be *down here*, but life's like that, isn't it? Gas is enjoyable, certainly, but we always have to take what goes with it.

Which is Whatley, thought Joe, shivering and staring dully at the apparatus. A tune ran through his head, one of Liffy's, but he couldn't quite remember the words. *Tarry in caves but beware of local bats*, was that it? *Beware of bats, my child?*

So the point is, Bletchley was saying, the gas will help you relax and be receptive in these unfamiliar surroundings, even though you're not feeling too well today. And it also serves as a security precaution. You'll be able to hear everything Whatley says and ask whatever questions you may have, but afterward your impression of Whatley's voice will be just a little distorted. As the chief here, he prefers it that way.

Being distorted? asked Joe. Why?

Now then, murmured Bletchley, just breathe normally through your nose.

Bletchley fitted a small rubber mask over Joe's nose. Joe sat there listening to a rhythmic sigh, growing stronger. After some moments had gone by, a door opened. A man with only one arm, immaculately dressed in starched khakis, was moving around on the edge of Joe's vision. Was that really the notorious Whatley at last, in the flesh?

Ah, said a voice from far away. And this must be our new Purple Seven Armenian who has traveled all the way from a mesa in Arizona to be with us. No please, Joe, don't bother to get up. You look quite comfortable where you are. And I believe you take your tea without sugar, is that right?

Joe nodded. *Beware of bats*, he thought.

Yes, continued the voice, it's a pleasure to have you with us at last. Now let's not waste any time, let's get right down to the bottom of things immediately. We're here to talk about Stern—the man, the agent, everything. Yes, everything. . . .

Most of Joe's memories of the Monastery were a blur after that. Later, after the briefing in the huge leather chair with the gas mask had ended, he did remember finding himself on a narrow stone terrace.

The terrace must have been quite high up in the Monastery, for there was a beautiful view of the desert. He and Bletchley were sitting alone there, side by side in canvas deck chairs. A camouflaged canvas awning provided shade and there were potted palms along the walls. The skin of a Bengal tiger was hanging at one end of the terrace. From the color of the sky, Joe guessed it must be almost twilight.

. . . and for those reasons, Bletchley was saying, I don't think you should be upset by the violence of Whatley's language when he speaks of Stern. Passions run high in wartime and poor Whatley has never gotten over losing his right arm to the Germans. In fact he told me once he can still feel the fingers on his missing hand twitching late at night. The forefinger especially, his trigger finger. It just never stops twitching, he said.

Nor will it, thought Joe. Not if it's missing.

He had no idea what the conversation was about or where it had started. There was a half-empty glass in his hand and he sniffed it. Quinine water. Bletchley was leaning forward and leisurely adding gin to his own glass, stretching and smiling, relaxing. All at once Joe had the sensation of being on a passenger liner bound for the East, for India. He and Bletchley were chance acquaintances sitting together on deck, chatting and having drinks before sundown, passing the time before they went in to dress for the late sitting

Tarry in open spaces, my child, thought Joe.

At least you must feel better after your nap, said Bletchley.

I do, but I'm still disturbed. Disturbed by Whatley, what?

Well I could see that, but I don't think Whatley was being intentionally evasive. I'm not privy to that much of it, but my impression is he wants you to come in fresh, without preconceptions about Stern and Stern's role in this affair. Strictly from the outside, so to speak.

Stern, muttered Joe, gazing out over the rolling desert. Someone from the outside, you say?

Exactly.

Or someone from the other side perhaps? added Joe. Wouldn't that be another way of putting it? What if the Germans suddenly took a special interest in Stern? What could the Germans come up with? What could they uncover?

I suppose it's something along those lines, said Bletchley. I don't know specifically what the nature of the operation is, but my impression of its general drift is about the same as yours.

That's it, thought Joe. The Monastery's having me play a part similar to a German agent's. Look into Stern's activities from the point of view of the other side, and see what I can come up with. But why? They've got more than enough to do out here running operations against the Germans. Why go to the trouble of running an operation against Stern, one of their own men? The information he has must be very important. Even crucial, as the three men in white linen suits said back in Arizona.

A thought struck Joe.

And could it be that this information concerns the Monastery? Is that why these Monks are so tight-lipped about everything? Because they're afraid for themselves? Because Stern knows something about this place that nobody else knows? And if the Germans were ever to find out . . . ?

Bletchley sipped from his glass and began to talk about sunsets at sea. Once more they were on a passenger liner bound for the East, for India.

Changing the subject, thought Joe. Bletchley doesn't want me to become too curious about Stern's specific piece of information. Report back on Stern in general, that's all. Not recognize the nugget when I come across it. If I do.

Joe found himself drifting away again, losing touch.

We'll have to be leaving soon, said Bletchley. I don't like driving at night. It bothers my eye.

You don't like it but you do it, thought Joe, an image flashing through his mind, something Liffy had mentioned in passing. Liffy accompanying Bletchley to meetings with agents at night in an automobile, Bletchley in front acting as merely the driver while Liffy was in disguise in back with the agent, debriefing the man according to Bletchley's instructions. The agent concentrating on Liffy, giving Bletchley the opportunity to listen and to observe the agent through the rearview mirror. A simple trick and an old one, but effective.

Well the game's elaborate all right, thought Joe, but at least we know now why we're sitting up here on the captain's bridge with our hunting trophies and our potted palms. Bletchley's the real skipper out here and he's the one who's in charge of this operation and in charge of the Monastery for that matter, and Whatley's just someone on his staff, his deputy probably. . . . But why *is* the game so elaborate? These Monks have a war to worry about and Rommel's out there with his panzers churning closer all the time, so what's going on? Why are they so deathly afraid of Stern at a time like this? . . . One man after all, no more.

Have you ever heard of the Sisters? asked Bletchley.

Joe tried to think.

The Weird Sisters, you mean? That old expression for the Fates?

Bletchley laughed.

No, this has nothing to do with folklore. I was referring to two women who used to be the reigning queens of Cairo society a while back. They're twins and rather reclusive now. They live in a house-boat on the Nile, I'm told.

Oh. No I haven't heard of them, said Joe.

But surely the name Menelik Ziwar means something to you, doesn't it? That Egyptologist Stern used to know? He was also quite a society figure once . . . in his way.

Yes, I've heard of old Menelik, said Joe. What about him?

Bletchley didn't answer. He got to his feet and stretched.

We really must be leaving, he murmured. I don't like driving at night. It bothers my eye.

Joe didn't remember the drive back through the desert with Bletchley, or arriving in Old Cairo, or Ahmad helping him up to his room. Nor did he know that Liffy had come that evening to take up the vigil, Liffy quietly humming to himself as Joe tossed with fever and the night swirled more deeply over that decaying ruin known as the Hotel Babylon, as all the while down below the taciturn Ahmad sat erect on his high stool in the gloomy corridor that passed for his office in life, the yellowing sheets of a thirty-year-old newspaper spread out in front of him, opened as always to the society page.

8

Maud

She locked her back door and started down the outside stairs to the alley, where her neighbor's children were still out playing despite the late hour. As soon as they heard her footsteps in the darkness they came rushing up, laughing and shouting and trying to guess which of her hands held candies for them. And then their mother was leaning out of one of the narrow windows of yellow light on the alley, and Maud had to speak to her before she looked in their open kitchen door to exchange a few more words with the grandfather of the household, who was always proud of a chance to display his meager French.

In the quiet little square at the end of the alley, tucked away behind busier streets, there were other neighbors to greet, working people out for a stroll or simply standing around in small groups chatting and enjoying the evening breezes off the river, so welcome after the fierce heat of the day. The waiter inside the door of the little restaurant on the square was all smiles when he saw her.

No, he said, there'd been no mail for her that afternoon. And yes, his son was doing very well, already a help in the kitchen at the age of ten. Another few months and he was going to begin training the boy to set the tables. . . . The waiter leaned closer, a trace of graveness in his voice, a hint of intensity around his eyes.

You'll be coming to dinner soon? Perhaps this weekend?

If we can manage it, she said, knowing what he meant.

Oh good, good. I'm so glad. . . .

She crossed the cobblestones to the small outdoor café, taking a table at the back. The waiter there was also a friend who had to tell her his news while he wiped the table three or four times, shifting his weight from one foot to the other.

We have some special pastries tonight, he added. Shall I put one aside for you?

That would be kind, she said, and the waiter beamed. Since she never ate a sweet when she was alone at the café, he knew she was expecting her friend. Abruptly his manner also became intent, confidential.

Are things going well? He's . . . everything's all right?

Yes, said Maud, smiling.

Oh well, that's just fine then, praise be to God. . . .

The man left to bring her coffee, muttering to himself, and Maud gazed up the little square toward the street where the traffic passed. She never ceased to wonder at the concern people felt for Stern and his well-being, even people who hardly knew him. Yet the suggestion was always there, the suddenly alert tone and the almost anxious question which could have been an everyday pleasantry, but wasn't. . . . Everything's all right? . . . You'll be coming for dinner soon? . . . Which meant, Is *he* all right? Will *he* be coming back soon?

And the smile of relief when she answered yes. And the deeply felt whispers. . . . *Oh good, good. . . . Praise be to God.*

She sipped her coffee, happy to be alone in a place where she belonged, enjoying the nighttime sounds and rituals of her neighborhood. Then all at once she heard his voice above the murmur, deeper than the others, and there he was making his way between the tables and greeting the waiter and saying something to a group of old men which made them laugh, causing their cups to rattle. . . . *Stern at last.* The great dark head and the mysterious smile, the sweeping eyes and the hands that never stopped feeling things, that were always reaching out and touching, touching. . . .

He slipped into the chair beside her, his hand resting lightly on her shoulder.

. . . I was hoping to get away in time for dinner, but you know how it is these days for a clerk at the office. Nothing but more and more work on the ledgers. Sometimes it seems that contrary to what God says, accountants are going to inherit the earth.

He smiled and drank off the arak the waiter placed before him, still holding her shoulder with his other hand. The waiter seemed reluctant to leave and Stern made a remark in Arabic which made the man laugh, the slang too complicated for Maud to understand. Stern nodded, smiling up at the man.

. . . another? Why not. Now what did I do with my cigarettes?

He let go of her shoulder and felt his pockets.

. . . must have forgotten to pick some up, I'll just step up to the kiosk around the corner. But you're having a sweet, aren't you? Shall I tell him to bring it now? . . . I'll only be a moment.

Stern walked inside and spoke to the waiter, lingering with the man for a moment, neither of them acting out of the ordinary, then turned and left the café and went striding quickly up the square to the street. Two or three minutes later and he was on his way back, this time resting his hand on hers when he sat down. He always touched her when he was with her, it was a habit he had. His fingers moving ever so slightly, gently. Caressing, *feeling*. . . . And for some reason, this time, her eyes fell on his disfigured thumb with its cruel scars, made a few years ago when his thumbnail had been ripped away in some foolish accident.

Once he had told her how it had happened . . . trying to fix something and his thumb slipping, catching, the thumbnail tearing away and tearing flesh with it . . . she couldn't even remember the details now. In fact she had long since ceased even to notice that thumb with its scars, because it was just another part of Stern now. But all at once she did notice it at that moment, and it almost startled her. The contrast of those brutal scars and the gentle strokes of his thumb on her hand . . . all at once it seemed unbearably poignant.

Stern smiled warmly, happily, his eyes breathing her in.

. . . so *good* to be with you, he whispered. So *right*, the way life should be.

While they were talking, he reached up and stroked her hair. There was nothing unusual about the gesture and from a distance no one would have seen anything out of the ordinary, any change in his manner, but Stern was now whispering in an obscure Greek dialect native to the mountains of Crete. He used the dialect only when they were in a public place and he had something private to say. Maud didn't speak it as well as he did, but she understood it easily enough.

138

. . . I don't want you to worry but I'm not quite alone tonight. I'm being followed.

She felt a twinge inside. How long has it been going on? she asked, and watched him shrug.

. . . a few days.

But who are they, Stern? Is it all right?

. . . oh yes. Just some fellows from the Monastery.

Just that, she thought, aware of his hands ceaselessly moving, stroking her and touching the table and touching his glass, his cigarettes, her ring. Feeling the world around him now more than ever, as if he were afraid of losing it. Not wanting to let it go, *touching.* . . .

But why, what does it mean, Stern? Do you know?

. . . well I'm due to leave town later tonight and they probably want to make sure I get safely on my way.

He laughed harshly.

. . . you know, in hopes I won't come back.

She frowned at the remark, thinking how his humor had become bitter lately in a way she didn't like, but Stern seemed not to notice her frown. His eyes were moving around the square as he took out the old Morse-code key he always carried and began to turn it over and over, his other hand holding her shoulder.

What is it, Stern?

. . . oh. Well you haven't noticed anyone around, have you?

No.

. . . and the family next door to you, the grandfather, he hasn't mentioned seeing anyone?

No, but are they watching me too? Is that what you mean?

. . . I'm afraid they may be, so I'm told . . . but not that closely and there's no danger involved, it's just something to do with me.

She looked at him. None of it made any sense to her, but of course there was no reason why it should. Stern had always been careful never to talk to her in any detail about the work he did for the Monastery. Yet lately he had been alluding to his work more openly, which she found disturbing in itself.

. . . so it might be better, he added, if you didn't say anything about this at your office. It doesn't concern the Waterboys and they don't know anything about it, so why upset them? And you've seen nothing yourself so there's nothing to hide. Of course if something should seem out of the ordinary, it might be wise to mention it to the grandfather next door. He's around all the time and he knows everyone, and he would . . . but anyway, it's strictly between the Monks and myself and . . .

Stern didn't finish. He smiled his mysterious smile and changed the subject and they talked of other things, Stern drinking heavily all the while. Then too quickly midnight was near and their moment together was over. Once more it was time for Stern to leave.

I know you have to rush, she said, but there's still one thing you haven't told me tonight. How *are* you?

The question cut through Stern's restlessness. He slumped forward and looked down at the table, a weariness coming over him, his powerful eyes still for once, even his hands at rest.

. . . tired, Maud . . . *exhausted.* But it's not so much the physical part as . . . it's strange, you know. I always thought the body was supposed to give way first, especially when you have the kind of habits I do. But no, it seems the other illusions . . . it's not so much the armor of the soul as . . . well anyway, I'm going to be away for about two weeks, so . . .

She reached out for him and he held her tightly, silently trying to say all the things he hadn't been able to say in words, smiling as he stepped back and squeezed her hand a final time, quickly then moving off up the square . . . the restless stride and a nod or a word here and there to the late stragglers of the evening, turning and waving to her, the great dark head against the midnight sky of the city as he reached the corner and looked back, catching a final glimpse of her. . . .

Gone. She took a deep breath, gazing after him. How odd it is, she thought. For years the partings were always so hectic for us, wrenching in some painful way. But now when there's a war and the danger is greater than ever, it's almost quiet between us. Peaceful even.

Why? she wondered. Because so many of the decisions are no longer ours to make? Is that really the only way for life to be less tormenting? To have its choices taken out of your hands, its decisions taken from you?

She sat up late that night on her little balcony, the way she always did when Stern was leaving again. Two weeks this time, he had said, but who knew what that meant? Who could ever know with a man like Stern who was forever leaving on some dangerous new mission for the Monastery?

Mission. The Waterboys always used that term and so did the Monks. Everyone else always spoke of going on missions, but Stern never did. Somehow it was too grand a word for him and he spoke, instead, of traveling. . . . A man on his travels. . . . I have some traveling to do.

Stern . . . Joe . . . how very different they were in so many ways, yet the two of them had once been very close, years ago in Jerusalem. Joe had often talked to her then about his great friend Stern, and she remembered how surprised she had been when she and Stern had finally met much later, in Istanbul, after all three of them had taken their separate paths.

She didn't know what she had expected, probably some kind of genie after the way Joe had talked about him. Certainly not the Stern she had come to know, so much like other men when she saw him as she had tonight, hunched over a table in a small café and talking of little things, laughing and silent by turns, the two of them so much like everybody else in the way they reached out for each other and quietly held on as best they could, enjoying their brief moments together. Stern in the shabby suit of a clerk, pushing back his hair and joking about ledgers and making light of working late at the office. . . . Save for his restless eyes and his hands that were never quite still, the same as anybody else passing an hour in the little square at the end of her alley. Tonight at least for a moment . . . the same as anybody else.

And Joe? Why had she thought of him tonight? Or did she always think of him at this time of the year especially . . . remembering their long-ago trip to the Sinai and their month together in a tiny oasis on the Gulf of Aqaba. Brilliant waters and sands that burned and the stunning sunsets of the desert bursting over them, and the breezes of the all-healing sea, the eternal stillness of dawn in the beginning of love. . . .

Yes, that must have been why she had thought of Joe tonight. It was the time of the year and Stern leaving once more as Joe had left so often when he worked for Stern long ago in Jerusalem . . . some coincidence of little things in her mind. The tricks of memory mix-

141

ing the years together as she sat up late on her narrow balcony, gazing out over the great restless city and thinking of many things, but above all of Stern.

The voice, the eyes, the incessant touching . . . could it really be that he was finally coming apart like the world itself? Stern with his lifelong dream of a great peaceful new nation in the Middle East, the vision shaken in the monstrous slaughter of the First World War, only to be shattered in the madness of the Second World War. Nothing left for Stern now because no one wanted to hear of his hopeless dreams, not the Arabs and not the Jews . . . no one. And yet Stern had known all of that for years, so why did he go on doing what he did? Why did he struggle endlessly when there was no end for what he sought?

In the darkness Maud suddenly laughed at herself, laughing at her own musings.

Why does *he?* . . . but why do any of us? Why do we go on trying when what we hope for will always be beyond us? When we can never more than touch the lives of others in passing? When even our own life must forever be tentative and incomplete and out of reach, no more than a shadow of what we long for?

So perhaps it wasn't that hard in the end to understand why people felt so strongly about Stern, even men like the waiters in her little square, chance acquaintances who knew almost nothing about him. Quite simply, they saw in Stern something they wished they had been able to see in themselves. A refusal to accept the pathetic limits of life, a defiance to the pathetic failures of hope. . . .

We have to be more, he used to say. It's no longer enough to be what we were. We're dreaming creatures who have learned to reach beyond ourselves, unlike any other animal, who can therefore decide what we will become. And no matter how it terrifies us, there's no other way for us to be now. . . .

And the great dark head thrown back as the mysterious smile came over his face.

. . . so it isn't true any longer that we can *just* create ourselves. Now we must. Our childhood as a race is over and there's no going back, no escape into barbarism, no way to lose ourselves in the mindlessness of our animal past. Now we have to be free in order to be at all. The child within us prefers its instinctual cage, and the wars of this century are the final tantrums of our childhood's end, but the wars can't go on and on and we all sense that. Our killing toys have become too clever and our killing fields have become the entire earth, and now we either have to put aside our childish ways or refuse to, and in refusing, renounce life. I mean destroy ourselves utterly. . . .

Oh yes, she thought. Stern and his invincible dreams and the legions of little people who seize hope from the fires that go on consuming him in the dark places of his soul, Stern with his alcohol and his morphine and the crumbling defiance of his vision. . . . Tired, he had said. *Exhausted,* he had said.

From her little balcony Maud gazed out at the soft lights of the restless city, thinking of the wilderness not many miles away where great armies were slaughtering each other across the barren sands, as ferocious as blind animals ripping and clawing in the night.

Poor Stern, she thought, *poor all of us.* And have we really become like him . . . too grand a dream to survive?

9

Menelik

Joe awoke in his tiny room in the Hotel Babylon on a Sunday morning, having been lost in fever since Friday night. Liffy was still sitting at the table beside him, keeping watch, as he had been for most of that time. While Joe recounted the strange tale of his trip to the Monastery, Liffy squirmed uncomfortably and his face grew more and more pinched with pain. Finally he opened his mouth and let fly with a thunderous clap of gas, followed by an explosive barrage of gurgles and sighs. He smiled weakly, patting his stomach.

How's that, Joe? The *Bletch*, you say? Well it's ominous all right but I can't say it surprises me particularly, only because nothing having to do with war surprises me. An all-seeing one-eyed Bletch in charge of the Monastery? It's madness, that's all. It's all madness and I try not to think about it. . . .

Liffy's stomach went on rumbling noisily. Joe asked him if he had ever heard of the two women known as the Sisters, whom Bletchley had mentioned.

Heard of them certainly, said Liffy, but that's no help to you. Anyone who's spent any time in Cairo has heard of those social lionesses of yesteryear, the two of them so old and famous it's rumored they might once have been on intimate terms with the Sphinx back before he was turned to stone, as so often happens with good ideas. But that was yesteryear and now the fabled Sisters live in seclusion in a houseboat on the Nile, watching time go by, a counterpart to the Sphinx in the desert. . . . But what, pray, does it all amount to? Has Bletchley suddenly gone philosophical on us? Just lost his grip and decided that the darkest hour of a dark war is the time to do some serious brooding over the enigma of the Nile and the Sphinx? Somehow it seems unlikely.

Joe nodded.

It does, all right, but Bletchley has a way of not appearing to say much when in fact he's saying a great deal. Now the last thing he mentioned at the Monastery was old Menelik and the Sisters, almost in the same breath, but why? And what's the connection between them, and what's that got to do with Stern today?

Liffy grew thoughtful.

Today, he muttered. The here and the now. . . . That's always a confusing matter, isn't it, because who knows what's here or now in someone else's mind? . . .

Abruptly Liffy smiled, whistled.

Wait, don't move. When you and I saw Stern in the eye of the Sphinx, it was in a lookout old Menelik had fashioned for himself in the last century. But that wasn't the only secret place that was dear to the old sage's heart, was it? There's also his crypt right here in Cairo beside the Nile, that ancient mausoleum beneath a public garden where he lived his last years. Now what about *that,* Joe?

Joe rubbed his eyes and gazed at the bottle of gin on the table.

It sounds fine to me. What about it?

Ah well. Today, Ahmad uses that crypt as his secret workshop, the place where he keeps his printing press and his engraving tools and so forth. I'll get to that. But first, didn't Bletchley make some comment when he mentioned old Menelik and the Sisters? Some attribute they had in common? You alluded to it . . . what was it exactly?

Joe frowned.

You mean the fact that old Menelik was also something of a society figure in his day?

Liffy's hand shot out and he pointed at Joe.

Precisely. And who, by chance, just happens to be the expert on all Cairo social matters having to do with yesteryear? . . . Who, you say? Why Ahmad, of course. Ahmad, none other. The society pages of thirty-year-old newspapers are his specialty. . . . So then. What Bletchley seems to be saying is that to find out the truth about Stern, you must first find out the truth about old Menelik and the Sisters. And the key to that must be an excursion into Ahmad's past, because it is Ahmad who holds the key to Menelik's secret crypt today. Of course. Who else? This is Ahmad's clandestine workshop we're talking about, his underground truth.

Liffy laughed.

Too roundabout for you? Too devious and obscure? Well it wouldn't be for Bletchley and his Monks, I'd wager. Because lastly there's the fact that you're the only person staying in the Hotel Babylon, other than Ahmad himself, and *that* didn't happen by chance. That had to be arranged that way, by Bletchley of course. So whatever enigma Bletchley's brooding over, it starts right here in the Hotel Babylon with our local hermit-in-residence. And clearly, at this point on your journey east, all paths lead to Ahmad.

Liffy nodded thoughtfully.

Yes. That's exactly what Bletchley seems to be saying in his cryptic Monkish way. . . . Your journey now involves time, my child, not space. Not rivers and mountains and deserts to be crossed, but memories to be explored. For the moment has come to stop look and listen while tarrying in caves and open spaces, those of the past, and while marking well the local aphorisms. Ahmad's, no less. For now you must behold the very notion of this crumbling hermitage where you find yourself, this mythical Babylonian retreat which you share with only one other human being deep in a Cairo slum. . . . In short, what *is* the Hotel Babylon, my child? And who *is* Ahmad and what on earth is someone like him *doing* in these crumbling ruins while a terrible war rages across the world?

Liffy laughed, then turned serious.

In a way I envy you, Joe. I've never gotten to know Ahmad well, but I've always sensed there are whole worlds to be explored there, perhaps even a whole secret universe. And it may be that old Menelik is somehow at the center of this distant hieroglyphic past, a kind of black sun around whom many lives once revolved in some mysterious underground way. And although Ahmad has a strange ability to move from this world to others and back again, perhaps for that very reason you can't expect a coherent narrative for what you seek. Because it's Ahmad's memory that you hope to explore, isn't it, and memory never flows from beginning to middle to end, does it? It's always in transit in the middle of things, all of it is, and it deals exclusively in glimpses and suggestions, or shards, as Menelik might have called them. Fragments, in other words. Odd bits and pieces from which we must try to reconstruct the cup that once was, the fragile vessel that once held the wine of other lives in other eras. . . . Fragments, shards, yes. The elusive materials of the Egyptologist.

146

But after all, we're in Egypt so that's only natural, I suppose. Only to be expected, I imagine.

Joe watched him. He smiled.

My God, Liffy, your imagination has found a lot for me to do this Sunday afternoon.

Liffy looked up and nodded eagerly.

True? While I'm exploring a totally different kind of reality? But let's consider your business first, since yours *is* business and my plans involve nothing more than straightforward outright debauchery, merely erotic tumbling at its sweatiest. . . . Now then, how can I help? What can I tell you about Ahmad or the Hotel Babylon or the music of time? But wait, I have an idea. Why wouldn't a pianola be as good a way as any to get things rolling? . . .

Liffy snorted. He laughed.

You've seen it, I know you have. There it stands under decades of dust at the far end, the dark end, of the corridor downstairs, a pianola of all things. And what in God's name could it possibly be doing there?

Joe moved as if to stand up and Liffy immediately whirled and glared at the bottle of gin on the table.

Is there a genie trapped in that bottle? he asked.

It seems likely, muttered Joe.

And you want to let him out? Set him free?

It seemed like not such a bad idea.

Liffy frowned, shaking his head vigorously.

Business first, Joe. The pianola takes precedence. Now then. Every Sunday morning, after Ahmad has his coffee and his sesame wafers on his high stool behind the counter, he strolls back there into the gloom and ponderously plays the pianola for an hour or so. Peddling the past, he calls it, perhaps because the pianola only has one roll. *Home Sweet Home.* You might say Ahmad has a delicious nostalgia for bygone eras.

Liffy looked thoughtful.

Of course he also has his trade which he pursues in old Menelik's mausoleum, currently Ahmad's secret workshop. Down there Ahmad's a master forger second to none, said to be the best in Egypt. Money is his specialty, great heaps of counterfeit currencies for the use of fanatical Monks who have taken the vow of poverty. Spurious millions in the cause of bogus appearances, don't you see, rather like life itself. But Ahmad also turns out identity papers and other scraps of this and that, such as those coupons good for free drinks. Don't you remember me flashing one at the airport? *Say Ahmad sent you and you'll never be sorry?*

You mean those coupons actually work? asked Joe.

Always. Anywhere in Cairo.

Why?

Liffy smacked his lips.

I thought you'd never ask. They work because Ahmad's father, also an Ahmad, was once a famous dragoman in Cairo, the leading guide and interpreter for tourists in these parts and something of a patron saint to those in the pimp and alcohol trades. It seems they still revere his name because he was one of the forerunners of modern Egyptian nationalism, by way of the dragomen's benevolent society, which he founded. Anyway, Ahmad *père* used to hang around the verandas of tourist hotels, leering up business for himself in the last century, and one winter he chanced to have a torrid affair with a young German woman who was down for a holiday, and Ahmad *fils*, our Ahmad, has been a fiercely anti-German vegetarian ever since.

Why?

Because that young German woman became his mother. Soon after Ahmad *fils* was born, you see, she abandoned both Ahmads and returned to Germany. She thought it was best for all concerned, but certain political enemies of Ahmad *père* spread a rumor that she'd buzzed off home because she couldn't live without a daily chomp on the long thick blood sausages of her fatherland. Our Ahmad heard this malicious rumor while still a sensitive youth and took it as a personal insult, reading some kind of sexual innuendo into his mother's reputed craving for large Germanic blood sausages. He never forgave the poor woman for preferring them to him. In fact he has never forgiven women in general, or Germany in general, or meat. . . . Once more the meat problem looming large in human affairs, I'd say, and it does have a way of doing that, doesn't it, old horse? Meat, I mean. *Meat*, that's all. The *meat* of the matter, pure and simple. Even when someone's as spiritual as Ahmad is, it's just extraordinary how often meat can be fundamental to what ails us. . . . Yes, *meat*, my child. Consider it well while tarrying in spiritual caves and open spaces. . . .

Liffy sighed.

As I well know. As I know as well as anyone. . . . But in any case our Ahmad is generally referred to locally as Ahmad the Poet, although no one has ever seen him write any poetry. A matter of disposition, perhaps. And it's safe to say that on top of everything else, Ahmad's *very* keen on the Movement.

Which movement is that? asked Joe.

My dear fellow, *the* Movement. Is there ever more than one? *The* Movement may be defined as whatever explains history to the individual concerned. The Movement is revolutionary in nature, a dazzling innovation that no one has ever thought of before, again, save for the individual concerned. The Movement smashes through the old order of things and updates us, a kind of political trolley used by some to transport them from being young and no one, to being older and someone. I'm sure you've heard of people dedicated to the Movement, even if you haven't met one recently. *L'homme engagé*, for example, remember him from the '30s? Dashing French fellow in a beret who was always chain-smoking dramatically? Who used to turn up behind the intellectual barricades in moments of crisis to sum it all up by saying, *Life is absurd* or *Life is a Cambodian*, that sort of thing? But if all of this seems confusing to think about, why not relax and leave the thinking to Ahmad? I'm sure he'll tell you everything you could ever want to know about the Movement, and I do mean everything. Followers of the Movement are like that. . . . But what's the secret of the pyramids, master? *Everything*, my child. . . .

Liffy nodded to himself, his face thoughtful.

I should also add that Ahmad has been well described as an Egyptian gentleman in a flat straw hat who stands at a slight angle to the universe.

Who describes him that way? asked Joe.

The retired belly dancer up the street, replied Liffy. That very nice woman who sells tender young roast chickens for a living, as well as serving as the official hum-job historian for the rue Clapsius. She *always* says that about Ahmad.

Oh I see.

Yes. And the reason Ahmad never takes off his boater, his hat, she says, is because it's a memento from an earlier and quieter age when Ahmad served as the stroke and captain of a racing crew rivered by the dragomen's benevolent society against the British navy. In those days there used to be a ferocious rowing competition known as the Annual Battle for the Fleshpots of the Nile, and in 1912, I believe it was, Ahmad's crew *won*, the only time the British navy was ever beaten at its own game on the Nile, and by riffraff at that. The touts and pimps had done it at last. . . . And never, notes the former belly dancer, did the rue Clapsius hum with so much *verve* as it did that night. It was a heartening triumph for all true Cairenes, naturally, and a banner day for Egyptian nationalism. So the boater Ahmad wears is a precious memento from that fabled victory of yesteryear.

Liffy frowned.

But that *was* yesteryear and now he's *quiet,* Ahmad is. He's like a huge solemn cat silently licking his memories. So although all paths lead to Ahmad, according to Bletchley's clues, I'd still go gently with him when introducing Stern's name. Years ago the two of them were very close, but there was some kind of betrayal involved and it's still a touchy subject. I've never gotten to the bottom of it.

Liffy stood up. His face brightened.

Anyway, I have to tell you I telephoned Cynthia last night, hoping for a reconciliation, and she said she might take notice of me if I turned up on her doorstep as someone suitable this afternoon. I was considering playing the part of a Free French officer with the colonials. You know, a darkly handsome spahi officer of Algerian cavalry. They wear swirling red cloaks. . . . Irresistible on a Sunday afternoon, wouldn't you think?

Devastating, said Joe, smiling.

If you've recovered, that is, and don't need me. . . . And by the way, Bletchley seems to have someone keeping an eye on you. I spotted a young fellow hanging about up the street. He's missing most of his fingers and he may just be looking for a tender young chicken for lunch, or then again he may not be. Are you interested?

Not yet, said Joe. It's too soon.

Liffy laughed.

It is? Strange, but that's what Cynthia always says when we get into bed. *It's too soon. Talk to me first.*

And do you?

Liffy nodded vigorously.

Indeed, I tell her erotic tales from my travels. Would I be one to deny the myriad sexual acts mounted by spahi officers over the years in the desert? Beneath the swirl of a red cloak on Sundays?

Ha, and now I'm off to taste adventure, boomed Liffy, happily sweeping out the door and clattering down the rickety stairs.

At the foot of the stairs, behind the small counter tucked away in the shadowy corridor that led to the street, the enigmatic Ahmad sat silently playing solitaire, a thirty-year-old newspaper open at his elbow. From what Joe had seen, solitaire and thirty-year-old newspapers seemed to be the man's sole pastimes when he was not engaged in his professional duties as a deskman at the Hotel Babylon or as a forger in Menelik's mausoleum.

Ahmad was a large man, his appearance bizarre even by rue Clapsius standards. In addition to the battered flat straw hat that was always on his head, he wore great round tortoiseshell glasses, securely attached to his ears by pieces of red thread tied in identical bows. His hair was also a bright red, obviously dyed according to his own prescription, for the color was much too bright and uneven to have been the work of a professional hairdresser.

Although his massive face was far from young, it had remained smooth and unlined and was rooted in an enormous thrusting nose. The size of his hands was remarkable and the general impression he gave was of great muscular strength in repose. There was even a childlike eagerness to his face, as if his impressions of life were still new and not yet fully formed, with the result that he looked less like an older man and more like a boy who had aged.

Up until that Sunday Ahmad had always been withdrawn in Joe's presence, never saying more than was necessary. But Joe had guessed this might have to do with a natural shyness on Ahmad's part, and in fact Ahmad's manner changed completely, as Joe had hoped it would, when Joe leaned on the counter and mentioned in an offhand way that he had once heard many stories in Jerusalem about the masterly Egyptologist and revered black sage unknown to the world as Menelik Ziwar, dead now these many years.

Of course the fact that the mere mention of Menelik Ziwar's name could dramatically alter the nature of an afternoon, any afternoon, wasn't surprising. It was true that only a few people had ever heard of this fabled Cairene of the nineteenth century, even when he was still alive. But to those fortunate few he would forever remain an astounding man of unsurpassed accomplishments, a hero of legendary proportions.

And unforgettable in every respect. Joe only knew what he had been told about Menelik Ziwar a decade earlier in Jerusalem. But Ahmad's connection with old Menelik was much more personal, as it turned out, and inextricably entwined with his own most intimate concerns

Menelik Ziwar had begun life as a black slave named Boy, born in the Nile delta early in the nineteenth century. At the age of four he was tossed into a cottonfield and told to pick, and under normal conditions that is what he would have done for the rest of his days, about two decades at best, before dying of dysentery or cholera or typhoid. But somehow Boy managed to learn to write a few words, including *Ziwar*, the name of the rich cotton-fat family that owned him, and soon he was proudly inscribing this name as a kind of graffiti on every available surface on the plantation where he lived.

Before long one of the Ziwars took note of this ubiquitous salute to his name and was flattered by it. He had Boy transferred from the fields to his mansion, to service his opium pipe on a daily basis. Boy now had time to dream, and with his imagination fired by the rewards of literacy, he quickly went on to learn to read as well as to write. That accomplished, Boy felt he had earned the right to a better name and immediately chose *Menelik* for himself, after the mythical first emperor of Ethiopia, the only country in Africa not ruled by Europeans at the time.

When Menelik was freed his success was even more startling. He moved to Cairo as a young man and learned the European tongues in order to be able to support himself by working as a dragoman, while quietly launching his study of hieroglyphs between backstairs assignations with tourists. He then turned his attention to archeology, at the same time cornering the opium market in Cairo as a way to finance his expensive digs elsewhere, and soon became the leading Egyptologist of the century, a wizard of subterranean life.

Yet the habits of anonymity acquired in his youth stayed with him, and Menelik always allowed the dissolute young men of the Ziwar clan to take credit for his remarkable discoveries, preferring instead to remain invisibly in the background, sagely advising others where to dig and how much opium to smoke while doing so, the better to appreciate these splendid treasures hidden by the ages.

Menelik's career of unsurpassed brilliance continued until he was well into his nineties, but long before then he had gone underground completely to live out his days in even greater obscurity, choosing one of his own discoveries as his retirement home, a spacious ancient tomb now to be found beneath a busy public garden beside the Nile. There old Menelik had graciously held court until he died, royally entertaining the few people who knew he existed. And it was this same mausoleum beneath a public garden in Cairo that Ahmad now used as his secret workshop, forging spurious millions for the Monks, as Liffy said.

And thus had ended an astonishing life begun so simply in a child's graffiti of long ago, on that fateful day in the nineteenth century when a little black slave named Boy had dared to raise his eyes on the cotton plantation where he labored, thereby exuberantly defying law and order, and had dared to write on a wall those slashing bold words that were to set free the magic of his yearning soul forever.

HAY.
EYES TIE-ED DRAGIN COTTUN ROUN.
COTTUN AINT FAYROW,
EYE EM.

(s) ZIWAR UF DA DELTER.
MI, ZATS ALL.

10

Ahmad

But it was only one tiny part of old Menelik's career that seemed to appeal to Ahmad, not his phenomenal life in general.

Ahmad's intense admiration for the old Egyptologist was focused entirely on that extremely brief period when the young Menelik had worked as a dragoman one winter in Cairo, in order to support himself while beginning his study of hieroglyphs. For it was during that long-ago winter that Menelik and Ahmad's father had conceived the idea for the first dragomen's benevolent society, a forerunner of twentieth-century Egyptian nationalism.

Such vision, said Ahmad to Joe. And what heroic battles they had to fight to get the struggle out of the cafés and into the streets. In those days a dragoman could only find work during the winter tourist season. The rest of the year he had to do without, as did his neglected suffering children, the poor little waifs. For a dragoman in those days, it was rut or perish. During the winter, rich Europeans clamored for a dragoman's services and were willing to pay almost any price to get their hands on him. And then?

What did happen then? asked Joe.

Spring, thundered Ahmad. The cruelest season. And not only spring, but spring and summer and autumn. The tourists stopped coming to Cairo because it was too hot, and those same dragomen who had been the hottest items in town were suddenly rendered cold. Whereas before, a world-weary dragoman had hardly been able to set foot on the veranda of a tourist hotel without being pounced upon by wealthy Europeans in search of the rumored depravities of the Levant, now these same poor slaves to the lusts of foreign exploiters were summarily scorned. Jeered at. Made the butt of rude Italian gestures and abruptly tossed off hotel verandas as if they had become so much superfluous hanky-panky.

But *they* changed all that, boomed Ahmad. And if you think Trotsky and Lenin set the world on its head, you should have seen what old Menelik and my father did right here in Cairo decades earlier. Fearlessly they went from café to café, convincing their fellow dragomen the time had come to stand up, to shriek, to speak out against these intolerable forced vacations that stretched on from spring through summer to autumn. Oh it was a time of fervor, all right. A time when there was electricity in the air.

I'm beginning to feel it, said Joe. It sounds like a regular spring thundersquall bursting over Cairo, with intellectual lightning just everywhere.

Ahmad whirled on him, his eyes afire, his voice crackling with emotion.

Ram it, he thundered. Up until then dragomen had always been mere rams for hire during the winter season, while being scorned during all other seasons. But no longer. Not after old Menelik and my father launched *the Movement*. And how did the idea for this great revolutionary crusade begin? This secular *jihad* to free the toiling masses of dragomandom?

Small, I bet, said Joe. That always seems to be the way.

Ahmad was somber, thoughtful.

Would you believe me if I told you it began in a small way? But always my father was passionately hammering away at the same inspiring theme. . . . You have to get out of the cafés and into the streets, he said. If you want your power to be felt, *organize*. If you want to make them listen to you, *organize*. There's only one way to change history. *Organize*.

Straight ahead through the centuries, said Joe. But was old Menelik really so interested in politics as a young man? I'd always heard he was only a dragoman for a winter or so, to make ends meet while he was getting his hieroglyphs together. Do I have it wrong?

Abruptly Ahmad's face darkened.

Menelik went underground, that's all. Down into tombs. But he continued the struggle there.

Oh I see.

And his heart was always aboveground with my father and the cause, said Ahmad, who then began offering up a host of elaborate excuses to explain Menelik's speedy departure from the Movement, which made it clear Joe hadn't been wrong at all.

In fact although the idea for a dragomen's benevolent society had originally been Menelik's, the black scholar had lost interest in café agitation almost at once, due to his increasing fascination with buried graffiti and forgotten facts and subterranean reality in general, the everyday spadework of Egyptology. What Ahmad had been referring to when he admitted that the black scholar had gone underground.

But it was also apparent that Ahmad didn't like to dwell on this subterranean aspect of Menelik's life. And the reason Ahmad couldn't accept these underground truths, refusing even to acknowledge their existence beneath the shifting sands of Egypt, was because he wanted so desperately to believe the founding of a dragomen's benevolent society in Cairo had been the most dramatic event of the nineteenth century, and therefore the most significant cause that anyone could have taken part in then.

And all because that was what his father had done.

Democracy in action, boomed Ahmad, all his old enthusiasm returning. My father and his fellow dragomen discussed everything under the sun as they lounged away the hours in cafés, and there were superb speeches and vivid manifestos, not to mention all the poignant true-life stories that were constantly being retold and retold. The times were *alive* then, and there was even talk of founding a new nation or a new world-order dedicated to pure dragomanly ideals.

And so we had *verandaism*, thundered Ahmad. And we had radical nocturnalism and revolutionary hotel-lobby restructuralism, and a revisionist humanist wing with no furniture, and the inevitable backroom lobby filled with cigar smoke, for the disabled. . . . Oh it was *all* there. And each faction had its hour of shrill ascendency as the final truth took shape, and then finally the enraged shouts erupted and the fighting slogans were unwound, and the downtrodden dragomen of Cairo rose up as one angry man and marched out of the cafés and into the streets. They just weren't going to take it anymore, and thus was born the International Brotherhood of Dragomen and Touts. Or simply *the Brotherhood*, as they were known to their supporters. Or *the DTs*, as their detractors so viciously referred to them.

There's never been any respect for minorities, said Joe.

Ahmad's massive nose flared. He sighed, gripping his powerful fists together.

I have to tell you things didn't turn out well for my father, he said in a quiet voice. In his later years my father became increasingly bitter and eventually refused to see anyone at all, even Cohen and the Sisters, and that's shocking when you think of it. For hadn't their midnight sails on the Nile once been the very talk of Cairo? Those bawdy tender nights when the four of them had dressed up in costumes and drifted riotously on the currents of the great river, drinking champagne from alabaster cups of pure moonlight? Singing their songs to the stars and caressing the night with sensual laughter?

Oh yes, the four of them had been famous friends once, yet there came a time when my father stopped going out and refused to see even them. . . .

Ahmad lowered his eyes.

Underwear had always been my father's trademark in his professional life, the finest erotic underwear imported from Europe. But when he stopped leaving his rooms, he also stopped wearing underwear. At home, with just me around, he refused to wear any at all. The fantasy's gone, he used to say. My illusions have departed like an ancient scroll rolled up.

Ahmad hung his head.

And it was all because he felt the Movement had betrayed him. It's grown fat, he used to say. It's just not the same anymore, it's not what it used to be. And in his bitterness he began smoking more and more hemp, which increased his appetite so that he ate more and more, which made *him* fat.

Ahmad glowered.

Bloat. Revolting. The dragoman's anathema.

Ahmad's scowl deepened.

My father had worn a beard all his life, ever since he was a sleek young man. But when he rashly decided to shave it off thirty years later, what did he find lurking beneath his beard, time's cruel reward for his decades of selfless sacrifice on behalf of the Movement?

My God, said Joe, what did he find?

Wattles, thundered Ahmad. Deplorable. *I have wattles,* he confided to me one evening, his face all bandaged up to hide the fact, so heavily bandaged he looked like a mummy. In those later years people got into the habit of referring to him as Ahmad the Fat, and quite naturally they called me Ahmad the Thin. And since everyone else was using those names, we picked up the habit ourselves.

How is the fat one today? I would ask. Bitter and lonely, he would answer, and how is the thin one? . . . Meaning me.

Ahmad shook his head sadly.

Sometimes when you feel defeated the world just seems to bear down on you, insulting you and humiliating you. I saw that happen to my father and it was terrible. He became a recluse and there was nothing I could do to make it any better for him. He played solitaire and read old newspapers and kept his face bandaged like a mummy, and he smoked hemp and never wore underwear and never stirred from his rooms. At least a game of solitaire can't betray me, he used to say. At least thirty-year-old newspapers can't lie.

Ahmad sagged heavily against the counter, his voice sinking.

Toward the end, the only thing that gave him any pleasure was listening to donkey bells. There were donkeys everywhere in Cairo in those days and he loved listening to the gay tinkling sounds of their bells. Nothing else could ease his terrible loneliness.

Ahmad looked away.

The end came in the autumn. The Nile was still red with the topsoil of the Ethiopian highlands, and the nights were cool and no longer filled with desert grit. But the great river was ebbing swiftly and with it my father, a lonely beaten man with the life going out of him. He'd had an operation on his throat by then and he couldn't speak, so he penciled notes for me on a pad of paper he kept by his hand.

Raise me up off the pillows, he wrote that last evening. *Let me hear the lovely bells one final time. . . .*

And that was the end. He died in my arms.

Slowly Ahmad raised his eyes and looked at Joe, his huge boyish face tormented, his voice a whisper.

Don't you see? I only *pretend* the Movement was important in order to honor my father's memory, even though in my heart I know it was nothing more than a farcical oddity once used by someone to justify his life. . . . Every life has its Movement, of course it does. But what does it matter in the end? *Who cares?* . . . But what I really can't understand is why my father didn't spend his life with donkey bells? Why didn't he make them or sell them or do anything while riding around on a donkey, when he loved those gay tinkling sounds more than anything in the world?

158

Ahmad's lips quivered. Pain creased his massive face.

Why don't people do what would make them happy? Why do they let themselves get trapped into things? Why don't they just?....

But Ahmad was unable to go on. His whole body sagged and he covered his face with his hands, softly beginning to weep.

Noisily, Ahmad blew his nose.

Please forgive me that outburst of realism, he muttered. I try to keep them down to a minimum, given the way things are.

Ahmad blew his nose again and drew himself up on his high stool. His face brightened.

But see here, may I offer you an aperitif in some interesting attractive place, by way of apology?

You must be able to read minds, said Joe. Are you going off-duty then?

No, not exactly. But my town house is so conveniently situated, duty is no problem at all, said Ahmad, slipping off his high stool and disappearing down behind the counter. Joe thought Ahmad was retrieving his sandals, so he raised his voice.

A town house, you say? Does that mean there's a country house too?

Not now, Ahmad called up. But before the war I had a little cottage on the edge of the desert. The last war, that is, not this one. *My* war. The cottage was a delightful little hideaway where I could replenish my soul on weekends. In those days I not only wrote poetry and played tennis, I was also a champion cross-country tricyclist. I owned one of the first racing tricycles in Cairo, one of those swift machines you don't see anymore, the front wheel almost as tall as a man. And there I would be in my sleek racing goggles tearing down some road by the river at all hours of the day and night, the two white discs of my goggles reflecting the sun or the moon as I sped along laughing, a regular Sphinx on three wheels, just *flying*. . . . Oh yes, I was speed itself in those days. Hold on to your hats, they used to say, here comes Ahmad.

Is that what they used to say? Joe called out.

Always. Down by the river. But you have to picture the holiday crowds eating their grilled pigeons and their tehina salads in those cafés you find in limp gardens along the Nile, where clumsy birds of blue and gray hop along the red earth in front of you, taking flight at the very last moment with angry cries. Where kites and crows wheel black and slowly in the polished skies, the scarlet flamboyants in bloom and the sacred white herons dead still on the branches of the sagging trees. A holiday race, in other words, from the pyramids to the Nile. And picture the excitement rippling through the crowds by the river, and every head in every café turning, and a triumphant cry going up as the first tricycle came looming out of the desert. And screams and more cries as the thundering chant was taken up by one and all.

Hold on to your hats . . . here comes Ahmad.

I can see it, said Joe.
Speed, muttered Ahmad. Power. More and more speed and more and more power, I could never get enough of it.
He paused.
I also took great care with my clothes in those days. My appearance was important because I was not only an interior decorator but a leader of café society, which meant all kinds of people were always coming to me for advice and counsel. There used to be a saying in Cairo in those days. *When in doubt, ask Ahmad.*
Ahmad was still down behind the counter, apparently having trouble finding his sandals. While Joe listened he watched a large scruffy cat which had taken up a position just outside the front door on the cobblestones. The reddish cat was licking its paws and sunning itself. Suddenly it stopped and stared directly at Joe.
Your desert retreat must have been lovely, Joe called down.
Oh yes, Ahmad called up, his voice muffled. Cool nights and hot days, just like that song Liffy sings. But then a freak sandstorm came along and blew everything away, and I arrived at my hideaway one weekend to find there was no there there.
You decided not to rebuild?
I wasn't given the choice. It happened during the war, the last one, and tastes were changing and everything was changing and my inte-

rior decorating business was going from bad to worse. In fact I could no longer earn a penny. New people were coming along and I was out of fashion.

Joe jumped.

Ahmad's head, just his head, had appeared above the counter. He gazed solemnly at Joe for a moment from beneath his battered flat straw hat, then sank out of sight again, his voice drifting up from behind the counter.

I know it must be difficult to imagine when you look at me today, he called up, but I was quite fashionable before my troubles began. For a while I managed to keep up appearances with the help of friends, but life was changing drastically for them too, as it was for everybody. Some of them took up something new while others just wandered away and were never heard from again. While a few, like myself, could be seen still haunting the old spots, hoping to see a familiar face. . . . It's like that in wartime, even when the battles are thousands of miles away. Suddenly the world you knew is no longer there and you find yourself off in some little corner where nothing is quite right, not quite what it used to be, and a sad loneliness steals over your heart. . . . Sad, because you always thought your little world would go on forever. Because you never really understood how fragile it was . . . how fragile anything important is, because so much of it always exists only in your own imagination. But then all at once the dream is shattered and you're left with little bits and pieces in your hand, and an emptiness as vast as the night creeps into your soul. . . .

A sigh rose from down behind the counter.

I used to have long talks about it with a friend named Stern. . . . Quite simply, I'd failed in life and I didn't know what to do. A lonely time and long ago. . . .

Silence for a moment down behind the counter, then Ahmad began again, a lighter tone to his voice.

And what *did* I do? Well briefly I tried my hand at no-nonsense capitalism. Loot was my goal, nothing else mattered. Orphans and starving widows be damned. Let those whining misfits grub for their keep like the rest of us. If Carnegie could choke the poor and make ten million a year while throwing dimes to the mobs and being revered for it, why couldn't I? . . .

Instinctively, Joe jerked away from the counter. All at once the top of Ahmad's head had loomed up into view and was just sitting there, his enormous nose resting on the edge of the counter. He had removed his straw hat and was holding it aloft in some kind of salute, only the upper part of his head showing.

Fish and chips was the business, said Ahmad. Greasy fish and Levantine chips. Have you ever seen that old van Liffy drives sometimes?

Of course, said Joe. The Ahmadmobile.

Exactly. Well that van belonged to me before it was acquired by an unnamed secret service. Originally it had been an ambulance in the First World War, cheap to buy because it was war surplus, as I was myself. Well I had the van cleverly fitted out with a vat for deep-frying and an icebox for fish, and my goal was to be a self-made success. Strictly one man alone oozing his way to the top, the Carnegie of greasy fish and greasier chips. And when all was ready, off I drove through the rutted back streets of greater Cairo, merrily clanging my ambulance bell, ready to relieve the housewife's dinnertime burdens with tasty orders cooked on the spot. I was the originator, you see, of the modern fast-food business in the Middle East.

That's amazing, said Joe.

And I was also the instigator, from a religious point of view, of what might be called the Moslem movable feast of the contemporary era.

That's even more amazing, said Joe.

Well it seemed so to me, and for a time I thought the Ahmadmobile might become a household word in the back streets of greater Cairo. But what's that famous Latin expression for the inevitable changes of fate? *Sic semper Ahmadus?*

A look of profound disdain came over the upper half of Ahmad's face, the part that was showing above the counter. His huge nose twitched, as if assaulted by some disgusting smell.

What a *greasy* way to make a living, he said. In fact when you really put your nose in it, capitalism is a *very greasy* concept. Poetry and boiling oil just don't mix. But I suppose you Europeans must have already discovered that at least by the time of the Inquisition.

You mean you didn't have much luck? asked Joe.

Well I went around clanging my ambulance bell, making every effort to think of myself as an irresistible Pied Piper, and I tried every conceivable trick to cut expenses. I even lived in that smelly van for weeks on end, sleeping in the stretcher rack like any victim from the battlefield, hoping to get a better feel for capitalism. But all I ever felt was *greasy*, and between the rack and the fumes, my spirit was broken. Choked. Even though I oozed grease from every pore, I just had to accept the fact that I'd never be another Carnegie.

Weakly Ahmad waved his straw hat a final time and dropped out of sight below the counter. Joe breathed deeply several times, clearing his lungs. The large reddish cat was still staring at him from the cobblestones.

My visionary instincts were right, Ahmad shouted up, but since they were visionary they were ahead of the times, which meant I was wrong. People are comfortable with the way things were done yesterday, but uneasy about whatever may be done tomorrow. Which is why vision never pays off, and why poetry never brings in any money. If you want to make money, the best thing to do is to repeat after others. Whatever they say, just keep repeating it. Others like that and they pay you for it.

Or better yet, said Ahmad, muttering to himself down below, repeat something that was done a very long time ago. Three or four thousand years ago, for example, the way Crazy Cohen did. That can really bring in the money.

Excuse me? Joe called down.

I was saying, shouted Ahmad, that my real problem with fish and chips was that I wasn't able to master the secret of capitalist success in this part of the world.

What's that? asked Joe. The secret?

Slimy suspicion, boomed Ahmad. Subterfuge as the supreme code of conduct.

Again a part of Ahmad's head abruptly reared into view. He rested his nose on the counter, his glasses bouncing up and down. He seemed to be laughing silently.

Because in his heart, every true Levantine knows that if the rest of the world is half as devious as he is, then the rest of the world bears very careful watching. In other words, we have much in common with the great leaders of the world, both those of the West and of the East. Hitler, Stalin, Genghis Khan. . . .

Ahmad sank out of sight, chuckling as he descended.

Joe was moving restlessly back and forth in the shadowy hallway, wondering why this strange conversation seemed to go on and on with Ahmad down below the counter. Certainly Ahmad seemed talkative enough, surprisingly so. But why was he hiding down there? Was he really so shy he could only talk with someone if he stayed out of sight most of the time?

What happened after that greasy failure? Joe called down.

Very little, Ahmad shouted up. I was in debt and there was no money coming in, and it didn't take long for me to realize there was no future in that. Specifically, I knew it one evening when I walked into a café where I used to go, and not a soul there recognized me. It had always been our special place and Cohen and I and Stern had always gone there, surrounded by our circle. And then not to be recognized by even one person? . . . I wasn't only embarrassed, I was ashamed and humiliated. I was nothing and I knew I was nothing.

Ahmad groaned down behind the counter.

Well the next morning I took a temporary job that normally I would have considered a ridiculous joke, but the joke turned out to be permanent and the beginning of my own Great Depression, foreshadowing the world's. As usual, I was ahead of my time.

Again Ahmad seemed to have lapsed into silence down below the counter.

What was the job you took? asked Joe.

A position as counterman in a sordid brothel in decline, later to be acquired by an anonymous secret service, this rotting structure we now see around us, absurdly named the Hotel Babylon.

Ahmad's head abruptly surfaced above the counter. He rested his chin and stared at Joe, his face expressionless, his battered straw hat tipped forward at an angle.

Since then I've come to terms with my lot, however, and occasion-

164

ally I'm even able to muster a little humor. But all things considered.
it's been a long captivity for me here. My own sort of Babylonian
Captivity, as I realized long ago.

He smiled as his head sank out of sight.

More time passed.

This is impossible, thought Joe, and finally leaned over the counter to see what Ahmad was doing. Ahmad was down on his hands
and knees with his back turned, removing screws from a panel in the
wall. The panel was covered with dirty fingerprints and its edges were
badly worn. Joe pulled back his head.

You might have been wondering, Ahmad called up, why I never
supported myself through forgery. I could have, since I'm quite good
at it. Ask anyone around town and he'll tell you no one makes better
money than Ahmad the Poet. Crisp clean lines and well-defined details, accurate portraits and artful images. . . .

Joe jumped. Once more Ahmad's face had suddenly appeared
above the counter, grinning this time, the straw hat on the back of
his head.

Were you wondering that? asked Ahmad. Why I didn't just forge
my way to stupendous wealth long ago?

Ah, yes, said Joe, looking first at Ahmad and then at the large
reddish cat still sitting outside in the sun, immobile, watching him.

Ahmad nodded eagerly.

I thought so. But to me, you see, forgery is only money for art's
sake, and I wouldn't feel comfortable spending such money. So the
lot destiny seems to have cast me in this world is poverty in the midst
of counterfeit riches. Genteel poverty when I'm able to relax with
my music, humiliating poverty the rest of the time. And that pretty
well describes the life of Ahmad the Poet.

He stared at Joe, his chin resting on the counter.

Now then, it's time for our aperitif so please come down to my
level in life.

Excuse me?

The swinging door under the counter, whispered Ahmad. You are now on the threshold of the lower depths, or what used to be called in Gothic novels, *the Secret Behind the Wall*. Just get down and join me here please, on the floor.

Joe looked at Ahmad, then crawled under the counter. The panel with its worn edges had been removed from the wall, revealing a square opening large enough to admit a man. Ahmad had lit a candle and was holding it in front of the black hole. A smile of boyish delight lit his face as he began to whisper.

This mysterious closet you are about to enter is left over from the old days when the hotel was still a brothel. Call it the local treasure chamber, if you like, and follow me but be warned. Abandon hope, all ye who enter here. And also, duck your head or lose it.

Ahmad laughed.

Avanti populo, he whispered, there's no turning back in life. The descent into the underworld begins.

Ahmad's secret closet, as it turned out, had played a significant part in the history of the Movement in the nineteenth century.

One of the very first rights won by the Brotherhood, whispered Ahmad, thrusting his candle into the blackness. It was here that dragomen the world over began their long struggle to free themselves from the bedrooms where they had been virtual prisoners.

How did it work? whispered Joe.

Well when the police came around to raid the district, the Nubian porter in the lobby went to the pianola and pedaled *Home Sweet Home* at full volume, alerting the dragomen on assignment upstairs in the bedrooms, who immediately flung aside their customers and grabbed their flowered nightshirts and rushed down here to hide in safety behind the wall, passing the time with gin and parcheesi until the all-clear was sounded. That way they couldn't be arrested on some trumped-up charge.

And the customers didn't mind being arrested alone?

The customers were wealthy foreign tourists, whispered Ahmad, so naturally the magistrates let them off. Smiles for tourists with loot and bugger the wogs. The usual double standard.

Ahmad chuckled and crawled through the opening, Joe going in

166

after him. The chamber turned out to be quite large for a closet, although it was still no more than a small windowless room. Ahmad's regular living quarters were in the basement, he explained, and this was but a private hideaway he used for listening to music and doing his exercises. The walls of the little chamber were stacked with dusty piles of newspapers, the most recent ones dated 1912, from what Joe could see. There was clutter everywhere, dozens and dozens of dusty Victorian and Oriental objects of every size and shape. A vague lavender scent permeated the cave and a chinning bar hung from the ceiling. Between the stacks of dusty newspapers, there was just enough space for a large man to stretch out and do push-ups.

Ahmad smiled happily.

My own little lair, he said, pulling out two tiny canvas stools for them to sit on. Joe nodded, dazed by the astounding clutter in the room. Ahmad, meanwhile, went on clearing his throat, apparently rehearsing what he was going to say. He seemed much more nervous than he had out front and when he finally spoke, there was a thin attempt at bravado in his voice.

Well now, so you've come from America, have you?

Yes, murmured Joe, his eyes drifting around the room in a trance.

Well now, isn't that a strange coincidence? The world is really very small. It just so happens I once was given a complete edition of the collected letters of George Washington, some thirty-odd volumes in all, and they certainly added up to some fascinating reading.

They did?

Oh very. Let's see now. Did you know, for example, that Washington's false teeth were made from hippopotamus teeth? He also used teeth made from walrus tusks and elephant ivory and even cow teeth, but he always preferred hippo. He claimed it gave him a superior bite and chew. With hippo, he said, even peanuts and gumdrops were possible.

Even peanuts and gumdrops? murmured Joe. President Washington?

So he stayed with hippo whenever he could.

And wisely so, I'm sure, murmured Joe, who was still so overwhelmed by the clutter in the room he couldn't concentrate on what Ahmad was saying. Again Ahmad cleared his throat.

Serious tourism began in Egypt around 700 B.C., mumbled Ahmad so it's perfectly understandable you'd want to come and see the sights. But beware, nostalgia is deceptive. Nearly everyone in nineteenth-century Europe had syphilis, and if we forget that then the fainting spells and the dim lighting of the Victorian era become mere quaint oddities.

Quaint, said Joe. That's true.

Or to put it another way, added Ahmad, the Vikings were once the most ferocious marauders in the world, but only a short millennium later most male Danes seem to be ballet dancers.

A nostalgic dance, murmured Joe. That's true.

Ahmad quickly cleared his throat, a suggestion of panic spreading across his face.

And speaking of ballet and the dance, were you wondering where the best belly dancing in Cairo is to be found? Of course, my information may be a little out of date, but before the last war the best belly dancing was to be found in the . . . what shall I call it, the *gut* of the fish-market district? . . . Well in the fish-market district then, in the little drinking places there. In those days belly dancing always came with the smell of fish. It was considered suggestive. . . .

Ahmad grinned broadly, but at once his grin faded. He rubbed his enormous nose and stared down at the floor in embarrassment.

It's *hopeless*, he muttered. I just can't do it anymore.

Joe stirred and looked at this large gentle man slumped over on the other little camp stool.

Forgive me, he said, I'm afraid I was distracted by all the things you have in here, it's almost like being inside a person's head. But what is it you can't do? What seems impossible to you?

Ahmad made a gesture of futility.

Trying to talk, he whispered. A simple little thing like being polite and making you feel comfortable. I'm very happy to have you here, it's just that I don't seem to know what to say, here among my things. It's not what I'm used to, it's not like being out front at the counter. This is all I have in here and I guess I'm not accustomed to sharing it with anyone. Not that I don't want to, I do very much. But I seem to have become clumsy in some terrible way over the years and everything I say comes out wrong, not what I really mean. It's just that it's been so long since anyone . . . well what I mean is . . .

Ahmad clenched his fists and stared at the floor, his voice trailing off. Joe reached out and touched his arm.

I know the feeling well enough, he said, but there are always things to talk about. Even here, where everything means so much to you.

Ahmad's face twisted in pain and the words burst out of him.

168

But *what?* I don't want to be another fool lost in the past. What could I possibly talk about that would be of interest to you? To anyone? *What?*

Ahmad buried his huge fists in his lap.

Do you realize, he whispered, that the adventures of my life are now limited to forays up the street to the greengrocer's? That I actually have to plan my daily trip to buy vegetables and prepare myself for whatever contingencies may turn up? And that when I'm home again safely, I say a little prayer of thanksgiving because no harm came to me? And that when I wash and chop and cook my little pile of fresh vegetables for the evening meal, those vegetables represent the sum total of my accomplishments for another day?

Ahmad stared at his lap.

Greengrocery espionage, you might call it. And if the accomplishment seems meager, I can only say that for some of us even a trip to the vegetable stand is a dangerous journey to make in daylight, a torturous undertaking which requires every bit of courage we possess.

Ahmad shook his massive head.

For the same reasons I only venture downtown at night to do my forgeries. Because the streets are deserted then and I can slip through the shadows unseen by the failures that crowd my life.

Ahmad made a small sound deep in his throat.

But I'm sure you understand my situation by now. And with everything the way it is, what can I possibly talk about that would be of any interest to you?

Well there were those times back before the last war, said Joe. That's a whole world that's gone now, just as there's another world ebbing away at this very moment, and that's always been intriguing to me, how things change and why. Couldn't you tell me a little about that? About those times you used to have with Stern?

Ahmad shrugged.

I guess I could, if it really interests you. . . . Actually there were three of us who were always together back then in the beginning. Three of us who were the nucleus, but even then Stern used to drop out of sight from time to time. For a day or two you'd notice him growing restless, then one morning he'd be gone. Where's Stern? someone would ask, and the answer was always the same. He's off to the desert but he'll be back. And like the night and the day, Stern always did come back. Another morning or another evening and there he'd be at one of the tables in our little café, smiling and laughing and carrying on in his usual outrageous manner.

Ahmad paused.

That was before he became so involved with political ideals, you understand. Before he began to travel in connection with his political work. This period I'm talking about was back when he was still a student, when he'd just arrived from the Yemen, where he grew up.

But he used to talk to you about these sudden disappearances? asked Joe.

Oh yes, because we were so close, and also because of my little retreat out on the edge of the desert. He used to ask me if he could stay there sometimes, during the week, when I wasn't using it, and of course I was more than happy to have him there. He didn't have much money in those days and it was the least I could do for a friend.

In those days? mused Ahmad. The truth is Stern has never had any money, he can't abide it. When a little comes his way he spends it at once on friends, he's always been like that.

Ahmad smiled, gazing into the distance.

Empty hands and eyes whispering of hope, as Cohen used to say. And Stern never slept in my cottage when he went there. Instead he'd tramp off over the dunes and camp out in the wilderness like a bedouin, taking almost nothing with him. But still, there's never been anything simple about Stern. People used to think they understood him when they didn't, because there are things in Stern that won't mix. It's always been that way. . . .

Once more Ahmad paused, and this time he seemed to falter, as if he was afraid he was losing himself in the past. He even sneaked a timid glance at Joe, who smiled, trying to encourage him.

And that was Stern, said Joe. And who was the second member of your inner circle?

Ahmad nodded eagerly.

Well that was Cohen of course. Not the one of my father's generation, not the one who went for midnight sails on the Nile with the Sisters and my father, but his son. He was Stern's age more or less.

And what was he like?

Oh he was a colorful rascal. Very elegant and witty and a great favorite of the ladies, they couldn't resist those long dark eyelashes of his. He was a very gifted painter too, a trifle morose on occasion but that only made him more appealing to the ladies. The handsome and moody young artist, you know.

And then there was you, said Joe.

Yes, lastly there was me. Much clumsier than them in almost every respect, in everything save for music really, yet somehow I was able to provide a certain rawboned paste to their mysterious leaven. And mysterious it was, magical even, when the three of us were together. Everyone remarked upon it and we were always mentioned in the same breath, because we did seem inseparable. And oh how we carried on in the grand tradition, roaming the boulevards with a word here and a smile there, the three of us in swirling cloaks and cocked hats in the dramatic manner of Verdi, our eyes afire for whatever mischief might suddenly leap into being in front of us, whatever gaiety might swoop our way on the amazing sidewalks of life.

Ahmad smiled gently.

Later Cohen dropped out of our group to get married and raise a family. Odd, but the men in his line always seemed to be doing that.

Ahmad laughed, rubbing his knees with pleasure.

And what a line it was, those infamous Cairo Cohens. . . . But see here, what kind of a host am I today? Where is your aperitif and where is our music? Forgive me, I seem to have forgotten myself.

Ahmad jumped to his feet, laughing. He dug behind a stack of newspapers and came up with a dusty bottle of banana liqueur, to all appearances as old as the newspapers. A little digging somewhere else and he found two small glasses, then busied himself over a dusty pile of primitive phonograph records, all of them warped by time. When he found the one he was looking for he placed it on an old-fashioned phonograph with a wind-up crank and a flaring sound trumpet. He vigorously worked the crank and a faint voice screeched from far away. Immediately Ahmad went into a crouch, his straw hat askew, one ear almost inside the gaping mouth of the sound trumpet.

How lovely, he said with profound satisfaction. It's Gounod's *Faust* and the Bulgarian who sings the part of Mephistopheles is superb. What do you suppose ever happened to him? . . .

On the wall facing Joe, a large heroic poster from the time of the First World War advocated membership in the Young Men's Moslem Association.

WE WANT YOU, said the authoritative mullah depicted on the poster, as he pointed a bony forefinger out at the viewer. Behind the mullah a group of plumpish Moslem youths lounged beneath a flowering tree in the courtyard of an imaginary Cairo mosque, happily admiring each other's large gold wristwatches. In the distance rows of sturdy industrial smokestacks puffed thick white smoke into the air, while overhead a small primitive triplane came racing in above the pyramids, bearing the morning mail to Cairo. In all, life was humming and exceptionally clean in the poster.

Ahmad glanced up from his crouching position next to the sound trumpet. For a moment he too contemplated the poster.

What *do* we get from the art that obsesses us? he shouted.

I firmly believe, he shouted again, that most abstractions are simply our pseudonyms, and that we are therefore time. For surely it is in our fancy, not in reality, that the basis of our lives is to be found . . .

He laughed.

Which can only mean that in addition to everytning else reality is, it's also unreal.

At last the faint scratchy aria came to an end. Ahmad switched off the phonograph and held up a bottle of lavender liquid he had found somewhere, an atomizer attached to its top. He pumped and great clouds of sweet-smelling mist shot in every direction.

Disinfectant, he said, sitting down again. These old buildings, you know. But to tell you the truth, I'm completely indifferent as to whether the ruler of the world is called Anthony or Octavius. What does interest me, and what I've always strived for, is a purity of heart which forgives and justifies and includes everything, because it understands. . . . Yes, but like all people who ponder life, I often feel frightened and alone.

Ahmad gazed at the floor and lapsed into silence.

Do you still write poetry? asked Joe.

Ahmad sighed.

No, I'm afraid I don't. For a long time I tried to fool myself, but the words would never come to life no matter how hard I labored over them. Then after that I thought I'd accept second-best, so I started work on a poetical dictionary. But I didn't even finish the letter *A*. The last entry I worked on was *Alexander the Great*. Somehow it was just too painful sitting out front at the counter night after night, contemplating all the things Alexander had done in such a brief lifetime.

Ahmad turned to Joe. He smiled sadly.

I think I recognize my condition. Quite simply, I'm a poet who can't write poetry. I was given the soul and sensitivity for it, but not the talent. So when all's said and done my profession remains that solitary one known through the ages as *the failed poet.* And there must be many people like me who live alone in their little corners, knowing they've never been anything but ordinary, and it's not that we can't contribute to the world in some minor way, for of course we can. The sadness comes from the fact that we can't contribute as we'd like to and create even one little moment of beauty that might live on in someone's heart. . . . But do you know what the real tragedy of the profession is? It's that we get used to it. It's that we go beyond self-pity and beauty and simply endure in our little caves.

Solemnly, Ahmad gazed around the tiny room.

Surrounded as always, he murmured, by a little universe of things we understand. . . .

He lapsed into silence again.

I've often wondered, said Joe, what it must be like to have grown up among all these wonders of antiquity, the pyramids and the Sphinx and all the rest of it. How does it affect you?

It affects your taste, said Ahmad.

You mean you tend to take less notice of passing fashions?

Well I don't know about that, I was being more specific. What I meant was the taste in your mouth.

Oh.

The fact that you never know who or what is going to blow into your mouth next.

Oh.

Yes. There you are walking down a street and suddenly some hot dry dust swirls into your mouth and coats your tongue, but who or what is it? Some deserted corner of the desert being sent to you on the wind so you can taste its desolation? All that's left of some ancient tomb? Or is this grit on your teeth the final remains of a unicorn of the XVII Dynasty? Or is this new unsavory coating on your tongue the very last memory of the Hyksos, who were always an obscure people?

Ahmad smiled.

Dust to dust, he said. In the desert only a part of the past gets buried and forgotten. Another part always gets eaten, and although we like to pretend we can forget that part too, we don't really.

Ahmad frowned.

So the past is always with us and never more so than during a war, when so much of the past is seemingly being destroyed. Just look at that old cardboard suitcase in the corner. I bought that suitcase thirty years ago in a hurry one evening when I was on my way to Alexandria for a night of pleasure. Then I was young and strong and not yet ugly, and for me that flimsy suitcase will always bring to mind the memory of a boy in a cinnamon-colored suit, shabby because he was so poor, who then revealed mended underwear and a faultless body.

And do you know what's in that suitcase now? Two folders of my useless poems, a collection of scribbles once meant to be more, a forgotten footnote to the conscience of the race. My life, in other words. . . .

Ah Cairo, *Cairo*, this sultry place of half-light where the windows have to be shuttered until sunset for most of the year, where white-tiled terraces violently throw back the heat and the hoofbeats of horses pulling old carriages clatter reassuringly in the darkness. This Cairo with its radiant winters and its glowing springs with their winds from the desert bringing the terrible heat of summer, yet also bringing cool nights and breezes off the river. . . .

Yes, my Cairo, my life. In the end all grand schemes of order are private, and all the systems which we pretend are universal have but the dimensions of my closet. And thus we never find new places, nor do we find another river, for the city follows us and we grow old in those byways where we wasted our youths.

Ahmad stared into the distance.

Wasted . . . so many things in so many places. And now there is but this body, this worn and tarnished locket hung upon my soul. How many thousands of times have I celebrated the glory of its treasures and the wonder of the gift, the blessing . . . the burden?

And lamented them, surely. How many times in these byways where I wasted my youth? . . .

Joe watched him. He shook his head.

Wasted, Ahmad? That's not what I've seen here. That's not what I've heard at all.

Ahmad stirred.

What do you mean? What have you seen, what have you heard?

Joe laughed. He spread his arms wide to take in the small crowded cave where so much of Ahmad's life lay heaped around them in dusty piles.

Ah yes, Ahmad, a world of your own making is what I've seen and heard, and what poet could hope for more than that? And when I look to the heart of that world I see a great wide boulevard with three young men striding down it. And their talk swirled into the night, for they were great companions in those days and they always made their rounds together, elegant and witty and matchless in their joy and laughter, three fearless kinds of the Orient of old. And one of them was a painter, and another a poet, and the third an extravagant dreamer from the desert. And people flocked to hear those three kings of old, to catch even a glimpse of their outrageous performances. For they were *Cohen and Ahmad and Stern* and they laughed and wept with the very gods themselves, for the world was an opera then and the sidewalks of life were rich with poetry and color and love, and they were the masters of the boulevards in those days and everyone knew it. *Knew it.* . . . Everyone who ever set eyes upon them.

And that's what I've seen, said Joe. And that's what I've heard.

Ahmad stared into space, his face solemn behind his great round tortoiseshell glasses, his enormous head swaying defiantly in an imaginary breeze, his battered flat straw hat standing at a slight angle to the universe. Gravely then he nodded to the left and to the right, as if welcoming the companions of his youth, his hand all the while straying down the wall to where an ancient dented trombone rested amidst the shadowy piles of debris. Solemnly Ahmad drew the dusty instrument to him and caressed it, blew a tentative note, rose to his feet.

And sounded a melancholy blast on the trombone, a powerful glissando, his hand sliding slowly downward in a lingering salute to the majesty of a lost world.

11

Trombone

When night fell they moved from Ahmad's cave to the courtyard behind the Hotel Babylon, where Ahmad built a small campfire and served a vegetarian supper, expertly mixing grains and spices and vegetables in an array of little dishes that Joe found delicious after his three days and two nights of fever. As for Ahmad, he was delighted to have an excuse to cook for a guest again, having not really done so, he said, since his tiny cottage on the edge of the desert had been swept away in the windstorms of the last war, along with the rest of his early life.

And so they camped like wandering bedouin in the narrow courtyard where vines and flowers had come to take root beneath the single palm tree, the two of them huddling around the glowing coals of their little campfire in the remote oasis they had found for themselves in the slums of the great city, whispering together under the stars and sipping endless cups of strong sweet coffee as the night deepened and Ahmad gently reminisced, his recollections ranging wide through the silent play of shadows that suggested other lives just beyond their small circle of light, Ahmad quietly conjuring up odd corners of memory in the reassuring darkness, in the vastness of that clear Egyptian night.

In addition to the bizarre curiosities of his own life, Ahmad talked especially about Menelik and the Sisters and the clan known as the Cairo Cohens. In one way or another, all of them had been intimately connected with Stern in the past, and it wasn't long before Joe had begun to sense a network in Stern's life. And not so strangely perhaps, as Joe recalled Liffy's prophecy that the moment had come for him to embark on a journey in time, this network of Stern's spanned more than a century, its members not all among the living, yet their presences still so powerful they echoed restlessly through other lives in a shadowy web of doing and feeling, that most profound of all secret human codes.

And so Ahmad went on conjuring up shapes from the shadows of the firelight, in the darkness, and again the next night they returned to sit up until dawn in their tiny oasis, the two of them once more traveling through long solitary silences as Ahmad searched his memory for turnings along the path, Joe gazing at the fire and trying to decipher the connections with Stern as Ahmad whispered back through the decades.

For there seemed to be clues in everything Ahmad said, quiet footfalls and unsuspected hints that were only to be recognized later, when Joe had traveled further in his attempt to uncover the truth about Stern. When the day had come to look back and ponder the weaving of Stern's wanderings, the network that would finally reveal what Stern had sought, the unique figure traced by every man on the infinite landscape of time.

Alone and exhausted in his room as the great city was awakening, before he fell asleep, Joe drowsily reflected upon these odysseys through the night.

Ahmad? . . . Stern?

Surely a journey in time, as Liffy had said. Not mountains and rivers and deserts to be crossed, but memories to be explored.

From the beginning he had noticed the changes that had come over Ahmad as they had moved from the gloomy corridor of the Hotel Babylon, Ahmad's apparent station in life . . . to Ahmad's secret musty lair tucked away behind a wall . . . and finally to the flowering courtyard outside the hotel, so naked to the immense Egyptian night. . . . Ahmad opening his heart more with each new descent of the darkness, each evening when the last of the sunlight died and the hour returned for them to camp anew beneath the stars.

Buy why, all at once, was Ahmad opening up like this? Joe wondered.

And the more he thought of it, the more it seemed there could be only one explanation . . . *Stern*. Ahmad knew how much Joe cared for Stern and obviously he felt a need to talk about Stern, to tell Joe something. But why did Ahmad feel that need so strongly now? What had suddenly caused him to abandon the habits of years, his decades of silence?

Memories, thought Joe, the past. . . . Fragments and shards on the journey, as Liffy had said. To be examined in retrospect in an attempt to reconstruct the cup that once had been . . . the vessel that once had held the wine of other lives in other eras.

Yes, in time, thought Joe. In his own erratic way, through glimpses and suggestions and his own peculiar rhythms, Ahmad will find where we have to go.

And meanwhile Joe listened through the nights and slept and pondered Ahmad's fragments during the days, trying to immerse himself in Ahmad's memories in order to grasp the span of Stern's network over the decades.

So elusive . . . time, thought Joe. And Stern's life has been so vast, and now with the war and everything disrupted, dying. . . .

As it turned out, he and Ahmad were to spend no more than a few nights together in the debris-strewn courtyard of the Hotel Babylon, that former brothel crumbling beneath the stars. Yet when Joe looked back on those few nights, they would expand into many worlds so distant and remote it was as if they had been scattered across a universe.

Ahmad's secret universe, as Liffy once had called it.

Joe learned that Ahmad had first met Stern, through Menelik, when Stern was a young student of Arabic studies in Cairo, before Stern had gone on to Europe and acquired his lifelong dream of a great new nation in the Middle East, made up of Moslems and Christians and Jews alike. And that Ahmad had been a witness to those early stirrings of conscience in Stern, so boyish and exuberant, that had later made Stern a dedicated revolutionary whose devotion never wavered.

Joe was fascinated. As well as he knew Stern, this early period of Stern's life had always been a mystery to him. And after all these years of knowing Stern in a particular way, he found it strange to try to picture him as a bumbling young man struggling to find himself, bewildered by others and making foolish mistakes. Or the young Stern sulking because his childish vanity had been wounded. Or acting with ludicrous bravado when it was obvious he had failed at some little thing. Joe listened to Ahmad describing these scenes from long ago, and even as he relived them with Ahmad beside the campfire he knew he would never be able to take them to heart, because the Stern he knew was such a different man.

It's curious, he thought, how the past of someone older, someone we love and respect and admire, so often appears mysterious to us and out of reach. As if they saw life more clearly than we do and weren't as confused and frightened as we are. As if life for them were more than the endless little things, the revolving wheel of little moments, that ours is.

A natural yearning, it seemed to Joe, within the universal mystery sometimes given the name of history. Man's past. Those little moments of infinite beauty and infinite sadness falsely ordered in retrospect to give life continuity, a recitation of finite moments that in fact had never existed.

And then an even more curious thought struck Joe.

What if it was this very yearning in man that caused his conceptions of God . . . of all the gods in men? Cruel and profane and vicious, as well as holy?

The war? mused Ahmad one evening. Frankly I take no particular notice of it. There's always one going on in this part of the world.

As for the Germans, it's impossible to think of them as anything other than the barbarians of our era, the Mongol hordes at our moment in time. And unfortunately barbarians do seem to serve a purpose in history, for when we have them as enemies at our gates we no longer have to judge ourselves. For a brief moment, anyway, our innate savagery is safely out there beyond the city walls and we can rejoice in our self-righteousness, and be smug in our petty civic virtues.

But *refined* barbarians? Men and women who listen to Mozart between murders?

We may think that's an innovation of our modern sensibility, but it's not. The beast has always been within each of us, born there a million years ago. Most of us make it as easy as we can for ourselves by ranting about the barbaric monsters at the gates who never stop threatening us, but as for myself, I'm glad I've never been in any position of power. With my fears and compulsions that would be dangerous, and I know it.

Ahmad smiled.

In other words, heaven save us from people who dream, especially failed artists, the worst of the lot. All tyrants seem to be failed artists of one kind or another. . . . But then, so are most of us in our souls.

People *change* so, said Ahmad on another evening. It always astonishes me how much people can change. Stern used to talk about poetry and opera and the important things in life, but then these changes came over him and now he seems forever preoccupied. Busy. Rushing from one place to another with no time to think.

You still see him then? asked Joe.

Oh yes, he'll send a note around and I'll go meet him in the crypt and we'll have an arak together and talk about the old days. But the place seems so empty now when we're there together. I don't mind being there alone, in fact I rather like it. But when Stern shows up there on a Sunday it makes me sad somehow, and he must feel it too, I know he must. He talks about Rommel and codes and those things he has on his mind, and it's just not the same. It's lonely for both of us.

Do you mean old Menelik's crypt? asked Joe.

Yes, old Menelik's mausoleum, my workshop now. The place where I keep my printing press and do my forgeries. Of course Stern still has his key to the crypt and he doesn't need me to let him in, and sometimes he goes there by himself on a Sunday. I can always tell when he's been there because some little thing will be out of place, some little thing only Stern would think of. It's his way of letting me know he's paid a call . . . his way of telling me he remembers too.

Remembers what? asked Joe.

Ahmad sighed. He gazed at the fire.

Those Sundays of long ago. Those wonderful afternoons when we were all there together.

All of you?

Yes. Cohen and myself and Stern and the Sisters and the one or two others who would show up. In those days people of Menelik's stature always had a time when they were *at home*, as we used to say, a time when friends came to call. Well Menelik's *at homes* were Sunday afternoons·and the crowd was always a young one. Of course Menelik was very old by then but he liked young people. The Sisters were an exception, but they've always been an exception in everything they've done.

A boyish grin crept over Ahmad's face.

Open tomb every Sunday, a charming social event with all the amenities observed. I can still see Menelik sitting majestically in his huge sarcophagus, which was also his bed in his later years, thoughtfully dispensing tea and wisdom as we sat around him in a circle. For all of us, it was the highlight of the week.

And you all had your own keys to the crypt?

Ahmad abruptly began to chuckle.

Keys? Oh yes, those of us who made up the inner circle. Menelik had arthritis and he didn't like to crawl out of his sarcophagus to answer the door.

Ahmad went on chuckling. Joe smiled.

What's that? What you were thinking of just now?

I was reminded of Menelik's underground stories, said Ahmad. They were really quite naughty, you know, shameless even. He claimed he'd picked them up from the hieroglyphic graffiti he'd been reading in pilfered tombs all his life. In other words, Menelik's dirty jokes were four or five thousand years old. He also added the disclaimer, sly man that he was, that the stories lost something in translation. But if they did we never noticed it. Quite frankly, he was a very funny man. Definitely on the ribald side, but funny.

Joe smiled. He nodded.

Off-color hieroglyphs from over the millennia, he thought. Inevitably a trifle coarse now. And keys to the crypt of the past once held by an inner circle, Stern still in possession of one of those keys.

And the others?

Ahmad grew somber, his memory jarred by his recollections of those long-ago Sunday afternoons in Menelik's subterranean home.

In the crypt, he murmured, back on those lovely afternoons in the tomb. And after an hour or so Stern would unpack his violin and that would be the sign for all of us to get ready. Stern would give us our note and we'd tune our instruments as Menelik sat in his sarcophagus, straightening the folds of the mummy's shroud he affected, a rapturous smile on his ancient face because that was what he'd really been waiting for all along, he so loved music. And then Stern would take out the old Morse-code key he always carried, his good-luck charm, and he'd rap it against the sarcophagus to get everyone's attention, and then he'd draw the first notes and Cohen and the Sisters and myself and the others would all join in, and off we'd go on one of our Sunday musicales. . .

Beautiful, murmured Ahmad. Harmonious and exquisite back before the war. The last one.

Ahmad shook himself. He poked the fire.

But you see how time interferes? How could any of us have imagined then that Stern would go on to do things that would land him in prison? Or that he'd risk his life escaping from prison?

When was that? asked Joe in a quiet voice.

In the summer of 1939 just before the war broke out. And that reckless escape was the prelude to what I've always thought of as Stern's Polish story. To me, a tale that sums up not only Stern but the very war itself. Desperate. Incomprehensible. A kind of madness. . . .

Ahmad began to twist and turn where he sat by the fire, as if he were drawing near to some uncomfortable truth about himself, some irrevocable confession.

It may be, he said, that I've given you the impression my failures in life have been of the material kind, but that just isn't so. My failures of the spirit have been far more profound and painful. And to what do I refer?

Ahmad gripped his fists together in a fierce pathetic gesture.

To Stern, of course. Doesn't everything always come back to him?

Ahmad's knuckles bulged and there was despair in his voice.

I committed a crime, he whispered. I've always been a sensitive person and I *know* there are certain things you don't do, especially to someone you love. When you act as I did with Stern, you shatter something deep inside a person. And when you do that. . . .

Ahmad faltered, clenching his powerful fists more tightly.

What I mean is, you can't humiliate someone you're close to, you can't *do* that, because it's more than we can bear as human beings. We can be defeated forever but we can't be insulted by someone we love, and the failure to give love when it's needed, *needed,* must always be one of our darkest sins. For in failing that we violate our very essence as human beings and cast ourselves out, and become no longer qualified to be called human. . . .

Again Ahmad faltered, and this time it seemed he would be unable to go on. He busied himself adding sticks to the fire, then carefully adjusted his flat straw hat to some new angle, then changed the subject.

Slowly slowly, thought Joe. But at least Ahmad was finally beginning to circle the forbidden subject Liffy had referred to as a betrayal of some kind, the cause of the old poet's irreparable rupture with Stern, now linked in some mysterious way with an adventure that Ahmad, his voice shaking with emotion, insisted on calling *Stern's Polish story.*

I know why they brought you to Cairo, Ahmad whispered one evening. No one has told me anything, but I know.

Joe looked at him and said nothing. Ahmad's face was troubled as he went on poking the fire, casting new shadows over their flowering oasis in the darkness. A shower of sparks shot into the air, once, twice, a third time. Ahmad watched them go out, then finally whispered again.

It's obvious, Joe, to me anyway. The Monastery called you in because they're afraid of Stern's secret connection with the nationalists in the Egyptian army, the Free Officers who want the British out of Egypt.

Ahmad glanced nervously around the debris-strewn courtyard. For several moments he listened intently to the night, then leaned closer to Joe.

Oh I've known all about that for some time, and I've always assumed the Monastery knew about it too and overlooked it for their own reasons, because Stern's so valuable to them. But now they must have this new fear that Stern has gone too far and joined the nationalists in some Egyptian-German conspiracy, some plot to turn the British codes over to the Germans. Well there's no use denying Stern could probably lay his hands on such information. After all these years of doing the kind of work he does, Stern has contacts at every level of Egyptian society, and given Stern's nature, a good many of those people must be indebted to him. But even if they weren't, Stern's knowledge of people is so great he could easily find a way to get what he wanted.

Again Ahmad glanced nervously around the little courtyard, and this time his whispers were even softer in the firelight.

Listen to me, Joe. Once or twice in the last months Stern has mentioned something called the Black Code in front of me. I have no idea what it is but I assume it must be some highly secret British cipher, because Stern also implied that much of Rommel's success comes from the fact that the Germans can read this Black Code. Now none of that means anything to me, but you're a friend of Stern's and you care about *him*, so I want to warn you it's more complicated than you think, perhaps even more complicated than the Monastery knows. The Zionists also want the British out of the Middle East, and as much as Stern has always done for their cause in Palestine, there are still Jewish extremists who would be glad to see Stern out of the way, because they distrust Stern's kind of cooperation with the Arabs. And as for the Germans . . . and the Monastery. . . .

Somberly, Ahmad shook his head.

It's *dangerous*, Joe, all of it. Monks . . . Rommel . . . Arab fanatics and Jewish fanatics . . . they all have their reasons for wanting to see Stern dead and gone, and he just has nowhere to turn, don't you see?

So it may not matter what you do now. I hate to say it, but it's probably too late for anything.

Ahmad looked sadly at Joe, shuddered, looked away. Joe touched his arm, holding his hand there.

I know that, Ahmad. I do. But as Stern himself used to say, we have to try anyway. Even if it makes no difference, even when it's to no end, we still have to try. . . . Because what else is there, Ahmad? What else . . . ever?

And there were moments of unexpected revelation when Ahmad came out with some remark that suddenly illuminated his entire life.

Sometimes I try to think of my mother, he once said, as simply the person she was. And I wonder then if this obsessive concern I've always had for her, for what she thought of me, has been enough to justify all these years of loneliness I've known, these decades of eccentric behavior.

By all accounts she was a plain and simple woman, an uneducated farm girl who chanced to come to Egypt one winter as a servant to a German family, and chanced to become pregnant, and then corrected matters as soon as she could by returning home to lead a regular life. Not a remarkable person in any way, nor was there anything exceptional in what she did. And it certainly would have been a mistake for her to take me with her. A brown baby on a small farm in Germany would have assured a dreadful life for both of us. Yet because this girl was my mother, and because of what happened, my entire life has taken a particular course.

Deep within us, it seems, we begin life with the false notion that our appearance in the world is of monumental significance, and so we assign universal meanings to the threads and colors of our early lives, assuming them to be a unique tapestry of mysterious import, rather than merely one more shoddy human patchwork in one more tiny corner of the world. There's nothing rational about the way we look at it, and perhaps because the belief is irrational, it takes much of our lives to unlearn it. But by the time we do unlearn it, that small commonplace irony may have grown into monstrous proportions. For by then we have long since stumbled out into life in such-and-such a manner, and our course may well be irrevocably set.

Consider.

If I were to meet a person such as my mother today, or even my mother herself as she was when she abandoned me, the ultimate cause of my obsession, would I suddenly find myself in a human presence so powerful, I could imagine it determining a man's whole life?

Ahmad's laughter boomed and thundered, then all at once his face was creased with scars.

No, a ridiculous notion . . . but the joke's on me. All you have to do is to look at me to know that. And seeing what you see before you, would you ever dare claim that some peasant girl from the backwoods of Germany, harboring thoughts no more complex than the blood sausage to be enjoyed next Saturday night, could conceivably fashion this complex brooding creature who now whispers to you deep in these Hanging Gardens of Babylon?

Ahmad shook his head.

No. Sheer nonsense. What we have here is simply a case of that grand murky importance we falsely assign to the parent of the opposite sex. . . . Do you realize I've probably spent thousands of hours seething with resentment over my mother, and *why*? Why have I secretly devoted so much of my life to her? Why have I harbored this absurd *notion* of her overwhelming significance in the scheme of things?

It's a terrible irony, that notion, and in my case it's an irony that was discovered too late. For this *mother* of superhuman proportions, this mythical woman who plotted all manner of things in the world and set loose a host of brooding demons within me, this *woman* never even existed. And thus have I spent a great part of my life secretly confounding a shadow of my own making. . . . A terrible irony, but at my age one that can't be undone.

You see I've had no restraint, no restraint. I've been a tree swayed by the wind. Most of us are afraid because someone else is in charge of our lives, and because we're terrified of failing alone. So we wait and wait for something to happen, thinking we can accomplish something by showing patience, but time passes and we grow old, and all we accomplish is ending up alone anyway.

Ahmad gazed at the campfire.

186

Destiny, he murmured, my destiny. What a droll thing life is. This mysterious and merciless arrangement of logic for a futile purpose.

For a long time now, he added, I've left this place as seldom as possible. Crowds confuse me, so I stay here among my things.

And inevitably as the echoes of the past softly gathered in the corners of their little courtyard, as a terrible war raged ever nearer in the nighttide of that desert sky, Ahmad returned again and again to what he had come to call Stern's Polish story.

> . . . *the desperate escape from a prison in Damascus* . . . *the informer in Istanbul who had turned up floating in the Bosporus* . . . *Stern's headlong trip to Poland on a mysterious mission of great importance* . . . *and finally, the secret meeting in* the house in the woods *near Warsaw, only days before Hitler invaded Poland to begin the war.* . . .

Ahmad stared at the fire.

Later, Stern tried to justify it to me, Joe. We were in the crypt on a Sunday afternoon, and what he was really trying to justify was his life. How he had changed over the years and why he felt it had all been necessary. And I could see how much it meant to him for me to understand, how hard he was struggling to make it sound reasonable to me. After all, I *knew* him, and I'd been his friend from the beginning.

But I couldn't bring myself to accept it, do you see? Not there in a place where we had known so much of what is beautiful in life. So I felt I had to tell him to stop because it was too painful for me, the way he had changed and the way I had changed, the way everything had changed. Of course it was wrong for me to do that, terribly wrong. I should have let him go on and explain it as best he could, and then I should have simply accepted it no matter how much pain it caused me, just accepted it as a kind of truth, Stern's truth. And perhaps the truth of the world today, whatever that may be.

But I didn't do that, Joe. I didn't have the courage. I was thinking only of myself and I was angry because of all I'd lost in the world, and Stern seemed to represent that to me because he'd always been such an important part of the world I'd loved and lost, perhaps even the most important part. . . . Who knows. Who can say.

So I should have heard him out whether I liked it or not, and then I should have taken him in my arms the way we used to do long ago when we were friends who held nothing back, who laughed and cried and held each other.

Ahmad's voice sank to a whisper.

But I didn't do that. Instead I told him to stop because I didn't want to hear what he was saying, and still he kept on trying in his halting awkward way, trying so hard to find the words that would let me understand. And then . . .

Ahmad hung his head. There were tears in his eyes.

. . . and then I turned on him. *Shut up,* I yelled. *Shut up.* And the strength went out of him and his whole body sagged, and there was a wretched yearning sadness in his eyes that no human being should ever have to know, a terrible sadness beyond any hope of redemption.

So I failed him, Joe, and you have to remember what it meant. For remember. Once there had been three young friends who were inseparable and who shared every feeling and dream, Cohen and myself and Stern. And Cohen had been dead for years and now I'd turned my back on Stern and left him alone. *I* had done that. *I* had destroyed a beautiful part of his life by taking away the one thing a poor man has, his memories, and I had cruelly shouted him down by yelling that those memories were *dead. Gone.* And he was nothing and utterly alone. . . .

Ahmad was quiet for a time.

No, I didn't realize the enormity of it then, but slowly I began to understand it. Slowly it crept into my heart. And now when we sit here looking into this fire, here with the darkness all around us and the power of the night boundless in its domain, the two of us huddling beside this little speck of light, two tiny insignificant creatures suspended for the briefest of moments in a realm of infinities and blackness, here in these small flames before us I see his face more clearly than ever. A burning human face passing and soon to be gone, and I *failed* him.

By not accepting him for what he is. By not having the courage and the grace to do that, but instead, turning away. Fully aware of the haunted sadness in his eyes and yet turning away, turning away and leaving him alone in his torment, alone in his anguish, a friend whom I have always loved. A friend and more, a fellow human being.

Ahmad shuddered.

And that's Stern's Polish story, a tale begun one Sunday afternoon in a crypt beside the Nile, begun and never brought to its conclusion. And it's my failure and a failure of the world, and we will both have to live with it.

Yet I know better than to blame the world, for the world is a metaphor and an abstraction that doesn't exist. We all have our moment to be the world, to do what is right and give love when giving seems impossible and love seems an intolerable mockery. We all have that moment once, and I did, and I failed it.

Ahmad opened his powerful hands and gazed at them in the shadows.

It's the briefest moment in our lives. And the simplest. Yet with it, we build our heavens and our hells forever. . . .

Who knows what Stern's really doing? muttered Ahmad one night not long before first light, just as they were getting ready to leave the courtyard and go inside.

What do you mean? asked Joe.

Ahmad leaned over the embers, glaring down at them, his face working in agitation.

All I mean is, who *really* knows? Of course he has contacts everywhere, and of course he has long served many causes in one way or another, to one extent or another, and of course he works for the British. But could there also be something beyond all that, some higher cause for Stern? An even more secret campaign to be waged . . . in his eyes? Something so profound, perhaps, as to be unmentionable save before God?

Well in fact he has alluded to certain things with me since the war started, and now more recently I've sensed a thread to these bits and pieces of his concerns, which he drops in front of me without intending to. For one thing, the Jews in Europe are constantly on his mind. And perhaps . . .

Suddenly Ahmad became defiant and the words burst out of him.

Well does he have some sort of *traitorous* relationship with the Nazis, then? With these Mongolian hordes who are storming the gates of civilization? . . . Stern says there are whole communities of Jews disappearing in Europe, and he alludes to unspeakable atrocities, and he's haunted like Liffy by images of empty railway stations late at night, from which people have been shipped away to oblivion and worse. And he says the Allies are doing nothing about it because the evidence isn't conclusive enough for them yet. And he says there's no time to wait anymore for a documentation of death, some kind of doggerel of statistics which will convince our bookkeepers in high places.

Well I know nothing about statistics, because that's not how I account for human beings. But many kinds of agents have passed through the Hotel Babylon since the war started, and some of them have escaped from Europe and some of them have been Jews. And I've asked them things and looked into their eyes to hear the answers, and I've seen *blackness*. So if Stern is involved with the Nazis, I know it must have to do with getting Jews out of Europe. There could be no other reason why a man like him would strike this terrible bargain with evil. . . . But as for what he gives the Nazis in return, God only knows. I don't even want to think about it. . . . His soul, probably.

Ahmad sank to a heap on the ground and covered his face. Great sobs shook him.

Don't you see, Joe? It's not like Stern to be mentioning these things in front of me, these bits and pieces about Black Codes and Rommel and all the rest of it. He's too clever and experienced for that. And if in front of me, in front of whom else? And how could he help but know the Monastery would have to hear about it sooner or later? . . . And take steps.

Ahmad stared at the dead fire.

But I refuse to believe Stern is acting this way because he knows it will get him killed. What I fear is that he may be cracking up, and that terrifies me because Stern has always been *hope* to me. Just knowing he's out there and will come back someday, the way he did when we were young and he went off into the desert, just that means everything to me.

In the shadows of the little courtyard, Ahmad reached out toward the dead fire.

Hope . . . hope. We can squander all of the gift of life and even more than that can be taken from us. But not hope. We must have hope or the heavens will spin silently and it will be as if we had never lived . . . a nothingness of nothing.

In the stillness of midnight Ahmad stirred and tipped his head, listening to a distant clock toll the long hour.

It's difficult to speak of all that is, he murmured. Silence is what I know best, whereas Stern . . .

Ahmad stopped and adjusted his flat straw hat.

What I mean is, the two of us have taken such different paths in life. Out of failure, I sought the secret adventures of order and the pale consolations of solitude, as did my father before me. But even though Stern's failures have been far greater than mine, because he dared to risk so much more, still he has never turned away from the chaos and futility of life. . . . What I have forsaken, just that has he embraced.

Ahmad looked at Joe.

I'm not used to speaking to people, that's what it comes down to. I'm not used to trying to make sense, because when we're alone with ourselves we never have to do that. But still, it *is* difficult to speak of all that is, even when we're trying to describe only one single moment, as I've been trying to do with you. These long nights, Joe, these hours deep in the desert in this little oasis we've found for ourselves . . . and every single thing I've said to you since first you approached my shabby counter in the Hotel Babylon, a way station on your journey, and asked directions for a path that would lead you to old Menelik's crypt, every word I've spoken to you . . . But tell me, have you sensed by now that all of it has to do with only *one* single moment? One actual, *specific* moment in time?

Joe glimpsed a movement in Ahmad's eyes, a glitter, a play of lights. . . . It may be now, he thought.

Yes, Ahmad, I think I have sensed that. For a moment can have so very many things to it and in it and behind it, can't it, making it what it is? Just as we do, as you just said. And trying to locate all those things that go into a moment, and give them a size and a shape, while leaving nothing out . . . Well that's an immense task surely. As immense as this midnight sky above us.

Ahmad nodded solemnly.

Yes it is, and so I'm going to try again. But this time, for once, I won't begin with all the things within and behind this *moment* of which I have spoken again and again, which I have approached in a thousand tentative ways because it haunts me like no other. This time I'll begin with the moment itself. Just there. Naked.

A smile came to Ahmad's face.

But first you must tell me, Joe, whether I've managed to circle it at all, for even a failed poet can have a touch of vanity hidden away somewhere. . . . So then, this *moment* of mine. Has there perhaps appeared a where or a when or a what to it, for you?

I think so, said Joe, I think I've begun to get a sense of that too. . . . And the where would be old Menelik's crypt, and the when might be a while ago, not last month but not too many years ago either. And the what, well that has to be Stern, and it might be Stern together with his Polish story. But above all, the what is *you.* Because that's the center, the eye on the universe that we've been talking about here . . . are talking about now. *Your* moment, Ahmad. *You.*

Ahmad gazed at Joe. After a while he turned to the fire and set his hat at some new angle. As if in a trance, his words ebbing and flowing, he began to whisper.

. . . it was just after the war started, toward the end of 1939 Stern and I were in the crypt and it was that afternoon when he tried to justify himself to me and I so cruelly shouted him down. . . . We all die alone and unjustified, I shouted, cleverly turning his own words against him, mocking the poor wounded creature with something he himself had once said. And the rest of it, everything that came before then, was just as I've described it to you. It was after that, that the *moment* came.

. . . he'd injured his thumb when he'd escaped from the prison in Damascus that summer, ripped it up horribly. By then, in the crypt that afternoon, the healing had gone on for some months and the dark purple streaks in his flesh were turning to scars. Ugly scars. Deep. It was the first I'd seen of Stern in quite some time, but a new wound was no surprise. Stern was always turning up with something . . . a cut and a bruise from some new battering, another part of him nicked away, a new clumsiness caused by an arm or a leg that wasn't working properly . . . always something. But he never took any particular notice of those things, nor did I. It was part of the way he lived, that's all, so there was nothing unusual about him appearing with a ripped thumb that afternoon. Not for him, not for me. It was merely another mark from his arcane travels. Simply a small memento from his latest sortie, this Polish adventure of his. An obscure footnote, perhaps, to the beginning of the Second World War.

. . . although in addition to the coincidence that Poland was where the war had started, there was also the fact of Damascus. Something profound indeed had happened to Stern since I'd seen him last, but not on the road to Damascus, rather in *getting away* from Damascus. Forgive a literary man his conceits, but the irony of that parallel hasn't been lost on me either. In retrospect, naturally.

. . . in any case, inexplicably at the time, Stern's small wound caught the corner of my eye that afternoon, and held it. All the time he was talking those dark purple streaks were somewhere on the edge of my vision . . . ugly, deep, hardening into scars just beyond my conscious thoughts. And he talked and I shouted my disgustingly selfish things at him, and he sagged and said no more and the encounter seemed over. Reluctantly he was gathering himself up to leave . . . broken, weary, alone. And I was raging inside and feeling terrible, already overwhelmed with regret and shame, feeling I'd damned myself by what I had done. . . . When all at once Stern stopped near the door of the crypt. Made some gesture near the door. A little thing, I think he raised his hand toward an old sign that's hanging there.

. . . and *that* was the moment. Somehow that thumb of his was there in front of us, and our eyes met and we both understood. We both *knew*. . . .

Ahmad sat immobile before the campfire, a large somber figure utterly still. The silence around them grew and grew and Joe, suddenly, was afraid Ahmad's mood was slipping away.

You knew? he whispered.

. . . *knew*, I tell you. Our eyes met and we *knew*. And then Stern reached out and gripped my shoulder and his hand was strong upon me like the good side of his name, stern and resolute and unyielding in the face of what can't be evaded or escaped in life. Unyielding, *strong*, I can feel the grip of that hand on my flesh even now . . . the hand with the ripped thumb. And he looked into my eyes and smiled that smile of his, so powerful and enduring despite the wretchedness

193

we both felt, a sad yet mysterious smile I've always known in my heart, *always*, and he nodded. . . . *Yes*, he said. . . . Just that one word. No more. And then the moment was over and his hand dropped away and the door to the crypt opened, closed, and he was gone.

Ahmad shuddered violently, as if he had been struck by a blast of wind from the dark reaches of the desert. He bowed his head and his voice trembled, but he managed to go on.

. . . how much time was there to be after that? Would there be weeks still to come? Months? Even a year or two perhaps? . . . No matter. It was decided and the mark had been made and we both understood. . . . Stern was to die. Stern had to die. Stern had become he who must die. It was decided and we both knew it.

Once more Ahmad lapsed into silence. Joe was as afraid as before to interrupt his mood, but he was even more afraid to let the moment pass. Urgently, he whispered.

But what gave you that sense of things, Ahmad? What *happened* to Stern in Poland?

Ahmad stirred and touched his nose, head bowed, still staring at the fire. His eyes flickered as he searched the flames for sensations, sounds, shapes, and this time when he spoke his voice was startlingly clear and ringing.

. . . *what happened* was that our world had come to an end. *What happened* was that we had tried to survive one war too many and we had lost. In the end, the barbarians had been too much for us. With their blackness and their forces of darkness the barbarians had come to lay siege, and they had stormed the gates of civilization and overwhelmed us, triumphing utterly. . . . Before, we had managed. Once, we had managed. But now no longer was it to be so. Stern and I, we were finished and it was over. The gates were going to burst open and we would fall there, our strength gone, our pathetic armor torn and ripped away, the life seeping out of us. And everywhere around us, vicious and unrelenting, there would echo the empty laughter of grinning barbarians, the primitive meaningless laughter of jackals, taunting us and *taunting us* as we lay dying.

Ahmad raised his head. He passed his hand in front of the campfire, as if committing his tortured revelations to the flames.

. . . a vision, then. A vision of what was and would be. A vision that seized both of us, born in that single moment when our eyes met and he said *Yes* and we both knew. . . . But when *we* knew, you understand, not anyone else, for Stern still appeared to be his old self then. He still looked the same and acted the same and there were none of those disturbing hints that have turned up more recently. In these last months the gestures of Stern's despair have become all too clear to anyone who knows him, but back then at the very beginning of the war? . . . No, certainly not. Not even the Sisters, as well as they know Stern, could have suspected so long ago that he was beginning to crack . . . come apart . . . *shatter.*

The fire sputtered and Ahmad stared, captivated anew by the flames. Yet again he had lapsed into silence as Joe waited restlessly, a feeling of desperation welling up inside him. At last Joe whispered, trying to be calm.

But Ahmad, what happened in Poland? What did Stern *do* there? What *was* it exactly?

Ahmad turned his gaze away from the fire, his trance broken. He rearranged his legs, his hat. With the tip of his forefinger, he touched his nose.

Exactly, you say? . . . Here now, what's this, Joe? What are the *details* of death, you mean, is that what you're asking me? What are the clauses and the subclauses of the pact Stern may have concluded with the Nazis? How many increments of the Black Code, or something else or whatever it is, equals how many Jewish lives on the first of every month? On the fifteenth of every month?

No, Joe, I don't know anything about these grim workmanlike orgies staged by the bookkeepers of the world, these despicable desecrations of the soul which alone seem capable of titillating the barbarians of our age, and worse, which seem to make up life in its entirety for them. This numbing banality of theirs which can delight only in a romance of the ledger and a romance of the rulebook, where abstract numbers can pile up with Germanic thoroughness, with that well-known Germanic attention to detail, with an implacable and industrious Germanic concern for categories, and for the corpses of categories . . . the mind's carrion, these things that are often called theories of history.

No no, Joe, I can't tell you anything about that. Stern and I have never talked about things like that. All I know is that he went to Poland to do something important, and he did it, and the outcome for him and for me is decided. But as for these details you seek, you'll have to go elsewhere for them. I'm not a bookkeeper who can measure human souls by using numbers, nor am I a political philosopher who can cleverly pretend to theorize into existence yet another new and nonexistent superman, or Sovietman, while logically explaining away mass murder, by the by. Stern can hold his own with these monsters of abstract theories, but I can't. There's a world I see and feel and know, but it's not that one. Stern and I, we've always opposed the barbarians in very different ways. He in many, but I in only one . . . in my soul. In *my* soul. You see, Stern is truly *more* than I am. I've never been but one man, whereas Stern has always been many men.

Joe listened. He nodded. It was useless, he knew, to try to draw from the old poet what wasn't there. Ahmad's knowledge was immense, but it was mostly self-knowledge and there were dimensions to Stern that simply didn't include him.

Well I understand now, said Joe, why these nights of ours have come about. And I want you to know how much it means to me that you've shared Stern here, your feelings for him, your love. But still, I . . .

Ahmad interrupted.

Yes, and I know what you're thinking now. Why is it, you wonder, that what Stern did in Poland decides my end as well as his own? That's what you want to ask, Joe, isn't it? . . . And what can I say that might satisfy you, or less, that might enlighten you just a little? Even the way I failed Stern, perhaps even that you find hard to comprehend. Because we *are* still brothers, Stern and I. That moment several years ago when we looked up from his thumb and our eyes met and we both knew our fate, that was *after* I'd shouted him down, wasn't it? In other words, even after our irreparable rupture, we were and are still brothers.

But you see, Joe, I failed him because I *feel* I failed him. It doesn't matter what anyone else thinks, it doesn't even matter what *he* thinks. What we feel is always true for us, it's real for us and genuine, *it exists*, and that's *our* universe.

I was always alone in the world, Joe. My father died when I was young and I never knew my mother, and there were no brothers and sisters, but then all at once there was *Cohen and Ahmad and Stern*, here in these byways that are my life. And the same music was in our veins and we were inseparable, and I was of them and every act and feeling of mine had a resonance in them, as did theirs in me. And

196

then Cohen was killed and Stern went away, yet still .

Ahmad tipped his head, listening to the night. Gently, he smiled.

Joe? I'm a *failed* poet finally, and I'm afraid I can't explain this any better than I have. But perhaps I could add one thought that might provide a glimmer of what I feel about Stern. . . . I've spoken of the hope Stern has always given me, just by being out there somewhere and being himself, just by being. And I *need* that hope because it's always been a special unspoken part of my life, an intimation of the richness in man, in all human beings. And when that hope goes, life will go . . . for me.

So what *is* Stern's Polish story, you ask? Well I can only answer for myself, and for me the answer is simply this. Three summers ago when the war was about to begin, Stern took his life in his hands in a Damascus prison and he weighed what he found there, in his hands, and immediately he broke out of that prison and went to Poland. And in Poland he acted as he felt he had to act, as was only right for him to act, given the human being *he* is. Yet given who *I* am, and the way I feel about him and the way I feel we've been connected through the years . . . well he was also acting for me, as it turned out. And doing so, almost certainly, with never a thought for me. After all, Stern is important in this world. So important, very few people will ever know.

But Joe? I'm *proud* of what he did, whatever it was. I'm *proud* he acted for me. On my own I never could have amounted to much in life. I dreamed of giving beauty to others but that was not to be. So I failed in what I wanted to do, and there's a cave not far away whose dusty contents will testify to the multitude of any man's lost dreams and lost adventures.

But wait, *listen.* Even here in the darkness, even here amidst the chaos of an unspeakable war, even now God's hand may be restlessly moving within me and touching my soul. For just by *knowing* Stern and being a part of him, haven't I then also taken part in giving beauty to many many lives through him, through what he is? Might not that also be so? And if perhaps it is, then who can say? . . .

Slowly, Ahmad nodded. He smiled, his face at peace, and gazed around the little courtyard.

A thumb . . . and a moment. So small, our world, and yet so vast. From the cave we know all too well to this mysterious sky we dream under. And Stern? . . . And myself? Well to be completely honest, I have no idea whether Stern feels his life has been justified by what he has done. He alone can decide that. But listen to me now, Joe, and *feel* the wondrous sweep of our majestic universe with its apparent contradictions.

For in the single moment I've spoken of, a single moment in time which is also my life, Stern *has justified* my existence, for *me.* . . . And *that*, that is truly the gift of gifts. For without it, we recede into dust. But with it, we take our place as dreaming creatures in the grandest of all schemes, and become one with the poetry of the universe.

Later that same night Ahmad turned to study the sky to the east. Not a hint of the grayness of dawn had appeared above the courtyard wall, but they both knew it couldn't be long in coming now. Then too, Ahmad must have realized that his journey into the past with Joe was nearing its end, probably with that very sunrise.

For me, said Ahmad, this hour always brings Stern to mind, but not for the reasons you may think. I know this is the hour when he turns to morphine . . . sadly. But that affliction is a burden of only the last decade or so, and I remind myself of all he has suffered, and I also recall the many other sides to Stern and how he has always been there in some obscure corner within me, whispering to me in his soft voice, or simply listening and forgiving me in his kindly way.

I have so many images of the man from over the years. From the boulevards and the cafés, from the riotous nights when he and I and Cohen drank and swaggered and raved away the hours, dreaming our way into eternity. Yet there will always be one image of Stern I cherish above all others. A startling image from long ago that speaks of man in the universe, a vision forever stunning in the simplicity of its mystery.

It's a memory of Stern as a young man going out into the desert in times of great sadness or joy, and playing his violin in the eye of the Sphinx in the last darkness before dawn, alone and soaring with his strong somber music, those awesome flights of tragedy and yearning that can only come from a human soul.

198

Stern's haunting canticle in the wilderness for the lost sunken moon . . . his only companions the unknowable Sphinx and the fleeing stars.

And there was still a solemn rite Ahmad kept to, in memory of all the fabled dreams of his youth.

Every Saturday toward the end of the afternoon he would excuse himself, going first to take a bath and then emerging toward sundown in a mended shirt and the one old suit he owned, both newly pressed and shiny, a spotted tie around his neck and his one pair of dilapidated shoes newly smudged with polish, his dyed red hair slicked down with water and his battered flat straw hat cocked at some odd angle, his spyglass in one hand and his dented old trombone in the other, a genteel spectacle of quiet dignity, a gentleman without means.

Slowly then, because it was difficult for him, he would labor up the stairs to the roof of the hotel, there to sit for hours in the soft evening breezes, peering at the city through his spyglass and playing his trombone in the darkness. He claimed he could see the little crowded squares where he had passed the evenings of his youth. He even claimed he could make out the cafés where he had once held forth with such success, amusing his friends far into the night with heroic couplets and sudden bursts of song from his favorite arias.

So Ahmad claimed, alone now on the narrow roof of the rotting Hotel Babylon with the melancholy sounds of his trombone, above the twinkling lights of the great restless city.

And of course it made no difference, Joe knew, whether Ahmad could really make out those little cafés in the darkness or whether he only imagined he saw them, alive once more with laughter and surging with music and poetry, no end to the glasses of wine and friendship and above all no end to the wonders of love, the soft air of his great city echoing with those evenings of long ago when the whole world had seemed to stretch before him, as he said, and he was still young and strong and not yet ugly.

12

Beggar

Joe stood close to a building across the way, studying the little restaurant Liffy had told him about. There was nothing unusual about it but he stood there staring anyway, fascinated.

It was a small quiet neighborhood tucked away behind busier streets. A moment ago he had been pushing through the crowds of shouting men in cloaks and turbans, the honking taxis and the sheep and camels and rickety lorries and Greek merchants and Coptic traders, goats gathered at crossings and Albanian planters and drunken Anzac soldiers, Italian bankers and Indian soldiers and Armenians and Turks and Jews, carts selling juice and carts selling nuts and carts selling fruits, barefoot laborers bent under huge heavy sacks and everywhere the poor wandering aimlessly, chanting the names of gods and saviors and the makings of an imaginary evening meal.

And then all at once he had turned a corner and here he was in a quiet little neighborhood where everyday people lived, the war far away. Seemingly so.

There wasn't much to see. A woman carrying vegetables home. An old woman shaking her head and muttering, a little group of women talking. Men reading newspapers at the tables of a tiny café. A small square and narrow cobblestone lanes, a water pipe where children filled bottles. Patches of shade and flowers, gray clothing hung up to dry. Little balconies and open stairways and half-open shutters, odd sounds clicking together. A beggar sitting alone in the dust.

Joe passed in front of the small restaurant, the kind of place where most of the customers were probably known by name, men with meager incomes who either lived alone or had no one at home to cook for them.

He peeked in. Some customers for the evening meal had already arrived, shabby dignified men who were lingering over each dish, trying to wait until they had finished their soup before they unfolded their newspapers out of boredom, loneliness. A small man in a gray suit was making a show of greeting a waiter as he removed his red fez and went through an evening ritual of pretending to select a table, probably the same table he had been going to for the last twenty years.

As Joe moved off into the shadows, he found himself wondering whether this was the kind of place where he would have expected Maud and Stern to come at the end of the day, to share a simple dinner and a carafe of wine. Later to move across the square to the little café to have a sweet, because Maud liked sweets after dinner. To sit together at one of those tiny tables and sip coffee and talk, and also just to be alone together under the stars.

And no, he wasn't surprised. It was the ordinary feeling of the little square that struck him, that and the blessed quiet which seemed so rare in Cairo. He could understand how it would appeal to them.

People coming and going and doing their commonplace things, far from the war. Lentils and barley and cigarettes, a glass of wine, little cups of sugary coffee. A man selling used clothes. Children laughing. Women sprinkling handfuls of water on the cobblestones to lay the dust at the end of the day. A hum of distant cries. A solitary beggar with downcast eyes.

No, it wasn't much of anywhere really, and none of it surprised him. The peculiar thing about Stern, after all, was that he appeared to be such an ordinary man in so many ways. The flamboyant figure who lived in Ahmad's imagination had long since disappeared with the years, and Joe knew that if he were to see Stern here on this street for the first time he would probably not even have noticed him. For Stern would have looked like anyone else in the little restaurant, the same as the man reaching up to take down his small inventory of secondhand suits, the same as the man making change in the little café or the clerk turning down an alley, the same as any of these people who were simply making a life, no more.

Making a life.

Stern's words, Joe realized. Stern's words spoken long ago in Jerusalem, in answer to Joe's eager questions about what Stern was really doing beneath it all. Words from another time and place altogether, spoken when Joe had been newly arrived in Jerusalem and groping to find his way in the world, and Stern had already been a man with years of hard experience behind him.

Of course, that wasn't all of it. The man who appeared in Bletchley's files, and in many files under other names, was also vastly different from anyone on this street. With the quiet lives these men and women lived, they couldn't have conceived of where Stern went and what he did. Yet in another way this quiet street was all of it, for Stern had the same fears and hopes as these people. He wanted things to be better and he tried hard to make them better. He had his small successes and his greater failures and one day when he was gone, nothing would have changed particularly. And in the meantime Stern came to this little restaurant to escape the noise and the crowds at the end of the day, to meet an old friend and talk about everything and nothing and silently share the minutes, at peace for a moment.

And Maudie?

No, it didn't surprise him to imagine her here either. Her life had also been unusual in so many ways, yet in other ways it wasn't at all. For surely she'd never wanted anything more than to be herself, to care and to live life fully.

Modest, like these people. Doing the best she could to make some sense out of the terrible mistakes of the past. So often a stranger again in the endless slippage of lives, the conflicting journeys of hope and need where people met and parted. Trying to face the wounding demons of the past, not escape them, because the past never went away. But trying to know herself well enough so those demons could no longer torment her. Struggling to stand alone and yet also to love—in the end, the explanation for all her wanderings. From the coal fields of a little town in Pennsylvania to the mountains of Albania, and Athens and Jerusalem and Smyrna, and Istanbul and Crete, and now here. A lifetime of searching, trying to find her place.

Joe gazed down the narrow little street. He looked up at the fading light and somehow everything seemed right. After all these years this was the kind of place where Maud and Stern would meet for a quiet evening together, here in this ordinary little neighborhood with its modest concerns, its small failures and triumphs. After all these years of struggle and pain and love, of losing and trying again, this was exactly where two people would come to celebrate life in the midst of a terrible war. To talk and sit silently, to smile and laugh and share for a moment those dreams that could never be wholly lost or forgotten, coming together in this simple place as the world raged and died just a little bit more beyond the corner . . . beyond the solitary beggar who sat at the end of the street in the dust, alone in the twilight, unmoving.

A beggar of no particular era, homeless and stateless and of no use to anyone, a beggar of life from nowhere who would one day return whence he had come. And yet also, strangely, the man for whom the war was being fought, the prize for all the great armies, the solitary man who would survive their terrible victories and their legions of victims.

Anonymous in his rags in the dust at twilight, a beggar surveying his limitless kingdom. . . .

Joe hovered off to the side, out of the way, waiting for her to come as Liffy had said she would. And then all at once she was there down the street, a small woman moving quickly in the way he remembered so well. That hadn't changed at all.

She stopped to greet a shopkeeper, her face lighting up, and that hadn't changed either. There was the same eagerness in her smile, the same concern as she tipped her head and made the shopkeeper laugh, some little thing said in passing.

Joe smiled too, he couldn't help it. When he had known her before, she had made an effort to take clothes seriously, even though somehow it had never seemed to work. But now apparently she had just given up on it. Yet she was beautiful, Joe couldn't believe how beautiful she had become with the years. Such a strong face and her eyes so expressive, so direct and smiling.

She was going into the restaurant and Joe turned away, excited and confused, frightened. Twenty years, it had been, and where had the time gone since they'd been together? She seemed a stranger now and yet she could never be that, they knew each other too well. They had a son who had been born in Jericho. They had met in Jerusalem and gone to the Sinai, to an oasis on the shores of the Gulf of Aqaba. Two decades ago and less than a year together . . . but still.

He wanted to walk up behind her and whisper her name, and see her smile and look into his eyes.

Maudie, it's me. . . . Maudie.

Instead he turned away, he had to. How could he explain what he was doing here? What could he say about Stern? No, he didn't know enough about Stern yet. He didn't know enough about any of it yet.

Joe moved quickly up the street, excited and afraid, confused. She seemed a stranger but she couldn't be that. He knew her, of course he did, and she knew him.

The beggar on the corner held out his hand as Joe rushed by, a long slender hand, calloused and hard and beautiful, as mysterious as an ancient map of some lost desert. Joe glanced at the beggar's shadowy face and gave him a coin and kept moving, his thoughts tumbling, racing. He had gone several blocks before he suddenly stopped in the midst of the swirling crowds, stopped dead still, alone and hearing nothing in the warm night air.

The beggar.

It was impossible. The beggar at the end of that quiet street had been Stern.

Stern? . . .

Joe had no idea how long he stood there in the middle of the crowded sidewalk, oblivious to everything around him. He turned.

No, there was no point in trying to go back, Stern would be gone by now. But what was he doing there? Why was he watching over Maud? And why was he back in Cairo when Bletchley had said he would be away for two weeks?

Bletchley?

No. Joe was sure he couldn't have been lying about Stern having gone away. Nothing would make any sense if he had been. So Stern must have returned to Cairo without Bletchley's knowledge, against

Bletchley's orders, and in fact Joe was beginning to think Stern could go almost anywhere without anyone knowing it. He was like Liffy with his disguises, only more so. With Liffy the disguises were always part of a role, but with Stern they were simply another part of him, another face on the turnings of his path.

And now Stern knew Joe was in Cairo, which meant he had to know why someone like Joe had been brought in, and that made everything backward because Joe himself didn't know why he was here, not really. How could he when he didn't know what Stern was doing, let alone why he was doing it? . . . Unless Ahmad had been hinting at something real when he spoke of Stern bartering away his soul to the Nazis. Unless there had been more in that than one of Ahmad's dramatic turns of speech. . . .

Joe drifted along through the crowds, feeling more lost by the moment. Everything was moving too quickly and he had to break out of these networks of the past which seemed to obscure Stern ever more deeply in the feelings of others. . . .

Talk to Bletchley then? Put it to Bletchley outright?

No, that was too dangerous. He didn't want to be the one who told Bletchley that Stern was back in Cairo. Not the way things were, the reasons for Stern's return unknown.

Talk to Liffy?

Yes, and for other reasons as well. Since becoming so deeply involved with Ahmad, Joe had begun to have an uneasy feeling that Liffy might not be telling him everything he knew about Stern, that he might be holding something back because he cared so much for Stern, an effect Stern often had on people. Instinctively they wanted to protect him, to safeguard that fragile essence Stern carried within him, perhaps for everyone. Joe himself had always felt that way and there was no reason why Liffy shouldn't, but the sooner he talked to Liffy the better.

Joe stopped at a public telephone, keeping his eye on the young Egyptian across the way who was following him on Bletchley's orders. It didn't bother him that Bletchley would know he had gone to the restaurant where Stern and Maud often met, or that he had waited there to catch a glimpse of Maud. Bletchley would have been expecting him to do something like that by now. Nor was he concerned about his behavior since then, for it could only tell Bletchley that seeing Maud had confused him.

He dialed Liffy's number and let the phone ring once before breaking the connection. He made a show of continuing to dial numbers, reaching Liffy's phone again and letting it ring twice before hanging up. So there was nothing to do now but wait and see if Liffy turned up in an hour where he was supposed to.

Nothing but one minor matter. Joe spent some time eluding the young Egyptian, and when he was sure he was no longer being followed he headed in the direction of the bar where he hoped Liffy would be waiting. It was down by the river and he hadn't been there before, but it was supposed to be a safe place where Europeans seldom went.

Strictly a refuge for the lowest of lowlifes, Liffy had said.

One of those downstairs dives, Joe, where the dregs of riverfront society and other serious alcoholics fade away in the shadows a little bit more every night. But also the kind of cave where a spirited actor who never succeeded, and an ex-shaman from an obscure American Indian tribe, could comfortably mutter together in sign language while blowing coded smoke signals in the air, without anyone noticing a thing. Certainly no self-respecting member of any superior race would ever show his face there, so it's our kind of place, Joe. A club that will have us without examining our forged credentials, a home of sorts for those who haven't been home since the Babylonians took Jerusalem, say about 586 B.C.? . . .

Joe smiled to himself as he moved along in the evening crowds. What in the world are all these people doing? he thought. Don't they have any idea there's a war on? . . . And so the evening had begun in an ordinary quiet neighborhood and Joe almost laughed out loud, thinking of Stern back there. A kind of relief, he knew, from the tensions building up inside him. But it was stunning all the same. . . . Stern dressed as a beggar? Sitting in rags in the dust at twilight at the end of a cobblestone lane?

A wonder, he thought, *that* beggar hasn't changed. He probably decided the moment he saw me to try to get a coin. He'd like that, Stern would, just the sort of thing that would give him a quiet chuckle. I'll have to ask him about it sometime.

But the giddy mood didn't last. Almost at once he felt the muscles in his stomach tighten.

Fear, he thought. Out-and-out fear and why not, this whole thing scares me to death. Nothing's looking easy now, just the opposite and getting worse.

Codes, he thought. Ahmad keeps saying Stern has codes on his mind. Well Stern must know his codes all right after all these years, especially these codes we call people and how to unlock their meanings, because that's what Stern's always been . . . a master cryptologist, a master decipherer of the human soul. Only maybe even more so now as the stakes climb higher. So we'll just have to find out why Stern was a beggar in the dust tonight, surveying his limitless kingdom, ah yes. . . .

Liffy was in the bar, standing at the counter. He smiled as Joe walked up.

Good evening, Mr Gulbenkian, Liffy called out, using the name that was on the false passport Bletchley had given Joe, part of his strange cover as a naturalized Lebanese citizen of Armenian extraction, a dealer in Coptic artifacts, *in transit.*

And a *very* good evening to you, said Liffy again, and welcome to the world of the underclasses. How fares the pursuit of Coptic artifacts on this fair night?

Let's go outside for a walk, said Joe.

They left the bar and moved away from the crowds, finding their way down the paths of a public garden beside the Nile.

Disaster? whispered Liffy uneasily, staring straight ahead.

Not that bad yet, replied Joe. It's not vodka time. Crisis only.

What happened?

Stern's back in Cairo. I saw him near the restaurant where he and Maud go. I didn't have a chance to talk to him because I didn't realize it was him until too late. He was disguised as a beggar. But Bletchley said Stern was going to be away for two weeks and now he's back without Bletchley knowing it, against Bletchley's orders. Why? Everything's moving fast and all of a sudden I don't have a couple of weeks to pick up the signals, nothing like it. I don't know enough yet to go to the Sisters, but I may have to try to see them soon anyway. I wanted to talk with you about it.

In answer, Liffy merely nodded. He was staring straight ahead as they moved along, withdrawn in a way that wasn't like him. A thought struck Joe.

It doesn't seem to be news to you, Liffy. Did you already know Stern was back in Cairo?

Liffy said nothing. For some moments they walked in silence.

I didn't know it for a fact, whispered Liffy at last.

Oh God, thought Joe. . . . Listen, he said quietly, I don't have to tell you Bletchley's been holding out on me from the very beginning, and now Bletchley's got to find out pretty soon that Stern isn't where he's supposed to be, and that's going to start all kinds of trouble. It makes things seem hopeless all of a sudden, because there's no time anymore and I'm nowhere and I can't help Stern this way. So if you can tell me anything. . . .

Liffy groaned. He turned.

Oh look, Joe, I feel very close to you and I feel very close to Stern, but this just isn't my kind of work. I don't really understand any of it and I don't really want to. I'm only a prop here, I told you that.

I know you did. And I respect the fact that you don't want to get pulled into Stern's affairs, and mine.

Only because I'd make a mess of it for both of you, said Liffy, because I know I'm no good at this sort of thing. You'd think I would be after all the time I've spent with disguises and playacting, but that's just it. What the Monks and the Waterboys do just isn't real to me and I can't take it seriously. Playing at it or laughing about it is fine, but no matter how hard I try I can't really convince myself that any of it makes any sense. Maybe that's because so much of the time I'm wearing some ridiculous costume in some ridiculous role. It's strange, but to me it's like being with Cynthia.

In what way, Liffy?

Well, you know when I go to see her she likes me to pretend this or that, because she thinks it's romantic, and I don't mind because it's still a game in the end, and I know that and so does she.

And this isn't? Is that it?

Well that's the point. This *is* a game to me but it doesn't seem to be to other people. Other people seem to take it seriously. To me, Cynthia is real. When we're holding each other late at night, *that's* real. But not the red cloak I might be twirling around in front of her earlier in the evening. That was just fun, nothing, a game.

I know, said Joe. I feel the same way.

You do?

Of course, Liffy. Nothing in this world is ever as real as a woman you hold in your arms. That's as close as we ever come to the truth of being alive, *knowing* it and not just thinking about it, which is always a second-rate activity.

But how can you manage it then? Doing this?

I can't very well, said Joe. And I know I can't and that's why I gave it up a long time ago. But I came here because I believe in Stern, and someone has to find out the truth about him for his sake, so he won't die thinking it's all been for nothing. Someone has to bear witness now and it doesn't matter whether it's you or me or Maud or somebody else, but I do know it has to be now if it's going to be. *Now,* God help us.

They were sitting on the bank of the river, gazing at the reflections of light on the water. Liffy was trembling, and when he spoke his voice was so weak Joe could hardly hear him.

. . . someone implied, yesterday, that Stern had just returned to Cairo . . . someone who trusts me, who would never imagine I'd say anything about it to anyone.

This man's involved with clandestine work?

Yes, whispered Liffy, but not the way we are, not with ours. At least that's what I think, I'm not really sure of anything.

This man knows what you do? Whom you work for?

Yes.

He knows Stern well?

Yes. That's how I met him originally. Through Stern.

Why does he believe you wouldn't say anything?

Liffy looked at Joe.

Because I'm a Jew and he knows me. Does that surprise you?

No, I thought it was probably that. He works for the Jewish Agency then?

Liffy made a nervous gesture with his hand, as if brushing something away from his face.

I don't think that's supposed to be known. I'm sure it's not.

Joe nodded.

Do you know which section he reports to? Is it the political section?

Some part of it, I imagine. Would Stern be involved with that?

It's likely, said Joe.

Once more Liffy made the nervous gesture, passing his hand over the side of his face.

Joe? I don't know what's right anymore, I have no idea what's right. . . . Oh why can't things be simple? Why can't they be the way they are on the war posters? *This is the job, let's get the job done.* Why can't life be like that? . . . Oh I just don't know what to do. Can't you tell me there's this and there's that, so I can choose and try to do what's right?

Sadly, Joe shook his head.

I wish I could, Liffy, but you know as well as I do that nobody can do that for us, not when the stakes are so important. Our decisions are always our own, and it begins and ends there. The clamor of the world just goes on and won't let up and still we have to find ourselves in it and find our name in the book of life, as impossible as that is, and nobody can do it for us and if we don't do it it's as if our name had never been there, as if we'd never existed at all. And meanwhile the clamor goes right on all around us and it always says the same thing, that nothing matters, so why decide anything? Stern, me, you . . . what difference does it make? How can one person ever matter? . . . But you know that's not true, Liffy. You know the two of us, right here, now, are the whole world. There's nobody here but us and that's the way it is and we're *all of it.* . . . But I don't have to tell you that. You know it better than I do.

Silence again between the two of them. Another long moment of silence as Liffy's mouth worked and he stared down at the river.

The man's name is Cohen, whispered Liffy. You could try to see him tonight. He's quite young. I'll tell you what I can about him.

And then Liffy turned and gripped Joe's arm, the anguish in his face so moving Joe would never forget it. Long after the two of them had parted for the last time that image of Liffy would still be with him, a reminder of a moment on the shores of the Nile, a memory of a terrible war and many things.

Joe? . . . O God have mercy.

Yes Liffy, I know, and truly I wish I didn't have to find out anything at all about Cohen and what he does, and I pray it will turn out all right for him and for all of us.

Liffy shook his head. His hands fell away. There were tears in his eyes.

But it won't be all right, it can't be. We're in too deeply now and I don't mean just Stern and you and me, or Cohen or Ahmad or any of the others. There are too many little spots of light on this vast river suddenly, too many reflections of the stars broken by these immense currents of time at our feet. Too many little sounds in the world that will be lost in the whirlwind forever, too many little echoes that will be removed from the book of life. This time it's not just Stern who won't survive. . . . Many of us won't, and many things.

I know it, he whispered, burying his face in his hands.

Joe said nothing. He put his arms around Liffy and held on to the flesh and bone with all his strength as Liffy wept in the shadows.

PART THREE

13

Cohen

It was a dark cobblestone lane with tiny shops squeezed one next to the other, the narrow alley barely lit by weak lights casting a feeble glow. The upper stories of the buildings overhung the alley to provide shade during the day, but at night they obscured the sky and closed in the alley, giving it the oppressive appearance of a tunnel.

The alley was deserted at that late hour, the storefronts dark. Most of the shops in the little quarter dealt in antique coins and semiprecious gems and various artifacts from antiquity. Here and there a thin line of yellow light showed between the locked shutters overhead, shining dimly from the bedrooms that fronted on the alley.

Joe picked his way carefully over the uneven cobblestones. It was an eerie feeling moving through the darkness there, knowing so many people were nearby and hearing the sounds they made, yet without a visible sign of life anywhere.

A pot striking stone. A muffled voice. A bolt sliding into place.

And his own footsteps surprisingly loud in the narrow alley and echoing in the darkness. A hundred eyes could have been watching him and there was no way he could ever have known it. But then all at once he was standing in front of a narrow shop with an old wooden sign overhead in the shape of a giant pair of eyeglasses, the gold lettering chipped and faded.

COHEN'S OPTIKS

He leaned forward and peered into the small shopwindow where a long brass spyglass was suspended on invisible wires, a printed legend beneath it.

Lenses made to order.
Fine lenses for all purposes.

To the left was a thick wooden door, not the entrance to the shop but the separate entrance to the living quarters upstairs. Joe raised the bronze hand of Fatima attached to the middle of the door and let it fall three times, causing echoes to boom up and down the alley. He intended to wait several minutes before knocking again, and he was already reaching out for the graceful bronze hand when he suddenly realized a little panel had been opened in the door in front of his eyes.

What is it? whispered a woman's voice in Arabic through the panel.

Joe couldn't see anyone in the darkness. He leaned forward.

I have to see Mr Cohen, he whispered in English.

Come to the shop tomorrow, whispered the woman, this time in English. It was a young woman's voice, he thought.

This concerns something else, he said. Please tell him Liffy sent me.

The panel closed silently, and in another moment the door opened just as silently. Bolt and lock and hinges all carefully greased, thought Joe. A thorough gent, as Liffy said, and this would be his younger sister.

He stepped inside and the door closed behind him. Vaguely, in the darkness, he could make out the upper half of a face.

Wearing a scarf? he wondered. Been out and only just returned?

I don't know anyone named Liffy, whispered the young woman. Who are you and what do you want?

I have some special business with your brother, Miss Cohen. The name's Gulbenkian. I'm soliciting charitable contributions on behalf of Armenian refugees from the massacres in Asia Minor.

You're twenty years too late then, whispered the young woman.

And that's exactly what I would have said until an hour or two ago, whispered Joe, when Liffy told me otherwise. That slaughter is already a couple of decades gone in the past, I was saying to Liffy, and the world has moved on to bigger and more impressive slaughters, so how can your friend Mr Cohen or anyone else be expected to remember the Armenians today? But Liffy smiled and shrugged, you know how he does, and he said your brother's concern for refugees has a way of transcending time, so to speak. He said your brother has a long memory when it comes to just causes, like all the Cairo Cohens. So please, Miss Cohen, if you could just tell him Liffy sent me I'm sure he'd agree that Liffy's not one to be sending idle visitors around to call at this dark hour of the night, not unless it was important.

I told you, we don't know anyone named Liffy.

That's what I mean. If you don't even know him, his visitors aren't likely to be idle. Of course I could also go rushing ahead and say I'm an old friend of Stern's, but that would be getting down to business straight off and I'm told that's not the way to go about things in the Levant. So now. I'll just stand here and wait in the dark until you have a word with him, if you don't mind.

He could hear her breathing. He was also beginning to be able to see her. She was a tall young woman who stood very straight, her hair falling down from beneath her scarf. She looked as if she had just returned from somewhere.

It's quite all right, he added, it's what I've been doing for most of my life. Waiting in the dark, I mean, for some kind of answer to come to me. Once I even spent seven years in a desert in Arizona, a good half of it in darkness, thinking about Stern and the many sides to the man. Amazing when you get into it, how many sides he does have. Do you mind if I smoke while I'm waiting?

Joe took out a cigarette and struck a match so she would be able to see his face. He was careful not to glance at her. She hesitated only a moment.

Good, he thought. Take the look you're given and come down on one side or the other. Has to be that way when you work alone.

I'll just be a moment, she said.

And I appreciate it.

He blew out the match.

The two of them sat in a back room on the ground floor, in the small workshop where fine lenses were ground for all purposes, as the sign out front said.

Cohen was tall and lean and angular, a generation younger than Stern. A dark lock of hair slipped over his forehead and he pushed it back. There was an unmistakable air of elegance about him, even when he was in shirtsleeves and worn slippers, surrounded by the buffers and trays and grinding wheels of his profession. Part of it was the graceful way he held himself, especially the way he moved his hands. He himself was so handsome women would have probably said he was beautiful.

Cohen smiled pleasantly, touching a long thin forefinger to his brow. Now that, thought Joe, would be devastating to the young ladies in the cafés, if he ever had time for cafés.

Well well, said Cohen. Here we are past midnight and at last I have a chance to meet a man called Gulbenkian. My sister tells me you're the new chief of the British Secret Service in the Middle East, or of Section A.M. for Asia Minor or After Midnight or whatever it is. Who can possibly stay current with all the vague intelligence units that keep popping up in this part of the world? I certainly can't. As your friend Liffy says, it seems to be a case of distorted images and refractions receding into infinity. All very mysterious and incomprehensible, according to Liffy.

How's that, Mr Cohen? I don't believe Liffy has slipped that one by me yet.

No? Well he was referring to the glare of the sun on the desert. It produces a multitude of little worlds, he says, which are all separate. Reflections, he calls them. But which world might yours be, and what might that have to do with me?

Well if the truth be known, said Joe, I came to discuss a magnifying glass your great-grandfather made in the nineteenth century.

Cohen laughed, relieved.

Is that all?

Yes. Only that, just imagine. But you see it was a very powerful magnifying glass, so powerful it has a way of letting us look right down through the years, from way back then when it was made, right up until the present. So powerful it can tell us who you are and who I am and why we're sitting here consulting together late on a clear Cairo night.

I wasn't aware we were consulting.

Oh yes, said Joe, no question about it. Now this magnifying glass I'm talking about is so powerful, mind you, that when a man puts it to his eye, his eye becomes a good two inches wide behind it, which is an eye so big it probably sees a good deal. Now your great-grandfather, who founded Cohen's Optiks right here where we sit, made this glass for a friend of his, an English botanist who happened to be skulking around these parts in the nineteenth century, one Strongbow by name. All right so far?

Cohen smiled.

Yes.

Good. And this man Strongbow wasn't an everyday fellow by any means, no more than was his friend Cohen, but one at a time. Strongbow started out as a botanist all right, but before long his wanderings got the best of him and he became an explorer, exploring just about everything in this part of the world and using his powerful magnifying glass to get a better look at the sights along the way. Then after doing that for about forty years he decided it was time for a change and he became an Arab holy man, whereupon he gave away his worldly goods as holy men tend to do, having no use for them on the paths they travel. And since his magnifying glass had always been so precious to him, he decided to pass it along to another of his dearest friends, who was also a great friend of your great-grandfather, a black Egyptologist by the name of Menelik Ziwar. Still all right?

Yes.

Fine. Now this Ziwar person was able to put the powerful glass to good use, using it to decipher the ancient mutterings in stone that he was always examining underground, hieroglyphs as they're called. And he did so until he died and the magnifying glass was laid to rest on his chest, in the sarcophagus where this Ziwar intended to pass the ages in a crypt beneath a public garden beside the Nile, right here in Cairo. This Ziwar you see, this old Menelik, was accustomed to talking to mummies as a result of his lifelong profession, but since his eyesight had been failing in his later years he thought it advisable to make his eternal voyage with a magnifying glass firmly in hand, the better to peer down through eternity without missing the details. So that's what he did and that's what lies on his chest today, that excellent and stirring device given to him long ago by his old friend

Strongbow, which had originally been devised by another great friend to the both of them, a superior craftsman by the name of Cohen. . . . Your great-grandfather.

Cohen smiled and touched the corner of his mouth. Right, thought Joe, devastating to the ladies if only he had time for them.

Excellent and stirring? asked Cohen. Isn't that a peculiar way to describe a magnifying glass?

It is, said Joe. But this magnifying glass was excellent because your great-grandfather, its first owner, had made it that way. And then it was stirring on top of that because its second owner, this botanist turned explorer turned Arab holy man, Strongbow, and its third owner, this black former slave turned archeologist, Menelik Ziwar, because all three of these great friends had an uncommon way of stirring up time to savor a new result of their own making, which was an Irish stew of history so to speak, although none of them was Irish.

But you're Irish, aren't you, Mr Gulbenkian?

That's right, and more so on some occasions than others. The weather seems to affect it, like an old wound. When it gets very dark out you begin to feel this stiffness at the base of your skull, and pretty soon it sneaks up toward your eyes, a sort of creeping paralysis of the mind, and drink seems to be the only way to waylay it.

Would you like a drink? asked Cohen.

Don't mind if I do, now that you mention it.

Cohen reached into a cupboard and brought out a bottle and a glass.

Is arak all right?

Thanks. Just by itself is fine.

Cohen poured and placed the bottle on a table beside Joe.

An Irish Gulbenkian, murmured Cohen. That's remarkable.

Joe raised his eyebrows as he sipped, his face lighting up with a kind of hope.

Do you think so? Still, we're much better at wishing and dreaming for things than at having them happen. Like most people, I suppose.

Then you're not really soliciting charitable contributions for Armenian refugees from Asia Minor?

Well I'm doing that too in a way, over the long haul, but I admit tonight it was just a bit of amiable subterfuge meant to get me in the door. Cover, Liffy calls it. Secret agents are always using one kind of cover or another, according to him. Again, like most people. But you used the word *remarkable*, and that's true, that's what they were all right, all three of them. Strongbow, old Menelik, your great-grand-father Cohen. Just a remarkable triumvirate back when they were young, before they went their separate ways. Back when they were about your age, it must have been.

Joe sipped again, his face thoughtful.

In those days, he said, those three friends used to get together every Sunday afternoon in a cheap Arab restaurant they'd found for themselves on the shores of the Nile, a pleasant filthy place they'd taken a liking to, and there they'd feast and drink and carry on, telling each other all the things they were going to do in this world. And when the afternoon was coming to an end and they were as drunk as lords, over the restaurant railing they'd go, just leaping into the Nile to drift away on the great swirling currents with contented smiles on their faces, enjoying the last good rays of the sun and belching and bubbling and snoozing ever so happily, just effortlessly pissing away their troubles so to speak, lords of the noble Nile for a moment in their youths. . . .

Cohen's long thin hands drew graceful shapes in the air. He smiled and shook his head.

I'm sorry but you must be mistaken, he said. You must have three other men in mind, because I know for a fact my great-grandfather always dined at home on Sunday. It was a family tradition.

That's right, said Joe, he never did all of it. Cohen started out in the restaurant with his two friends, but already being a family man, he didn't spend the afternoon carousing there but went home to have Sunday dinner with his fine young wife and young son, as you say. Then when Sunday dinner was over he'd suggest a pleasant walk down by the river, and in the course of this pleasant stroll the family would pass a felluca tied up, ready for hire, and the son would beg for a little sail and Cohen would kindly agree, and the whole family would climb on board for a lovely cruise in the late afternoon.

Well it would just so happen that while they were out there sailing on the Nile, Cohen would spot a couple of belching bubbling bodies floating by on the great river, his good friends Strongbow and Ziwar dead drunk on the currents of time, and the felluca would take a turn or two and Cohen would pluck his friends out of the water and lay them out on the floorboards to sleep it off. And a good thing it was, too, for if Cohen hadn't done that then Strongbow and Ziwar might have gone right on floating down the Nile and out to sea and been lost to history forever, which would have been a loss for all of us. So that's how those Sundays worked and that was Cohen's Sunday role, an essential one, because without him those other two wouldn't have been around to see Monday. . . . . Your great-grandfather. A faithful friend.

He was a good family man, murmured Cohen.

Oh he was definitely that, said Joe, like all the men of the Cairo Cohens. And he was also on his pious way to becoming the patriarch of his clan as well as a hugely wealthy man, after first being viewed as crazy. For it seems he had two mysterious dreams one night, the first depicting seven fat cattle coming up out of the Nile and being eaten by seven lean cattle that followed them, and then right on top of that another dream, this time of seven full ears of corn being devoured by seven lean ears.

Cohen smiled, relaxing and enjoying himself.

Do I hear an echo from the Bible? he asked.

And so you do, replied Joe, and of course messages from God were often said twice in those days so nobody would get them wrong. Well knowing the good book as your great-grandfather did and the history of his people in Egypt and all, and being himself in Egypt, he didn't need a prophet to tell him what his two dreams were all about. So the very next morning this Cohen put aside the lenses of his trade and headed out into the fields of Egypt to buy grain. He'd decided to give up grinding glass, you see, in favor of grinding grain.

Cohen drew some shapes in the air, a quizzical expression coming over his face.

Right, continued Joe. And at the time there happened to be plenty of grain in Egypt, yet here was this Cohen going deeper and deeper into debt to buy up all he could and store it away in warehouses. And he went on doing that for seven years and naturally everybody in the country got into the habit of calling him *Crazy* Cohen, for who in his right mind would fill up more and more warehouses with grain when all the fields were heaped with it already?

Well obviously no one who's sane, that's who. Obviously only a *Crazy* Cohen, a ward of God who'd been snatching messages out of thin air, thinking he'd been chosen to hear them. But he carried on in his delusions, Crazy Cohen did, never forgetting for a moment his back-to-back dreams in sevens, and lo and behold and surprise of surprises, all at once there was a terrible turn to the harvests in Egypt that wouldn't let up, with the result that almost no grain grew in Egypt for another seven whole years. And during that second stretch of seven years, the lean stretch, all that stood between Egypt and starvation was Crazy Cohen and his demented pious foresight, and his warehouses.

Joe leaned back and smiled.

Chosen, it seems, he was. And thus by keeping the faith and keeping his mind on my namesake, he made a stupendous fortune. . . . A pious gambler. Your great-grandfather.

Cohen nodded thoughtfully.

Your name is Joseph?

More commonly, Joe. Also O'Sullivan Beare. But my coat isn't many-colored, as you can see.

Cohen nodded again.

Do you also have eleven brothers, Joe?

More, I'm afraid. Or at least I used to. Over the years a lot of them seem to have fallen off roofs in the New World, while drunk. Thought they were reaching for the stars, don't you know. Queer place, the New World. Some people actually believe it's that.

Cohen gazed at Joe and drew a circle in the air.

So history comes around, he said, and that much is history. But I don't see what any of it has to do with us.

Right, said Joe. History hiding its real intent behind a cover, like secret agents and most people. Now let's just recall those three young gents who were such close friends in the nineteenth century, said Strongbow and Ziwar and Cohen. Of the three of them, Ziwar was a Christian and Cohen was a Jew, and Strongbow, although born an Englishman, was on his way to becoming a Moslem holy man. So already, to those of a religious bent, we have something of a representative gathering for this part of the world.

Cohen laughed. Friendly fellow, thought Joe, and so far so good. He poured more arak for himself as Cohen gestured at the buffers and grinding wheels in the workshop.

Religion aside, do these tools speak of great wealth to you?

No they do not, said Joe. But there used to be a saying in Cairo, I'm told, which explains that. *A little madness is a dangerous thing. Remember the Cohens.* . . . Which saying was as accurate as can be, for what happened in Cairo in those days was that old Crazy Cohen's son, who was partly practical and only a little mad and therefore known as Half-Crazy Cohen, what happened was that Half-Crazy went on to spend the entire family fortune while in the company of a great friend of his named Ahmad and two beautiful young women known as the Sisters. Some of the fortune went to the racetracks and the casinos, and some of it for champagne to fill alabaster cups of pure moonlight when the four of them were out carousing on the Nile, so long ago. . . . Such madcap living by your grandfather in his youth, in other words, said Half-Crazy Cohen, that all the Cohen fortune got spent. So that later when your father came of age he had to find a trade to support himself, and what better trade to turn to than the one that got the Cohens started in Egypt in the first place? Lenses. Nothing grand about it but honest work all the same, so back your father came to this very house where your great-grandfather had started and resurrected a faded old sign in the shape of a pair of giant spectacles, a symbol of eyes that can see, the sign we find hanging out front tonight. . . . And that, I believe, is the tale of the Cairo Cohens over the course of four generations and more than a century, stated in its essentials. Rags to riches to rags it goes, and whoever said we all begin the same and end the same knew what he was talking about.

Cohen smiled, opening a silver cigarette case. He offered it to Joe, who took a cigarette and struck a match for both of them.

Are you also an itinerant Irish historian, Joe?

More so on some occasions than others, but it's really the present that interests me, so let's head that way and consider the time when your father was a young man in Cairo, before the First World War. Now at this point old Menelik Ziwar was living in retirement in a crypt beneath a public garden beside the Nile, using a gigantic cork-lined sarcophagus as his bedroom, where he was known to be *at home* on Sunday afternoons, as they used to say, meaning he was ready to welcome friends and serve them a bracing cup of underground tea. And since so few people had ever heard of old Menelik to begin with, we shouldn't be surprised to find that most of his guests were the children of former friends.

A suggestion of a frown flickered in Cohen's face, even though he was still smiling. Joe pretended not to notice it.

So for one, said Joe, there was the grandson of his old friend Crazy Cohen, your father. And there was the son of an old friend and fellow dragoman-in-arms named Ahmad, the son also Ahmad. Then there was the son of the great explorer Strongbow, the child born to the Jewish shepherdess Strongbow married late in life, young Stern. And of course the Sisters from their strange houseboat, older than the other guests and the only ones who had known Menelik in his prime, long-term residents on the Nile who never wanted to miss a good thing near the river and seldom did. And that was the inner circle gathered around old Menelik's cork-lined sarcophagus on Sunday afternoons back before the First World War. There were some others who dropped in now and then, but we don't have to concern ourselves with them tonight.

For the first time Cohen stopped smiling. But his composure was still remarkable and Joe admired him for it. Stern's influence, thought Joe. There's no mistaking it.

And after these friends had tipped away their tea, Joe went on, they would unpack their musical instruments and get ready for the weekly concert that was so dear to the heart of old Menelik. For as that wise living mummy used to say in his five-thousand-year-old tomb—I wouldn't dream of trying to pass eternity without the music of life. Eternity, old Menelik used to say, just doesn't work without music. Examine anyone's notion of the great beyond, even the vaguest, and you'll hear melodious strings soaring in the background, or at least a lute being plucked. . . . Thus the concerts those friends always put on for old Menelik when they came to call, Stern quite naturally the leader. Stern tuning his violin and using his old Morse-code key to tap on Menelik's sarcophagus and get everyone's attention, old Menelik himself ecstatic at the prospect, the music soaring as everyone joined in their separate moods. . . . Stern and Ahmad and your father and the Sisters. . . . Your father thoughtful as he played his oboe, that very oboe we now see resting in a place of honor in its case on the wall behind you.

Joe paused.

But your father never had a chance to teach you to play it, did he, David?

No, said Cohen. He never did.

Joe sipped arak. Cohen was still as calm as ever, so calm Joe was inevitably reminded of Stern. And in fact from the very moment he had entered the house Joe had felt Stern's invisible presence, which was heartening to him. It meant Stern was loved and cared for here and Joe was grateful for that. But he still had to make it possible for Cohen to trust him enough to talk about Stern, and that wouldn't be easy because Cohen would never say anything that might bring the least bit of harm to Stern. Joe was certain of that and it only increased his respect for Cohen.

Well, he thought, I've made what connections I can with the past and now there's nothing for it but to bring us up to the here and the now and pray he'll tell me some little thing. Pray is all.

Joe reached down for the cylindrical leather case he had brought with him. He unzipped the case and let it fall away, holding up Ahmad's spyglass and extending it to full length.

Cohen, puzzled, stared at the spyglass and then at Joe.

And now, said Joe, we come to another excellent and stirring device, also made here in Cohen's Optiks. Used for enlargement or its opposite, and also useful for just plain seeing things. . . . I hope.

Joe put the large end of the spyglass, the wrong end, to his eye. He gazed through it at Cohen.

It's true, he said, that the world looks exceptionally neat and tidy this way. Ever wondered why?

Why? asked Cohen.

Because small things always look tidy. That's why we try so hard to reduce things and put them in categories and give them labels, so we can pretend we know them and they won't bother us. Order, it's called, *the* explanation or *an* explanation, the reason for and the reason why. It's comforting to us, naturally it is, who wants to live with chaos all the time? . . . Well not much of anyone in fact, because it suggests we're not in charge and can't understand everything. So we have this little game we play, rather like children lining up their toys on a rainy afternoon and giving each toy a name, and then calling them by these made-up names and telling them what they are and why. . . . And sometimes we pretend we can do that with life, lining up people as it suits us and telling ourselves what they do and calling it history. Like children with their toys, making it more comfortable for ourselves by *pretending* we order the chaos when we hand out names.

Joe lowered the spyglass, collapsed it, put it back in its leather case.

Know what, David?

What?

Life isn't like that. It's just not like that at all and neither is Stern and what he does. A label just won't do for Stern. Ten or twenty contradictory adjectives might be accurate, but how much would that help us to place him?

Joe shook his head.

Not much at all. Because the truth is Stern's as complex and chaotic as life itself. And he's human and he's going to die.

Joe stared hard at Cohen. He smiled.

And yet *I* know there'll never be an end to him.

Joe looked down at the spyglass on the floor.

Good workmanship, that. Made by your father for his friend Ahmad. The same Ahmad who is now a forgotten desk clerk at a Biblical ruin called the Hotel Babylon.

Cohen stared down at the spyglass, confused, unsure of himself.

But why. . . ?

Why did your father make it for Ahmad, you mean? Because Ahmad was the very king of the boulevards in those days, and a king should have the wherewithal to survey his kingdom. So the spyglass was a joke at the time, but now Ahmad uses the spyglass when he goes up to the roof of the Hotel Babylon on Saturday evenings to look for his lost homeland, like the Jews of old. And he takes his trombone with him and he wears his only suit, a flower in his buttonhole and a smudge of polish on his shoes and his dyed red hair slicked down with water, and he peers through his precious spyglass and pretends he can see the great city where he once ruled as king, alone there in the night of his captivity, a desperately yearning and haunted captive of the past.

Cohen lowered his eyes. Joe spoke very softly.

Your father died in the First World War, I know that. He was in the British army. The campaign to take Palestine?

Yes, whispered Cohen.

A young man, then. About your age?

Yes. It was a freakish accident. The Turks had evacuated Jerusalem but a deserter was hiding in the hills and fired off a round. One shot and then he threw up his rifle and surrendered. An illiterate man, a peasant. He didn't know his army had already left the city.

Your father and Stern were the same age?

Yes.

And after that Stern saw to your upbringing, is that it?

Cohen raised his eyes and gazed at Joe.

Why do you say that?

Because that's the kind of thing Stern would do. It's Stern's way.

Cohen dropped his gaze. He spoke with great feeling.

If it hadn't been for him we wouldn't have been able to stay together. He supported my mother and made it possible for us to keep the shop, and then when my mother died he took care of Anna's and my education. . . . Just everything.

Cohen picked up the silver cigarette case.

This was my father's. He had it with him the day he was killed. Stern gave it to me when I was a child. I don't know how he ever recovered it.

Cohen held out the case to Joe. There was Hebrew lettering engraved in the corner.

It was a present from Stern to my father on the day he enlisted. Do you read Hebrew?

No, but I can read that. *Life,* or your father's first name. Or both.

Cohen took back the case. He looked at Joe uneasily.

Shouldn't you tell me why you're here?

Yes I should, said Joe, and I think I ought to start at the beginning, back when I was much younger than you are and didn't know the smallest part of what you know about the world. Back when Stern and I first met in a mythical city.

Cohen watched him. He smiled.

Where did you say you met Stern?

Joe nodded.

That's right, you heard it correctly. I met him in a mythical city.

Slowly then, Joe smiled too.

And now like a child with his toys, shall we give it a name? Shall we call it Jerusalem?

Joe spoke quickly. When he had finished he leaned back and sipped from his glass, giving Cohen time to absorb it all. Cohen sat with his elbows on a workbench, his chin propped up in his hands, deep in thought.

I like him, thought Joe, continually recognizing little things that reminded him of Stern. I like him and why not, he could almost be Stern's son.

Finally Cohen moved.

But why not get in touch with him? Speak to him directly?

Could you arrange that?

Yes. He was here yesterday but that was a personal call. There's a way I can leave a message for him though, and he'd contact me within twenty-four hours. Isn't that soon enough?

It might be, said Joe, but I'm not sure that's the way to go about it. You know how Stern is. If I spoke to him now he'd probably thank me for the information about Bletchley and then be up and on his way, not wanting to cause me any trouble. He'd keep his problems to himself unless I could show him I was already part of the game.

Well do you trust this man Bletchley? asked Cohen.

To do his job. And his job right now is Stern.

But you don't know what part of Stern's work he's interested in.

True enough, said Joe. All I really know is that Bletchley's deathly afraid of something Stern knows, or something he thinks Stern knows, same thing. Yet Stern's been working with Bletchley's people for years and why this suspicion about him all of a sudden? What triggered it?

Joe shrugged in answer to his own question.

No matter. There are any number of possibilities and an informer's just one of them, but that's neither here nor there now. Bletchley's made it clear he's not going to tell me why he has a case against Stern, and that's something Stern wouldn't tell me either. So I have to find it out myself, elsewhere, or I won't be able to help Stern because he wouldn't let me. He'd try to keep me out of it, and I didn't come here for that.

But what is Bletchley after? asked Cohen. Could it have anything to do with Stern's work for us?

Joe shook his head.

Not strictly speaking, not Palestine or the Jewish Agency directly. The British concern is the war and it has to be something to do with the Germans. Just for openers, let's begin with Stern's Polish story.

Cohen looked puzzled.

Do you mean the time he disappeared just before the war broke out?

Yes. I assume you know he escaped from a prison in Damascus in order to get to Poland when he did, but did you know that escape almost cost him his life?

No. I had no idea it had been that dangerous.

It was. Didn't you notice his thumb later, when he got back to Cairo? The way he'd ripped it up?

Yes of course, but that was an accident of some kind. He explained it to me but I don't recall exactly . . .

Not an accident, said Joe. He did that clawing his way out of prison, and the strange thing is he'd been due for release within twenty-four hours. But Stern just doesn't take chances without a reason. Did he ever talk to you about that trip to Poland? Why he had been in such a desperate hurry?

Cohen frowned.

All I really remember is that he was very excited.

Excited?

Yes. As if he had taken part in something very important, almost as if there had been some kind of priceless breakthrough. You know how quiet Stern is about what he does. Well that time when he finally turned up again, he could barely contain his excitement. I remember Anna mentioning it, saying how wonderful it was to see him as his old self again. So exuberant and lighthearted, so enthusiastic. It was the way we'd always remembered him from before.

Before?

Yes. Back before all the changes came over him during these last years. Back before everything began to weigh on him so heavily.

Ah yes, thought Joe, back when Stern was so lighthearted and exuberant. Back when he was *his old self.* . . .

And for a moment, Joe found his own memories slipping back through the years.

Of course it wasn't just that Stern had changed since David and Anna were younger. It was also that the two of them had ceased to be children and had learned to see more deeply, to sense Stern's complexity and the contradictions in what he did, what he believed in.

Then too, as children they wouldn't have known about his morphine addiction and all that implied. As children they would have seen only Stern's kindness and love, not the despair that went with it in the bare rented rooms where he passed his nights in one dreary slum after another. Not the worn old shoes, sad reminders of journeys to nowhere, or the battered suitcase which held all he owned in the world, tied together from year to year with the same old piece of rope which was forever being carefully knotted, carefully unknotted, when it was time for him to move yet again. As children they would have known a very different Stern, as had Joe's own son, Bernini. When Joe had seen him in New York, Bernini had talked a great deal about Stern as he always did, recalling Stern in a very particular way from his childhood. . . .

Stern?

Bernini had smiled rapturously.

A great bear of a man who was always smiling and laughing when they had gone to meet his ship in Piraeus. The gangways clanging and noise and confusion everywhere as people rushed back and forth, and then all at once there was Stern in the midst of all the shouting passengers, laughing and waving and struggling down the gangway with his arms full of gifts, Stern's wondrous presents from everywhere. Trinkets and charms and incense and a little sheik's costume for Bernini to wear, and the Great Pyramid made of building blocks, complete with secret passageways and hidden treasure chambers. And lovely gifts for Mother too, as Bernini had said, rare wines and delicacies and a beautiful thin gold bracelet, the bracelet making a special impression upon Bernini because Maud seemed so touched by its simplicity. And then back at their little house that afternoon, after all the presents had been admired, Stern opening the first of the bottles of champagne and banging around in the kitchen as he began to conjure up the feast they always had on the night of his arrival, Stern laughing and dashing spices here and there as his cooking filled the house with delicious aromas from all the lands of the Mediterranean.

Bernini had smiled happily.

Stern's feasts? There had never been anything like them.

And it would go on like that for two or three days, nothing but champagne and delicacies and one treat after another, until finally the hectic visit was over and once more little Bernini would be standing with Maud on a pier in Piraeus, the crowds solemn now as they waved good-bye to the passengers along the railings, Stern a little apart from the others but waving and smiling as always . . . laughing, as always.

And that was what Bernini remembered. Unaware, as he was, of all the things Stern and Maud had talked about late at night in the candlelight of the narrow garden by the sea. Unaware, as well, that Stern had once again squandered all his money, spending what little he had on others as he always did. . . .

Stern?

Oh yes, Bernini knew Stern. He was a big jovial man whose sudden appearances always meant laughter and toys and feasts, and above all, magic. The exquisite magic of tales that spoke of the infinite wonders a child could one day discover and make his own. . . . So it was no surprise to Joe the way Cohen and his sister remembered Stern from their childhoods, from the time when Stern had been exuberant and lighthearted, as Cohen said. When he had still been his old self, as Cohen said, and had not yet grown somber under the weight of his burdens. For Stern had always tried hard to keep hidden the dark corners of his heart, and David and Anna had never suspected what lay behind the kindly words and the tender hands. But now in the last few years they had begun to see it, and sadly so, Joe imagined. Reluctantly so. . . .

Joe looked up.

Priceless, you said? Stern acted as if he had achieved some kind of priceless breakthrough in Poland? But there's only one thing Stern would consider priceless. Life. Just that.

Yes, murmured Cohen, still deep in thought.

But isn't there anything you can recall, asked Joe, about that trip of his to Poland? Does the Pyry forest mean anything to you? A place known as *the house in the woods*, near Warsaw? Any of that?

I'm sorry. Nothing.

I see. Well let's put Poland aside for the moment, it doesn't seem to be getting us anywhere. Let's talk about codes.

Codes? said Cohen, suddenly alert and wary.

Yes, codes. That doesn't bother you, does it?

No of course not, replied Cohen, too quickly perhaps.

Joe nodded, recalling Ahmad's fears that Stern might be talking about forbidden things in front of others because he knew it would get him killed, because he didn't have the strength to go on anymore.

Oh well then, said Joe. . . . You see I already know Stern's talking a lot about codes these days, but I also know he's always been fascinated by them, and we do have so many different kinds, don't we? Codes of law and ethics and behavior, codes that apply to secret thought patterns and just on and on. In fact you might even say codes are a metaphor for what we are beneath the surface of things. And some of them seem so universal we think they can be written in stone, while others are so obscure no one but ourselves may ever know they exist. So private, for that matter, that *we* may not even know they exist because most of the time there's no need for us to know. Because most of us can go through our whole lives without that kind of situation ever arising.

Cohen moved uneasily.

What kind of situation?

Oh I don't know. Something extreme, say, something that's more than just ambiguous. Something that goes beyond any notion of right and wrong into a kind of no-man's-land of morality where nothing's recognizable, where there's not the slightest hint of better or worse or terrible and not so terrible. Just way out there beyond all that where a man's alone and nowhere, with nothing but the deepest part of himself for company.

Cohen moved impatiently.

This is too abstract, I don't know what you're trying to say. Can't you be more specific?

Joe nodded.

I guess I can and I guess I'm working myself up to it. I guess I don't even like to imagine such a Godforsaken place because it terrifies me and that's the truth, David. Sometimes I don't like to remember where I've been. . . .

Joe broke off. Cohen was moving restlessly back and forth, becoming as disturbed as Joe was. But Joe knew he had to go on, there was no avoiding it.

I'll try to be more specific, David. Say your personal code was based on a reverence for life. On never harming or molesting life and certainly never taking it. But then there came a time, a moment, when if you ordered death for some, many more would be saved. What would you do?

Order it, said Cohen immediately, relieved. But isn't that what war is, any kind of war? Why are you bringing that up now and agonizing over it? Aren't men making those terrible decisions every moment in Cairo and in the desert? In Europe? Everywhere?

Yes, said Joe. God help us, *yes*. But what if the situation were the same but not quite the same? What if you stood alone over a little girl who was maimed and dying and there was no hope of saving her and her pain was unbearable and she whispered *Please*, and there was a knife in front of you and nothing else in the world because the world was gone, and you were alone and nothing worked and nothing counted and there was nothing but screams and suffering and dying and a little girl's twisted body and her eyes in unbearable pain and her whispers, *Please*, and a knife, and you picked up the knife and pulled back her head and her throat was in front of you as frail as all of life, and it *was* life. Would you do it, God help us? *Would you?*

Cohen was straining forward as if he were going to scream, so harsh and unrelenting had Joe become, his voice and his eyes, every part of him. And Cohen might have screamed if Joe hadn't suddenly shuddered and moaned and clutched his hands together in a wild violent movement. For a moment Joe seemed utterly exhausted and unable to go on, but then all at once he was whispering again, leaning forward and staring, all the harshness back in his voice.

Cohen moved in his chair. He looked down at the floor.

It's horrible, he whispered, *horrible.* How can anyone answer something like that? It's not fair to talk about it in an abstract way.

Cohen made a futile gesture in front of his face as if he were brushing something away.

In fact this is all too abstract. There's a world war going on and the suffering is incalculable and we all know that, so what's the point? This talk about a little girl. . . .

Suddenly Cohen sensed something. He looked up and found Joe's eyes hard upon him, and a fearful suggestion of doubt swept through him.

That's right, said Joe softly. There aren't many people in this world who have Stern's faith, and it was a fiery night at the end of the world when I saw him pick up that knife twenty years ago in Smyrna. A night of death and screams deep in the blackness of nowhere, and Stern was alone and I was alone and the little girl was lying between us, and I didn't have the strength to touch that knife and I wouldn't today. But I'm no match for Stern in many ways, nor are you, nor are most of us. And there's nothing more to be said about that, one way or another. We all do what we can in life. We try to no purpose and we do what we can and what we can't do, we don't. . . .

A muscle twitched in Joe's face. He looked away, lowered his eyes.

He seemed calmer now, but Cohen himself was still shaking. Never had he witnessed anything like the intensity he had seen in Joe's eyes and heard in Joe's voice, a terrifying glimpse of some world he never wanted to see himself. And as Cohen sat there watching Joe, it suddenly struck him how small Joe was. He hadn't thought of it before because it wasn't the impression Joe gave, not at all. But Cohen noticed it now and it seemed strange to him somehow. . . . Such a small thin man, even frail in appearance.

Joe was sitting quietly, gazing down at the floor. Slowly, he looked up again.

Codes, said Joe. They can be like names in what they tell us about people and don't tell us. . . . Take Rommel. Everybody calls him the

235

Desert Fox because of the uncanny way he anticipates every move the British make. He doesn't have half the forces the British have, but somehow he always manages to have his armor in the right place at the right time to give the British another mauling. But is he really so clever? Or is somebody reading the British codes for him?

Cohen reeled, shocked.

What are you talking about now?

Codes. Maybe something called the Black Code. But wait, one step at a time. Let's just assume for a moment that Stern considers an Allied victory inevitable.

But it *isn't* inevitable, Cohen blurted out.

I know it isn't, but let's just assume Stern looks at it that way for whatever reasons. Because he thinks Hitler's armies will die in Russia as Napoleon's armies did. Because he knew it was inevitable for the Americans to come into the war and shift the tide to the side of the Allies. Or more simply, because he doesn't believe the beast inside us can triumph in the end, not even with the Black Code. Because he believes in the Holy City of man and his faith is unshakable.

Stop, hissed Cohen.

No wait, slowly. It's possible a man could believe that much, it's possible Stern could. And if he did and if he were certain deep in his heart that Hitler was going to lose, then let's take another step and say . . .

Stern's a Jew, shouted Cohen. His mother was a Jew and he's a Jew and the Nazis are slaughtering thousands of Jews.

And then let's say there was a way, continued Joe quietly, to save a large number of Jews by giving the Germans something in return. . . .

Cohen leapt to his feet.

A way, whispered Joe, to keep those thousands and thousands of Jews from becoming . . . millions.

Cohen stared down at Joe. He stood with his arms by his sides, glaring down at Joe in horror, his anger raging out of control.

Millions? *Millions?* Are you *mad?* What on *earth* are you talking about? The Nazis are beasts and Hitler's insane but the country is Germany. *Germany.* My own family is German, we lived there for centuries. The Nazis are monsters but the Germans aren't howling barbarians on horseback. They're not Mongols and this isn't the thirteenth century.

True, said Joe. It's the twentieth century and the Germans are methodical and industrious and orderly. And they organize well and they work hard and they pay attention to detail and they keep good records and they're very thorough. They're not Mongolian hordes racing around on horseback.

The veins bulged in Cohen's neck.

And so?

And so I have to find out about Stern and the Black Code, said Joe quietly.

Get out, shrieked Cohen, pale and shaking with rage as he stood over Joe, his fists clenched.

You're mad. Get out of here.

And then Cohen's fury exploded and he stooped and grabbed the spyglass and swung it.

The blow struck Joe full on the side of the head and knocked him out of the chair. He went crashing down to the floor, spinning, upsetting a tray that sent glass shattering down around him. He was dazed and lying facedown, not really aware what had happened, not having seen the blow coming. He pushed out his hand and cut it on broken glass.

Clumsily he lurched to his knees, to all fours. There was a roar in his head and the pain was intense and sinking deeper. He choked, spitting out blood. Blindly he reached up and gripped something, a workbench, got one foot under him and pulled himself to his feet. He stood there holding on, swaying and choking and coughing up blood, trying to see. Somewhere near him was Cohen, a tall figure, a blur. The roar in his head was deafening and he couldn't think. A hand twisted his arm and pushed him across the room.

Joe was staggering, limping, bumping into things. A sharp metal corner drove into his thigh and there was another loud crash of shattering glass. His head banged into a door and he fell heavily against it, hanging there. The spyglass was being stuffed under his arm.

Cohen had abandoned him. Cohen was somewhere back in the room speaking through another door, saying something to his sister. Joe finally found the door knob and turned it, staggered into the corridor and almost fell on his face in the darkness. He caught himself, felt a wall, leaned against the cool stones and pressed his forehead there, trying not to fall, trying to breathe.

The door behind him closed. A hand touched him and Anna's voice whispered.

It's all right now, I'll help you. This way.

Joe let himself be led down the corridor in the darkness. When

237

they reached the door to the street she moved closer to him. She seemed to want to say something.

My right ear, mumbled Joe. I can't hear anything in the other one. He could feel her breath.

I'm sorry, she whispered. My brother has many worries and Stern has always been like a father to us. Perhaps you could come back tomorrow.

No. It wouldn't make any difference.

She seemed to agree. She whispered again.

I was listening, I heard what you said. I think you're wrong about Stern but I also think you want to help him.

She hesitated.

Might as well say it, whispered Joe. If I don't find out the truth others are going to come looking for it, and they're not going to care about Stern.

He felt her breath on his ear. She was still hesitating.

Oh say it, he whispered, dear God just say it. Does the silence of this world have to go on forever?

He swayed, bumped into her, sank back against the wall.

Please listen to me, Anna. I like your brother and I know Stern's been like a father to both of you, but what I said isn't unthinkable because nothing is, nothing ever. Look at the Nazis. And I know your brother's too young to take all this in, and you are, and it's not something any sane person should ever have to hear because it's beyond the human kind, God help us. . . .

Joe reached out in desperation and seized her by the arm.

But listen to me for Stern's sake, Anna, because he's going to die, and soon. There are depths to the human soul beyond all imagination, and you think you know Stern and you do know him in your way, but he's also more than that and *I* know it, *I've* seen it. And yes, he could barter away his soul and that may be exactly what he's done, God have mercy. . . .

Please try to calm down, she whispered.

I *am* trying, I *am*. It's just that I can't see and I can't hear and there's a shrieking in my head and I'm blinded by the darkness and I *know* what's going to happen and I'm frightened . . . afraid. . . .

He loosened his grip on her arm, but he didn't let go of her. Hunched there against the stones, unable to see, the whole side of his head torn with pain, he didn't dare let go of her.

Anna? Forgive me for saying those things back there. I'm sorry I had to say them but Stern is what he is and there's no way to . . .

Anna? I'm afraid he's coming apart and I want to find out the truth about him. If there were only some little thing, Anna, just something to go on while there's still time. . . .

Joe was sobbing for breath, no longer able to hold himself in, giving way as Cohen had before him. He heard the bolt on the door slide open, felt her hand tighten over his. Her lips were next to his ear.

He's never mentioned anything about a Black Code, she whispered, but there was something he said a few weeks ago. The three of us were having breakfast and Stern was in a good mood. My brother happened to step out of the room and Stern suddenly laughed. I remembered the remark because it seemed so odd. . . .

Yes?

He said Rommel must be enjoying breakfast that morning with his *little fellers.* At first I thought I'd heard *fellahs,* meaning fellaheen, but it wasn't that. It was *little fellers.* He didn't explain it and I don't know what it means, but it might lead you to something. The American military attaché in Cairo is a Colonel Fellers.

Oh?

David didn't even hear the remark. And please try to help Stern, try to help him. Good-bye.

Joe didn't have time to thank her. She squeezed his hand and the door closed behind him and all at once he was alone with the eerie sudden sounds of the city at night, peering up and down the narrow alley, trying to remember which way he had come.

14

Bletchley

Bletchley's smirk was monstrous in its contempt. His mouth sagged and his single eye bulged grotesquely.

Bletchley's face of concern, Joe reminded himself. . . . Bletchley's face of sympathy.

Another man would have shown his feelings by softening his expression then, but Bletchley could never do that. Not in his shattered ruin of a face with its severed muscles and missing bones. In Bletchley's half-dead face everything always came out looking wrong. Concern appeared as a grin of contempt, sympathy took on a smirk of disgust.

No wonder little children ran away from him on the street, thought Joe. No wonder strangers turned their eyes away in horror. Bletchley's shattered face couldn't speak the truth and he couldn't go around shouting it out every day of his life. So he smiled at the world, or tried to smile, and his humiliation never ended.

He was gazing at Joe's bandaged ear.

You weren't able to get a look at them?

No, said Joe. Common thieves in the night, I suppose. I don't even know whether there were two or three of them, or only one for that matter.

Bletchley sighed.

Well please don't go taking yourself down deserted alleys again at night. If you have to go out for a walk stay in an area where there's some life, where the patrols come by. There's no sense getting banged up like this.

Bletchley was using a handkerchief to clean the skin around his black eye patch. Sometimes when he did that he reminded Joe of a battered old tomcat trying to clean himself, ripped and torn and scarred from his battles but still trying to keep himself presentable. Of course Bletchley wasn't old. He just gave that impression because of his half-dead face that no one had ever been able to fix.

I would have taken more care, said Joe, but I didn't think I was looking all that prosperous these days.

Bletchley peeked over the top of his handkerchief and saw that Joe was smiling, mocking himself. He laughed, a snorting sound accompanied by an idiotic lopsided grin.

Well you don't look that prosperous, for a European. But prosperity is relative, isn't it? Anyway, you're beginning to look more like the rest of us now. Like the rest of us, that's it.

Bletchley went on snorting noisily. Joe smiled.

I am? How's that?

Your ear, said Bletchley. It looks as if it might be missing under that bandage, as if you'd just lost it at the front. Perhaps you don't remember your interview with Whatley too clearly, but Whatley only has one arm.

Oh. No, I don't remember that too clearly. A one-armed Whatley, you say, once the fastest gun in the west but it's only a memory now? Sounds like one of Liffy's songs.

Bletchley snorted.

It is odd when you think of it, but all the Monks do seem to be missing a part or a limb. Crippled, that's it.

Joe heard a ringing in his ear.

True? Do you suppose that means there's some sort of secret law that you have to be a cripple to be in intelligence?

Bletchley snorted.

To be intelligent, you mean? Well you may be right, I never thought of it that way before.

Bletchley finished dabbing around his eye patch and put away his handkerchief. The look of contempt came back into his face. Concern, Joe reminded himself.

Don't you think we ought to have a doctor look at it?

No need to bother, said Joe. Nothing to it really, and Ahmad seems to have a sure touch with bandages.

Yes, a man of unsuspected talents. He did some volunteer nursing work in the last war, as I recall. Drove an ambulance mostly. Men of a literary bent used to like to do that, apparently.

Sounds more like the Spanish Civil War, said Joe. Were you ever in Spain then?

Bletchley looked uncomfortable.

No. I was having some operations done.

It itches, said Joe, grimacing, pointing to his ear.

As usual, they were sitting in the small cellar room on the far side of the courtyard behind the Hotel Babylon. A single naked light bulb hung from the low ceiling, a cord leading down to the electric ring on the table where the kettle was steaming. There was also the chipped teapot and the two dented metal cups between them. As always, a newspaper lay at Bletchley's elbow and the meeting was being held at night, the customary time for dealings with the Monks, as Liffy had said.

What's new that's not in the papers? asked Joe.

Nothing good, said Bletchley. Nothing but one disaster after another. Bir Hacheim has been wiped out with its Free French and its Jewish Brigade, and now it looks like Rommel's going to be able to isolate Tobruk. We'll have to try to hold the line at El Alamein.

Can Tobruk take a siege?

It did last year for seven months. It's not as strong now, but Rommel shouldn't know that.

Bletchley looked down at the table.

Of course there are other things he shouldn't know, this Desert Fox who has become such a hero to the Egyptians.

And the El Alamein line? asked Joe.

It depends on several factors, supplies for one. Ours and theirs. If Rommel has the fuel to keep pushing, well, we'll flood the delta and lose the Canal and take what we can to Palestine and Iraq. The implications are unthinkable and that's what we're thinking about now.

I see.

Joe glanced at the newspaper.

What about the personal columns? Any better news there?

Bletchley's face twisted into a kind of blank stare, his eye widening. An expression of sorrow, Joe knew.

This isn't being reported yet, so don't say anything about it. All right?

Yes.

Bletchley hesitated.

We had a large-scale operation under way behind their lines, para-

242

military units, special strike forces, that kind of thing. We were trying to get at some of the more important bases they've been using to raid Malta, to stop our supplies from getting through. Well it was an absolute failure from beginning to end. They were waiting for us. . . . Waiting for us, that's it.

Bletchley stared blankly at his metal cup and the two of them sat in silence for a time. Joe had made his report, such as it was, not mentioning the Cohens and not really going into any detail about Ahmad. Bletchley had listened in only a half-attentive way, and his questions had appeared to be more concerned with Joe's impressions of Old Cairo, rather than with Stern. It seemed peculiar to Joe, but then, he always found Bletchley's manner peculiar. Something to do with Bletchley's mask, a face that never reflected what the man was feeling or thinking.

Bletchley was moving his metal cup around, nudging it a few inches to one side, a few inches to the other. The scraping noise made by the cup was the only sound in the room.

Night, thought Joe. Everything happens under cover of darkness when you're dealing with the Monks.

You shouldn't be so hard on yourself, Bletchley said finally. After all, you've only been in Egypt a little over two weeks, which is nothing for an assignment as complicated as yours. No one expects results right away and two weeks is barely enough time to learn your way around.

Joe nodded.

I know, but somehow it seems much longer than that. Probably because of where I'm staying. . . .

Bletchley scowled. Thoughtful, Joe reminded himself.

It is an odd old structure, Bletchley murmured in a noncommittal way.

He looked up from his cup.

Does your ear still itch?

Yes.

Isn't that supposed to mean someone's talking about you?

I hope not, said Joe. I'm supposed to be an unknown visitor here, just A. O. Gulbenkian in transit.

Bletchley continued to scowl.

A strange cover, said Joe. Whose idea was it anyway?

I'm not sure, answered Bletchley, still preoccupied. But don't try to expect too much from yourself too soon. Two weeks is nothing.

Why does he keep saying that? wondered Joe. What's he talking about? Rommel's getting ready to overrun Egypt and he keeps saying there's all the time in the world. It makes no sense, or isn't he worried about Rommel reading the British codes anymore? What's changed that I don't know about?

Bletchley was pushing his cup back and forth. The meeting seemed over. Joe got to his feet and lingered beside the table, not sure whether Bletchley had anything more to say.

Well I'll be on my way then. . . .

He started toward the stairs. Bletchley was still staring down at the table, his eye wide, empty.

See here, Joe, I could find you another room. This accident of yours, this isn't always the best part of town to be in. What do you say?

Joe shrugged.

Oh I don't think it matters. We are where we are, I guess, but thanks anyway.

Joe climbed the narrow stairs and stepped into the alley. Later he would often recall that quiet moment in the small bare cellar and Bletchley's concern, Bletchley's sorrow, his questions about Joe's welfare and his offer of another room elsewhere. At the time it had sounded like such a little thing, but had Bletchley meant something more by it? Something a great deal more important?

Could it even have made a difference and saved a life?

Two lives? Three lives?

As soon as Joe stepped into the night he heard the rumble of trucks in the distance. Everywhere now there were trucks moving into Cairo, pouring in from the desert with wounded soldiers and stragglers who had lost their units. Guns of all sorts and RAF wagons and recovery vehicles, armored cars and countless lorries crammed with exhausted sleeping men, crowding the roads outside the city beyond the pyramids, transports rolling in from the wreckage of the long campaigns in the Western Desert.

And smoke above the British Embassy where documents were being burned. And huge crowds in front of the British Consulate where refugees waited silently, hoping for transit visas to Palestine. And rumors that the British fleet was already preparing to sail from Alexandria to the harbors of Haifa and Port Said, to escape Rommel's advancing panzers.

Unmistakable signs, thought Joe. The fingerprints of war. And everywhere in Cairo the same whispered question.

When will he arrive? When will he get here?

But Joe had no thoughts for Rommel. It was Bletchley's melancholy remarks that obsessed him, the failure of the special operation behind enemy lines which Bletchley had talked about. For that must have been the mission that was going to have kept Stern away from Cairo for two weeks, and its collapse meant that Stern's last mission for the Monastery had officially ended.

Hours ago? Days ago?

In any case, Stern was now due back in Cairo so far as Bletchley was concerned, and whatever Stern had been secretly doing was now finished and at an end. Bletchley would see to that. Bletchley who did his job well, and who seemed to have arrived at a new sense of calm despite the news from the front. So for Joe there was very little time left. And sadly, as he had known all along, the outcome would be the same for Stern no matter what he learned now.

Indelibly the same, Stern's passage, Stern's fate, the mysterious weaving of Stern's journey over the years. Even Liffy had finally come to realize that when he had found Joe limping down the alley to the Hotel Babylon that morning, before daybreak. Liffy rushing up to help Joe after having waited all night in the shadows for Joe to return from his visit to the Cohens, fearful and more, frantic that something might have gone wrong.

As indeed it had. Dreadfully wrong. A small cry escaping Liffy then, when he had learned what had happened.

That's not like David, Liffy had said of the blow that wounded him so deeply.

Violence, Liffy had whispered with a shudder. It's terrifying. Even when we abhor it, it can seize us.

And then he had fixed Joe with his eyes there in the alley, gripping

Joe and whispering urgently and looking for all the world like some tormented prophet of antiquity who had just seen a vision of the coming destruction of his beloved Jerusalem.

Whatever Stern has done, Joe, you must prove it's right for the sake of all of us. It doesn't even matter if you and I are the only ones who ever know the truth, or if just one of us does, even that would be enough. For I have this haunting feeling that unless Stern's right in what he's done, with all *he* knows, there can be no hope for any of us in this monstrous war without end.

15

The Sisters

Flowers, boomed Ahmad. . . . *Flowers* are the keys to this particular queendom, therefore you must select the makings of your nosegay with special care. These two old dears are shamelessly sentimental and always have been.

Ahmad raised his head and solemnly sniffed the air, considering the matter further.

Or better yet, take two nosegays, he said to Joe. They may be twins and they may be in their nineties, but that doesn't mean they've always gotten along in every respect. They've had their differences over the decades and I suspect there's still a certain sisterly sense of competition, especially when a man comes to call.

On second thought, why not let me prepare your nosegays? Although it's been awhile, I'm familiar with their tastes and also with the color schemes on the houseboat. I did their interior decorating, you know, the last time they had it done, which must have been around the turn of the century. I don't recall exactly when it was, but one of them would surely remember. Between the two of them they remember everything. In fact there used to be a popular saying in Cairo which was a great favorite among boatmen, particularly.

> *Fear not, nothing can be lost on the Nile.*
> *For what the Sphinx forgets, the Sisters*
> *remember.*

In other words, mused Ahmad, see all . . . hear all . . . speak what? In some respects, you might say, these two old dears are rather like the Nile itself.

And with that Ahmad's massive face swayed majestically with the beginnings of a smile.

Two nosegays.

A darkened dilapidated houseboat, a rambling pleasure barge of yesteryear, where memories included everything.

Two tiny ancient women, twins, whose shadowy floating realm on the Nile had gradually come to be Joe's ultimate destination in his search for the truth about Stern.

The prospect of Joe visiting the legendary Sisters had even caused Liffy to emerge from his somber mood. Either that or Liffy had brought all his acting abilities to bear for Joe's benefit and was staging a bravura performance, laughing and joking and dipping into a variety of roles to encourage Joe.

The three of them, Ahmad and Liffy and Joe, had met for a strategy session in the narrow courtyard behind the Hotel Babylon, late in the afternoon as the sun was sinking. There amidst the creeping vines and the hanging flowers, the rustling old newspapers and the heaps of debris crumbling in the corners, they sat beneath the single palm tree as the shadows gathered in the slums of Old Cairo, Ahmad solemnly serving tea from a heavy silver tea service that had once belonged to old Menelik, the tea service resurrected by Ahmad from the epic clutter of his dusty little closet especially to mark the occasion.

Ahmad's manner had never been more dignified. Obviously to him an official visit to the Sisters, a social call by Joe or anyone, was an event of the most profound significance.

Ahmad poured.

Teatime, he announced in his ponderous voice, gesturing at the cups. Tea in time and need I point out that vast empires have risen and fallen on just such queer civilized rituals as this? Now then, mates, who will take what? Cream, sugar, what?

Before Joe could say anything Liffy had made a quick pass over

Joe's teacup, and his own, with what appeared to be a small pocket flask. Liffy flashed a brilliant smile.

A new invention, he explained quickly to Ahmad. A tricky combination of essences that takes the place of the usual sugar and things. Discovered, some say, in a remote desert in the New World where it is known locally as Irish-Hopi tea. Perhaps you'd like to try a splash yourself?

Ahmad's huge nose twitched above the little table where they huddled. He hovered, sniffing. He frowned.

Cognac?

Liffy nodded.

Egyptian cognac?

Liffy nodded again.

Foul, muttered Ahmad. Deplorable. But drink away at your cups of wretched Irish hope, the two of you, and meanwhile let's get down to business, *social* business, the only kind worth mentioning. Now then, before Joe can hand over his flowers he must first get in the door. And since he hasn't been invited to the houseboat, how will he accomplish that?

Ahmad smiled knowingly in answer to his own question. With a flourish he reached under his faded lavender nightshirt and produced a tattered piece of hard thick paper, which he placed on the table with great ceremony. The paper was badly stained, its faint engraved lettering illegible. Liffy and Joe leaned forward, studying it.

What in the world can that be? asked Liffy, mystified. Is it a secret pass of some kind? Your own ultimate forgery, good for anywhere in a universe of receding stars? Is that why the lettering is so dim? A *carte blanche,* perhaps, issued by the last pharaoh on his deathbed and good for immediate access to all secret tombs? A reissue of the same, promulgated by the last caesar on *his* deathbed? Or perhaps a highly prized invitation to Queen Victoria's birth? . . . What on earth is it, Ahmad? What could this curious document be?

A formal invitation, announced Ahmad triumphantly, to the grand costume gala that was held in old Menelik's crypt to honor him on his ninety-fifth birthday. Now *that* was music, and if anything will get Joe across the gangplank and into the houseboat, this will.

It will? asked Joe in wonder. Is it possible someone could still read it?

No one has to read it, said Ahmad. A piece of memorabilia as

249

unforgettable as this need only be recognized by its general size and shape and disposition. And it *will* be recognized by those who know it, by those who have traveled that joyous underground route, as the saying goes.

Excellent, said Liffy. Excellent. An invitation in time saves . . . well yes, of course it does. Now then, Joe, let me brief you on the more current intelligence making the rounds in the bazaars. But first, a warning. The Sisters are to be visited only at night. All informers agree on this fact, straight off and straightaway.

At night? repeated Ahmad thoughtfully. That, I daresay, is true.

Liffy nodded at Ahmad, his manner grave.

Precisely. There'll be a moon tonight and lunar facts, after all, are lunatic by definition.

Liffy turned back to Joe.

Simply a matter of vanity, perhaps? A sure knowledge that sunlight would show up unwanted wrinkles?

Possibly, intoned Liffy. Or possibly the information these tiny twins are heir to can only be grasped in the sudden intuitive glimpses that come where moonlight reigns.

In any case, continued Liffy, night is the milieu for this approach of yours. Night with its curious echoes and its soothing breezes off the Nile. If anyone tries to visit the Sisters at any other time, according to reliable gossip, they just won't be there. Of course they have to be there really, somewhere on the houseboat, because they never leave it and haven't in decades. But it seems the place has as many hidden passageways as the Great Pyramid, so when the Sisters are being elusive, well, they're as inaccessible as Cheops, at least so far as modern man is concerned.

Cheops, the prototypical *little* man obsessed with erections, muttered Ahmad with disdain, stirring his tea.

Precisely, said Liffy, throwing Ahmad a vigorous nod.

He turned back to Joe.

Now then, as for the houseboat itself, as for this shadowy structure looming at the end of a gangplank, this floating vision Ahmad so tactfully refers to as *their* particular queendom. . . . It seems this houseboat has had a very special relationship with British intelligence for some time. In fact there are those who claim that without this houseboat, there would be *no* British intelligence in this part of the world. Just none at all, nothing but blather and sand. So I guess it would have to be called the premier safeboat in the Levant.

Liffy delicately touched the ends of his fingers together, one hand against the other, making a sphere. A demented gleam crept into his eyes.

And now we may be drawing near the very heart of the clandestine matter. Breathe evenly, please, let the muscles in your neck relax and just consider the year 1911, if you will.

Ahmad sighed.

Now *that's* a year worth mentioning, he muttered. Not quite as grand as 1912, but a stunning performance all the same.

Precisely, said Liffy, vigorously nodding at Ahmad again. That *was* a year, too. I can see we're on solid ground here. Now then.

He turned back to Joe.

The year for what, you say? Well for one thing, that was when Churchill was given the Admiralty for the first time. And during his first year in his new post, that august presence set two goals for himself. The first was to convert the fleet from coal to oil, and the second was to secure a certain world-famous houseboat on the Nile as his secret flagship.

Abruptly Liffy puffed out his jowls in Churchill's familiar scowl. His head sank into his shoulders and he glowered resolutely at Joe.

As is well known, young man, he boomed, I achieved the first goal. As of 1911, oil was in and coal was out. But as is less well known, I also achieved my second goal. That houseboat did become my secret flagship, and a very pleasant home away from home it always was, too. Once the particulars had been arranged, I immediately fired off a congratulatory cable of welcome to my new companions-in-arms.

THE SISTERS,
THE NILE.

LADIES:

GLAD TO WELCOME YOU ON BOARD. THIS IS GOING TO BE MORE FUN THAN CHINESE GORDON'S LAST STAND AT KHARTOUM IN '85.

YOUR OLD PAL,
WINSTON.

The following day, boomed Liffy, glowering, jowls set, I received a return cable at the Admiralty in London.

YOU CHERUBIC LITTLE UPSTART. YOU WERE STILL IN SHORT PANTS IN '85, SO HOW COULD YOU POSSIBLY KNOW WHOSE STAND WAS FUN THAT YEAR, LAST OR OTHERWISE?

ANYWAY, NOW THAT YOU'RE IN CHARGE OF THE BOATS OF THE EMPIRE, KEEP A FIRM HAND ON THE THROTTLE AND CRANK UP THE STEAM, GIVE THE BOILERS HEAD AND STOP DRAGGING ANCHOR.

AND WE'RE GLAD TO HAVE YOU ON BOARD, WINNIE. ANY OLD TIME.

US.

THE NILE.

Liffy laughed.

Awesome, he said in his own voice. They seem to have known everyone in their time. But remember, only at night.

Oh, and one other thing, added Ahmad.

Be careful not to make any stray remarks about Catherine the Great or Cleopatra, or about lost family fortunes or about someone called Uncle George. At least not until you have a sound feel for the conversation. I'm not sure those topics are still sensitive, but they might be. Of course, any allusion to human height or size would be out of the question, just cause for immediate dismissal from their queendom, but I don't have to tell you that.

Ahmad smiled happily. He sighed.

They're foolish old dears, no doubt about it. But they're a rare pair and basically very friendly, and certainly likable when you get to know them.

Precisely, agreed Liffy, nodding. All rumors have verified that since long before Churchill got out of short pants and began reaching toward the tiller.

He turned back to Joe.

Now then. Let's start at the beginning again and make sure we've left nothing out, because memories which include everything can be tricky.

Liffy paused.

Now in the beginning there was Egypt and the Nile, and the Sphinx and the pyramids. . . . But also in the beginning, strangely, curiously, there were these two tiny women, twins, called Big Belle and Little Alice. And in the beginning these sisters, who are *the* Sisters . . .

Free the serfs, thundered Big Belle to no one in particular as she moved stiffly across the room, the declaration apparently a mere pleasantry meant to take the place of a remark on the weather.

Of the two tiny sisters, Big Belle was slightly shorter. But she was also bulkier, which perhaps explained why she was commonly known as *Big* to her sister Alice's *Little,* although neither one of them was ever so known to her face, according to Ahmad. Both of the tiny ancient women were wearing old shawls and cotton slippers.

Big Belle stopped in front of the chair where Joe was sitting and held out a glass, her face severe.

You said whiskey, young man. Will that do? It's Irish, but I have to warn you, it's Protestant. Jameson's. Can you manage?

I can, said Joe. As far as I'm concerned, drink is beyond tribal strife.

Big Belle put her hands on her hips and beamed. Standing, she seemed about as tall as Joe was sitting.

Good for you, she boomed. I always appreciate a man who leaves politics and religion at home when he comes calling on a woman.

Chirping noises rose from across the room, from the chair where Little Alice was sitting.

Women, trilled Little Alice. When a man comes calling on *women.* You know as well as I do, Belle, that Joe came to call on both of us. He brought *two* beautiful nosegays, or are you trying to ignore that?

Little Alice smiled sweetly across the room at Joe.

You'll have to forgive my sister, she chirped. Belle's so short, poor dear, she sometimes tries to forget there are taller women in the room. But I suppose it's only human nature to try to ignore the things that bother us. I'm almost five feet tall, you see, and I've always had a willowy figure.

Big Belle still stood with her hands on her hips, beaming, in front of Joe.

You're not a hair over four-feet-eleven, she called out over her shoulder, and you've been skinny since the day you were born.

Little Alice sat up straight in her chair.

Well at least I'm not four-feet-ten like some people, and I've never been stout because of all the chocolates I eat.

Better than that dairy mess you pick at, boomed Belle over her shoulder.

Yogurt is very healthy, Alice called out. And it has always kept me willowy.

Willowy? thundered Belle. How can anyone who's four-feet-eleven be willowy? Anyway, I'm sure Joe didn't come here to hear about your obsession with being skinny.

Belle smiled at Joe.

You'll have to forgive my sister. The reason she starves herself into being skinny is because she thinks it makes her look younger. Can't face her age, never could. Younger sisters are like that, I suppose. Just desperate to stay young forever.

How much younger is she? asked Joe in a normal tone of voice. The two sisters had been shouting at each other across the room, apparently because one of them was hard of hearing.

How much younger? said Belle. Eight minutes, more or less. But the way she talks, you'd think it was forty years.

Some people whisper, Alice called out, because they're afraid their lies will be overheard. Where's your knitting, Belle?

Belle left Joe and went to look for it. Joe sipped his whiskey and gazed around the room.

It was an unusual sitting room they had led him to, an airy old-fashioned sunroom on the side of the houseboat that faced the river. High narrow windows rose one beside the other from floor to ceiling, interrupted in the middle by a windowed alcove where a pair of tall French doors, as tall as the windows, opened onto a narrow veranda beside the water. The moon had already set at that late hour, but since the sunroom was mostly windows and all the curtains were pulled back, the stars and their reflections off the water would have been more than enough to have lit the parlor. A few candles flickered here and there but their only purpose seemed to be romantic, to cast a soft play of shadows over the scene.

Most of the furniture in the room was made of light airy wicker, ghostlike and insubstantial, painted white. Occasionally some handsome old mahogany piece would turn up in the dream, solidly rooted among the floating wicker shapes.

A small portrait of Catherine the Great hung at one end of the room, a portrait of Cleopatra at the other end. Both had been done long ago in pen and ink, apparently by the same artist, and both were badly faded. The portraits weren't meant to be realistic, the figures represented being strictly Victorian in dress and concept, the one imperial and opulent and haughty, an autocratic woman at court, the other playful and hinting at sensual delights in a vaguely Oriental manner, thoroughly proper in keeping with Victorian precepts, yet also suggestive of the hidden recesses of a nineteenth-century Turkish harem.

Both portraits, in fact, might have been meant to represent unsuspected aspects of a giggly little Queen Victoria in the frolicsome days of her youth, before she took on the burdens of empire, the tiny future queen having decided to succumb to fantasy one rainy afternoon in some castle or other, and abandoned herself to the secret joys of dressing up, as little girls were known to do. This impression was reinforced by the fact that the young faces in the two portraits were close enough in appearance to be the faces of twins. Tiny twins. Yet even in the portraits, the girlish figure of Catherine the Great was noticeably bulkier than the girlish figure of Cleopatra.

There was also a beautiful antique harpsichord in one corner of the parlor.

All together the sunroom was a magical setting by starlight, despite the number of wicker chairs and wicker settees crammed into it. Joe guessed that as many as thirty or forty people could have found a place to sit in the room at any one time, more if any degree of intimacy had been allowed. Of course the Sisters had been famous hostesses when they were younger, so perhaps this vast array of spectator seats beside the Nile was only to be expected.

Yet with only the three of them now in the room, a certain melancholy air to the parlor was unmistakable. An inevitable feeling of time having slipped away on the currents beyond the open French doors, taking with it a host of memories of laughter and gaiety and leaving behind these hauntingly empty wicker shapes as ghostly reminders of other worlds and other eras, forgotten now elsewhere, surviving only in the hearts of these two tiny ancient women.

Big Belle found her knitting and stiffly arranged herself in a wicker chair beneath the portrait of Catherine the Great. Little Alice cocked her head at the portrait of Cleopatra and nodded wistfully, as if hearing some echo flit across the water. Joe, meanwhile, smiled at them both and gazed out through the open French doors at the night and the river.

You've hurt your ear, said Belle somberly. Were you trying to listen to something too closely?

I'm afraid so, answered Joe.

It's like that, is it?

I'm afraid.

Belle continued to stare at him.

You remind me of my Uncle George, she announced abruptly. He used to wear a short beard and a shirt without a collar, and there was generally a makeshift bandage someplace on his head. He had your coloring and your build and he must have been about your age when he passed on.

Jesus, thought Joe. And I bet he gambled away the family fortune and dabbled in underage barmaids and drank himself to death. Sounds like the voice of doom and this is no way to get things started. But the important thing is, did they like this Uncle George or not?

Belle still stared at him severely.

Oh help, thought Joe, the curse of Uncle George is upon me. But mightn't that compulsive lecher have been a wee mite endearing to his lovely young nieces just once in a while? Maybe a friendly smile in their direction as he lurched down the gloomy winter corridors of their family estate, before he fired up the samovar and locked himself in the study to mutter over Paracelsus and rage with his vodka bottles? An uncle-ly pat perhaps, warm and respectable, before he went crashing out into the night to attack the peasant girls in their hovels? *Before* he stole all the family jewels and all the deeds to the family estates and fled on the spring train from St Petersburg, racing to Nice of course, there to madly gamble everything away in a monumental fit of drunken hysteria?

Belle's face softened.

The poor dear drank to excess but we were always very fond of him, she said, as if reading Joe's thoughts.

Three cheers for the rascal then, Joe almost shouted, I always knew Uncle George would pull it out in the end. Of *course* he drank to excess, but didn't all the great souls in Russia either drink or love to excess in the nineteenth century? Of *course* they did, poor dears, but the fact is we're still very fond of them.

Joe smiled.

That's a handsome harpsichord in the corner. Do you play it?

Oh no, Alice does. My instrument is that little one you see on top of the harpsichord. It's a kind of old-fashioned bassoon.

Known as a piccolo faggotina in F, Alice called out gaily. Leave it to Belle to find an instrument with a name like that. Belle *will* have her own way, Mother used to say. She *will* do exactly as she pleases.

Little Alice laughed.

Belle and her *fagottina*, she chirped. Her fago*ttina*, the *piccolo* instrument she plays. I mean things weren't said that directly in the old days. One just didn't step into a parlor and blurt out things like that, but of course Belle always did. And *in F*, mind you, so there was no way to misinterpret what she was saying. I mean *realll*-ly.

Little Alice tossed her curls.

Do you like shepherdesses? she called out to Joe.

Big Belle sniffed, studying her knitting.

And how is the poor man supposed to interpret that, Alice? My sister, she called out to Joe, is referring to those porcelain figures on the table beside you.

Joe inspected the figures. He picked one up and admired it.

Oh that one? Little Alice called out, twirling a ribbon on her shawl. That one was an Easter present from a Serbian prince.

A birthday present, declared Belle. And he was hardly a prince.

Little Alice pushed back her curls. She smiled prettily at Joe.

Belle is so contrary, she just can't help it. Belle *will* find fault, Mother used to say. She *will* be stubborn.

Affectionately, Little Alice gazed at her sister.

Should you be drinking that gin straight, dear? You know what the doctor said.

The doctor be hanged, proclaimed Big Belle emphatically, and Little Alice sighed, a faraway look in her eyes.

Well perhaps that porcelain was a present for my birthday, but I still remember that Serbian prince as if it were yesterday. His older brother had gambled away the family fortune, the castles and estates and everything, and then he had sneaked away to Nice where he lived in shame in a small garret room he rented, occasionally writing sketches on Balkan intrigue for the local newspapers. Dimitri had to go to work on the stock exchange in Cairo but he never held it against his older brother. He used to visit Nice every spring to pay off his brother's tradesmen. He would have liked to have given his brother money but he knew his brother would just gamble it away. Finally the brother died of consumption in his garret one dark winter night, leaving a note that said, *Forgive me, brother.* Dimitri cried, but really it was a blessing for everyone.

The brother died at noon on a summer solstice, stated Big Belle conclusively. He fell under a carriage in Nice while chasing a young French sailor across the street, in full view of everyone. As for Dimitri, he was in no way an aristocrat. He got his start by making a corner on coffee, the Piraeus, 1849.

I said he worked on the stock exchange, mused Little Alice, which is the same thing really. Anyway, I can picture him as if it were yesterday. A plump figure of a gentleman in a white coat that shined from ironing, waving his long white ivory-handled flyswatter as he came down the club steps on the stock-exchange side of the street. The peddlers would be running after him, offering him early asparagus and mangoes and calling him count or baron. Of course, he was no such thing. Just a rich Greek who had made a killing in cotton.

Annex the Crimea, thundered Big Belle. *Damn those Turks. Organize a colony called Alaska.*

But a generous man, mused Little Alice. He was always giving me porcelain shepherdesses.

Big Belle looked up from her knitting.

Who's that you're talking about, dear? One of your beaux?

Yes, Dimitri. That rich stockbroker from the Balkans whose nationality I always mix up. I've just never been able to get the Balkans straight in my mind. Was he a Serbian or an Albanian or a Croat, or was he some other odd thing? You remember him, Belle.

I certainly do. I probably knew him better than you did, although I was only his paramour's sister. He always came to me for advice before he made one of his periodic plunges in the market.

Well what was he, Belle? Was he an Albanian?

No. He was a Montenegrin peasant and he got his start in coffee, the Piraeus, 1849. He was something of a pirate and the only cotton he ever saw must have been in his children's underwear. He himself wore silk. . . . Dimitri, yes. Married late. A good catch. Everybody had an eye on him. The advice he wanted from me would sometimes get out of hand. After a while I had to refuse to meet him in private.

Big Belle turned to Joe.

You'll have to forgive my sister. She makes things up, always has. Flighty.

I am not, Little Alice called out, sitting up straight in her chair.

Thick-thighed, added Alice under her breath.

What's that? said Belle over her knitting.

Dimitri gave me that porcelain in 1879, mused Alice. I remember because that was the year he asked me to move into the villa where the drawing room was done in the Turkish style. All the things in it, the woods and the velvets and the lamps of pink and blue Bohemian glass, everything was faded and opaque and dusty. And the rooms on the first floor all smelled of cinnamon and Arab cooking.

You're making things up again, said Big Belle. The year was 1878, the year Pius IX died. You're trying to move up dates to make yourself seem younger than you are.

Thick-thighed, whispered Little Alice.

Belle gazed at her sister affectionately.

I'll have you know the men I've been acquainted with have always preferred women with some meat on their bones.

Tra-la, twittered Alice. And especially the bones women sit on?

And what's that supposed to mean?

Just that if they hadn't fancied a plump bottom to begin with, they wouldn't have been coming around to see you in the first place. After all, you were known as *Big* Belle for a reason.

259

Belle smiled with satisfaction.

On that account, I never heard a single complaint from any man. They were always pleased and often ecstatic.

I'm sure they were, said Alice. Why wouldn't they be? *Those* kinds of men always did prefer you.

When men go oystering, replied Belle, there are those kind and then there are the other kind. And as I recall, the latter were always talking about you in the cafés. Pretty *Little* Alice and her pretty *little* mouth. Oh I remember.

Do you now? But how did you know what they were saying in the cafés, Belle? I always thought cafés were for silly people and you only went into town to see your stockbroker?

And a good thing I did, too. If I hadn't, I can't imagine where we'd be today. The Lord only knows what would have become of us if our future had been left in your hands.

Belle, really. This houseboat was a gift to whom, I might ask?

And who has paid the bills on it for the last forty years, if I might ask?

Alice tossed her head.

Money has never meant anything to me, that's true enough. I've always been a gypsy at heart. Who cares about money? *Who cares?*

Belle sniffed.

That's easy for you to say. Nothing more substantial than a day-dream has ever meant anything to you.

Dimitri, mused Alice. His ironing woman was a Copt, I remember. She had the Coptic cross tattooed on her wrists and she spoke Italian because she'd been educated by nuns.

You'd be the one to know, said Belle. You always did like to poke around in the servants' quarters.

Because I always found them interesting, that's why. More interesting than the people who strut in drawing rooms and put on airs. Servants have fascinating things to tell you. That's where I learned to read hands and Tarot cards.

Put on airs? What's that supposed to mean?

Just that that Croat or whatever he was, that Dimitri, was a terrible bore. Oh Belle, he was. Admit it for once.

He was Montenegrin and fabulously wealthy, and if you'd had an ounce of sense you could have asked him for that villa and he would have given it to you, instead of just those little porcelain trinkets.

Money money money, never anything but money. I like my shepherdesses and I don't give a hoot about money.

Of course you don't, why should you? Haven't I always been here
to see that we're provided for?

But he was such a bore, Belle. All he could talk about was his
tedious researches into the Balkan aristocracy. I mean really, who
could care about such a ludicrous notion? That and his daubs, as he
called them, those cheap paintings he bought in Europe and insisted
on attributing to unknown pupils of various seventeenth-century
masters. Dimitri indeed. That *Croat*.

You may say that now, but I'll have you know the stocks I recommended he give you that Christmas paid excellent dividends for decades. Right up until the last war, thank you.

Well you ought to thank me, Belle. If there were any dividends, I
certainly earned them. Do you know he actually told me once that
Albania was a good place to buy paintings? Ah ha, I thought, now
it's all going to come out. A mysterious tale about stolen master-
pieces and a secret castle high in the Albanian Alps known only to
dissolute Russian princes and unscrupulous Levantine art dealers.
That's what I imagined, but when I asked him why Albania was a
good place to buy paintings, his answer was that they were cheap
there. Can you believe it? Of course paintings were cheap in Albania,
why wouldn't they be? What kind of a painting could you have
found in Albania sixty years ago? Or today, for that matter? Of
course they were cheap, how ridiculous. They were utterly worthless.

Stop prattling, said Belle. There are no Alps in Albania. Don't
become overexcited just because we have a male guest, you're not a
fifteen-year-old flirt anymore. Stop squirming and try to compose
yourself. Would you like more sherry?

I think I will have a little more. Being reminded of Dimitri makes
me thirsty. . . . *Arghh*. Always that sticky starchy taste gumming up
my throat before the guests arrived for dinner. And there was never
any relief from it. An hour later, between soup and fish, just when I
was beginning to be able to swallow normally again, Dimitri would
come prancing down to my end of the table and wiggle his eyebrows
and whisper something about a quick private stroll down to the
bushes at the end of the garden. Between soup and fish, mind you,
and I would even have to make up the excuse we gave our guests.
Dimitri indeed. . . . *Arghh*. What a Croat. You're right that there was

nothing aristocratic about the way he got through a dinner.

Belle had put aside her knitting and was stiffly crossing the room to Alice's chair, a decanter in her hand. Her left arm was hanging down in some strange way, Joe noticed, and she almost seemed to be dragging her left foot. She poured from the decanter into Alice's glass.

Is that all I get, just a half? My throat's suddenly dry as can be.

Your nerves, dear. Remember what the doctor said.

He's a silly young fool.

That's as it may be, but we know what happens when you drink too much sherry. Remember what happened that last evening with Dimitri.

I do remember too, said Alice. We were getting to the end of dinner and the savory was just about to be brought in, when Dimitri came prancing down to my end of the table and wiggled his eyebrows and whispered the usual whisper, and I just stood up and smiled and spoke very clearly to the guests, most of whom were his business associates.

Please excuse us, dears, but Dimitri simply insists we race down to the end of the garden so I can taste his very own savory behind the bushes, the sticky starchy kind, tra-la. But start right in because we'll be back in a minute. Dimitri's always very fast in the garden, or anywhere.

Little Alice laughed.

And that was the last I saw of him and his boring stockbroker crowd. Dimitri bolted faster than he'd ever done anything in his life, even behind the bushes.

Alice, said Belle affectionately. Try to behave yourself. I just can't imagine what Joe must be thinking.

Belle was stiffly, slowly, returning to her chair. Was her face set like that because of pain? wondered Joe.

Alice emptied her sherry glass at a gulp. She smiled across the room at Joe.

I did drink too much sherry that evening, she confided, and I *am* excitable. And I'm also impulsive and changeable and not the most practical person in the world, just as Belle says. But we are what we are, aren't we? Belle has a head for solid facts and dates and things like that, and I just don't. When I remember things I think of colors and patterns and impressions. It's just the way I am.

Belle had resumed her knitting. Joe noticed her loving glance at her sister.

You used to paint beautifully, said Belle.

Oh no, not beautifully, but I enjoyed it and that was the important thing. It was a way of expressing myself. I always used to say I'd be a recognized painter by the time I was fifty.

Little Alice looked down at her lap.

But it didn't work out that way, she added in a quiet voice.

Alice has crippled hands, said Belle softly. Arthritis. It happened years ago. It was very unfair.

Oh well, murmured Alice, we can't have everything. And there's always a reason why something should be so, rather than otherwise. At least that's what I've always told myself.

She smiled. A bright smile.

I'm a dreamer, she said, Belle's right about that too. When I was little I used to get up early and go out and run through the fields to feel the wind in my hair, and then I'd climb a tree somewhere to spy on people. But I wasn't spying on them really, it was just that I liked to look over walls. I hate walls, I've always hated walls. So I used to climb trees so there'd be no walls, and I'd look down into people's yards and make up stories about what they were doing. When I went out for my run Belle would still be in bed, but then when I got back she would be sitting on the front porch, reading a book. Belle was always reading as a child. She *will* be bookish, Mother used to say. She *will* be stubborn and not go out and play like other children. You always had your nose in a book then, didn't you, dear? And I could never understand it. I always wanted to be out running and exploring and living like a gypsy, and I could never understand how someone could just sit around all day and read.

Belle wrinkled her nose. She sniffed contentedly.

You silly. What do you think reading is? I could go all over the world in books.

History books, said Alice. You always read history. And when I came back from my morning run we'd sit on the porch and Mother would bring us cookies and milk, and I'd tell you all the things I'd seen, and you'd say I'd made them up. And then you'd tell me some stories from your history books, and I'd say you'd made *them* up.

Alice laughed.

What a pair we were. So very different from the very beginning.

Yes, murmured Belle. Uncle George always used to say that. He used to say he could never believe we were twins, we were so different.

And on rainy afternoons, said Alice, you'd bring the brown stool in from the front room and put it next to the kitchen table, and you'd climb up there and pretend you were an empress sitting on your throne, remember? A great empress of all the somethings, and I would be your lady-in-waiting and bring your jewels.

Did you mind? asked Belle.

Oh no, I loved it. Especially when you asked for your crown and I brought it in on a cushion the way you said, and I waited in the doorway until all your ministers had taken their places and you told me to advance, and in I marched in front of all of them, very carefully because I was always afraid I might trip, and I stepped up on the stool and the moment had come at last, and I put the crown on your head. Oh I was so *proud* then. And later when court was dismissed we'd go into the bedroom and you'd drape me with scarves in front of the mirror, and I'd dance. I wonder why I always imagined Cleopatra wore scarves and danced?

I don't know, said Belle. Perhaps you saw a picture somewhere. But dancing in scarves is nice and you were so pretty.

Oh no, not pretty.

But you were. You were a beautiful little dream in gossamer veils, and you just floated through the air.

No no, murmured Alice, I was just myself. But the books never claimed Cleopatra was pretty, did they? They just said she was charming and had a lightness about her, and that's what always appealed to me, the lightness, the light. Any fool can be born with a pretty face. That's nothing.

Abruptly, Belle's hands went still above her knitting. She was staring down at the floor and Alice noticed it at once.

What is it, dear? Is your side bothering you again?

No, it's not that. I was thinking about the little brown stool and climbing up to sit on the kitchen table, to play at being the great empress of all the somethings, nearly ninety years ago now. How foolish it seems. The empress of what, I ask you? Our little front porch?

Belle's face was sad. She stared at the floor.

Well you *were,* said Alice softly. You were, you know.

I was what, dear?

The empress of our front porch. For me, you were.

Well, murmured Belle. Well. That's something, I guess.

And it is, said Alice, it *is* something too. I've never been so proud in all my life as when the time came to enter the court with your crown and all the ministers bowed low, and I walked in holding the cushion high, so afraid I'd trip, and you smiled at me, Belle, right there in front of everybody. And it made me feel wonderful inside and suddenly I knew I wouldn't trip and everything was going to be all right.

It was the proudest moment of my life, whispered Little Alice, and it always will be. *Always.*

When three or four clocks in the parlor struck the hour, Belle excused herself to take some medicine. As soon as she had left the room Alice came over to sit beside Joe. She put her hand on his arm.

Tip your head, please? I want to whisper.

Joe did so.

It's about my sister. I know she seems grouchy sometimes but she doesn't really mean it, it's just that she's in such terrible pain. First she broke one hip and then she broke the other, and there were all these operations when they put in plates and wires and I don't know what, and the doctors said she'd never walk again because nothing's supposed to heal at our age. But they didn't know Belle, did they? When Belle's determined to do something she just sets her jaw and goes ahead and does it. It doesn't matter who says it can't be done, she just does it. Belle *will* refuse to listen to others, Mother used to say. She *will* just get that look on her face and do exactly what she wants to.

Little Alice smiled warmly.

Even Uncle George, the poor dear, used to say the same thing. Well after she had all those operations, Belle decided she was going to walk again. And she went on trying and trying with her lips tight and her jaw set, and finally she did it. The doctors said it was a miracle but I knew it was just Belle being herself. Belle likes to pretend, you see, that she doesn't believe in miracles. She likes to think she's too rational for things like that.

Little Alice laughed merrily, then turned serious.

So she learned to walk again, and soon after that she had a stroke. That's what you notice about her left side, she's partly paralyzed. Usually I get her medicine for her, but tonight she didn't want me to because you're here, I could tell. And that's why I let her bring you your whiskey and pour my sherry, because I could tell she wanted so much to do it. Belle's proud that way. She wants to keep up appearances.

I just thought you should know, added Little Alice. So you wouldn't think badly of her.

I could never do that, said Joe.

And she was always so talented, continued Little Alice. Everyone admired her for it. She used to write beautiful stories in French and Russian which she'd learned mostly on her own, from books, because she's so clever with languages. And comedies that were witty and subtle and made you laugh and laugh long after you'd finished them. Belle was going to be a writer, you see, and I was going to be a painter. Privately, we always had those dreams, just between the two of us.

Little Alice looked down at her hands.

Those particular dreams didn't work out for either of us. But there were other things to compensate, and Belle has never stopped writing. The work that has come to mean the most to her is a history of the life of Alexander the Great, for children, which she has worked on for years and years. She's completed three or four volumes but she hasn't gotten to the end yet, and it's all told simply and directly so that a child can understand it and appreciate the great accomplishments. Not the military victories so much as the journeys to strange lands and all the strange peoples Alexander met, so children can appreciate what it means to try hard and live your own life. Someday she may finish it, I don't know.

Shyly, Alice looked up.

Or maybe not? Maybe she can't bring herself to finish it and the story of Alexander the Great will just go on and on forever, like the Nile?

Little Alice smiled.

It's true that people are affected by where they live, and we've lived here so long it's almost like a dream. Oh yes, we're ancient and we know it. Sometimes I think we're as old as the pyramids, so much has passed by us here.

She laughed.

But I'm chattering again, aren't I? Belle's right, I just can't help myself. But you see I never wanted to become old and even now I don't *feel* old, even though I look a hundred and ten, more or less. I know it sounds strange, but inside I feel exactly the same as I did when I used to go for my runs early in the morning and I'd come back and find Belle sitting on the porch, reading, and Mother would bring us cookies and milk. Inside, it's still me.

Little Alice frowned.

And I could *never* picture myself living like those little old ladies you used to see around here, who never appeared in public until the sun went down. You used to see them gathering like old crows on the corners of small empty streets just after sunset, shaking their ancient hats and chatting in French with Greek or Armenian accents, or Syrian or Maltese accents, and then they'd go strolling off in a cluster along the flowered railings to their daily card game in some damp darkened room that you knew would be cluttered with heavy Moorish-style furniture, the arabesques and mother-of-pearl gleaming feebly in the gloom, the fragile inlaid filigree all gummed up with dust.

I hate dark rooms, whispered Little Alice. And I don't want to look like an old crow in some ridiculous old-fashioned hat, and I hate those tiresome card games old women play and the heavy gloomy furniture that always goes with them. I like things light and airy and I never wanted to be old, and somehow I've never been able to picture myself that way. I know I'm as ancient as the hills but I don't *feel* that way. I feel as if I'm just still me.

Little Alice abruptly smiled.

But here I am prattling again. Tell me, do you like Egypt? It's changed so much since we first came here. Originally, Belle and I were on the stage and that's why we never married. In those days actresses never got into families. Nowadays it's different, but it used to be like that.

You must have been very young when you came to Egypt, said Joe.

Oh yes, we were. With white camellias in our shining dark hair. And it was unforgettable, that first sparkling winter we were here, nearly three-quarters of a century ago.

Was it that long ago?

Yes, that's when it was. We came for the opening of *Aïda*, for the first performance of *Aïda* that was ever given anywhere. But we didn't come as wealthy tourists or as the guests of someone who was wealthy. We were poor then and we didn't know a soul in Egypt and we came as slave-girls in *Aïda*, just two little slave-girls off at the back of the stage. *Aïda* opened at the khedivial opera house in honor of the opening of the Suez Canal, and there were guests from all over the world in Cairo then, and not one of them paid a penny for anything. Everything was free, given by the Magnificent, the khedive Ismail. The shops and hotels all over Egypt just sent in their bills to the minister of finance, who paid the lot of them without a murmur. The road to the pyramids was built then, so the Empress Eugénie could visit them in her carriage.

Little Alice nodded to herself.

And even though we were just slave-girls in the production, we began to attract a certain amount of attention, because we were twins, I suppose. And before long we were being invited around to dinners and to sunset sails on the Nile, and then later came the beautiful houses, the villas that were museums of china and carpets, the rarest in the world. And Belle had her residences and I had mine, and it was lavish, I can tell you. We used to call on each other in our carriages or meet along the river somewhere, and then in the evenings we'd be sitting in our separate boxes at the opera, in the first tier, our breasts covered with diamonds and every pair of glasses in the house turning from one of us to the other, looking to see what we were wearing and watching to see which gentlemen we spoke to, and with how much enthusiasm.

Little Alice smiled shyly.

People used to talk about us in those days but I don't suppose they do anymore. I don't suppose people even remember we're still alive.

Oh yes they do, said Joe. And there are all kinds of mysterious tales about the mysterious sisters who live in a rambling houseboat on the Nile.

Little Alice clapped her hands in delight.

There are? Still? Even though we're a hundred and ten, more or less?

Little Alice grew wistful.

What kinds of tales? Where do they say we came from?

Ah, now that's the most mysterious part of all. Nobody claims to know where you really came from, but one story is that you were

Russian princesses running away from a family scandal. An uncle had gambled everything away in Nice, or some such thing, so friends bundled the two of you into a sealed train in St Petersburg one cold winter night, at the Finland Station, and you went abroad with the best of old Russia in your suitcases and never went back again.

It sounds like a nineteenth-century novel, whispered Alice happily.

It does, doesn't it? And then there's a totally different story, just as intriguing, about the two of you being Hungarian actresses who went to Paris at a young age and became a hit there. And another story begins in Venice, and another in Vienna, and just on and on. There's no end to them really, and one is more exotic than the other.

Little Alice smiled, looking down at her hands.

Just imagine, she murmured. Isn't that lovely. . . . Uncle George would have liked that, she added with great feeling.

And who was Uncle George, said Joe, if you don't mind my asking?

No, I don't mind. We loved him a great deal and we both like to talk about him now. It didn't used to be so easy. . . . He was our mother's brother and he was the only relative we had, the only family. He ran the pub in the village where we grew up. It wasn't much of a pub but that's what we used to call it. When Belle and I were children we cleaned up for him there. We mopped the floors and carried in the firewood and did the washing up. We always thought it was very exciting to be in such an adult place.

You were English, then, originally?

Yes, from a little village near York. Our father had worked in a factory and he was killed in an accident when we were babies, so Mother took us back to her village. The only thing we ever knew about our father was that he was a laborer and drank a lot because he was unhappy. Mother never talked about him, Uncle George told us what we know. Apparently our father used to beat Mother when he drank, we overheard Mother and Uncle George talking about it once. And then after he died Mother made quilts and things like that to sell, but it was really Uncle George who made life possible for us. He was a bachelor and he helped out with our food and our clothes and other things, and the presents Santa Claus gave us at Christmas, and the presents we received on our birthday, were always from Uncle George.

It was Uncle George's cottage that we lived in when Mother took us back to her village. It was small so he moved out back into the shed and let us use the cottage. He made wonderful things with his hands, mostly for us, but he must have been unhappy too because he also drank a lot. He was a kind man and very gentle and he was always so good to us. When we were children, there wouldn't have been any Christmases for us without Uncle George.

Little Alice gazed down at her hands.

He drowned himself in the millpond one New Year's Eve. He went down there alone in the darkness and drowned himself and they found him on New Year's Day. He would have been forty that year. And after that Mother said she wanted to leave the village forever, she said she just couldn't live there anymore. Well she had her own dreams, Mother did, and she wasn't just like other people, and there was a little money from the cottage and from Uncle George's share of the pub, and she used that to take us to Italy, which was an unheard-of thing to do in those days for people like us, common people who were poor and uneducated and didn't know anyone. But she was a brave woman and she wanted her daughters to make something of their lives, so she took us to Italy because she loved the sun, and an Italian man she met gave us singing lessons, Belle and me, and that's where it all began for us. All of it.

Little Alice tipped her head.

It's strange, isn't it, those exotic tales people tell about Russian princesses and Hungarian actresses, and Venice and Paris and Vienna and all the rest of it. Of course, I'd be speaking less than the truth if I didn't tell you we used to encourage that sort of thing when we first came here.

Little Alice looked up at Joe.

Two little girls, she whispered. Two little girls mopping the floor of a pub in a village near York, a long time ago. And then later the singing lessons, and eventually appearing as slave-girls in the first performance of *Aïda* that was ever given anywhere, just tiny parts for two young girls. And so it all began, and so it goes.

Suddenly her smile was gone and she was gazing up at Joe with a childlike face, in a questioning way.

So it's no wonder, is it, that we never left? That we stayed in Cairo, in faraway Egypt?

No wonder at all, said Joe. After all, not everyone has the chance to be Cleopatra beside the Nile.

Little Alice stared at her cramped gnarled hands.

Oh yes, she whispered, *oh yes*. And that's what I always used to tell myself when I sat in my box at the opera and everyone looked at me and envied me for my diamonds and I felt nothing but rage and sorrow because I could never get married. And later when I was home again in whatever villa it was, and the man had left to go home to his family and the servants were in bed, and it was very late and I was all alone again and crying and crying in bed because I knew I could never get married, that's what I used to tell myself. Ten thousand times I must have said it as I cried myself to sleep. We can't have everything in life, so remember how lucky you are. Think of the good things you have and just remember. *Remember*. . . . Or as Uncle George used to say, You can take what you want from life. All you have to do is pay for it. . . .

Joe reached out and plucked a tear from her cheek.

There now, he murmured, there now. And so we do remember, and so we do pay. And what a beautiful night it is to be here with the two of you in this wondrous room, the stars so bright and magical upon the river.

Big Belle cleared her throat by the door, a noisy growling sound. Slowly, she came limping back into the room, smiling broadly.

Here now, what's this? Are the two of you holding hands already? I'm gone for no more than a minute and my little sister is already flirting with some gentleman caller?

My fault entirely, said Joe. We got to talking about the past and I'm hopelessly sentimental, I have to tell you that.

You're Irish, thundered Belle.

Well that's right.

Well don't be redundant then, we heard you the first time. Now let me take your glass and refill it for you. It's getting late and we have some talking to do.

Alice moved away to her chair. Belle returned with the new glass of whiskey.

Will that do?

It will. A mite large as before, but then.

But then, life *should* be large, boomed Belle. Otherwise, what's the point? Now you've been sitting here patiently letting two old sisters carry on the way they're used to doing, and you've hardly said a word, which must mean you're out looking for things. My guess is, you have some questions to ask. Do you?

Yes, as a matter of fact.

Fact? thundered Belle. Fact, you say? Well since Alice and I have lived a total of almost two hundred years, and gossip being what it is in Cairo, and men being what they are anywhere, Alice and I have come across a few facts in our time. But first, tell me this. Do you work for this man Bletchley?

In a way, I do. But in a way, not.

What do your questions have to do with, then?

Joe looked from one sister to the other. Straight out and straight ahead, he thought. They drink their gin straight here and they serve their whiskey straight and they call a Dimitri a Dimitri, at the dinner table or anywhere else, so it's not a time for niceties now.

Joe looked from one sister to the other.

Stern, he said. My questions have to do with Stern.

Belle's knitting needles stopped clicking. Immediately the two sisters were on guard and a silence settled over the room.

Stern is a very dear friend, Alice said quietly after a moment.

I'm aware of that, replied Joe. That's why I'm here.

Do you know him well? asked Belle.

I did. I haven't seen him in a few years.

Where did you know him?

In Jerusalem, it was.

In what connection?

I worked for him for a time. Later we became just friends.

Worked for him? Doing what?

Smuggling arms into Palestine. For the Haganah.

Big Belle stirred. She seemed to be recalling something.

Do you know anything about scarabs?

One only, answered Joe. A giant stone scarab with a mysterious smile carved into its face. A great huge and hollow giant stone scarab. That's what I smuggled the arms in. Stern had set me up to pass myself off as a dealer in antiquities.

When exactly?

After the last war.

Belle studied Joe more closely.

What does the Home for Crimean War Heroes mean to you?

It means a charity in Jerusalem, said Joe, where I lived when I first arrived in the city. I was on the run from the British and in disguise, and I lived there until I met Stern. They gave me a used khaki blanket which I still have. Their standard award of merit, it was.

Little Alice was becoming so excited she could hardly sit still. A smile was growing on Belle's face.

Do you play cards? asked Belle.

I don't now but I did once. Poker. Twelve years of it in Jerusalem.

Big Belle suddenly beamed. She whooped as a crescendo of chirping noises erupted in Little Alice's corner.

That Joe, thundered Belle, the Irishman who lived on a roof in the Old City. *Free the serfs. Annex the Crimea and the hell with the Turks.* Why didn't you say you were *that* Joe and not just some odd rowing companion of young Ahmad? We've heard a good deal from Stern in the past about *that* Joe.

Happily Belle grabbed the gin bottle at her elbow and upended it, taking a drink straight from the bottle. Little Alice's mouth fell open.

Belle. What on *earth?*

Big Belle smacked her lips. She sighed noisily and licked her lips with an enormous smile.

I know, dear. Forgive me.

But Belle, *realll*-ly. I haven't seen you do that in sixty-five years.

Belle laughed.

Sixty-seven, dear.

Not since that very first time when you were going to spend a night with Menelik, said Alice. Not since that afternoon when we were somewhere together and Menelik sent a note around just begging you to spend a quiet candlelit evening with him in his sarcophagus, to celebrate his retirement from his digs in the field.

I know, dear, and what a grand invitation it was to a young woman not much more than twenty. Hieroglyphs engraved on a heavy slab of stone, no less, in Menelik's very own hand, with accompanying translations engraved beneath it in demotic Egyptian and ancient Greek. Menelik's very own Rosetta Stone of love. Just think of all the time and thought it must have taken him to turn that heavy basalt slab into an invitation. No young woman in her right mind could ever have responded to that with anything less than a resounding, *Yes I said Yes I will Yes.*

I remember, mused Alice dreamily.

Indeed you do, said Belle, and so do I. It isn't often that a suitor presents his case to a woman with words actually written in stone.

To the woman of my dreams,
the incomparable Belle.

Dearest:

Today I retire from a lifetime of active archeology and go underground for good and forever. Won't you please help me inaugurate my future life in the crypt by the Nile that is to be my new home? Among its many delights is a most spacious sarcophagus, cork-lined, which is to serve as both my bed and bedroom, and which will simply take your breath away. Large, my dear, as well as timeless, and need I add that they don't make them like that anymore?

Until an hour after sunset then, my most beautiful Belle, for a time we will both cherish as the night of a lifetime.

Easily. Clearly. And until that moment when I hear your sweet knock on the door of my anonymous crypt, I remain,

Your most ardent and devoted of admirers above or beneath the sands of Egypt, both ancient and modern,

$\qquad$ *All my love,*
$\qquad$ *(s) Menelik Ziwar.*

P.S. Don't bother to dress. After a life of determined Egyptology, all of history is at my disposal and we can wander wherever we choose, adopting such costumes and manners and methods as may suit our purposes, our moods, our tastes, and above all our grand designs for lovemaking throughout eternity.

Belle sighed. She smacked her lips.

No, she said, you don't see invitations like that anymore, no more than you meet a man like Menelik. Menelik was different, and his unusual invitation was just the beginning of the unusual delights we were to know together that evening. One might have thought a sarcophagus would be a trifle cramped for the tour through history Menelik had in mind, but that was beforehand. Before Menelik got his hands moving and the champagne flowing and started peeling grapes and dipping them here and there.

Belle. I just don't know what to say. I mean, *realll*-ly. What can Joe possibly be thinking?

I know, dear, but Menelik was an out-and-out contortionist and there's no use denying it. I've never known anything like it, he was just everywhere at once. It must have been all those years he spent excavating ancient tombs, bending himself around in tight quarters. Not to mention doing so in the dark much of the time, when he had to depend on his fingertips to do his seeing for him. *Oh,* Menelik's fingertips. It makes me shiver to think of them even now.

Belle? Are you sure you're all right?

I am, dear, perfectly, I haven't felt so good in sixty-seven years. It's also that first rush the gin gives you when you gulp it straight from the bottle, there's nothing like it. I never could abide sipping from glasses in order to appear ladylike. Menelik used to say there was only one way to deal with a bottle of gin. The same way you deal with me, he used to say. Just grab the fellow firmly and upend the rascal and swallow for the life of you.

Belle.

Big Belle smacked her lips. She laughed.

Now *he* was a man, Menelik was. Who could ever imagine such a thrilling night in a sarcophagus? And a sarcophagus that had originally belonged to Cheops' mother, of all things? Oh yes, there was never a moment's rest when you were with Menelik and he was mulling over five thousand years of Egyptian history. Just when you thought all that coming and going through the ages might have tired him a little, he'd twist himself around somehow and all at once he'd be whispering in your ear again. Do you know what they used to do, he'd whisper, back during the XII Dynasty? No? Well it's rather clever. All you do is move this leg a little like that, and your left hand here, and your other hand . . . oh yes. *Oh yes. Ooooo. . . .*

Belle. Please.

Big Belle sighed. She licked her lips and beamed.

And then there was that specialty Menelik used to claim had been invented during an even earlier dynasty, but which was really nothing more than a very elaborate hum-job with a few sacred props thrown in. . . . *Oh,* Menelik. It's exhausting just to think of him. Perhaps I ought to have one more, all at once I'm feeling thirsty. These memories. . . .

Abruptly Belle hoisted the bottle of gin and drank again. She sighed and placed the bottle back on the table.

But why didn't you tell us you were *that* Joe? That Joe, just imagine. . . . Well all right then, all right. On to business.

Belle's knitting needles began to click in the stillness. Alice glanced at her sister and straightened her shawl, going through a final flurry of flutters before subsiding quietly into an alert position. Belle cleared her throat

Are you ready, Alice?

Ready, Belle.

Belle gazed at Joe.

Stern's in trouble?

Yes.

You think it's serious?

Yes.

How serious?

Joe looked at her and then at Alice.

I'm afraid it's the end.

Belle's fingers stopped moving. She stared through the open French doors at the river, her jaw set.

I refuse to believe that, she said. Please begin with your questions.

I'm on unsure ground here, said Joe. I've got some bits and pieces but I don't have an overall shape to what I'm looking for. You might say it's the same as it used to be for Menelik back when he was digging up the past and everything he found was partial and broken and dusted by time, and he had to try to put it together so that it would make some sense. To see who the people of that particular dynasty were, and what they had been up to. A little bit like that maybe. I suppose we all have to delve into the Egyptologist's craft now and then, and there even seem to be some hieroglyphs involved. A code, so to speak. Things I can't decipher because there's no Rosetta Stone for this one.

This one? asked Belle. What's that, *this one*? What is the code? What does it cover?

Stern's life, I guess you'd have to say, I suppose that's what it really is. And since you know Stern as well as you do, you can understand it's not a simple matter to sift the sands through your fingers and come up with something with a shape to it, a coherency that translates into words. The end result has to be simple enough because Stern's just a man. But that's only once you know how to read the hieroglyphs.

A Greek word meaning *sacred writing*, murmured Belle.

Joe nodded.

Yes, Greek. Like a good many things in this part of the world.

But the writings the word denotes are much older, mused Belle.

Much older, said Joe. So my task is a little bit the same as Menelik's used to be. Of course the best thing would be to talk to people who aren't here, but you can never do that. And it's also true that what Menelik dealt with happened four or five thousand years ago, while what I'm looking for happened yesterday or a month or a year or two ago, but it's the same thing really. Ancient history always begins yesterday, doesn't it?

Or even with your afternoon nap, murmured Alice. Sometimes everything that happened before then is like a dream, little shards of this and that. And Menelik, bless his soul, would have been the first to say so.

True, said Joe. The evidence never is in, not by half. So, like Menelik, I have to blow the dust off the shards and nudge the bits and pieces around and see if I can make a picture out of them.

Belle's patient, said Alice. She's always been clever at jigsaw puzzles. I have no patience at all but I can sense patterns sometimes. They just come to me.

Well? said Belle

Joe nodded.

Yes. There's this, for example. Rommel knows things he shouldn't know and it has something to do with codes. British codes. It's as if Rommel could read them. The important one may be called the Black Code, and somehow a Colonel Fellers may be involved, he's the American military attaché here in Cairo. Because Stern said recently to someone, first thing in the morning, that Rommel was probably enjoying his *little fellers* at that very moment, over breakfast.

Arab boys? asked Alice.

Too simple, declared Belle.

Oh.

The little things over breakfast, said Belle, have to refer to the American colonel.

Oh of course.

Belle closed her eyes to concentrate. A few moments later she opened them.

Nothing. Alice?

Alice was staring dreamily across the room toward the door. They followed her gaze. Belle sniffed thoughtfully, quietly.

Is it the door, Alice?

No, the doorstop.

Belle and Joe studied the doorstop. It was made of wood and hand-painted, a small upright tableau depicting two vivacious young girls from the nineteenth century, smiling in long curls and flowery hats and voluminous dresses, carrying parasols. The clothes and the sky had been done in delicate pastels, faded now by three-quarters of a century of Egyptian sunlight. The painted earth at the bottom of the block of wood, the weight of the doorstop, was richly dark and blackened by the passage of time.

We must have worn a dozen petticoats in those days, said Alice. How old were we when I painted that?

Fourteen, replied Belle. We were in Rome.

That's right, and I painted a lot of them one summer, trying to make a little money. I used to go around to the tables in the pensione at teatime and sell them, remember? But that's the only one left now, the only one we brought to Egypt. Just look at those hats, Belle, and those ridiculous dresses. How did we ever move around dressed like that?

It was clumsy. We were very restricted.

Oh we were, we were. I used to hate wearing all those petticoats. And just look how rich and black the earth is, not red and sandy the way it is here. Oh how strange this is.

It is strange, Alice. I wonder what brought all of that to mind just at this moment?

I have no idea, I can't imagine. But didn't we think we were very grown-up when we could dress like that?

Yes, petticoats and everything.

That's right. And we were only fourteen years old, and the Italian men were always . . . and now Joe has mentioned a Black Code and the black in that painting seems to remind me of something, Belle. Something having to do with sex in Rome.

278

Sex way back then, dear? That's a rather extensive subject, I'm afraid. Or are you thinking of something we might have heard about more recently?

Yes, more recently. Within the last year, perhaps. Oh that's maddening, it's right on the tip of my tongue. Why do we have to be so old and have so many things to remember? But you must know what I'm thinking about, Belle. *Sex. Rome.* Can't you remember?

There are hundreds of incidents to remember, dear, but which one of them is on your mind now? Maybe it might help if you narrowed things down. What kind of sex was it, exactly?

Italian sex. Seduction. Age leering at youth and innocence corrupted. A poor young cleaning woman just in from the country and a suave older man spending money on her and giving her an evening beyond her wildest dreams, and then taking her back to his candlelit flat overlooking the Piazza Navonna and whispering *bella bella* and making fantastic promises while pulling off her petticoats and exacting a few concrete promises in return. Oh just think, Belle, *think.* I know you can recall it.

Suddenly Belle's knitting needles clicked once.

Of course. That's it, Alice, you've found it.

Little Alice smiled shyly. Big Belle turned to Joe with a triumphant expression.

Isn't she a marvel? The Black Code is some kind of American cipher which the Italians managed to get their hands on in Rome. They stole it from the American Embassy with the help of a cleaning woman who was on the night shift. That was five or six months ago, around the beginning of the year, and the Americans still don't know about it, apparently. Now one would assume the Italians passed along their discovery to their allies, the Germans. What's the job of a military attaché, exactly?

He reports on the military situation in the country where he's stationed, answered Joe.

Ha, peeped Alice. Do Belle and I look like military secrets?

Indeed, said Belle, the attachés we've known always seemed to be up to something quite different. But let's assume this Colonel Fellers is more conscientious than most and actually does his job. What if he's been sending reports back to Washington on a daily basis? His reports would naturally include a synopsis of British intentions, the locations of British units and their strength and morale, and British plans for offense and defense. He would send his reports by commercial wire, which means that practically any clerk in the Egyptian Telegraph Company would have access to them. Or anyone else along the commercial telegraph route to Washington. Furthermore, it's likely that he would file his reports at the end of the working day, which is to say early every evening.

In the Black Code, chirped Alice. Seduction made me think of it.

And so, concluded Belle, allowing for some deciphering and translating in the dark hours, the timing would be just right for Rommel to have his *little fellers* sitting beside his herring at breakfast the following morning. Everything that would be useful for Rommel to know, carefully compiled by Colonel Fellers.

Belle smiled, Alice smiled. Joe was utterly astonished. He looked from one sister to the other and whistled softly.

And there, said Belle, is the secret behind the Desert Fox's uncanny foresight. He can read. And thus it seems it may not always be wise to praise famous men.

Or to put it another way, chirped Alice gaily, you know a man by what he puts his nose into first thing in the morning. *Little fellers?* Herring? . . .

What do you think? Belle asked Joe.

In answer Joe whistled again, very softly.

I think the two of you are astounding, he said. And I also think the Black Code is about to join Hammurabi's code as one more chunk of ancient history in the sandy Middle East. From now on it's herring only for Rommel's breakfast, and a once dashing hero is back to looking like a surly thug when not in uniform.

Well there, twittered Alice brightly.

Belle clicked her knitting needles with conviction.

Next? she said.

Joe nodded. He frowned.

I'm sorry, but a few things are still a little unclear to me. Bletchley has told me almost nothing and I haven't been able to talk to Stern yet, so the hieroglyphs are still a mite mysterious. The truth is, I still can't make out Stern's role exactly.

Ask questions then, suggested Belle. Isn't that why you're here?

It is, said Joe, and I have to admit I feel a little bit like some ancient Greek traveler come to pay a call on the Sphinx.

Little Alice laughed.

Come now, we're not as enigmatic as all that, are we? Two forgotten little old women with their aches and pains and their lives behind them?

Joe smiled.

No one would ever describe you that way. The two of you are a legend, you must know that.

To others maybe, said Alice, looking down at her cramped hands, her laughter gone.

Just look at those, she whispered sadly. Two ugly claws, that's what they are.

There there, said Belle in a quiet voice. We mustn't dwell on the unfortunate things, dear. After all, life has been very kind to us in so many ways.

Alice looked up at her sister, who smiled and nodded in encouragement.

Belle sitting stiffly erect.

What a will of iron, thought Joe. Two broken hips and part of her paralyzed and nothing holding her together at all really but that fierce mind of hers, that iron soul that won't give up because she knows her little sister couldn't manage without her. Because she knows Little Alice would just float away like the beautiful dream she's always been. Wind in her hair and running through the fields and climbing trees to see over walls, a pretty singing bird who'd just take flight on the rays of the sun and float off in the summer air forever if it weren't for her older sister waiting back there on the porch where she's always been, solid and substantial and just a mind now, just a soul that won't give in. *Big Belle,* they've always called her and that's what she is, determined and fierce and all mind and soul now. And precious little else now, God have mercy.

Belle turned to him.

You have questions?

I do, said Joe. I was wondering if Stern has known all along that the Germans have the Black Code?

Not all along. He found out not too long ago, as we did, by way of the Italians. They're good at so many things, but war isn't one of them. Winston summed up the matter once with his usual flair for words. *An Italian blitzkrieg* was the phrase he used, which is certainly the most hopeless of concepts, and also one reason I've always liked the Italians. A people incapable of making war well are blessed by God. In any case, Alice and I knew only that this American cipher had been stolen in Rome. We didn't know what use it was being put to, or about this Colonel Fellers here in Cairo. But Stern would have been aware of all that. And more important, the Germans would have known that he was.

You're certain of that?

I am now. It's simple enough to reconstruct it in retrospect. I would say the Germans were probably present when the truth slipped out in front of Stern. So if he had spoken to the British, the Germans would have known immediately who had given the secret away. You understand, I'm sure, that Stern's extraordinary value to the Allies has always been that he's thoroughly trusted by the other side. It's this very unusual quality he has about him. This ability to inspire trust.

I know, said Joe.

So knowing that the Black Code had been compromised, Stern was placed in a terrible position.

Stern's usual position, it seems. But the two of you suspected this?

Yes, we both sensed it. We could see how tormented he'd become. It was obvious something was torturing him, but we didn't know what it was until tonight.

This is an idle speculation, said Joe, but do you think Stern was planning to tell the British eventually?

That's neither idle nor speculation, replied Belle. The reason Stern returned to Cairo a few days ago was precisely to do that. Again, this has only become clear to us tonight. Until a few days ago he'd been hoping the British would uncover the truth about the Black Code through other channels, other sources. He'd been desperately waiting and praying for that. But when this last mission turned out to be such a disaster, he decided he couldn't wait any longer. His mission was part of a larger scheme, apparently, which was a total failure.

Yes, I know about it, said Joe. There were special strike forces and the like against the German and Italian bases being used to attack Malta. Bletchley mentioned it. Stern was probably serving as a pathfinder, the contact for one of the commando groups behind enemy lines.

He was devastated when he returned, continued Belle. Truly

282

wretched. He said he feared the tide might really have turned in favor of the Germans. So he had decided to talk to Bletchley.

Joe was puzzled.

Yet I was with Bletchley yesterday evening and there was no hint at all that he even knew Stern was back in Cairo.

No, Bletchley didn't know Stern was back, or at least he didn't know then. As it turned out, Stern didn't have to go to Bletchley. As soon as Stern reappeared in Cairo he learned that what he'd been so desperately waiting for had finally happened. The British had finally learned about the breaking of the Black Code through other channels.

That would explain Bletchley's new sense of calm last night, said Joe. But at the same time Bletchley has been implying all along that this was exactly the kind of thing that worried him about Stern. This business that's now cleared up by the fact that Colonel Fellers and the Black Code were the source of all the trouble. So it just seems strange that Bletchley didn't say anything about it, or give me some hint that the situation had changed and Stern was no longer under suspicion.

Joe nodded to himself, puzzled anew. But Belle said nothing and he noticed that her face was impassive as she stared at her knitting.

Trouble, thought Joe, for the first time sensing that the Sisters were withholding something from him.

What could it be? he wondered. Obviously it had to do with protecting Stern, but why? From what?

And why had Bletchley said nothing if the revelations about the Black Code cleared Stern of suspicion? Didn't it have to mean that Bletchley had some deeper concern about Stern? Some fear that far transcended the Black Code?

The writing on the wall. The hieroglyphs of Stern's life. Joe still couldn't read them, they were still a mystery. And he was sure now the Sisters were holding something back, guarding some secret because of their love for Stern. Cherishing Stern, as so many people did.

And then there was Belle's mention of *other channels*. Bletchley, the British, had learned about the Germans deciphering the Black Code through *other channels.* Did that mean some low-level informer who was secretly working for the British, or was much more than that involved? Was that why Bletchley had said nothing to Joe? Because these *other channels* were so very important Bletchley couldn't even hint at their existence?

Belle sat rigidly in her chair, her mouth set.

Perhaps it's the timing that's confusing me, said Joe, the sequence of events. The Black Code was stolen in Rome toward the beginning of the year?

Belle nodded.

No earlier?

Belle shook her head.

It doesn't fit, he thought. That was when the three men in white linen suits had turned up in Arizona, just about the same time the Germans were getting their hands on the Black Code and putting it to use in North Africa.

So obviously Bletchley had studied Stern's file and picked out Joe's name and asked that Joe be recruited to come to Cairo for another reason altogether. For something that didn't have anything to do with a serious security leak in Cairo, and the suspicion that Stern might be behind it. The appearance of the Black Code affair was merely a coincidence, something that had turned up in the interim and been cleverly put to use by Bletchley to mask his real concern from Joe. So Bletchley's real concern must have always been elsewhere, his fear of Stern something more profound.

And as so often the same thought returned to Joe, an inexplicable episode in Stern's life that wouldn't go away—Stern's Polish story. He wondered whether the Sisters would discuss it. He wondered if they even knew anything about it, so mysterious was it becoming in Joe's mind.

Belle still sat with her mouth set, waiting.

I don't mean to pry, said Joe, but it seems you've seen Stern more than once since he's been back.

That's true enough, said Belle. He's in the habit of coming here quite often, he's always done that. But it has nothing to do with Bletchley or what he does for Bletchley. Stern's visits here go back to a time before he began his revolutionary work. To the days when he was a young student in Cairo.

I see. I didn't know that. To be frank, as well as I knew Stern in Jerusalem, he never mentioned you.

Belle smiled.

He's like that, isn't he. Very private and protective of those he loves. And I imagine there have been other revelations for you concerning Stern since you've been here.

Yes. Many. And I have a feeling the most important ones are yet to come.

Belle frowned. She gazed at Joe.

How long have you been in Cairo? she asked.

A little over two weeks.

Such a short time. . . . Tell me, how do you feel about these revelations you've had concerning Stern?

Joe shrugged.

Ah well, he said, that's hard to put into words because Stern's life is more complex than most. But all lives are secret tapestries that swirl and sweep through the years with souls and strivings as the colors, the threads. And there may be little knots of tangled meaning everywhere beneath the surface, tying the colors and threads together, but the little knots aren't important finally, only the sweep itself, the tapestry as a whole. So what saddens me about Stern is that I may never even *glimpse* the sweep to his life. Not even have a glimpse of the tapestry as a whole. . . . That's how I feel.

Belle nodded, gazing at him, deep in thought.

She's trying to decide what to do, thought Joe. They know exactly what I need but they're protecting Stern the way everybody does.

Little Alice stirred, a faraway look in her eyes.

And oh he was such a handsome boy, she murmured. I remember so well the first time we met him, right here in this very room. Menelik had brought him to meet us. Menelik and Stern's father had been great friends in the old days, and when Stern came to Cairo to study, Menelik was like an uncle to him. He brought Stern here the very day Stern arrived in Cairo from the desert. . . .

To this very room. And Stern was so young and strong and pure, so determined to be honest and kind in life. And those beautiful ideals of his, and that wonderful enthusiasm. Of course there were other sides to him as well, I suppose there had to be, growing up in the desert the way he did, in a tent on a dusty little hillside in the Yemen where there were no other children to play with, so much alone from the very beginning and accustomed to that, because it was the way it had always been. A kind of solitude you could see in his eyes, a mark of sadness perhaps, a touch of the barren desert deep within him that would always be there, no matter what. A quietude, a stillness, and it did have its lonely side to it. You had to admit that.

But there was also so much warmth and tenderness in him because people were so precious to him, because of his loneliness as a child, I imagine. And you only had to look at him and listen to him talk for just a moment to be filled with joy. You couldn't help yourself, you were just swept away. This is what life can be, you felt. This joy and this beauty and this freedom, this exquisite music drawn from the silence of the desert.

Even though life doesn't turn out that way for most of us. Even though things happen and get in the way and we seem to arrive at some little place in life, by chance as much as anything else, and just stay there. Never having done as much as we would have liked, never doing all the things we dreamed of doing once. Even though it is like that for most of us in the end, when we look back.

Even so, you felt something different when Stern was with you. You only had to look at him to know there could be so much more, truly beautiful things. It was hope that he gave you. *Hope*. You felt it. You just knew it.

And he stood right there that first afternoon, I remember. It was his first day in Cairo and he stood in those open doors by the river, his eyes shining, and he said how wonderful it was to see all that water, to just stand beside the Nile and look at it. And he laughed and he said that might sound foolish to us, but that when you had grown up in the desert the glory of all that water was simply miraculous, simply beyond imagination. Truly a wonder, he said, laughing. Truly a gift of God. A gift of His variety and splendor.

He had an Arabic name as well then, I don't remember what. Menelik would remember but Menelik's dead now. And he stood there in the open doors with his eyes shining, laughing and gazing at the Nile and just feasting on all of it like a hungry man brought to a great table. And he told us all the beautiful things he was going to do in life. Hope. *Hope*. . . .

So very young then, back in the beginning. A thin excited boy with everything ahead of him, filling our hearts to overflowing with joy, his joy, the magic of just being able to look and see and feel and love. That's how rich the world was for Stern. So miraculous for him and so unexpected in its gifts, its blessings. . . .

Yes, we all felt it that first afternoon. Menelik and Belle and myself, we all felt it although not one of us said a word. But we understood the magic of that moment. Watching him, listening to him, we all knew he was precious to this world and it would always be so. *Precious*. A special human being, a man apart. Always to be so. . . .

Silence then in the room. Silence for a time.

Finally Belle picked up her knitting. The rhythmic clicking began again.

There's more you wish to know? she asked.

A few things perhaps, said Joe.

Joe scratched his beard. He picked up his empty whiskey glass and put it down again.

There's a trip Stern made to Poland, he said. Nearly three years ago, just before the war broke out. I'm convinced it's at the heart of everything because Stern was reckless for once, and that's not his way.

Joe stopped.

Are you familiar at all with any of this?

Alice looked at Belle, whose face was impassive.

Why would Stern have done that? asked Belle after a moment.

To save lives, said Joe. To preserve the lives of others. And I understand he felt there was some kind of priceless breakthrough while he was in Poland. Do you know anything about it?

First, said Belle, there's a question we have to ask. How important is it for you to find out about this?

Very.

Very, yes. All kinds of things seem important along the way, but in the end? You might be surprised what's important to Alice and me when we look back on life.

I don't think so, said Joe.

Alice sighed.

Nor do I, she said, and Belle doesn't either. But what she's asking in her delicate way, Joe, is this. What if it meant your life?

I know that's what she's asking, and the answer has to be the same. I came to Cairo to find out about Stern, that's all.

But why is that so all-important to you?

Because he deserves it. Because the end is coming for him and he deserves a witness to the truth of his life.

But *why*? Why do you feel that so strongly?

Because he's explored the human soul more deeply than anyone I've ever known. Because his life looks like nothing but failure, and I can't accept that without knowing it to be true. Because long ago in Smyrna during the massacres, deep in the night that began our age of genocide, I watched him pull back the head of a dying little girl and slit her throat, and that moment has forever haunted me. Because unless there's some meaning in his life, I can't see where there would ever be any meaning anywhere.

And does there have to be? asked Belle.

No.

For you or for anyone?

No.

Do you feel it's our right, just because we were born?

No. But I feel we should seek it.

And yet you yourself, Joe, find Stern's life to be a chaotic tapestry. And in such a vast network of colors and threads and souls and strivings, what can you expect to find?

Nothing perhaps.

But if you did find out . . . about him, what would it tell you?

It might begin to tell me what life is, and how it should be lived.

Belle stared at him and then she turned away to gaze through the open French doors at the river. Alice had also turned away and was looking out at the river, and again there was silence in the strange room so crowded with ghostly wicker chairs, the dozens and dozens of pale shadowy shapes drifting with the reflections of the stars off the water, airily floating in the soft yellow glow of the few candles that still burned in memory of other eras, dimly now and low with the late hour.

And it's decided now, thought Joe. The weaving's done and they know what they're going to say or not say to protect the rare fragile thing they cherish.

It was Alice whose small voice finally broke the silence. Little Alice gazing at the river and speaking quietly in the stillness.

How hard we try, she murmured. How *hard* we try.

The two ancient women seemed far away, lost in thought. Abruptly Belle's knitting needles clicked once.

All right, she said. All right, young Joe, you'll have what you want to know. But whatever we tell you now is for Stern's sake. It doesn't concern the war, not this war or any war, because we have nothing to do with such things. So for Stern's sake, then, because we love him and because he's always been like a son to us, and there's no limit to that kind of love.

Belle paused, her hands holding her knitting. Alice sat erect, watching her.

Over the years, said Belle, we've known many people from many lands who have come to tarry here in the course of their restless journeys and be touched by the timelessness of the place. And there's nothing new about that, people have always done that. Alexander the Great stopped here, wondering whether he might recognize something, before setting out to reshape the world. But it was already a tradition by then and long before young Alexander there had been visitors in search of man's past, his nature, come to view the enigmatic pyramids and the enigmatic Sphinx and the great river that gives life in the desert. A Greek word, *enigma*. A riddle, something obscure. Do you know the origins of the word?

No, said Joe.

It means *to speak darkly*, murmured Little Alice. To speak allusively. And the root of that is the Greek word for *a tale*.

Yes, said Belle. Oddly enough, the ancient Greeks had the idea that such was the nature of an account of life. To recite a tale, to speak of life, was to speak darkly because the essentials forever lay just beyond the clear light of the mind, tempting and allusive and beyond. To them, a tale was felt and experienced and its truths were known that way. But a tale could never be reduced through recitation to mere landscapes and seascapes and other topographies of the soul, however mighty, however brilliant the telling of it. Nor could the shadows and the echoes of a tale be removed in the speaking of it.

Belle studied Joe.

By chance, we know the name of their first great teller of tales, don't we? Or at least time and tradition have assigned a name to this blind man who would otherwise be anonymous, who must have sat in the dust of some wayside recounting what he had overheard from the din raised by those who passed him by, or what he imagined he had overheard. And curiously enough, since you mention Smyrna, it was that very same ancient Greek city in Asia Minor where this obscure blind man was said to have been born. Blind Homer seeing deeply behind his dead eyes, seeing brilliantly in the dust of the wayside through the perpetual shadows of his mind. Homer's blind eyes at play for all time on the dancing glittering seascapes, on the hard unyielding landscapes of the ancient world where others passed him by on their journeys, passed him by while imagining they sailed and strived in the clear white light of their days. When in fact he was the one who saw the journey, not them, because he was blind and they had only lived it.

And that ancient Greek image of blind Homer seeing more than the great heroes of whom he spoke, seeing more than those who have eyes, is an enigma in itself. And as an enigma it whispers to us and hints at things and suggests far more than we might want to acknowledge readily, and it remains an enigma untouched by millennia, no less of a truth today and yet no more resolvable than it was then, three thousand years ago. An enigma as dark and allusive and true, still, as it ever was. And with that we are brought to the code you now look for in Cairo.

Belle paused, gazing at Joe.

Today? This century? Stern? A sudden unexplained trip to Poland just before the war broke out? A priceless breakthrough?

Enigma, she said, is the name of the code machine used by the Germans. Just before the war broke out, a Polish intelligence service acquired one of these machines. Stern learned of its existence through contacts and he knew the machine had to be turned over to the British before Poland fell. Consequently, he went to Poland at once and there were hectic clandestine meetings in Warsaw that finally resulted in the most important meeting of all, held in a secret signals–intelligence post buried underground in the Pyry forest, a concrete bunker referred to as *the house in the woods.* Stern wasn't at that final meeting himself, but he played some part in arranging it. Just what part I can't tell you, because Alice and I don't know that. In addition to the Poles at the meeting there were three men from London, two of them professional experts in cryptology. The third man from London, an observer rather than a participant, was there in the guise of a professor from Oxford.

Joe was listening intently, deep in thought.

He knits, said Joe suddenly.

Both Belle and Alice stared at him.

What's that? asked Belle, startled.

Joe looked confused, embarrassed. He had spoken as if from a trance. Now he passed his hand over the side of his face, a nervous gesture, as if he were brushing something away. Even as he made the movement with his hand, he realized it was something he had seen both Liffy and Cohen do in the last few days.

Do you know about this? asked Belle.

No, none of it, said Joe quickly. A thought just came to me, that's all. I'm sorry I interrupted you, I didn't mean to.

Who knits? asked Belle, curious all at once.

That third Englishman who was in the bunker, the one who was pretending to be a professor from Oxford. Actually he's a Scotsman.

He is?

Yes.

How do you know that?

The way he speaks.

And he knits?

Yes.

How do you know?

I've met him. He knits and listens and doesn't say much. And he smokes a strong brand of cigarettes, or rather, he inhales them without lighting them. He never lights his cigarettes. They call him *Ming* on the other side of the Atlantic, the American-Canadian side. He's a chief of some kind, high up, probably at the top, he has that way about him. When I saw him he was traveling with an American and a Canadian who must be equally high up, who go by the names of Big Bill and Little Bill.

How do you know it's the same man?

I don't, I just have this feeling it must be.

Belle stared at Joe, curious and more.

You're beginning to sound like Alice, she said in a quiet respectful voice. And where did you meet this Scotsman called Ming, who knits?

On top of a mesa in Arizona, said Joe. Underground, in the sky. In a kiva.

A what?

The Hopi Indians call them a kiva. It's a sacred underground chamber. At the time I met him I joked with myself that they were the Three Fates come to call on me. One Fate spins the net of life, one measures it, one cuts it. I joked with myself that he was the one who spins, because he knitted and listened in the kiva and didn't say much. He gave me a shawl then that he'd knitted, a black shawl, it was a gift. They came to visit me in Arizona to get me to come to Cairo to find out about Stern.

Before I left the mesa I gave the shawl away, added Joe for no reason. I'm sorry, I didn't mean to interrupt you. Please go on.

But Belle didn't go on. She was still staring at him, fascinated.

You gave the shawl away before you left that place? To whom?

A little Indian girl in the village. A little Indian girl.

Yes, what happened?

Nothing really, said Joe. I was sitting on the edge of the mesa one night and the sun was going down and a little girl came out of the shadows and stood beside me. I took her hand and the air was getting chilly so I gave her the shawl and she was there with me for a while. She didn't say anything, neither of us said anything, we were watching the last of the light. After it grew dark she went home and I went to the kiva for a meeting with the tribal elders.

I gave her the shawl because it was cold, he added simply. It was my last night before I left the mesa, as it turned out. I was trying to decide whether to leave or not, whether to come to Cairo.

You were thinking of Stern, said Belle, and of the dying little girl in Smyrna twenty years ago. The one whom Stern . . .

Belle stopped. She stared at her lap.

Yes, you're right, said Joe. I thought a lot about Stern that night.

Nervously, Joe passed his hand over the side of his face again.

292

Please, he said, I'm sorry to have interrupted. I'm terribly anxious to hear the rest of it. What happened at the secret meeting in the woods near Warsaw? The Poles agreed to turn over their *Enigma* to the British?

Belle looked at him. She leaned back in her chair.

Yes. Eventually the machine reached London and since then the British have been reading everything the Germans tell each other. The secret is truly priceless, and very few men in the British commands know of the existence of *Enigma*. But Stern knows, and the British have learned that he knows, and how can they possibly allow that to be when Stern lives the kind of life he does? The secret is far too important, the danger far too great. And then there's also the future and Stern's Zionist connections to be considered. Today, British and Zionist interests coincide, but they didn't before the war and they may not again. So with everything taken together, it's a situation the British would feel they would have to bring to an end.

A cry escaped Little Alice.

An end, she whispered, gazing out at the river.

Oh an end, *an end. . . .*

Joe got to his feet. He walked quickly over to the open French doors and turned, restlessly beginning to pace around the room.

It's clear enough now, he said. Bletchley's been having me trace people down to see what he has to worry about. He didn't have time himself to do the follow-up work so he had me called in to do the excavating for him, to find out which of Stern's friends might know what. A natural precaution for a professional like him. He didn't want to make his move against Stern until he was sure he could finish things once and for all. You can't afford loose ends when the secret's as big as this one, so he had me out gathering the bits and pieces, and then when he felt he had enough of the picture. . . .

Oh my God, cried Joe, I've been digging Stern's grave. I've been digging into Stern's past so Bletchley can get ahold of it and . . .

Joe sank into a chair, appalled at what he had done. He gripped his hands together, trying to get some control over himself, and suddenly he remembered where he was. He looked up, staring wildly at one sister and then the other.

293

There's danger, he said. There's danger to all the people I've talked to, I can't say it strongly enough. Obviously Bletchley's been watching me much more closely than I imagined, since that was the whole point of the thing. And there's danger to the two of you, and we've got to . . .

Belle shook her head.

No.

But there is, I tell you. If Bletchley suspects . . .

No, repeated Belle. We understood this situation before you came here, Joe, that's why we asked how important it was for you to learn the truth about Stern's trip to Poland. We've known all along what the implications of that were, as has Stern. So nothing has changed for him tonight, or for us, but much has changed for you and those you've been in touch with. For unfortunately we never act alone, do we? The colors and threads of the tapestry are too closely interwoven for that, so no matter what we do, we always act for others as well, although generally without their knowledge, and often without even knowing it ourselves. But that's the nature of souls and strivings, isn't it, Joe? None of them is ever separate and every act casts echoes in many places, through many lives.

Joe jumped to his feet.

But the two of you, he began. We must . . .

Belle stopped him again. She shook her head.

No, not us, Joe. There's nothing for us to fear. Just look around you and you can see that for yourself. Alice and I are from another time altogether. We've lived our lives and there's nothing anyone can do to us that matters, surely you understand that. And even if there were, I doubt Bletchley would dare to take a decision like that upon himself. In fact, I'm quite certain he wouldn't.

Belle nodded slowly and went on in her quiet voice.

But even that's not the point. Alice and I aren't really a part of any of this, don't you see that? At the beginning I told you that what we were going to say had only to do with Stern, not with the war, not with this war or any war. And I said we would tell you for *his* sake, Joe, because we love him and because you wanted to know the truth about him for your own reasons. Your own personal reasons. Isn't that so?

Yes . . . yes it is.

And we believe in those reasons of yours, Joe, and so we went on and spoke to you.

294

Joe had collapsed in a chair. He looked up and found both Belle and Alice watching him.

I'm sorry. I'm sorry but I . . .

It's *all right*, whispered Little Alice suddenly. Don't take so much on yourself, Joe, just let Belle finish.

Joe turned from one of them to the other.

Yes, I'm sorry. Please go on.

Belle nodded.

This may sound strange to you, but the truth is Stern is more important to us than the war, this war or any war. His life means more to us, quite simply, than all the clamor of all the great armies which are ravaging the world for the sake of a noble cause, bless them, and for the sake of an evil cause, damn them. And that's true even though vast numbers of innocent people are suffering and dying, and even though many more will suffer and die before it's over one way or the other, if it ever is.

A sad smile played on Belle's face.

That may sound narrow and selfish to you, Joe, and it may even offend you. But we're not philosophers, Alice and I, and that's the way it is for us. Certainly we would wish better for the world, and we know what a terrible tragedy it is when these bestial nightmares seize men. But the two of us are old, Joe. We're *old*, and we've lived too long to embrace the entire earth and everyone on it. These times are a tragedy for man, but we're simply too small and our eyes are too old and dim to gather that grand sweep in. We've never been great empresses of all the somethings, or magnificent queens by the Nile. We're just two sisters who never married and never had children, who began by mopping floors and went on to find roles in an opera of life, who dreamed a few harmless dreams along the way and then ended somewhere, having done the best we could.

And in the end there's nothing more to say than that, nothing except one thing. *We love Stern, our son.* We would do anything for him but there's nothing we can do for him now but weep, and so we do that. With the darkness closing around us, in our hearts, we weep for him and we weep. *For him. . . .*

Joe sat with his head in his hands, listening to the words of the Sisters and thinking of many things. Of Ahmad and Liffy and David and Anna, of Bletchley and his desert fortress and his bands of anonymous Monks, of Maud and Stern and the quiet little Cairo square where the two of them had once passed evenings together. And of the young Stern years ago in this very room, standing in the open doors beside the great expanse of river and laughing, his eyes shining. . . . Stern laughing and feasting on the riches of life, giving joy and hope to all who knew him.

Joe felt two tiny hands on his shoulders, gestures by the Sisters in passing, the two of them stopping to touch him for a moment as they moved slowly across the room, Big Belle going stiffly on ahead, Little Alice lingering to speak to him softly.

We're in the habit of ending our evenings with music, she said. It's soothing to us and helps us to sleep, but mostly we do it because it brings back so many good memories of beautiful moments we have known. So please excuse us, Joe, and leave whenever you like. We know you have much that concerns you and much to consider. Young men always do. . . .

A mysterious blend of sounds then filled the shadowy sunroom in that strange houseboat anchored on the shores of the Nile, Little Alice brightly trilling on her harpsichord as Big Belle sounded the somber notes of her small bassoon, a twinkling haunting strain to their music as Joe gazed out at the river and listened to their elegy under the stars, their allusive recitation at the end of the long night.

16

Two Candles

As soon as Joe left the houseboat he picked out one of the men who was following him. He waved to the man and began walking quickly.

Several buses later and he had also lost the second man. Of course it had to be obvious what he was doing and Bletchley would be getting telephone calls from the surveillance team, but that didn't matter to Joe. He was angry now, too angry to care if it showed as he worked his way deeper into the city, waiting, doubling back, looking for eyes that avoided his, a head that turned away.

Nothing. No one. Where was the third man, or was Bletchley using two-man teams to cover him?

No, not good enough. Using replacements, then? The men telephoning in and having someone take their place ahead of Joe? Waiting for him, keeping the trail alive that way?

No, Bletchley wouldn't have the manpower for that, not with all the demands there had to be on the Monastery these days. Bletchley might be willing to assign more men to him but not until he was sure Joe was really on the run. And Bletchley couldn't know that yet, despite the telephone calls coming in from his surveillance team that morning.

Monks, thought Joe. Bletchley's bloody Monks from the desert. A secret order of initiates with their own rules and their own hierarchy, looking like everybody else but not like anybody else at all. Solitaries

297

who pursued their missions alone, silently conversing with their co-religionists through secret signs. . . . Even their vows had a monastic quality to them. Obedience and silence, and poverty in a way, chastity in a way. A secret brotherhood with secret goals, the anonymous Monks of war. . . . The bloody anonymous Monks of war.

So where was the third man then, the leader of the team?

Joe quickened his step and turned corners, angry that somewhere near a man was watching him, hunting him, one of Bletchley's anonymous Monks. And then all at once he saw him. A small man moving awkwardly on the other side of the crowded street.

Joe felt a sudden rush of blood. Now he was a hunter himself and he could strike, wound.

There was a café on the corner. He turned in and went to the back where the telephones were, slipped out the rear entrance of the café and moved behind a truck which was rolling forward to cross the street. He walked slowly keeping pace with the truck, hidden by it. Only a minute or two had passed since he had first seen the man.

Joe was now across the street from the café, behind the small young man who had joined a group of people waiting at a bus stop. The small man had opened a newspaper and was pretending to read it as he watched the café. Joe moved up behind him and dropped his chin onto the small man's shoulder, rested his chin there, looked down at the newspaper open in front of both of them. The man's eyes flew sideways but no cry escaped him.

Too clever by half, thought Joe. I know they told you to look the enemy straight in the eye, but a lunatic resting his chin on your shoulder is something else.

Joe smiled, still looking down at the newspaper.

Gulbenkian's the name, he said. Do you mind if I sneak a quick glance at the headlines to see what Rommel had his nose into at breakfast this morning?

People at the bus stop turned to stare. The small man recovered and spoke with indignation.

Excuse me? Is there something you wanted?

Too late, little rabbit, thought Joe. Forget what they told you about showing no emotion. Madmen are disturbing to everybody.

Joe smiled more broadly.

All I wanted is the secret to Rommel's success, he said. Does it mention in the papers what he ate for breakfast?

Excuse me, said the young man forcefully, angrily. He had closed his newspaper and was trying to move away from Joe, but Joe held him tightly from behind and moved with him, his chin still on the young man's shoulder. Joe noticed for the first time that he had a limp. The people at the bus stop had formed a circle around them. Joe grinned sideways into the small man's face, only inches away.

Would you believe me, he said, if I told you I've just been up all night listening to Catherine the Great and Cleopatra explain what Rommel puts his nose into first thing in the morning? Maps or herring, most people might think, but it's not like that at all. Just *shocking* information, as a matter of fact.

The small man had finally pulled away from Joe and now stood facing him, his fists clenched, hatred in his eyes. A large crowd had gathered around them, pushing and pressing forward, trying to find out what was happening. Joe raised his arms and stepped back, shouting at the crowd.

O worthy Cairenes, O noble sons and daughters of the Nile. Today a great liberator moves ever closer to Cairo and oppression may soon be at an end. But what has this agent of British imperialism just whispered in my ear at this very bus stop? What manner of slander has he dared to whisper right here in broad daylight?

Silence fell over the crowds pressing in from every side. Joe waved his arms and shouted.

O worthy Cairenes. Is it right for this secret agent to say the great General Rommel puts his nose into little fellahs first thing every morning? Is it right to say such wicked things about a great generalissimo panzer liberator? Can't the great General Rommel eat what he wants for breakfast?

Angry mutterings ran through the crowd. Hisses. Groans. Again Joe waved his arms and shouted.

And verily I say unto you, a great field-marshal generalissimo panzer savior, our very own Rommel, can eat what he wants for breakfast and British imperialism be damned. And I've said it before and I'll say it again, and I'll keep on saying it no matter what they do to me.

Rommel eats what he wants for breakfast.
Eats what he wants,
Eats what he wants. . .

To the hungry masses thronging the crossroads that morning, the visceral appeal of Joe's booming message was immense and immediate. In only a few words Joe had managed to express the first principle of every poor Egyptian's dream for a better future, *food*, the dream disguised as usual as homage for a savior, the first principle disguised as the first meal of the day, breakfast. So it was no surprise to Joe when several daring voices took up the revolutionary cry out of hunger, and in another moment the entire hungry mob had broken into a thunderous chant secretly demanding an adequate breakfast, hundreds of clenched fists raised against the clear blue morning sky.

We've said it before and we'll say it again.

Rommel eats what he wants for breakfast.
Eats what he wants,
Eats what he wants. . . .

Joe noticed some policemen forming across the way, getting ready to charge into the crowds before a riot broke out. Already the mobs were surging back and forth in a fierce din of shrieks and sirens and horns. Joe winked at Bletchley's small Monk, who was still trapped in front of him, and slipped away into the crowds. A block up the street, the shouts and horns behind him, Joe suddenly stopped and leaned against a building. All at once he felt dizzy, as if he had been running for hours.

A silly trick, he thought. There would only be more anonymous Monks waiting for him near the hotel, the first telephone call from the surveillance team would have seen to that. So why had he done it? Why had he lost control so quickly?

It was more than exhaustion, he knew that. The night had been filled with many things but the excitement was gone now. For the first time since leaving the houseboat, he felt he could see things clearly. And then he listened to the animal cries behind him and realized what had happened.

Joe choked and groped for the wall, violently beginning to vomit.

300

As he hurried along he thought of the young man he had just humiliated, a small man with a limp, with a bad leg or no leg, a false one in its place. Had he lost the leg in a tank? There wasn't much room in a tank and small men managed better, so that's where they were often assigned.

The boy hadn't done very well at the bus stop, thought Joe, but of course he was new to the game. Probably he'd learned about tanks first, then how to walk again, then a quick course with the Monks before he was sent out to walk the streets for Bletchley. . . . He could imagine the boy's file being sent to Bletchley and Bletchley going through it and seeing his own life laid out in front of him. The boy patched up and out of the hospital and able to walk, an earnest young soldier who still wanted to help, could Bletchley use him? And Bletchley looking at the file and seeing his own life twenty-five years ago, everybody gets his own war. For Bletchley had also wanted to stay on in the army back then, it was just that they hadn't been keeping men with only half a face, no more than one leg would do it today. So Bletchley had known exactly how the boy felt and had taken pity and made him an offer.

God help us, thought Joe, but that's exactly how it works. Sign on as a war hero and lose a leg and if you're lucky you get promoted to streetwalker, simple as that.

And the kid was just doing his job back there, thought Joe. He doesn't know who I am and he's never heard of Stern and he's got nothing to do with any of us, but I put hatred into his eyes, I did that. And he'll pass it along all right but the worst part is I was enjoying myself, I *wanted* to wound, and laughing I was because I was so clever. . . . Clever for sure, whipping a crippled kid like that in front of a lot of people.

He stopped, exhausted again, feeling empty and ashamed. It seemed so futile sometimes. All these years and something like that could happen so quickly. It was frightening.

But he didn't have time to think about it. He had to keep moving now. There was just so little time left for anything.

The alleys of Old Cairo, as always, looked as if they had been gnawed by rats during the night. Joe was near the hotel. He turned a corner.

A haggard Arab figure suddenly loomed up in front of him, blocking his way, the man's hair long and matted, his filthy cloak a patchwork of faded rags. Desperately the Arab clawed at the air in front of Joe's face, his eyes burning as he ripped at the sunshine. But it was the creature's mouth that horrified Joe, snapping and gnawing at the sunlight. Joe tried to back away but a flaying claw came slashing down and hooked him, the Arab's bony fingers burning into his skin. Joe winced at the shock. The Arab's face was only inches away . . . a wild vision of some hermit who had lost his way in the centuries and come staggering in from the desert to haunt the byways of the city. But then all at once the Arab's eyes seemed strangely familiar.

Liffy?

For a moment the frantic burning eyes held Joe, then the claw slipped away and the mysterious gaze was broken.

Me, gasped Liffy . . . an asthma attack . . . in here.

He pulled Joe sideways into an alley and dragged him along.

Are you all right?

. . . better now . . . can't go back to the hotel. . . . Here.

He pulled Joe into a dark room off the alley, separated from the alley by a shabby curtain. There were small bare tables in the room and a counter with bottles in a row, stacked chairs, a mirror behind the counter. An Egyptian faced the mirror, his back turned. The floor glistened from water splashed around to lay the dust.

The Egyptian behind the counter glanced into the mirror to see them and went on wiping glasses. The mirror was old and cracked and deeply grained with time, its edges blackened in the gloom. Joe guessed the place was some kind of cheap bar used by laborers, probably mostly at night, empty now save for its owner. Liffy wheezed and sputtered and ordered coffee.

Joe found himself gazing into the mirror, fascinated by the odd distortions floating in its hazy interiors. A peculiar thought flashed through his mind. What if Stern were to sit with him looking into that mirror? . . . Liffy dragged him along to a table at the back, away from the shabby curtain separating the room from the alley. Liffy was still pale and gasping for breath. Joe held his arm.

Are you all right? Can I do anything?

Liffy closed his eyes, chewing at the air.

. . . better now . . . passing . . . an attack.

Joe glanced over his shoulder at the counter, where the owner of the bar was putting a tiny metal pot to boil, removing it when the froth bubbled up and letting the froth subside before returning it to the flame, boiling the mixture of coffee and sugar three times in all. The color was coming back into Liffy's face. Finally he opened his eyes and stared at Joe.

Better?

Yes, whispered Liffy. I was beginning to think you were never going to show up.

What's this costume you're wearing?

Nothing, just something left over from last night. I was doing a job for the Waterboys and didn't have time to change. Wait.

Joe heard the movement behind him. The owner brought over the two little cups of coffee and placed them on the table, a disheveled man with puffy eyes. As soon as he had left them, Liffy leaned forward.

I was afraid I'd missed you. Something's happened.

What?

Ahmad, whispered Liffy. I came to see you late last night when I finished work. I didn't think you'd be all night and I was going to wait in your room, but I never got there. Ahmad wasn't at his desk when I walked in and there was something wrong, I could feel it. There didn't seem to be anybody there.

Joe gripped his hands together under the table.

You looked around?

Not inside, I didn't like it. Then I thought he might be out back in the courtyard and I went around and climbed up to look in.

Liffy's hands were trembling. He lowered his eyes. Joe stared.

Ahmad, whispered Liffy. He was lying there all crumpled up. It looked as if he had fallen off the roof. His spyglass was still in his hand and his trombone was beside him.

A spasm jerked in Joe's stomach.

Dead?

He was lying the wrong way. His legs and his head were all twisted around but his straw hat wasn't there. I didn't stay, I left and came to wait for you. I've been waiting for hours, I didn't go back. I have no idea what's going on there.

What was he wearing, Liffy?

His faded lavender nightshirt. That old thing he always wears when he's on duty.

Liffy hung his head. He pulled his hands off the table and hid them, his voice trembling.

I know what you're thinking. Ahmad never went up there without putting on his suit, it was his special place after all. And where was his hat, Joe? What happened to his old straw hat?

Liffy's voice cracked. He clutched Joe's arm, begging him, imploring him.

He went up there on a whim? Just decided to do it and leaned out too far . . . lost his balance?

Joe closed his hand over Liffy's.

An accident? pleaded Liffy in desperation.

No, said Joe, squeezing Liffy's hand more tightly.

No? Liffy almost shrieked. Just this one time? *No?*

Joe gripped Liffy's shoulder. Tears were streaming down Liffy's face.

He was *pushed?* shrieked Liffy in a whisper. A harmless man like Ahmad? But what's the *sense* of that, Joe? What's the *sense* of it?

Joe was on his feet. He dropped some coins on the table.

There's no time, I have to leave.

Liffy's head jerked back.

Where are you going?

I have to see someone.

Who?

There was terror in Liffy's eyes.

Who? Say it. I know anyway.

David, whispered Joe.

Liffy leapt to his feet.

I'm going with you, then. I am.

You shouldn't, Liffy, not now. It would be better if you didn't.

Better? David? . . . *Better?*

All right but we have to hurry, whispered Joe, and started down the room toward the shabby curtain separating them from the alley, a sudden image catching Joe's eye as they rushed past the mirror, the vision of a ghostlike figure drifting through the half-light behind him, wild hair streaming and a billowing cloak and a tormented face glowing in the dimness. . . . Liffy in flight through time. The unworldly figure of Liffy whirling through one of the last of his mysterious incarnations. . . .

The door to Cohen's Optiks was ajar. A bell tinkled when Joe pushed it open. There was no one in the shop.

Another door, half open, led to the workshop in the back where Joe had talked to Cohen. The workshop was also empty, the door at the rear of the workshop closed. Joe knocked, waited, turned the handle.

It was a storeroom, the place where Anna had listened to Joe's conversation with her brother. There were boxes and dusty trays, discarded grinding wheels, a clock on the wall which no longer worked. Anna sat on a box, staring at the floor. She looked up, bewildered.

I only just heard. . . . Were you there?

She stared at Joe blankly and he shook his head. She stared at Liffy.

You weren't there? . . . Wasn't anybody with him?

No, said Joe softly. What happened?

Oh. Oh a lorry struck him. The police just told me. He was crossing a street. They said it was nobody's fault.

Her face was empty. She stared at the floor. Joe heard a muffled cry beside him and all at once Liffy was on his knees beside Anna, gathering her up in his arms, the two of them rocking back and forth and wailing and crying out . . . crying and crying.

Joe looked at the motionless clock on the wall and felt himself sinking. He pressed his eyes shut, too weak to stand, his heart crushed by the eternal sound of their weeping.

The tiny Greek church they had sought for refuge was deserted save for the two of them, the floor of the nave bare as was the custom, the few high-backed wooden chairs pushed back against the walls like thrones at a convocation of wary medieval kings. Shouts from playing children pierced the cool darkness.

Liffy sat on his throne with his hands in his lap, the life drained out of him since they had left Anna. Beside him Joe moved uneasily on his throne, thinking how stark the tiny church was without its priest and worshipers, its canticles and incense, with only vanished chants to fill the shadows. Liffy stirred, whispered.

Joe? What are you going to do now?

Well I'm going to try to see Stern tonight, one way or another, but in the meantime I need a sanctuary. In another era this little cave would have been fine, but the concept's no longer honored, sadly. Seems holy places have a way of getting lost over time, don't they, so you always have to be seeking new ones. . . . Can you think of a place, Liffy?

A refuge, you mean?

Yes.

Liffy was gazing up at the low dome, at the fresco there depicting the austere figure of Christ as Pantokrator, the Paraclete or Inter-cessor, the stylized face expressionless, the enormous powerful eyes staring down at them.

You could try old Menelik's mausoleum, whispered Liffy. That would probably be as safe as anywhere.

It might be at that, thought Joe.

But Ahmad kept his forgery equipment there, he whispered. Won't Bletchley think of that?

Liffy stirred.

There's no reason for him to bother with it. There's nothing but a small printing press which runs by hand, so old and battered no one but Ahmad could ever work it. I imagine they'd just leave the place locked and forget about it. It doesn't mean anything to any of them.

Seems likely, thought Joe.

But how could I get in then?

I have a key, murmured Liffy.

You do?

Yes. I had a duplicate made of Ahmad's once. He used to let me borrow his and I was always afraid of losing it.

You used to go there by yourself, you mean?

Sometimes, to get away from everything. Ahmad took pity on me and let me use it. I used to go there to read.

Joe looked at him, surprised.

What did you read down there?

Buber, mostly. It was very quiet and I could feel at peace.

Joe nodded. I've been thinking about the Waterboys, he whispered, wondering if they could help in some way.

Liffy moved on his throne, still gazing up at the dome.

Why them?

Because I doubt they know anything about this, security being what it is. And because there'd have to be some sense of rivalry between them and the Monastery, human nature being what it is. And also because Stern's done work for them in the past, which means they'd have a high opinion of him. And because Maud works there. I know she only does translations, but that still means they'd trust her. Is there any officer there you know particularly well?

The Major, murmured Liffy. He'd be the one to contact. We get along and I think he reports directly to the Colonel, Bletchley's equivalent. In fact I think he's the Colonel's personal assistant. I can give you his private phone number and you could pretend you were me, asking for an emergency meeting. I've never had to set one up in the clear over the phone, but you could do it. We have the arrangement.

I couldn't imitate your voice, whispered Joe.

You wouldn't have to. Whenever I call him I use a different voice. It's a kind of game between the two of us.

Joe nodded. Liffy's gaze was still fixed on the fresco overhead.

Joe? What will you do if Menelik's crypt doesn't work out? If you have to find another place to hide? Where will you go?

I've been thinking about it and I suppose I might have to try the houseboat. The Sisters would take me in all right, the trouble is Bletchley would think of it. I know no harm will come to them, I'm sure they're right about that, Bletchley wouldn't dare. But the houseboat just sits there on the water and if Bletchley's men came looking, well, they'd find me soon enough.

And so?

And so I'll just have to hope old Menelik can keep me hidden down there in his five thousand years of murky history.

Liffy looked at him.

I know, whispered Joe, it's a hope that doesn't make much sense. History doesn't hide you, just the opposite. Gives away your hiding place, if anything. But what other hope is there?

Liffy didn't answer.

And when they question you, added Joe, remember, just tell them the truth. You know I talked a lot with Ahmad, and that I talked with David once, and that I went to see the Sisters last night. But you don't know anyone else I might have seen and you don't know what the Sisters might have told me, and that's the truth. You don't know, Liffy, that's all. It's not your affair. This business is between Stern and me, and Stern and me and Bletchley, and that's the way it's been from the beginning. So just tell them the truth and Bletchley's not going to give you any trouble when he understands how things are. There's nothing wrong with Bletchley, it's just that he's got his own job to do and we're sitting in different places. So just the truth, Liffy, and it'll be all right.

Liffy nodded, distracted. He opened a little leather pouch which was hanging from his neck and placed a key in Joe's hand.

Menelik's crypt?

Yes.

Liffy stared at Joe, then whispered again.

There's one thing I have to know. Is Stern . . . did it turn out to be . . . is it all right? Did he know in the end, Joe, did he have it right? You have to tell me the truth for Ahmad's sake, for David's . . . ours.

Joe smiled.

We never doubted that, Liffy. Deep inside, neither one of us ever doubted that. Stern's on the only side there is, the right side. Life. Hope. The right side. And we knew that, Liffy, we *knew* it. Do you remember what you told me about Stern the first time you ever mentioned him? How the two of you used to go to poor Arab bars late at night and just sit and talk about nothing, and in particular, never about the war? And you said he liked your imitations, they made him laugh. And you said that meant a great deal to you, bringing laughter to a man like Stern, knowing the life he's had. It made you happy, you said. Do you remember?

Yes.

And then you said something else, Liffy. Do you remember?

Yes. I said it was an unusual kind of laughter. I said it was gentle, and I said his eyes were gentle.

That's right, said Joe, and so they are. And so there's nothing to be afraid about now because it's going to be all right.

Joe smiled. Liffy looked at him. And, of course, there was that last question lingering between the two of them, when would they meet again, and where? But they understood each other too well to bother with that, and instead they made their final arrangements and sat a few minutes in silence, gazing around the tiny church with its little dome and its darkened fresco of the Paraclete, the Intercessor, sharing the coolness and the quiet of the place, a moment of calm for both of them.

Finally, reluctantly, Joe squeezed Liffy's arm and slipped off his throne.

I have to be going now, he whispered.

Liffy drifted along with him toward the door. There was a small stand for prayer candles and Liffy stopped to light two of them, one for Ahmad and one for David, and they stood looking down at the candles before they embraced. And that was where they parted and where Joe left him, a frail man in a tattered cloak with his matted hair streaming around his face, a sorrowing hermit from the wilderness crouched over the flickering candles of memory, of love.

Liffy silently weeping for Ahmad and David in the somber light of that little cave. Liffy once more the haunted prophet of old, a frail man stricken with the terrible knowledge of the names of things . . . his ancient dusty face running with tears that glistened like tiny rivers come to water the desert.

17

Mementos

The vast bands of homeless pilgrims roaming the outer circles of the Irrigation Works seemed to keep no regular hours.

They were also all said to be in search of water. Or at least that was what they claimed whenever they were stopped and asked what they were doing, those milling bands of Slavs and Rumanians and Danes and Greeks, Belgians and Armenians and Dutch, some determined and some merely dazed, others wild-eyed or tame by turns as they chaotically croaked their messages and banged their long staves on the floor, pilgrims far from home swaying as stalks of grain in the wind, those confusing groups of Maltese and Czechs and French and Norwegians, Cypriots and Hungarians and Poles, the many stateless wanderers and the occasional homespun Albanian.

According to Liffy, they kept no regular hours in the outer offices of the Irrigation Works. But in the inner offices where Maud worked, the practice was to take an hour or two off in the afternoon, to escape the heat, before returning to work into the evening.

Thus, after taking many precautions, Joe was sitting in the living room of Maud's small apartment when the front door opened that afternoon. He heard her put down some packages and walk along the corridor, quietly singing to herself. The room where Joe sat was shuttered against the sun and the heat. Maud stepped into the room and stopped singing. She stared.

She was smaller than he remembered, close up like this. She put her hand to her mouth, startled, wonder and astonishment playing on her face. Joe took a step forward and reached out.

It's me, Maudie. I didn't mean to scare you.

She stared, her hand at her mouth. A familiar smile came to the corners of her eyes.

Joe? It's you? It's really you?

He took another step, reaching for her hands, her green eyes brighter than he remembered. Sparkling, stunning.

I didn't want to just turn up, Maudie, but I couldn't write and there was no other way to let you know.

He smiled more broadly.

It is a surprise, isn't it. Twenty years later and here in Cairo, whoever would have thought it?

She watched him, intensely curious. He glanced around the room in his embarrassment.

It's nice, it's a nice place you have. How are you? You look fine.

She was still staring at him. At last she found some words.

But how? . . . why? . . . what are you doing here?

Joe nodded, smiling.

I know, it's strange, you just walking in like this and me just sitting here. It's as if we'd seen each other last month or last winter or something. How are you? You look fine.

Suddenly she laughed. He remembered her laughter but not the astonishing richness of it.

I'm fine, but what are you doing here, Joe? Are you in the army? I thought you were still in the States somewhere. You've hurt your ear. Here, let me look at you.

She pulled away and studied him, still holding his hands. She laughed and wrinkled her nose, a beautiful little movement that surprised him at first, but then he remembered that too. She used to do it when something unexpected pleased her. It was just that he hadn't seen it in such a long time.

He looked away, embarrassed. She was still studying him.

Would you know me, Maudie?

Your eyes, I'd know your eyes anywhere but I don't think I'd have recognized you on the street. Your face has changed and you have a leaner look, although you were always thin.

Joe laughed.

It's the lines, he said, they cut deeper now. But you look just the same. I'd recognize you anywhere.

Oh no, she said, freeing one of her hands and pushing back her hair. I've changed completely. . . . But heavens, oh my, has it really been twenty years? It doesn't seem that long, I don't feel that old. . . . You look very distinguished though. Age becomes you.

Distinguished? Dressed like this?

Your face. I didn't notice what you were wearing.

She laughed.

Your clothes never did fit you, you know. Remember that funny old uniform you used to wear in Jerusalem? The one that had belonged to that ancient Franciscan priest, that Irish friend of yours who'd been in the Crimean War?

Yes, the baking priest. He'd worn it at Balaklava.

That's right. The one who survived the Charge of the Light Brigade because he was drunk. His horse was shot out from under him and he was too drunk to keep up on foot, so they gave him a medal for heroism because he lived. Then afterward he became a priest and was sent to Jerusalem and put in charge of the bakery in the Franciscan enclave in the Old City. And he'd been baking bread ever since, always in the four shapes of the Cross and Ireland and the Crimea and the Old City, the four concerns of his life, as he said. That uniform he gave you, that was too big for you too.

Joe nodded, smiling.

Well I guess I haven't changed all that much then, I'm still wearing hand-me-downs. This suit belongs to an Armenian dealer in Coptic artifacts, in transit, or at least that's what my papers claim he is.

The Armenians, she said abruptly, were the first people to embrace Christianity as a people. Fourth century.

Joe looked at her in surprise.

That's an obscure piece of information. How did you know that?

You told me.

Oh.

They gazed at each other.

Would you like something to drink?

That would be grand.

A glass of lemonade? I have some made.

That would be lovely.

But she didn't move. They were standing a little apart and she went on staring at him, fascinated.

No, I don't think I would have recognized you on the street, not unless I'd looked into your eyes. The rest of you is different. There's a leanness to your face that changes your whole expression.

You look like someone who's been living in the desert, she added in a quiet voice

Joe smiled.

Well I guess that's only right because that's what I've been doing. Not here, over in Arizona. I finally found an Indian tribe that would take me in.

You used to say you'd do that someday.

I know I did. And I got the idea originally from hearing about your Indian grandmother. Remember how I used to ask questions about her all the time? . . . Ah Maudie, where did the years go? Where did they ever go?

I don't know. But here you are again all of a sudden, and you're still asking questions the way you always did. You were always looking for answers then.

I was young, Maudie.

Yes, we both were. And you could never get enough of anything, you wanted things so much. And I suppose I did too, and maybe that's what was wrong with it. Both of us so young and wanting things so much, too much, I don't know. Are you still like that, always looking for answers?

In a way, I imagine. But in a way it's also different.

Yes, I would have guessed that. And there's a calmness you didn't have before and you're leaner, harder. In a good way, I mean, inside. The desert must have done that for you.

Probably.

She looked down at her hands, her face thoughtful.

You've been tending your soul, haven't you? You used to talk about doing that and that's what you've done. You went away and did it.

I suppose.

Yes, it shows. It shows in your eyes and your face and I guess we all do that in our way, and I guess that's where the years go. . . . Oh my, but we were young then. We were, Joe, so very young, and we didn't know much of anything. . . . Oh my. We were children playing in the fields of the Lord and there was never a day or a night for us, never darkness or light, just love and the joy of being together and wanting to be together. . . .

She stared at the floor.

It was beautiful, she whispered. . . . It didn't last, but it was beautiful.

Joe moved closer. He put his arm around her shoulders.

I brought some pictures, Maudie, some photographs of Bernini. I took them before I left the States. He's playing baseball, wearing what they wear when they do that. He's called a catcher. Can you imagine your son doing that, just like any American boy? He was very excited when I told him I was going to see you. He sends you his love. He also sent this.

Joe took a bracelet from his pocket, a thin gold-colored band without any markings on it, made from some cheap metal.

He picked it out himself, said Joe. I asked if I could help him choose something but he said this was what he wanted. He said he knew you'd like it because it's simple, and you like simple things. And then he talked a lot about the little house by the sea in Piraeus, where you used to live. He has such a good memory for some things. And he insisted on paying for the bracelet out of a little money he'd earned. He says he's already learned enough to get paid for it sometimes. Of course it must be something they do at the school to encourage them, paying them a little now and then, but he is doing well, Maudie. I went to the workshop and watched them repairing watches and he's getting on with it all right. It's not going to make the least bit of difference, the things he can't do, they're not going to hold him up at all. In other ways he's just marvelous, the way he thinks is just marvelous. Oh he's a jewel, little Bernini is.

Maud took the bracelet and held it, gazing down at it. She wondered whether Joe knew that Stern had once given her a bracelet like that in Piraeus, although one made of gold. And of course Bernini had remembered that other bracelet, and now with this simple gift he was saying to her that he too. . . . But of course Joe must have known all of that . . . and understood it.

Joe felt a quiver pass through her shoulders as he held her. All at once she seemed smaller than ever to him, her shoulders thinner than he remembered.

Here now, Maudie, what's this you're doing?

Tears were welling up in her eyes. She shook her head, as if to send the feeling away.

I get so frightened sometimes, she whispered. He's not little anymore, not just a child, and sometimes I get so frightened when I think about it. The world's not made for people like him, it's not. It's hard enough to get by when you start with all the regular things. . . .

314

Joe held her tightly. She was crying and shaking her head, unable to shake herself free from the echoes she didn't want to hear.

Ah Maudie, I know how you feel and it's right for you to feel that way, you're his mother and nothing else would be right. But it's also true that people succeed in all kinds of ways. It's just breathtaking how they do it and Bernini's a fine lad, that's all, and he's going to do just fine. It doesn't matter that he can't read and write the way others can, or that he doesn't have a head for figures particularly. All the one means is that he'll never be an accountant hidden away in the back of some dusty office. And as for the other, well Homer was blind and he couldn't read or write, but he still saw everything there was to see and read the world much better than most of us. What I mean is, Bernini has other gifts and it's a rich world he has, just teeming with beauty. And it's going to be a rich life he finds for himself, I know it.

Maud had stopped her tears. Suddenly she looked up and smiled.

My God you're beautiful, thought Joe. Just trying so hard to take in all of life and make the best of it, and never hiding to be safe. It's the difficult way but it's also where the riches are, God bless.

She raised her hand. Joe smiled.

In the old days, he thought, you would have put your finger on my nose when you said whatever it is you're going to say. It's your way of getting close to people, the best thing God ever made.

Maud dropped her hand self-consciously. She looked confused.

The lemonade, she said. What happened to the lemonade?

I don't believe we've had the pleasure yet.

She laughed.

Poor Joe. You come to visit on a hot afternoon and you don't even get something cool to drink. I'm sorry, I'll just be a minute.

While she was gone he wandered around the room looking at her little treasures, the simple things that spoke of years of trying to find a place. Mementos he remembered from Jerusalem and Jericho, even a seashell from a tiny oasis on the shores of the Gulf of Aqaba. And mementos from Smyrna and Istanbul and Crete and the islands and Attica, and now from Cairo, from Egypt.

Once more, then, Joe found his thoughts slipping back through the years. To Jerusalem where they had met, and to Jericho where they had gone in the autumn when the nights had turned cold, because it was always summer in Jericho and Maud was going to have their child. A little house with flowers around it and lemon trees not far from the Jordan, a heady lemon scent near the river of promise and hope.

But it hadn't worked out for them in Jericho. Joe had been away running guns for a mythical man named Stern and Maud had grown desperate, afraid that one day he might not return and love would be taken from her again, as it always had been before. Joe too young to understand her fears and Maud too young to explain them, the two of them wrenched apart because they loved each other so deeply, until finally Maud in her anguish had abandoned Joe without even leaving a note, because words were too painful for what was being lost. . . . Maud overwhelmed with sadness as she trudged up the path away from the little house and its flowers, carrying the infant son she had named Bernini in the secret hope that someday he at least might build beautiful fountains and stairways in life. . . . Bernini at least.

And so to Smyrna, and to the islands and Istanbul and Greece, more restless years of uncertainty as her wanderings stretched on and on and seemed as if they would never end. Stern entering her life then through one of those mysterious turnings of fate so common in the ancient lands of the Eastern Mediterranean where everyone seemed to meet sooner or later, perhaps because they were all secret wanderers and it was a place for that, for seeking.

Stern and Maud meeting for the first time on a bleak afternoon beside the Bosporus where Maud had gone to stare at the swirling waters, feeling too weak to go on, too tired to pick herself up and try again, too beaten and alone for that. The darkness falling and a stranger coming out of the rain who was thinking exactly what she was thinking, who came up to the railing beside her and began talking quietly about suicide, speaking simply because he understood so well that sad solution, that haunting companion of the lonely. . . . So Stern had saved her life that afternoon and eventually Maud had been able to try again. Once more there had been a little house with flowers, by the sea this time in Piraeus, where she and Bernini were happy together and Stern had come to visit.

And those had been the best years really, the happiest years for

Maud when she looked back. Bernini still young enough so it didn't matter if he wasn't quite like other children, but then all too quickly that had ended. . . . War was coming.

Stern there to help as always, finding a job for Maud in Cairo and suggesting a school for Bernini in America, now that he was too old to sit daydreaming by the sea. A special school where Bernini could live and learn a trade, so that someday he would be able to support himself and make his way, in America where it was safe. Stern offering to pay for the school since Maud didn't have the money.

In the end she had agreed because it was the best thing for Bernini. And she had always thanked Stern, even though she had known from the beginning that the money must really have come from Joe. Because Stern didn't have money like that, despite what he told her, and Joe was the kind of man who would find it. Joe trying to make it easier for her by sending the money to Stern, and asking Stern to make the offer in his place. . . . And thus Bernini had come to have two fathers who cared for him, two men whose lives had been inextricably entwined with Maud's through the years. . . .

Echoes, thought Joe. Echoes of the sun and the sand and the sea and a glorious spring on the shores of the Gulf of Aqaba . . . echoes from the brief span of a moon above the Sinai so long ago. . . .

Joe held the seashell to his ear, listening and listening, then replaced Maud's little treasure.

She was distracted when she came back from the kitchen. She sat down beside him and pushed back her hair.

What is it? she asked suddenly, looking startled.

Joe smiled.

Nothing.

Did I do something strange?

Joe laughed.

Not that I know of.

Oh the lemonade, she said. I forgot the lemonade. I must have been thinking of something else and had a glass of water and just turned around and come back. How silly of me. It's dreadful how my mind wanders.

Nonsense. What were you thinking about?

Maud's face was serious.

Bernini. What you said about him. I understand that, you know.

Of course you do, Maudie. Sometimes it seems to me that everybody always understands everything. It makes sense, after all, when you think of it, because we do have all of the past and all of the future within us, so what happens is that we just get reminded of things in life we already know, and remind others in turn. Stern taught me that, and you did, and then I learned a little more about it sitting in the desert for seven years. The sounds in a desert are small and you have to listen ever so softly to hear the whispers of the real things, even though they're already inside you.

Joe? I know Bernini's special and it's only sometimes that I feel confused, and right now the confusion has more to do with seeing you.

Yes, there are just so many feelings, aren't there, Maudie. What we had and what we lost, and what we've done since then and haven't done. . . . It's confusing, I know, and it's sad.

But now there's something else, she said quietly. You don't have to tell me why you're here. No one has said anything but it has to be because of Stern, it can't be anything else. And I suppose you can't talk about it and frankly I don't want to hear about it anyway. I know what Stern has meant to me and I'll always know, and nothing can change that. . . . But Joe? Just tell me one thing.

She turned away and shook her head. The tears had begun to well up in her eyes.

Oh what does it matter, you don't even have to tell me that. I already know the answer.

No, Maudie, go ahead and ask it anyway. It's better to say some things outright and not just hint at them, even when we know the answers.

She stared at the floor.

All right. . . . Last night I saw Stern. We went out to the desert and we sat up all night near the pyramids, and he talked as if it were all over and he even said it was the last night of his life. I tried to tell him we don't know things like that, but he said he knew it anyway, and then at dawn he took a photograph of me out there with my camera, so I'd have. . . . But Joe, is it true? Is it all over for Stern?

Joe nodded. . . . Yes.

You mean he's finished, just like that, and there's no way to . . . no chance at all?

Not with what's happened. No.

Oh, I didn't want to believe him. It's so hard to imagine with someone like Stern who has always been there and always managed to come back. Somehow you just never think . . .

Joe took her hands.

But how does he know? she asked. How does he know that?

I guess it's just always been that way with Stern. There's no explanation for it. He just knows things, that's all.

Oh my, I feel lost. . . .

Maudie, try to hear me, I need your help. I want to see him and there's no time. I came all this way to see him and find out about him and there's almost no time left, so can you help me do that? It may mean trouble with the people you work for, because of the Monks, serious trouble even. But can you do that for me anyway, for Stern's sake, for all of us?

Maud hung her head. Her voice was far away.

. . . I can get a message to him.

Where is he now? Do you know?

Maud turned and gazed at the shuttered window. Thin lines of sunlight framed its solid darkness.

Out there, she whispered. Out there dressed as a beggar in some nameless city where he's always been. He tried so hard to find his holy place and he never did, but he never stopped believing in it, Joe, and something terrible has happened now. He's out there alone and he thinks he's failed. He sees his life as so many ruins around him and he thinks it's come to nothing, and all the pain and suffering were for nothing. He's wearing a beggar's rags and he's not afraid, but he's lonely and defeated and he shouldn't feel that way. . . . Oh Joe. *Oh my.*

Maud pushed away her tears.

Last night he said so many things he'd never said before. Some of them I already knew without him having to tell me, but some of them I didn't. And now he's out there thinking he's failed and there was nothing I could do to convince him it isn't so. I felt completely helpless. Stern, of all people. *Stern.* He's done so much for others and now he feels nothing means anything to him. . . .

Oh Joe, make him see. Let him *see.* Don't let him die feeling this way. . . .

Maud jumped to her feet.

Wait, I'll get the lemonade. The little things have to go on . . . they have to, otherwise it's too much.

After he had left, Maud sat looking at the thin gold-colored bracelet on her wrist, turning it around and around and thinking how strange life was, how contradictory. For the thin bracelet reminded her of the trade Bernini was learning, repairing watches, and the time told by watches was something Bernini didn't even believe in, dwelling as he did in another kind of time where the hour of the day was only to be found in one's heart.

And she wondered as well what this gift from her son might mean now, coming when it did. Could it be that this simple little band was to be the final memento of all the many worlds she had known with Stern, with Joe?

Maud alone in the half-light turning the little bracelet and pondering the meaning of love in its long ago beginnings. . . . A miracle to be cherished above all others . . . to be found only to be lost and lost again through the years.

18

Crypt/Mirror

Old Menelik's spacious crypt from antiquity, hidden away beneath a public garden beside the Nile.

A secret and soundless vault unearthed by the great Egyptologist early in the course of his brilliant career of anonymous discovery in the nineteenth century. Later chosen by the former slave and graffiti expert as his retirement home, when he finally decided to forsake sunlight altogether and go underground once and for all, permanently on principle.

In the middle of the crypt the massive stone sarcophagus that had once belonged to Cheops' mother, its roomy cork-lined interior having served for many years as old Menelik's cozy bedroom in retirement, after he had abandoned the elegant pharaonic society he had sought in his youth and had set himself up on a heap of pillows in the evening of life, to sip tea in his sarcophagus and nibble an occasional madeleine in the comforting stillness, to ruminate and recall stray words from over the years. A soothing womb of refuge that had quite naturally evolved into old Menelik's tomb in the end, its enormous stone lid now firmly lowered into place for what might well be eternity.

On the far side of the crypt a small manual printing press, until recently the clandestine work corner of the melancholy Ahmad, former master forger and reigning night clerk of an obscure way station known as the Hotel Babylon, a run-down lodging whose Hanging Gardens had already been in an advanced state of decay at least as far back as the turn of the century, when its sordid rooms had always been available for balmy interludes in the unhurried darkness of Old

Cairo, rentable by the half-hour without reservations on anyone's part.

Save for the printing press, the crypt exactly the same as it had been in old Menelik's day. In another corner a handsome harpsichord which had once been played by Little Alice.

Here and there clusters of stately Victorian garden furniture, its paint flaking away, originally Sherwood Forest green. The furniture consisting entirely of sturdy park benches, monstrously heavy and all but immovable due to the solid cast-iron slats binding their undersides in unbending Victorian decorum. These park benches arranged so visitors could circulate with ease when Menelik had held his *open tomb every Sunday,* as he used to say, sitting upright and alert in his huge stone bed while entertaining friends at his famous weekly musicales.

Everywhere on the walls of the crypt the exquisite hieroglyphs and pharaonic wall paintings that testified to old Menelik's unparalleled success as a social figure in other ages.

On the park bench next to Joe lay the book Liffy had been in the habit of reading in the crypt on quiet afternoons. Buber, thought Joe. A wonderful old crank who actually believes man and God should talk together. No wonder Liffy used to like to slip away from the mayhem aboveground and have a little quiet discussion down here, why not? Never was much good for his people, that mayhem up there.

Joe looked down at the thick wad of forged foreign currency he was holding in his hand. He had picked up the money at random from the neat piles stacked along the walls of the vault, crisp counterfeit bills left over from Ahmad's last run on the printing press, uncounted sums of Bulgarian leva and Rumanian bani and Turkish paras, all of it apparently worth something somewhere.

The Balkans, thought Joe. Always was a confusing concept, as Alice says, and its money is just as confusing as the rest of it. What's one to make of leva and bani in the end? Or for that matter, of paras above all?

He studied the money, aware that something about it wasn't quite right.

Coins, he thought all at once. In real Balkan life this money was never issued in anything but coins, but here's Ahmad turning it out as paper money. Surely the old poet must have had a strong sense of

322

private reality to be able to forge coins as bills, even if they are Balkan bills.

Joe stuffed the money into his pocket and moved uncomfortably around on the hard park bench, his attention drawn to the crude sign hanging over the iron door at the entrance to the crypt.

THE PANORAMA HAS MOVED.

It was an old sign clumsily painted, a slab of whitewashed wood with uneven block letters in green, badly faded by years of exposure to powerful sunlight. Where had the sign come from and why had old Menelik seen fit to hang it over the door of his retirement home? What memories had it held for the greatest archeologist and subterranean graffiti specialist of the nineteenth century?

Joe frowned.

There's something sad about that sign, he thought. Something ciphered too, I would imagine. Surely it's no mere slip of stray sentiment adrift in the gloom, considering what this place has meant to so many people. Of course things would tend to be cryptic in a crypt, that's only to be expected. But all the same I'll wager that sign has a hidden message to it. It would have to down here in old Menelik's mausoleum of stoned coincidences, as Ahmad used to call it, quoting his father who had lapsed into a heavy use of hashish toward the end.

THE PANORAMA HAS MOVED.

Mysterious graffiti, thought Joe, and what might its origins be? Pharaonic? Nilotic? A Biblical writing on the wall after the manner of *mene, mene, tekel, upharsin?*

Who knows? thought Joe. Best to ask Stern about it when he shows up. When in doubt about a sign faded by sunlight deep in a crypt underground, best to ask a master cryptographer what's really going on, as some old Cairo saying must have it.

Joe turned uneasily. A sound seemed to have come from the corner where the small printing press stood . . . metal rubbing lightly against metal . . . a soft crunching noise.

Impossible, he thought, gripping the arm of his park bench. Yet a part of the machinery in the corner seemed to be moving, almost as if the manual press were preparing to crank through a cycle.

My God, he thought, of course that's impossible, and steady there, I can't go losing my bloody mind now. These antique shadows are playing tricks on me

But then he jumped, startled, unable to believe it. The small hand-driven printing press was actually beginning to turn over. Meshed parts were moving methodically in some kind of inscrutable order, up and down and sideways, backward and around and in. There was a loud groan and then the machine clattered noisily, cranking out a slip of paper. The paper fluttered and floated down to the floor.

Message from the past, thought Joe, leaping to his feet and rushing over to snatch up the slip of paper . . . a Greek banknote newly printed. *One hundred drachmas.* The ink was still wet.

Joe whirled where he stood, taking in the crypt at a glance. The thick iron door was still solidly locked, the massive stone lid was still on the sarcophagus and as so often in life, everything seemed still the same when it wasn't.

THE PANORAMA HAS MOVED.

Joe spun around, peering in every direction. *Oh help,* he shouted silently, turning over the strange banknote in his hand only to find there was a different currency printed on its other side. . . Albanian money. *Ten thousand leks.*

Ha, he thought. Inflation in the Balkans as usual and so much for classical Greek values too. They've gone to the Albanians like everything else we once admired. Just nothing's worth what it used to be and that's a fact in this world. . . .

Joe jumped, became rigid. Deep laughter was booming through the crypt, great surges of rolling laughter. A hand was reaching out of a hole in the wall behind the press, stealthily removing block after block of stone and widening the hole, methodically pushing the blocks aside and stacking them up on the floor. After a moment a ghostly head emerged from the blackness, an apparition in the age-old rags of a mummy. Without warning the ghostly head jerked back to reveal a dusty masklike face staring directly up at Joe, fierce dark eyes glittering in the dimness, beneath them the third eye of a gun barrel pointed at Joe's head.

Joe's mouth fell open. The revolver disappeared. The ghostly figure crawled forward and then all at once there was Stern standing in front of him, laughing and dusting off his tattered Arab cloak, laughing and laughing and shaking his great dark head.

. . . sorry about that, Joe. I didn't mean to scare you.

Joe hopped up and down.

How's that, Stern? Didn't mean to, you say? Well do you always go around cranking off counterfeit money when you break into a tomb? Just in case you have to pay your way in eternity?

. . . a mistake, said Stern, throwing back his head, laughing. . . . I was groping around and my hand happened to fall on the printing press handle.

Happened to fall, you say? Well after seven years in the desert I just happened to drop in down here to say hello, so *hello*, you stranger.

Joe laughed too and they embraced, hugging each other.

They sat on a park bench near the huge stone sarcophagus. Stern sniffed the bottle of arak in his hands and passed it to Joe.

The honor's yours, you must be thirsty. There's an Arab saying that nothing quickens a man's thirst like seven years in the wilderness.

Joe smiled and took the bottle, admiring it. When Stern had begun rummaging around in the crannies of Ahmad's little printing press, poking into its recesses and finally holding up the bottle in triumph, it hadn't surprised Joe particularly. Somehow it was the kind of thing he would have expected of Stern. An unlikely act in an unlikely place.

Joe glanced sideways at Stern.

Strikes you as a scene you've come across before, does it? Two down-and-out tramps sharing a bottle on a park bench?

Stern smiled.

What happened to that wondrous thirst?

Right. It's got me in its grip.

Joe drank. He turned his head and coughed.

My God that's strong stuff, Stern. But it helps a printing press think more clearly, you say?

Stern laughed.

Ahmad was very fond of his old printing press and he always claimed arak was the best solvent for cleaning counterfeit type.

And I don't doubt it for a moment, said Joe. It's a first-rate solvent for all kinds of things, brains being one and Balkan reality another. But aren't you the tricky one now? Imagine just sneaking in here through a secret passageway like a regular tomb robber on the prowl.

Stern took a drink from the bottle. He lit a cigarette and a smoke ring floated up over the sarcophagus.

I was afraid the front entrance might be watched. It seemed wiser to come in the back way.

Tricky, all right. Has that secret passageway always been there? From the time when the tomb was built, I mean?

No, Menelik had it put in as an emergency exit. But from the looks of it, I don't think he or anyone else has ever used it.

Right, dusty as dusty and the very past itself. It's just that I didn't know there was another exit of any kind down here, and that's what scared me.

Stern moved, shifting his weight.

But isn't there always another exit, Joe, if you look for it hard enough?

Joe whistled softly. He pretended to make a face.

And there you go, Stern, starting up first thing. You *are* tricky, you know that? As long as I can remember you've been saying things that arrive or leave more ways than one. It's not that you're ambiguous really, it's more a matter of searching out different paths in your quiet undercover way. That and keeping your eye all the while on more than one lodestar up there in the unfathomable deep. I suppose it must be a habit you picked up in the business you keep.

Stern's dusty face softened.

And which business is that, Joe?

Right you are, and that's exactly what I meant. Which business among the many and how's a body to know which one is being referred to?

Joe laughed happily, more relaxed than he had been in weeks despite the circumstances. They drank and talked about the past, passing the bottle back and forth, recalling the years since they had seen one another in Jerusalem. There had been letters back and forth during those years, but inevitably much that had been left unsaid by both of them. On Stern's part, because so many of his

326

concerns could never be committed to paper, and for Joe, because many of his experiences in Arizona weren't of the kind that could be readily described in letters. The conversation could have gone on much longer and Stern seemed reluctant to have it end, but there was so much Joe wanted to know he finally interrupted their talk by standing and sitting down again. He took a drink from the bottle.

Stern? Can you spare one of those awful Arab cigarettes you carry?

Stern handed him the packet. Joe lit one and coughed.

Wretched, same as always. Tears the lungs right out of a man. They always were the worst.

Stern watched him. Joe glanced at Stern's scarred thumb and looked away.

What is it? asked Stern.

I was thinking about last night at the Hotel Babylon, and this morning at Cohen's Optiks. I assume you know all about that.

Stern shifted his weight. He spoke slowly, haltingly, and there was a calmness in his manner that bothered Joe.

You mean Ahmad? . . . Yes, I know about that, and I know about David. . . .

Stern moved again, a ponderous motion.

I wanted to see Anna, he said quietly, but I knew I couldn't. David was such a wonderful young man, so much the way his father used to be. He always reminded me of his father. And Ahmad, well, we go back a long way. Ahmad was one of the first people I met in Cairo, along with Belle and Alice and David's father. They were all Menelik's friends to begin with. . . .

Stern was gazing at the sarcophagus in front of them, thoughtful, somber. Joe waited for him to continue but he didn't.

Silence, thought Joe. Dead whispers as he slips. Better a roar of outrage than that, better anything than deafening quiet. He's just too cool and calm by half and I don't like it. Silence is the enemy here tonight.

Ahmad and David were Bletchley's doing, I take it, said Joe.

Stern nodded.

So what's next then? asked Joe.

Stern moved, hesitated. He looked at Joe for a long moment and when at last he spoke his voice was matter-of-fact.

Next? Well let's see. How much do you know?

Most of it, I think. About *Enigma* anyway.

Well that's most of it now. At least it's the part that counts.

So?

So Bletchley will do what it's right for him to do. He's fighting evil, after all, the Nazi madness in the human soul

And so?

And so I'm next, said Stern.

Joe looked at him. Too calm, he thought. Too calm by half.

And that's all? Just like that?

Stern shrugged.

Yes, I guess so. Sadly, even good purposes conflict. Good and evil just aren't as simple as we'd like them to be. We try hard to pretend otherwise, but it's never really true.

Stern smiled again, a peculiar smile that Joe remembered.

But tell me, Joe, why did you ever allow yourself to get drawn into all of this? So often I used to envy you over there in Arizona. It seemed like such a good life, exactly the kind of thing a man should do with his days, not at all what I've done with the years. And even after you did come here you could have pulled back, given Bletchley something and then. . . . Bletchley probably expected it, in fact. Why didn't you, Joe? You must have sensed where things were heading.

More or less, I suppose.

Well?

Well I didn't pull back, that's all.

But why?

I don't know really. How can we ever give a true answer to something like that? Because I wanted to see it through to the end. Because it seemed right to do that.

I'm afraid it doesn't surprise me, said Stern. From the time I saw you on the street near Maud's, I'm afraid it's what I thought you'd do.

Why afraid?

That's obvious, isn't it?

I guess. But did you know I was in Cairo then? Before you saw me on the street that evening?

No, I had no idea, it was a shock. But the moment I did see you I knew why you were here and who'd arranged it and what the circumstances had to be. I'd realized all along that eventually someone might find out some facts about that trip of mine to Poland and look into it, as Bletchley did, and then start something like this. I didn't imagine they'd go so far afield as to look you up, but then, it makes sense when you think about it, doesn't it?

I suppose it does, Stern, at least as much sense as anything else. And then the first time we did come face-to-face, there you were playing the beggar, sitting in the dust in those rags with your hand out, and I took pity and gave you money. And you, you shameless rascal, you even *took* my money.

Stern laughed.

I was hungry. I just don't have much pride anymore.

Well that's not true but we'll let it pass, the same way I passed you by then. But why didn't you get in touch with me after that?

I thought about it but I was hoping you'd find out enough to give Bletchley some satisfaction, and then quit before you got in all the way. I didn't expect it to happen, but there was always a chance.

Joe reached for the bottle.

So where does that leave us now, Stern? Just a couple of losers having a last glass together on a park bench underground? Just mulling it over and trying to get a grip on before we go topside and get run down by a lorry or take a tumble off a roof?

Stern opened his hands and looked at them.

Maybe. Probably. It's the danger in living among people, isn't it? In the desert you can run out of food or water but it's not all that easy to do, really. You can get by on very little and it takes longer to die. Men, civilization, speed things up.

Stern smiled.

But I still wouldn't say this is our last drink.

No? Well I'm glad to hear that, I never did like the idea of closing time. And how many carefree hours might we have ahead of us then?

Oh I don't know, said Stern. We could probably even manage a day or two if we stayed down here.

But how could we do that? Isn't this one place Bletchley's bound to look if we don't show up elsewhere?

I imagine, so I guess we only have hours. But we do have some time, so we might as well relax.

Well it may sound strange, Stern, but the fact is I *am* relaxed. I didn't get a nod of sleep last night but I feel as if I've been doing nothing else.

You stayed up all night with Belle and Alice?

Almost all night, but how did you know I was there? You haven't been following me too, have you?

No, but I have friends in the city who keep an eye out for me . . . beggars . . . fellow beggars. It's an occupation that allows a good deal of time for observation.

Joe nodded. . . . Stern's secret army, he thought. Some people have tanks, some have Monks, he has beggars. Must depend on which dusty byway you choose to sit in at the end of the day.

Beggars, are they? said Joe. And do you know what happened then on my way back from the houseboat this morning?

Stern laughed.

A dreadful commotion. You nearly caused a riot, shouting about Rommel's breakfast.

There was that as well, said Joe, but it wasn't the important thing. What happened was that I made a fool out of one of Bletchley's young Monks who was following me. Lost my head and humiliated him for no reason at all. I was terribly ashamed.

Stern looked at him.

Well you should forget that now, Joe. It's over and done with.

I know it is, and there's something else I wanted to mention. That letter you wrote to me about Colly's death. That was a beautiful letter, Stern, and I'll never forget it.

Well I'll never forget Colly. Along with many other people who knew him.

Joe nodded.

He was his own man all right, said Joe, and an unusual one. But you know, I did a little quiet asking into his death after I got here, and Bletchley gave me the impression you might have made a special trip to Crete, using an operation as an excuse, just to find out what happened to Colly. Any truth to that?

Stern moved awkwardly on the bench.

There could be.

Could be, yes. Could be, surely. But did you or didn't you? I don't think I caught your answer.

I did make the trip, said Stern.

I see. And naturally that was just a little thing. But what about Bletchley himself in all this?

I like him. He's a decent man.

Do you trust him?

To do his job, yes.

And his job is us, now?

In answer, Stern reached out and touched Joe's arm.

And more silence, thought Joe, just more and more of that shadowy shape that won't be. But he's got to start somewhere.

Well even if that's how it is, said Joe, there's still one thing that's been bothering me this evening in this cozy vault. That sign over the door. I know it's suggestive, but of what? And where'd it come from?

Stern turned and gazed across the crypt. After a moment he began to speak in a faraway voice.

The Panorama used to be a restaurant, he said. It was right on the river, a cheap place, mostly a refuge for off-duty dragomen. A dirty open-air restaurant with trellises and vines and banks of flowers, and a pool where ducks paddled and a cage with squawking peacocks, and strong dark wine by the flagon and huge platters of spicy lamb. A century ago three young men got into the habit of spending long Sunday afternoons there, eating and drinking and talking and talking, and they liked it so much they always went back when they could later in life.

Ah, said Joe, so that's the Panorama being referred to. I've heard of that restaurant all right, but I never knew its proper name. And the three young men in question would have been your father, once called Strongbow, and Menelik and the Cohen of the day, the one who was later known as Crazy, before they all set out on their journeys. And they kept going back to that restaurant for a full four decades, as I understand it, and that was the legendary forty-year conversation on the banks of the Nile that Ahmad used to talk about. That I also heard about years ago in Jerusalem, for that matter.

Yes, mused Stern, it did last on and off for forty years, right up until my father became an Arab holy man and disappeared into the desert. But then toward the end of his long life he decided he wanted to see Menelik one last time, Cohen being dead by then, and he traveled up from the Yemen to Cairo and he and Menelik returned to their same old restaurant one Sunday afternoon, not long before the First World War.

And they found that sign waiting for them?

Yes, said Stern. That sign and an empty lot.

Joe whistled softly.

So how did they celebrate then? Did they go look for the restaurant?

Stern shook his head, his voice far away.

No, they didn't do that, they didn't go anywhere. They were too old to drink by then and too old to have any particular interest in food, and they knew each other so well there wasn't much point in even talking anymore. So what they did was sit down in that empty lot and rest their backs on that sign and spend the afternoon enjoying the view. Now and then one of them would chuckle over some memory that came to mind, first one of them and then the other, and that was how the afternoon passed. Then when the sun began to sink they got up and left the place, Menelik to return here to his sarcophagus, my father to return to his tent in the Yemen. And for them, that was the end of the nineteenth century.

Joe whistled very softly.

And there we have it straight out, he said. And after forty years of honest raucous talk beside the Nile, there hangs the sign of a tale in time, deep underground and out of sight. And it is amazing when you think of it, how such an immensity of swirling moments can reside in a legend as brief in the telling as that one. And sure the Panorama did move . . . and sure it has and does.

Suddenly Stern's manner changed. A dark mood seized him, some violent memory from over the years. He lurched heavily to his feet and began pacing around the crypt, oblivious to Joe and everything else, his eyes working feverishly in the gloom, his thoughts fixed on some distant landscape.

Joe watched him in fascination. It's strange, he thought, how much Stern can look like a beggar when he wants to, how easy it is for him to become the very poorest of the poor or anything else. . . . And it was frightening as well, for there had always been something profoundly disturbing to Joe in Stern's sudden transformations.

Joe sat quietly watching, waiting, as Stern moved restlessly through the shadows. . . . A gaunt face hollowed to the bone, so lean no more could be dug from it. Hard slender hands and scarred feet and a faded cloak made threadbare by innumerable beatings on stone, weathered by a relentless sun until it was as soft and pale as the sands of the desert. But for Joe, there was more to Stern than just his striking appearance. There had always been a hunger haunting the man that knew no bounds, a fierce and pitiless hunger that could never be satisfied.

Here, now, Stern was a beggar in a crypt. And he *is* that beggar, thought Joe. With Stern it's never just a disguise. As he limps there in his rags, he is that wretchedly poor man with nothing.

Yet, as Joe also knew, Stern was truly many men in many places, truly a vast and changeable spirit who had ventured so deeply into the byways of the human soul that every sound he heard there had long ago become but an echo from his own heart. A strange and mystifying presence who had touched many lives, yet there were so few of them that Joe knew anything about. Years ago in Jerusalem there had been one or two, and again in Smyrna, and now in Cairo there were a few others, friends of Stern whose lives had always been involved with his wanderings, some even for a lifetime.

And Maud.

No one had been closer to Stern during these last years than she had, and yet it was only within the last twenty-four hours that Stern had sat down with her and told her about the massacres in Smyrna two decades ago, when Stern had picked up a knife and pulled back a little girl's head and made the sudden awful slash that had cut through his entire life, a terrible and merciful act but also just one among tens of thousands in Stern's turbulent life with its wrenching changes . . . these few people in Cairo and Jerusalem and Smyrna the only ones Joe happened to know about. How many others had there been in other places? How many people helped in some small way by his devotion and love? How many lives marked through the years . . . how many hearts touched by Stern?

A strange and restless soul, thought Joe, as he watched Stern pacing in the shadowy dimness of the vault. Perhaps even a soul lingering on the stormbeaten threshold of sanctity.

For as the poet said, hadn't that threshold always been terrible? . . . Even crime-haunted?

Suddenly Stern whirled.

I've got to get out of here. I can't stand it down here any longer.

Joe got to his feet.

Fine. Where do we go?

Stern thought for a moment.

There's a place I used to go to years ago when I was a student, a cheap Arab bar, I've been back there once or twice. It's small and out of the way and as safe as anywhere else. In fact it's not far from the Hotel Babylon, which is good. Bletchley won't be looking for us that close to home.

Fine. It doesn't have an old cracked mirror behind the counter, does it?

Yes, don't all bars? How else could we ponder that mysterious stranger who enters our lives whenever we sit alone and brood?

True. And by any chance, did you ever take Liffy to this bar?

I may have. Why?

Because if it's the same place, I was there with him this morning.

Stern stopped. He gazed at Joe and smiled.

That's curious.

You're right, it is, said Joe, also smiling. Well then, is it time to leave old Menelik's mausoleum on a clear Cairo night in 1942? Time, is it, as we used to say?

Yes. Just give me a minute.

Sure, said Joe, I'll just wander over and give Ahmad's miraculous printing press a last inspection. Who knows? After you and I leave here no one may ever see that magical machine again. This crypt may just stay locked forever and that may be the end of Greek leks and Albanian drachmas and Balkan reality in general, who can say. Odd money in any case, Ahmad's private tender. . . .

Joe kept talking as he walked away, talking and scraping his feet and shuffling, making noise. Out of the corner of his eye he saw Stern moving quickly in the other direction, his face to the side, not so much avoiding Joe as making it easier for Joe to avoid him. Joe stopped in front of the printing press and began turning a handle, turning and turning it, making noise.

He glanced over his shoulder. Stern was crouching by a table near the door, beside a candle, hunched over and intent as he worked on something in his hands. A small black case lay open in front of him.

God have mercy, thought Joe. . . . *Morphine to steady the blood, oh God.*

Joe squeezed his eyes shut and turned the handle of the printing press around and around, methodically making noise and cranking out counterfeit banknotes, spewing out more and more of the ridiculous money onto the floor.

THE PANORAMA HAS MOVED.

Oh have mercy, whispered Joe silently. He's tried so hard and he's given and given but he's finished now and he just has no more to give. And when the time comes let a whirlwind descend on the desert at night and let the blessed stillness of dawn be on the sands where he's walked. And let a moment of peace be on him before then, just one small moment of peace before the wind howls an end to him in the darkness . . . *an end* to all he was and wanted. . . .

It was the same poor Arab bar where Joe had gone with Liffy that morning. A narrow barren place where laborers slumped along the walls in stony silence, somberly smoking and drinking in the half-light, stirring only to nod at their uselessness within the passing hours.

The two of them sat at the counter, facing the cracked grainy mirror on the wall. Now I have to get this right the first time, thought Joe. There are opposing points of the compass to be touched and not much time to do it in, so how to get things started with Stern? One way or another we've just got to break through that *silence* of his, damn it to the end of the world. He's just got to know and believe in what he's done, but how to help him go where he needs to go this one last time?

The mirror, thought Joe, recalling the visit that morning with Liffy. The mirror will have to tell him . . . *the mirror*. See all, hear all, speak what?

Joe laughed and spread his arms, gathering in the room with the gesture.

So this is your secret world, Stern? This is where you dreamed away the wee hours of your youth? Well it's a murky place for sure, and certainly a place for dreaming. Certainly there'd be no other direction you'd want your fancy to take in the late hours here, in an alley as sordid as this one, in a rat-infested slum in Cairo or anywhere else.

And speaking of murkiness, Stern, there's something that's been weighing more and more on me since I arrived in Cairo. It has to do with the tiny glimpses we're given of people, and the fact that everyone seems to be a secret agent in life in a way. With their own private betrayals and their own private loyalties that we don't know anything about, and their own secret code copied down from a private onetime pad, which we both know is all but unbreakable. And with their status in this world not unlike my own in Cairo, *in transit*, as the good document describes it ever so nicely.

Ahmad, for example. When you looked at him you saw only a silent melancholy man endlessly playing solitaire and nodding over newspapers that were absurdly out of date, like all newspapers. But when he opened the secret panel to his clandestine little cave, hidden away behind the wall in the shabby corridor that passes for a lobby in the Hotel Babylon, with all the treasures he'd stored up over the years in that private little closet . . . well, a whole world of experiences suddenly came to life right in front of your eyes.

I was lucky enough to catch a glimpse of that private world, Joe went on, but it would have been just as easy to have missed it altogether, as I'm sure many people did. And to them Ahmad will always be merely what he appeared to be, a taciturn man without any feelings particularly, some kind of large and immobile oddity not worth knowing.

Even the implements of the clandestine trade are there, continued Joe, cast in their own unique shapes as is only proper. An old dented trombone, say, that served as the unlikely key to Ahmad's secret code, because it provided the notes to the tunes that others had forgotten, but not him. Or an old cardboard suitcase, empty save for a few sheaves of paper with some poems on them, the black bag of Ahmad's particular escape and evasion operation over the years, its very emptiness bulging with voluminous secret memories that only Ahmad could decipher.

So it strikes me there are no commonplace people in the crowd, said Joe, and no innocents in the game of life really. We all seem to be double and triple agents with unknown sources and unsuspected lines of control, reporting a little here and a little there as we try to manage our secret networks of feeling and doing, our own little complex networks of life. . . .

Ahmad? An immobile taciturn man without any feelings particularly? *Ahmad?* That eloquent and gentle poet? That shy swaying poet of stately lost dreams and elegant lost causes? A man who so heroically defended his mythical lost city of the soul?

No, Ahmad wasn't what he appeared to be at all. And don't we all use covers in a way, Stern? Don't we all use our own secret codes? And don't we all protect the secret sources of our strength and keep them separate one from another because they're so dear to us, while all the while we secretly plan the little clandestine operations of our lives, our daring forays up the street to the greengrocer's? And isn't betrayal, as Ahmad also said, still the most painful wound of all, and self-betrayal the very worst kind there can be? So devastating to us it forever remains incomprehensible in our hearts? The one sin we can never forgive in ourselves, therefore the one sin we can never accept from anyone?

Well it does strike me that this secret-agent way of doing things is true for all of us in some fashion, said Joe, and part of it often comes from fear, I know, the fear that others may discover who we really are. But all of it isn't fear, not generally, and in your case none of it is. So what's the other part of it, Stern, the part that isn't greengrocery espionage? The part that takes us beyond the obvious similarities in people and gets us closer to that figure you were talking about earlier. That mysterious stranger who manifests himself in the mirror behind the bar and just plonks himself down to stare at us when we're brooding alone. Who *is* that stranger and why is it so difficult to know *anyone* in the end? Even ourselves.

Stern moved, sipping his drink. He smiled.

Answers, Joe? Pulling my cover as a greengrocer in order to find answers? Well I suppose the other part must come from that very mirror behind the bar, from the images there and the voices. When you look at this mirror in front of us, you see me and you see yourself. But since this is a place I once knew, when I look at this mirror, inevitably I see many people.

Now it's beginning, thought Joe. And slowly, easy now, if we're to hear the first whisper through the silence. . . .

I wouldn't doubt that for a moment, Stern. So tell me, of the many people in that mirror for you, can you see the first woman you ever loved? Is she still there?

Stern lowered his eyes.

Yes, he whispered.

And there it is, thought Joe, and now he's listening to the echoes and straining to hear their beginnings, now when everything seems to be coming to an end. So slowly then, from the deepness of the silence. . . .

You can see her, Stern? What was her name, I wonder?

Stern was still gazing down at the counter.

Eleni, he whispered.

Ahh, and that's a beautiful name, Stern. A name from ancient times that has always meant beauty to everyone and especially to Homer, who launched a thousand ships in his mind because of her. And where did you fall in love with her, and who might she have been?

Awkwardly Stern shifted his weight, his eyes fixed on the counter.

It was in Smyrna. She was from one of the leading Greek families there, back when it was still a Greek city. We were married. It was before you and I met.

Joe was astounded. He had never known that Stern had been married.

What happened?

It was when I first returned from studying in Europe, whispered Stern, when I was just setting out and beginning to learn about revolutionary work. We fell in love and we were married and for a while it was wonderful. But my life didn't seem to allow for a marriage, at least not for two people as young as we were. There was trouble between us and she left me and came back, then finally she left for good.

Where is she now?

Dead. She's been dead for years.

She must have been young.

She was, whispered Stern. Much too young.

What was it?

Stern turned uneasily and looked at Joe.

I'm not sure, I've never been sure. Footprints in the sky that I couldn't see? The sound of perfect sunlight? Laughter and joy and the eternal tragedy of the Aegean?

Abruptly Stern turned away from Joe and stared hard into the shadowy interiors of the mirror. He raised his hand and reached out, as if he were groping for something there.

It seems everybody doesn't make it, he whispered. It seems everybody can't. . . .

He had been in Athens when he finally heard the end was coming for Eleni. She had left him during the First World War, left him and Smyrna and gone to live in Italy. She hated war and she hated killing and she had learned to hate Stern's work, even though it was her uncle, Sivi, who had taken Stern in as a young student returning from Europe and had first trained him in that very work.

In Athens, years later, Stern chanced to meet a man who had seen Eleni recently, an acquaintance who had known them both in Smyrna before the war.

I'm afraid it's all over for her, said the man. The drinking just gets worse and you can't really talk to her anymore. But it can't last this way. She's killing herself.

They talked awhile longer and then Stern said good-bye to the man and walked back to the small hotel where he was staying in Athens. Only a year earlier he had become a morphine addict although he hadn't admitted it to himself yet, although he was still pretending he could face the grayness in the window at dawn, the coming of a new day, alone.

But that night he did admit it to himself as he sat up in the little hotel room in Athens, thinking of Eleni. That night he admitted many things to himself while thinking of her, because he had to.

A kind of prayer. That's what he'd had in mind.

He wanted to remember how beautiful Eleni had been when they had first met in Sivi's lovely villa by the sea. And he wanted to remember the long nights of love they had known that first spring and summer and autumn, and winter. The closeness and the tenderness, the excitement, all of it.

A kind of prayer to send to her to bring the good times back to life, by remembering them. So perhaps that one night at least Eleni might also be able to remember the good times, for it had been a wonderful love they had known.

And so Stern had recalled it all and been drawn back to the very beginning of their love, back to a spring day in Smyrna before the First World War. . . .

A brilliant afternoon. The two of them young and laughing and falling in love, wandering through the empty alleys near the harbor and coming to a little café, deserted at that siesta hour. And sitting down at a small table in the shade of a narrow old building, quietly laughing in the stillness of the little square, a breeze off the water and the warm colors of sunlit stones against the blue sky.

A sudden thud. Eleni and Stern turning with smiles on their faces.

Two cats, still coupled, had slipped off the roof of the building above them and fallen, fallen, and come crashing down into the cobblestones no more than ten feet away. One of the cats was unmoving. The other cat was trying to raise itself on its front paws, its hind quarters crushed in the sudden fall from sunlight to shadow, quietly screeching and trying to raise its head and sinking back, trying to sniff for life as its eyes closed. The one cat dead and the other dying.

Stern staggering to his feet and stumbling away, sick to his stomach and sick in his heart and utterly bewildered in the small shaded square. Eleni running after him and taking him by the arm and holding him tightly, pressing herself to him as he wandered lost by the sparkling sea. . . .

Yes, Stern had remembered it all and left nothing out in the darkness of the bare little hotel room in Athens. And once he had even imagined reaching out and touching Eleni in the stillness, and she had looked at him the way she used to and they were young again and in love and the world was made for them, and they would go on forever doing all the wonderful things they had known on the shores of the Aegean, with wine and love and soft whispers in the shadows, and little boats in the harbor. . . .

A kind of prayer, then, down through the hours of that long night in Athens. And he hoped his whispers had reached Eleni and helped her in some small way as the darkness closed in and the end drew near. Nothing left out of his prayer, all the bright dark moments of love, the exquisite joy and the infinite sadness. . . .

It wasn't much but he hoped it had helped a little, for soon after that Eleni had slipped and lost her way, and the end had come for her.

Joe shook his head, stunned by this revelation from Stern's past.

Somehow it's all hard to take in, he said at last. I've just never thought of you as having had a wife. The way you've moved about and forever uprooted yourself, always traveling. . . . I don't know.

Stern groped for his glass, a clumsy motion, his other hand edging back and forth on the counter.

Well it was a long time ago and you never lose what you had together, but you go on as best you can, if you can. Everybody doesn't seem to be able to, and it's not a matter of courage or worth that decides it, or of being more or less of a person. I don't know what decides things like that. People come up with all sorts of answers but I've never found one that works for me. Eleni was a beautiful human being, that's all. She had so much to give the world and she was no weaker than the rest of us, so why did it happen to her?

Yes, said Joe, it's always the same *Why.*

And what is that feeling anyway? asked Stern. The belief that there's a purpose to it all, or should be?

Stern moved his hand on the counter, edging it back and forth.

I've always envied people who have it, but I've never been able to see things that clearly myself. It all seems chaotic to me, and only in retrospect does life take on any kind of purpose or design. Of course that could mean I've just never been able to fathom it. Or it could mean the purpose and design aren't there, and it's only our need for them as dreaming creatures that casts some kind of coherency over life when we look back.

Stern shrugged.

341

When we do look back, he said, we always know there were certain moments that determined our lives, and certain things that did become inevitable for us, eventually that. . . . But when did it become so? When did it begin, I wonder. . . .

Stern took out the worn Morse-code key he always carried and held it in his hand, feeling its balance. Joe smiled.

Bit of the past still traveling with you?

What's that?

The Morse-code key. I see you still carry it.

Stern gazed down at the smooth slip of metal shining from years of being rubbed between his fingers, gently polished by the oils of his skin. His eyes were thoughtful, far away.

I didn't realize I'd taken it out. I seem to have become distracted lately, or maybe relaxed is a better word. There's been little chance for that since the war started.

Joe nodded. Sign both good and bad, he thought. Good, because it means he's leaning back and taking a look at things. Bad, because he feels none of it matters anymore.

Stern studied the key as if listening to something, then put it away.

There are no inanimate objects, murmured Stern. Everything around us whispers continually, it's just that we don't have time to listen. In the desert it's different. In the desert you have the time and you listen long and hard because your life depends on it.

Joe watched him.

Why these thoughts, Stern?

Stern frowned, moving awkwardly around on his stool.

I'm not sure. I guess I was thinking about home, the idea of a home, what it means for all the people who have lost theirs in the war and will never have one again. . . . I chose my life and I knew what I was doing, but it's still true you never get used to being homeless. You can get used to being away from home, whatever home happens to mean to you, that's easy enough. You can even do it forever, if you have to. But there's a difference between that and not having a home at all.

Well I can see what you're saying, Stern, but I'd never have thought you could consider yourself an alien out here. Not when you can pass yourself off as a native no matter where you go. What's more, as a native of just about any background or standing.

Joe smiled.

After all, you haven't always been a beggar in rags the way you are tonight. As I recall, some other incarnations of yours have been quite grand.

I guess.

Well?

It's what you just said. I can pass myself off as a native. But being one, feeling that you belong in a place, is different.

That it is, and that brings us back to a stranger in the bazaars and deserts, aloneness amidst the clamor and the silence. What's it all about, Stern? Why these thoughts tonight and what was the particular inanimate object you had in mind?

Stern frowned, moved.

A rug. I was thinking about a rug.

Joe watched him.

A rug, you say. Simply that.

Yes. Rugs always remind me of someone's home because that's where I've always seen them, in someone's home. Most of my life has been spent in places like this, bare rooms with bare floors and almost no furniture, not places for living. It's just a little thing, one of those innumerable details we almost never think about. One of those tiny physical details that define us eventually, strangely.

That old faded red wool hat of yours, Joe, that's a physical detail. The one you used to wear in Jerusalem when you were living alone in that odd little room on a roof in the Armenian Quarter. Do you still have that hat?

Yes.

With you here in Cairo?

Yes.

And you wear it?

Well I did all right, back when I was taking my ease in the Hotel Babylon and seeing the world with the help of Liffy's miraculous gift of faces and gift of tongues. Or when I was out back in the courtyard with Ahmad late at night, sitting in our tiny oasis and listening with him to the stars.

Why did you wear it, Joe?

Habit, I suppose. Reminded me of things, I suppose. Must make me feel comfortable wearing it.

And uncomfortable too sometimes?

Oh yes. The incarnations come and go and it's not always easy to recall where those other people in your body have been, and what they did and what seemed so crucial at the time. Of course some of it *was* crucial, all of it in its way, but is that what you meant about physical details? That my red wool hat is a way of reminding myself that a kid on the run in the hills of southern Ireland, and an obsessed young man playing longterm poker in Jerusalem, and the medicine man of the Hopi Indians, and an Armenian agent known as Gulbenkian in wartime Cairo, that these odd types are all related in some obscure way? Moreover, that they all grew out of a boy who passed his childhood tossing around in a fishing boat on the tides off the Aran Islands? Tides and more, despite all? Despite even adverse winds and the peculiar sunspots of time? That all these boys and men and notions I've just mentioned, despite the years, still have something in common? Namely me, because they *are* me? Is that what you meant?

Stern laughed.

You have a way of putting it, Joe. But yes, something like that.

Sure, thought Joe, something like that, but what exactly? Which rug are you thinking of, and why? All of Europe has lost the rug it's standing on, but you've got one specific one in mind. . . .

Well sure then, said Joe. In that sense nothing would be inanimate and there'd be no such thing as just plain furniture in life. An old wool hat or a shiny Morse-code key, they'd have their changing tales locked inside of them all right. But it was a bare floor you were talking about, a rug and a bare floor and homelessness. And it would seem to me that someone who grew up in the desert the way you did, in a tent made of goats' skins, wouldn't have any serious interest in floors, bare or otherwise. So how did that get into your thinking tonight, and just where was that bare floor? You must have looked at it hard and more than once. Where was it, Stern?

In Smyrna.

Then it must have to do with Eleni, thought Joe. Or with her uncle, Sivi, who got you started in this business.

Where in Smyrna, Stern?

Stern moved.

344

In Sivi's villa, he said, in the bedroom I always used when I stayed with him. A long room with a high ceiling and tall French doors and a small balcony overlooking the harbor. At one point, after Eleni left me, I used to spend a great deal of time sitting out on that balcony in the early mornings when the harbor was coming to life, and then again late at night after everything had closed and there was only an occasional wanderer poking along the waterfront. I liked the quiet, the peace, the new light of the morning and the old light of the stars. Harbors have always fascinated me with their ships from far and wide and no end to where they might go. Any journey under the sun conceivable, every destination in the world a possibility.

Stern smiled.

It's the ancient Greek in me, he said, that fascination with what lies beyond the horizon. Or what may lie out there, if you dare to look for it.

Greek too, Stern? Being English and Arab and a Yemeni Jew isn't enough of a heritage for you? You want to take on the Greeks too?

Yes, why not, said Stern. And anyway, everybody in this part of the world has a bit of the ancient Greeks in them. The Greeks were the ones who went everywhere after all, who couldn't stop themselves from trying to go everywhere. The light and the sea, but above all that astonishing light that makes you think you can see forever. It just drew them on and on and not just across the surface of the earth. What interested them was what lay beyond things, behind things, beneath things. The soul was their sea and the voyage never ended. Returning home to Ithaca was only an excuse for the Odyssey, the voyage itself was what counted. Homer, with his blind eyes, couldn't help but see that.

Homer, Stern? He's said to have been born in Smyrna. And what of that little balcony in Sivi's villa where you sat in the late and early hours, listening to Homer's seascape and keeping watch in your mind's eye?

Stern frowned.

A peaceful place on the surface, he said, but I wasn't at peace then. Eleni had left me for the last time and I hadn't become used to any of it yet, particularly going back to Smyrna and not having her there. Eleni *was* Smyrna to me, and the whole excitement of the place and the beautiful way of life people had there then, before the massacres, was inseparable in my mind from Eleni. When I was away, traveling, it wasn't so bad. But whenever I went back to Smyrna to see Sivi, I could only think of her and all the little places where we'd been together. Every little corner held some memory and no matter where I looked it was there waiting for me . . . some feeling, some sensation that brought her back to me.

I had no control over it, said Stern. It was a mood I couldn't overcome. Her loss was always in front of me in Smyrna, tearing at me and never letting up. All I wanted to do when I was there was hide. Sivi tried to help but he couldn't really. The days terrified me, especially the sunlight on bright days . . . Homer's sunlight. The nights were easier in a way as they always are, less harsh and less brutal, but it was also at night when the most dangerous moments came. The truly black moments when nothing mattered and it began to seem perfectly reasonable to just end it all . . . just end it. End everything. . . .

Stern fell silent. He touched the ragged sleeve of his cloak and leaned forward, staring intently into the shadowy mirror.

The end of December. One of the last nights of that dark year when Eleni had left him for the last time.

Stern had just arrived back in Smyrna to spend the holidays with Sivi, through Epiphany. Sivi was always careful to arrange some event for the evenings, so Stern wouldn't be left to sit alone in his room and brood. But that evening friends had invited Stern to dinner, so Sivi felt it safe to go off to the theater.

Stern was able to manage only a few hours at the house of his friends before his courage left him. He gave them an excuse and returned early in the evening to Sivi's, to sit on the small balcony of his bedroom looking out at the harbor.

He was strangely calm that night and the decision came to him in a natural way as he sat there gazing at the lights on the water and listening to the sounds of the sea. There was nothing dramatic about it. On the contrary, it seemed reasonable and commonplace. A new year was coming and there was no point in facing it. No point at all.

So he went inside and emptied a bottle of pills into his hand and swallowed them one by one, without water, the way he always took pills. Then he poured himself some whiskey and sat down on the side of the bed to savor the drink, lighting a cigarette to go with it.

Suicide? A desperate act brought on by intolerable despair?

No, not at all. That wasn't the way he had felt about it then. He was calm and his feelings were commonplace, his mood reasonable. A drink and a cigarette before lying down to sleep was the same as hundreds of other nights. Exactly the same, only this time he wouldn't wake up.

He sat there on the side of the bed gazing out through the open French doors at the harbor, not particularly sad, relieved more than anything else. Soothed, at peace. The soft lights swayed on the water and the gentle night embraced him, a tranquil murmur of whispers rising from the cafés below in the darkness, anonymous and remote like the world itself.

It's so easy, he thought, as he sipped and smoked. Real decisions are always so easy, unlike the little things. And death is comforting and death is peace, only life is not. . . .

Stern remembered nothing after that until he awoke the following morning. Sivi had stopped by his room when he returned from the theater and had found Stern sitting on the side of the bed, dressed and unconscious. Sivi had immediately guessed what had happened and had made Stern vomit and called his housekeeper, and the two of them had pushed Stern into a cold shower and walked him up and down in his room for more than an hour, until the danger had passed, only then letting Stern lie down to sleep.

The housekeeper had told Stern about it the following day, when he questioned her. As for Sivi, he had never mentioned the incident and never alluded to it in any way. Instead he was his usual jovial self the next day, laughing and joking and trying to buoy Stern up as he always did, as if nothing at all had happened during the night.

But whenever Stern had returned to Smyrna and his bedroom in Sivi's villa, he had picked up the corner of the new rug beside

the bed and looked at the stain on the floorboards, a
permanent stain made by his vomit, by the life going out of
him one night in order that he might live.

I used to close the door and sit there staring at it, said Stern, trying
to find some design in that map of my life on the floorboards. But no
matter how hard I looked it was still a shape without a shape, shad-
ings that turned in upon themselves, a swirl of dark tones that was all
suggestion, like clouds in the sky. So I tried to see something there
but I never could. I could never read anything into it at all.

At first that stain was so ugly to me I hated to be in the room with
it. It shamed me and frightened me and I was always aware it was
there, under the rug, and always very careful to step around it. But
after a while I forgot about it and I'd actually find myself standing
on it, not thinking where I was. . . . In a way that made it better, but
it also saddened me because it meant I'd learned to live with the
stain. The psyche doing what it had to do in order for me to survive.
Forgetting. What it always has to do when something horrible becomes an everyday companion in our lives. . . . But there was also
another cause to the sadness. Whenever I found myself standing on
that stain, I also found myself thinking of my childhood and how far
I had come from a dusty little hillside in the Yemen. By a bed now in
a room that wasn't my own, near some open doors overlooking a
harbor. . . . But why this harbor and why this room? . . . I used to ask
myself that and a whole host of questions would follow. Where is
this? Where are you? And the answers were devastating. . . . I was
anywhere. I was standing on a map that was me, my life, and it had
nothing to tell me. So I wasn't someplace, I was just anywhere. . . .

Stern drew back. He touched the neck of his ragged cloak and
turned away from the mirror, pulling himself away from its peculiar
fascination.

As for that attempt at suicide, he said, the first one, it caused me
to think about many things. What I'd really done and what it
meant, and what I'd learned about myself and the human condition,
and maybe more than anything else, what I'd learned from Sivi.

There was so much wisdom in the old man I've often wondered whether he was actually aware of it. Whether he did what he did out of some intuition, or whether he knew that the way he acted after that night was the only thing making it possible for me to go on. . . . Sivi acting *as if*. Acting as if nothing had happened. . . . How could he have known to do that unless he himself had once been where I was then?

But that's a whole other subject, said Stern, and it leads to the massacres and Sivi going mad during the massacres. Wisdom that profound is so tenuous it's often impossible for it to survive the brutality of life, the fears within us. And with Sivi it didn't. and he went mad. . . .

Of course, that night on the balcony happened a long time ago, when I was just beginning to become a man. And looking back on it and what followed, I realized just how hard we try not to grow. How desperately we go on trying to clasp the certainties of childhood to our hearts, bravely trying to face the world with that pathetic armor. I *know*, we say, I may not be able to explain it but I know what I mean.

And yet if we can't explain it, said Stern, there is no understanding. Instead there are rigid dead dreams, the sand castles of our childhoods to which we add a turret or two in our youths, and a rampart or two later on before we die, passing on to our children the same outwardly dreamy shape with the same inwardly dense and incomprehensible structure.

Stern frowned. He stared down at the counter and his voice was tense, hushed.

Why is it we don't understand how destructive it is to cling to things? Why is it we don't understand that even revolutionaries do that, and that in fact there is often no one more reactionary than a revolutionary? A man who yearns for order, often innocently, and therefore justifies violence and murder and terrible repression through his yearning for the imagined symmetry, the imagined beauty, of a sand castle in a child's mind?

Images, said Stern . . . things we imagine. These hosts of ethereal wonders and horrible monstrosities born of our unfathomable imaginations. Belief in everything and in nothing is the curse of our age. Righteously, arrogantly, we play in our minds with the zeal of pious hermits who have seen nothing of the world and refuse to do so and refuse to hear any echo of what has come before us. So enormous is our arrogance, and so pathetic, we even pretend we can jettison our own past and make ourselves into *anything*, just by saying it's so.

But it isn't so and we can't do it because we know so much less than we think we do about man's freedom and responsibility, and his guilt. Yet we go right on *pretending* in our arrogance, making terrible presumptions that demand hundreds of thousands of victims, even millions of victims. The victims our age seems to want . . . and worse, seems to need.

Why? Why is our guilt so great today we have to practice human sacrifice on such a monstrous scale? What are we sacrificing to? Why do we feel this brutal guilt so implacably it causes us to raise up a Hitler or a Stalin to work our slaughter for us? Is freedom really so terrifying in the twentieth century that we have to have concentration camps and whole political systems that are nothing but prisons? These huge grinding inhuman machines that people willingly flock to, willingly embrace and die for, calling them the future? Are we really so terrified by freedom that we have to make the world into a vast penal colony? Are we really that desperate to recapture the order of the animal kingdom . . . our lost innocence and ignorance?

Revolution, said Stern. We can't even comprehend what it is, not what it means or what it suggests. We pretend it means total change but it's so much more than that, so vastly more complex, and yes, so much simpler too. It's not just the total change from night to day as our earth spins in its revolutions around a minor star. It's also our little star revolving around its own unknowable center and so with all the stars in their billions, and so with the galaxies and the universe itself. Change revolves and truly there is nothing but revolution. All movement is revolution and so is time, and although those laws are impossibly complex and beyond us, their result is simple. For us, very simple.

We arrive at a new dawn only to see it turn to darkness, or more specifically, *in order* to see it turn to darkness. And we live in darkness in order to know light. . . . For a moment. As time spins forth opposites, with no end or beginning that we will ever perceive.

Revolution? Dedication? Belief in humanity and in gods that die and gods that fail?

Innocence is the origin of our sin, said Stern, and our hope as well as our curse. From that innocence comes all that is evil and all that is good, and living with it is our fate. For the God who is and all the gods who have ever been and will be are within us, seeing with our eyes and hearing with our hearts and speaking with our tongues. . . . *Ours.* I know. I've been as dedicated as anyone. . . .

Stern stopped. Muscles tightened in his face and his eyes moved restlessly.

He's disturbed all right, thought Joe, we're getting in deeply now. And sirens are going off in his head and flares are exploding and gunfire's rattling everywhere. A man looks like that when he's been under siege too long. Shell shock, a doctor might say. Of the soul, Liffy might say.

Joe rested his hand on Stern's arm.

You know, he said, awhile ago when I mentioned Ahmad and David, it surprised me that you passed over them so quickly. But I have to keep reminding myself that you and I have lived very different lives these last years, and you've been close to a lot of that. My times have been quiet and I don't have to tell you how hard that makes it to deal with violence. In matters of feeling, I know, we tend to think everyone's concerns are our own, a way we have of trying to bring people around to our own size and shape. Seems to be human nature to want to make people into a standard issue so we can pretend we understand them, which would be reassuring, naturally. So I have to keep reminding myself of that scorching freezing desert you've been living in, with its death and its dying and its own bloody rules. And I know it's been bad, but what's been the worst part about it for you?

The sounds people make, whispered Stern. The sounds they make when they're lying there ripped up and dying. It's something you never get used to, and once you hear it it never goes away.

No, I don't imagine it does, said Joe. At least not out in that no-man's-land where you've been living for all of your life. But you know, most people have never heard that. Most people hear whines and whimpers and excuses in the end, things you can say something about. Not that animal sound from deep down that just sits there worse than death and has nothing to do with words, ever. . . . Do you remember that saying, though, about abstractions being our pseudonyms? The tendency we have to project our own personal cause as the general cause at large? Which is why Marx, say, badly constipated as he was from so much sitting around and thinking, tended to feel a future explosion in the lower regions or classes was a scientific necessity? The historical movement of pent-up bowels objectively determined by the grunts of the dialectical potty, and so forth? Do you recall that saying at all?

Stern stopped moving around for a moment. He glanced at Joe and looked away.

It sounds familiar, he murmured.

Does it? Well I thought it might because you were the one who said it.

I was?

Yes. One night when we were sitting up late over lamp fuel in Jerusalem. And wretched drink it was that night, same as now. Also called Arab cognac and I'll never know how those two names got together to ease the pain in the dark hours. Talk about opposites. *Arab* cognac? Arab *cognac?* Just hearing that causes a revolution in the head, a real revolution, the kind you were talking about, not to mention ongoing turmoil in the stomach. But yes, you did say that once, and Ahmad after you more recently. As I recall, you were quoting from your father's memoirs.

Oh.

Stern moved restlessly back and forth. He made a sign to the owner of the bar, who drifted down the counter to fill their glasses. Joe touched Stern's arm, smiling.

But I can't let you off too easily, Stern, now can I? I mean this feeling you have that you've failed. It's only to be expected I'd have to worry that one a bit, Marx and the war aside. So tell me something. When you were young, did you ever think of becoming a recluse off in the desert somewhere, the way your father ended up? Something along those lines? It would have been easier, certainly, than dealing with people.

Stern looked surprised. At least I'm getting his attention again, thought Joe.

No, said Stern. Never.

Why not, I wonder.

352

Stern gazed down at the pool of water on the counter. And he's beginning to do more than just remember, thought Joe. It's not all sirens and bombs and flares going off.

Not enough guilt, said Stern. That wasn't my father's reason for doing what he did, but it would have had to have been mine. He sought the desert, after all. I was born there.

Right. Stands to feeling. So I guess what we're talking about here is regret, isn't it? Things haven't turned out as well as you'd hoped.

Stern shuddered violently.

As well? What in God's name do you mean, Joe?

Right. Things have turned out awful, in fact. The worst. And yet what you've done in the last few years is a hundred times what most men can do in a lifetime. Of course it's also true not many people will ever know about it. Bletchley and Belle and Alice and myself, and Maud and Liffy in a partial way, and some others that I'm not aware of. Not many surely, a handful at best, and even so they're never going to be able to say anything about it except to themselves. Whisper it to themselves maybe, when they're alone and sad and taking the long view. And doesn't that bother you a little? It'd be only natural if it did.

Stern moved his finger through a pool of water on the counter, tracing a circle.

Yes, he said. I suppose it does.

Well sure, Stern, why not. Anybody would like it known they've left something real behind, something more than just the dust of gold and real estate, something tangible to the heart. Still, another man could be puffing himself up with pride if he'd done what you have, but you don't even see yourself as having accomplished much.

Joe rested his hand on Stern's arm.

Tell me, why this talk about Sivi tonight? It's been a long time, ten years since he died, twenty since he went mad. On the face of it, those events would seem more than a little distant to be taking up so much of your thoughts tonight. Or are we looking back to the real beginnings of your Polish story? . . . Ahmad used to call it that, you know, and he wasn't referring just to the actual trip to Poland. For him, your Polish story seemed to suggest a great deal more. Maybe that was because Ahmad always had a long-range way of looking at things, so although the war appeared to start in Poland, he knew its true beginnings had to be much more deeply buried in time. . . . But anyway, Sivi then. What keeps bringing him to mind? Or is it Smyrna we're really talking about?

Stern moved his finger through the pool of water, tracing circles, his restless eyes never still.

Somber and feeling useless all right, thought Joe, just as Maudie said. But telling him it isn't so won't help. No sense telling a hungry man he isn't hungry, when did that ever mean anything? The flares and the sirens may have let up a bit in his corner of the desert, but he's still expecting the next barrage and he's weary to the soul, that's certain.

Stern?

Yes. Sivi, you said. I was thinking about it.

And?

I think it's because I started out with him and learned most of it from him. And then too, that period in Smyrna is all of a piece in my mind. Eleni and Sivi and the wonderful times we used to have before the massacres, before that whole way of life disappeared forever. And the Aegean must have something to do with it, that mysterious light that has always made men want to go farther. And living with the sea in Smyrna and just the sea itself, the closest we ever come to the sound of infinity. And I was young then, so everything was significant, and I was in love. . . .

Yes.

So all of it together made every sensation intense. Everything seemed clearer and surer somehow, but it's that feeling of intensity I remember the most. Experiencing every moment to the fullest, even the smallest things, the way we always should and so seldom do Everything *alive*, Joe.

Yes.

But then the changes began to come and the parts no longer fit and no longer made up a whole. . . . Eleni and I drawing apart and seeing that terrible pain in each other's eyes, and knowing full well what was slipping away but powerless to do anything about it because the past of someone else is forever beyond us, untouched by our best intentions. Helpless, the two of us, even though the ruin of the dream was unbearable. . . . So that ended and then the darkness came to Smyrna, the massacres, and Sivi went mad and everything ended there for me, and there was nothing to do but go on.

Yes, said Joe. And now Smyrna is the world and massacres come every day like the night, and whole ways of life are lost in the darkness. But you're no stranger to that night, Stern. You've known that darkness for a long time now.

Stern was gazing down at the counter, unmoving at last, finally at rest in the half-light of that barren room. Are we there? thought Joe, watching Stern. He waited and a long moment seemed to pass before Stern raised his eyes.

That's true, whispered Stern. And sometimes I can look back with a measure of calm and justify most of it to myself. Life has always been pretty much the same, after all. Three thousand years ago on those same shores of Smyrna, the Greeks went through every bit of it and raged and wept and then launched their ships anyway, at least some of them did, those who hadn't blinded themselves or locked themselves away in cages because of the horror. . . . So this has happened countless times in the past and innumerable others have sat here like this, as you and I are, and I've tried to see with Homer's eyes and you've tried to help me see, and I know all that, Joe, I know it. It's just that sometimes . . .

Slowly then, Stern turned and looked at Joe and never had Joe seen eyes that were so exhausted.

. . . it's just that sometimes I can't feel the balance anymore, the *balance*, Joe. It's all too dark and unyielding and there seems to be no reason for anything and I just can't pretend to myself that there is. Can't *pretend* anymore, Joe, do you understand? And I look back and I can't see that anything means anything at all. . . .

Too close, thought Joe, we're getting too close. He's got to pull back or he'll shatter right here in front of me.

Well I know it, said Joe, I can feel that in you, and we both know you've been out there living with this century too much. It's not what most people do after all. Most people spend their lives in other ages, muttering back through the past while sitting up straight in yesterday's furniture, perusing yesterday's timetable and mulling over yesterday's thoughts. Animals are conservative, as you say, and we'd always prefer to do things the way we did them the last time, given half a chance. And I know what you mean about how dangerous that's become and the paradox of violence growing out of innocence, out of these pathetic certainties we cling to, the sand castles of the race.

Joe?

Yes I know it, and I know that sad paradox whereby prophets delve into the childhood of the race and turn memories into visions of the future, imagining the lovely total order of an imagined Garden of Eden. And we do seem to have gotten into the habit of rummaging around in our heads too much, not listening to the echoes from outside and playing with ideas as if they were toys. Try one and try another and if white doesn't work, try black, and if God won't do the job, try Hitler and Stalin.

Joe?

Words, Stern. They're just words, a child's building blocks, just names for misplaced memories because we want so desperately to believe that someone somewhere is in charge . . . or might be . . . or could be. Words are our shadows in the twentieth century, as if giving something a name gave it a place and put it in that place. As if saying something took care of it. As if repeating incantations could set us free. As if we were no longer dealing with human beings. . . . Because that's the real trouble, isn't it, Stern? Ideas are always easier to deal with than people, because ideas are words and can be numbered and defined and reworked to our liking and assigned colors and playing stripes, and categorized and put safely away in drawers. And so we deal with ideas and pretend we're dealing with something real, and Lenin's a mummy like any of the pharaohs, and Hitler will be a mummy for the thousand years of his Third Reich if he can manage it, both of them with their own Great Pyramid of skulls so we can remember them, and meanwhile human beings are massacred along the way. . . . *Massacred*, surprise of surprises, on the way to the sand castle.

But Joe?

Right. I need another drink myself and here comes your man with the lamp fuel, time-honored. And human beings are dark and unyielding and that's the truth of it, and that's also the real code and the only one that matters. And because human beings are what they are, we take the easier way and play with these niceties we call ideas, building blocks after all, the dead weight of our pyramids and also good for raising our very own Tower of Babel. Clean and simple lines progressing logically upward in an orderly fashion, we say, according to the laws of reason. . . .

Reason, Stern? Logic? Touch a human soul in any spot that counts and you know how reasonable an answer you get. A scream is what you get, a cry of despair and hope. But we pretend otherwise and pretend we can build ideas one on top of another until we have a magnificent cathedral to kneel in or an imposing people's emporium to cheer in. Sand castles, as you say. Or maybe, like today, just these huge grinding machines of death, outright. And all the while human beings are being slaughtered for the sake of . . . For the sake of *what,* Stern? *What,* my God? *Ever?*

Joe, I . . .

No wait, Stern. I've come a long way to sit in this bare room tonight and savor the smells of this slum and knock back some lamp fuel with the friend I've known longest in this world. A long way in time and in space, so you can't expect me to let you off easily, now can you? Or to put it another way, I'm here now and I'm real and you've got to deal with me. With *me,* Stern.

Joe nodded, he smiled. He held Stern's arm and slowly, Stern smiled too.

Got him, thought Joe. There's no way he can deny himself in the end. Not him. He knows too much for that.

Right, said Joe, leaning back. And here we are and what a place to come to when in need of bucking up the soul. I mean it's not exactly bracing, is it, to be where we are in the dark hour of a dark war? The two of us sitting not far from the Nile lamenting the eternal state of affairs? Everything changing and nothing the way it used to be? The ancient Egyptians had what, thirty dynasties more or less? And every one of them an end of an age, the end of an era, with its share of gents like us sitting up with the lamp fuel and lamenting the death and the dying and pondering the permanent revolutions of the heavens, round and round? Makes you wonder if times change at all really, and if you and I haven't been in the custom of dropping in here over the ages to reflect upon the ends of all those dynasties. Makes you wonder, in fact, if this room or one like it hasn't been here for four or five thousand years, so a couple of gents like us could drop in and take stock of the latest end game not far from the river

Joe glanced around the room. He made a face.

And there's not much of it in the end, is there? Stock, I mean This place is just plain *bare.* Except, that is, for what's going on in this mirror in front of us. A shadowy screen, that one, with its cracked edges and its grainy textures, surely a worn cinema of the mind with its reels of fleeting shapes and its projection lamp in need of more lamp fuel to make more light, now as always. So yes, I think I may just have one more glass even though you're not yet ready yourself. But why are you smiling, Stern? Because you *know* we've been sitting here for four or five thousand years? And why is that smile even giving way to a little laughter? Because that seems like a long time to you?

Joe turned sideways on his stool, facing Stern. He pointed at the mirror.

And just what *have* we seen on this worn reel of the mind's eye? . . . Well first of all we started with a bare floor, *bare* like this room where we've been rambling over things for millennia, preparing a land and seascape for Homer. And that led you to a rug that was somebody else's, in a home that was never yours, and with that we saw a pair of open French doors and a small balcony overlooking a harbor that could have been anywhere, but wasn't. Smyrna, we'll call the place. And Eleni going off and killing herself over time, and the massacres coming and Sivi going mad in that place, and you acquiring a morphine habit and everything slowly dying like that second cat in the story, the one that didn't die straight off. . . . I mean my God, Stern, what is this tale of the century you're telling me tonight? Morphine and suicide and alcohol and madness, and despair and murder and death. . . . What *is* this? What *kind* of a tale, for God's sake?

Stern was very calm now. He was smiling his peculiar smile and listening to Joe, watching him, his face intent.

I'm not sure, said Stern quietly. Perhaps you can see it more clearly than I do, Joe. The tale of a man who wanted to believe? Who tried to believe?

Did believe, Stern. *Does* believe. And there should be no more of this talk of trying anymore, that's all behind you. Who sent that prayer to Eleni, have you forgotten that? And who took a frightened Irish kid on the run in Palestine and gave him his first lessons in life? And what about Belle and Alice, and David and Anna and their father? And Liffy and Ahmad and Maud and Bernini, and all the others I don't know anything about? Where would they have been without you? Don't you know you're the stuff of dreams to Bernini, don't you know that? You *are* dreams to him, you're what can be done in this world. Forget the secret codes and what you've done in the desert, the apparent *Enigma*. That aside, do you have any notion what you've given to people just by being who you are? Do you remember Sivi's first words that horrible night in Smyrna? When *he* was raving? Do you remember?

No.

Find Stern, he said. *Call Stern.* That's what Sivi was saying when he was going mad that night and not coming back. That's what he was reaching for on his way down. For *you*, Stern, and don't you *know* it, man? Don't you *know* it by now? Don't you know it's always been like that for so many people?

Stern was staring at the counter. He frowned and moved his finger through the water, tracing circles and fighting his weariness, struggling with himself. Joe could see it. . . .

And somewhere outside a commotion was slowly beginning to gather in the darkness. . . . Shouts and curses and drunken laughter, the victorious yells of men out celebrating an escape from death, some kind of triumphant drunken brawl working its way through the night.

Men turned nervously to glance at the shabby curtain hanging in the doorway of the bar, all that separated the half-lit room from the alley outside. The owner of the bar stopped what he was doing and turned uneasily to look at the curtain. Even Joe swung around to see what was happening, but Stern didn't both to look. Stern went on staring down at the counter, tracing circles of water with his finger.

What is that out there anyway? asked Joe, irritated by the interruption.

Nothing, whispered Stern. Probably some soldiers back from the front, happy because they're alive. . . .

Well? said Joe. You do know how much you've done, don't you? You don't really feel it all comes down to trying to no end, do you?

Sometimes it does seem that way, whispered Stern, despite what you say. Other people and how they feel . . . well you know other people can never justify our lives for us. We have to do that for ourselves.

I do know, said Joe. You taught me that a long time ago. And as for the blackness sometimes, this dark and unyielding part of us that's always inside just waiting for us to give it a name and a dominion out there, well I'd certainly agree with you now with this war around us. And I'd also agree if we were talking about great peaceful new nations that should exist and don't, in this part of the world or anywhere else. But that's politics, Stern, and the temporal kind at that, and politics have never been more than a cover name, *words*, a code for systems which aren't systems at all and can never be that, because the stuff in them, of them, is *us*. Not an abstraction but *us*, and we can't be reduced to systems through words, codes, covers, any of it. . . . In fact if there's one part of your thinking I'll never understand, it's how you could ever have mistaken that cover for reality. You, who've spent your life with these things and know about codes and covers and disguises, and what's real and what isn't. . . .

The shouts and the screams and the shuffling outside were louder now and moving closer. More of the men in the bar were watching the curtain that separated the room from the night. Joe swung around to look again, saw nothing, turned back to Stern. His voice was urgent, intent.

A place on the map, Stern, a country in that sense? Is that what you really wanted? Border guards and visas and customs officials in uniforms? Is that really what your dream comes down to? You, who've spent your whole life crisscrossing every conceivable kind of border and proving they're fictitious, arbitrary, meaningless? Other people may be confused by reality, Stern, but you *know*. How have you gotten yourself into thinking that real estate has anything to do with anything? Is that what those ancient Greeks went in search of? Place names? Is that why they launched their ships? The soul was their sea, you said that, and your whole life testifies that it's what's inside people that's important. Not the code names or the cover jobs or the uniforms, not the colors on a map or the words in passports listing conflicting names of God. . . . Just look at yourself in those rags, Stern. Don't they *show* you haven't failed? Don't they *prove* the land you sought is in men's hearts? And isn't that what your beloved Jerusalem is and always has been, a dream of peace for all people? Touch a human soul and you hear despair and hope, and although this real estate may be the world to us, it's still just a speck of dust lost somewhere in an unknown corner of an unfathomable universe. So arrogance aside, there can be no certainties, and hope is what you've always given people. Always, Stern. . . .

More screams and laughter and muffled shouts outside, moving nearer. Drunken curses and the sound of breaking glass, a window shattering somewhere up the alley in the darkness. Stern was sitting sideways on his stool now, looking at Joe and the curtain beyond Joe's shoulder. Joe spun around again, glanced at the doorway, turned back to face Stern.

Damn that noise.

It's nothing, Joe, just the night. Men celebrating because they're alive. . . .

I know, I know. So the point is, even good causes conflict and oppose each other, as you've often said. Just as love can oppose itself, even love. But don't you *feel* it, Stern? Don't you really know beneath and behind it all what you've done? Who you *really* are?

In answer Stern smiled his peculiar smile, and all at once he did seem truly at peace. There was a serenity in his gaze, a powerful enduring strength.

What a strange and paradoxical man, thought Joe. As mysterious and yearning as life itself.

And as Joe sat there looking at this elusive man whose secret he had sought for so long, he was reminded of the moment when he had passed Stern by without recognizing him at the top of the little street where Maud lived, Stern sitting in his rags at the end of the day keeping watch over one he loved, a solitary beggar who was homeless and stateless and who was yet the ultimate prize for all the great armies . . . anonymous in the end. A man alone in the dust at twilight surveying his limitless kingdom, a beggar of life from nowhere who would one day return whence he had come.

Joe held Stern's arm. There were tears in his eyes.

Ah that's good, Stern. You do know, I can see it. So it's been a clear night for us to see things after all and you've done it, Stern, and you know you have.

Stern nodded gently. He smiled his strange smile.

Maybe I have, Joe. And it's true we make our heavens and hells and spin them grandly in our hearts, sparing no extravagance or excess, no act of memory too daring and no disguise too extreme, every vista in the vast dream fashioned by us alone, out of love. . . .

Shouts. Screams. Men scuffling and yelling in the darkness.

Joe?

A smile on Stern's face and Stern's fist crashing into Joe.

Shouts. Laughter. *Bloody wogs.*

Joe stunned and reeling across the floor, not yet realizing that Stern had reared back and struck him full in the chest with all his strength, knocking the air out of Joe and sending him tumbling backward across the room, Joe knocking over chairs and glasses as he went slamming into the wall, into a corner. Joe with his back to the door, not having seen the shabby curtain pulled aside and the hand grenade that had come sailing in from the darkness, no one in the room moving except Stern. No one knowing what it was except Stern.

Bright blinding light then in the mirror behind the bar. A roar pressing Joe into the corner and glass shattering and debris falling and men screaming as they rushed to escape. Joe staggering to his feet in the smoke and staring at the spot where Stern had been a few seconds ago, before the hand grenade had exploded in his chest.

And even fiercer shrieks in the alley and yells everywhere and running feet, the barren room quickly emptying and the anonymous soldiers who had thrown the grenade disappearing in the darkness, people running and screaming and a roar ringing in Joe's head. Amidst the screams of terror, one cry higher than the others and eerily floating in the clear night, taken up again and again and passed on in the darkness

A beggar's been killed, a beggar. . . .

The cry leaping through the alleys and piercing the stillness of midnight, haunting unlit doorways and dark stairwells and tiny rooms where people huddled against the night in the slum, listening to the sudden cry of death.

A beggar . . . a beggar. . .

Joe standing in the corner in the smoke, in the haze, staring at the spot where Stern had been, Stern gone now in the roar of shattering glass and blinding light and the echo of disappearing footsteps. Joe smiling and whispering to himself.

He knew in the end. It was in his eyes.

The cry outside already so distant it seemed but an echo. And dust and chaos and Joe struggling to breathe, a sudden stillness to the world as the roar in his ears crowded out all else. Joe smiling, the thin cry far away now in the darkness dying, its moment over in the night.

A beggar . . . a beggar. . . .

PART FOUR

19

A Golden Bell
and a Pomegranate

Tobruk had fallen. The panzers of Rommel's Afrika Korps were little more than fifty miles from Alexandria. The routed British army was digging in to try to hold the line at El Alamein, but if that last resistance failed the Germans would overrun Egypt and seize the Suez Canal, and perhaps the entire Middle East.

Nearly all the British troops had left Alexandria. The streets of Cairo were jammed with vehicles pouring in from the desert. Civilians with money and documents were leaving for Khartoum and Kenya, South Africa and Palestine. Long columns of trucks retreated in the direction of Palestine.

The British fleet had sailed for the safety of Haifa. Military and civilian staffs were being evacuated. Huge crowds of European refugees stood in lines seeking transit papers and an escape to Palestine.

Belle and Alice weren't surprised to see Joe, but they were surprised to see him turn up so soon again at the houseboat. Joe was moving and speaking quickly, his words confused as he stumbled around the sunroom of the houseboat bumping into wicker furniture. Even his voice seemed not quite his own.

It was Belle who would recall that later. It was almost as if he had been possessed, she said later.

Both Belle and Alice tried to question him but his answers made little sense, and in any case it was impossible to hold his attention. Joe kept turning away and shaking his head, his voice sinking to a whisper. Occasionally one of the women caught a few words.

Danger . . . escape. . . .

They were shocked by the changes that had come over him in such a short time. Shuffling and disheveled, gaunt from lack of sleep, he looked as if he might collapse at any moment. His thin shoulders drooped, his shapeless clothes hung on him. His hands kept opening and closing as he picked up things and put them down again somewhere else, touching objects, touching everything, pointing at nothing and groaning, muttering to himself.

Escape . . . the exodus. . . .

It was as if events had finally overpowered him and he had shrunk into himself, retreating to some private world. For the first time both sisters realized how small he was.

But Joe, what happened to Stern? asked Belle. What happened to Stern?

Gone . . . everyone's leaving. . . .

He moved quickly away to the corner and stood there staring down at the harpsichord and the tiny bassoon resting on the polished wood. A bewildered expression crossed his face and he backed away, abruptly fixing his gaze on the portrait of Cleopatra. He went up to it and pushed his face close, examining the portrait.

The panorama's moved. . . .

What did you say? asked Alice.

But Joe was moving again, hurrying away, retreating to the other side of the room. He bumped into furniture and knocked over a porcelain figure, shattering it, coming to a sudden halt in front of the portrait of Catherine the Great. He shook his head, his mouth working all the while, biting and chewing, his tongue licking his lips.

But what happened to Stern? repeated Belle.

Gone and gone, even him . . . and by day
a pillar of smoke, by night a pillar of fire.

Joe swung around, his face harried and pale, puzzled. A spasm
twitched in the taut muscles of his neck. His hand went to his throat
and he gasped, fought for breath.

Joe?

He reached out desperately for support, caught himself, lurched
into the back of a chair. He whirled and knocked another porcelain
to the floor, shattering it.

Joe, Belle called out. *Stop,* for the love of heaven. Sit down, rest
for a moment.

But he couldn't stop, he couldn't rest. He groped through the air
in a frenzy and stared wildly around the room, recognizing none of it,
muttering to himself.

A ransom of souls . . . a crypt and
a mirror. I and Thou. . . .

His mouth fell open, his head slipped to the side. He gaped as
images tumbled through his tortured mind, obscuring the room. . . .
Wounded animals in the desert and flames shooting high in the sky,
trails of wreckage and twisted bodies, ripped tanks and abandoned
cannons, sirens and echoes and screaming men lying blind on the
sands. . . . And elsewhere to the east, endless columns of trucks
winding away into the Sinai, fleeing headlong into the wilderness on
the ancient paths that had always led to Palestine and the promised
land of Canaan.

Joe raised his hand, as if preaching to some invisible congregation.
He whispered.

Their lives have been bitter with
hard bondage. . . .

Whose lives? asked Belle.

Joe staggered, fell to one knee, pulled himself to his feet again
with an enormous effort.

They're leaving. . . .

367

Who's leaving? asked Alice. Where are they going?

> *To the land of their pilgrimage . . .*
> *a good land and large, flowing with*
> *milk and honey. . . .*

He uttered a cry and spun around, stumbling toward the tall French doors that opened onto the small veranda beside the river. Alice rose to her feet in alarm but Belle shook her head, stopping her. Joe stood in the open doors gazing down at the Nile.

> *And all the waters that were in the*
> *river were turned to blood . . . and*
> *there was blood throughout all the*
> *land of Egypt. . . .*

Alice tried to plead with him.
Joe? Rest for a moment. Sit down and rest, please?
But he was moving again away from the veranda. He stopped in the middle of the room and raised his hand once more as if addressing an invisible congregation, his obsessed eyes staring into the distance, glittering and fixed.

> *Don't you see them? Can't you see*
> *them? . . . They're beautiful jewels,*
> *they're precious stones. . . .*

Belle watched Joe's eyes, her face filled with sorrow.
What jewels, Joe? What do you mean?
Look at his eyes, whispered Alice, terrified.
What jewels? repeated Belle, loudly.
Joe murmured, his hand raised, his voice gathering strength.

Precious stones, settings of stones. . . . A sardius and a topaz and a carbuncle, an emerald and a sapphire and a diamond, a ligure and an agate and an amethyst, a beryl and an onyx and a jasper. . . . These precious stones, beautiful and ancient. And the stones shall be with the names of the children of Israel, twelve, according to their names. Every one with his name shall they be, according to the twelve tribes. . . .

Joe dropped his hand and turned away, his eyes shining. In despair, Belle shook her head. Alice was ready to break into tears. Belle made a gesture and immediately Alice rose and fled to her sister, holding her tightly.

I'm frightened, whispered Alice. He looks ghastly and it frightens me the way he moves his hands, the way his mouth keeps working. What's the matter with him?

He's ill, whispered Belle. He's not himself.

But his eyes, Belle, the way they shine and the way they stare, it frightens me. What does he see? What does he think he sees? Why are his eyes so strange? Whom is he speaking to?

He may have a concussion, whispered Belle. He may have been struck on the head or been near some kind of explosion.

Shouldn't we call a doctor, Belle?

In a moment. We can't leave him alone now.

Belle tried to comfort her sister, but she was just as disturbed by Joe's strange appearance and his even stranger behavior. Much more than mere physical exhaustion had to be involved, she knew that. It was his jerky movements that disturbed her, the spasms that seemed to seize him every few moments and spin him around, sending his disconnected thoughts careening off in some new direction. And above all there were his eyes, as Alice had said. There was a wholly unnatural luster to Joe's eyes, a feverish glow that was much too bright and seemed to devour everything his gaze fell upon.

Suddenly Belle raised her head. What's that? she whispered.

It was the sound of an automobile stopping nearby. In front of the houseboat perhaps. On the road beside the river.

Belle stiffened.

It's no use. There's no time to try to hide him and he wouldn't go with us anyway.

Joe wandered among the pale white wicker shapes, the ghostly furniture that crowded the room with wispy shadows of other lives and other eras. Again he raised his hand, whispering.

For I know their sorrows, and I am
come down to deliver them out of the
hand of the Egyptians, and to bring
them up out of that land. . . .

A car door closed, another. Whoever was out on the road in front of the houseboat seemed to be making as much noise as possible, although Joe's wounded mind was too far away to hear it. He stopped again, turned again, moving more slowly now. He looked out at the river, taking a step toward it.

> *Behold, I send an angel before thee*
> *to keep thee in the way, and to bring*
> *thee into the place which I have*
> *prepared. . . .*

The front door to the houseboat banged open. Another door banged and a sharp voice barked an indistinct order. Footfalls could be heard in the corridor, hurried footsteps growing louder. Alice buried her head in Belle's shoulder. Belle stared straight ahead at Joe.

He was smiling now, smiling for the first time, wandering among the ghostly wicker shapes and talking to himself. And the jerky movements seemed to have passed for the moment, the spasms to have subsided. Once more he was moving toward the open French doors but calmly now, gracefully now, the Joe they remembered, calmly drawn to the edge of the water.

He smiled as he gazed out over the river, his voice strong, the words spoken as if to someone he loved.

> *A golden bell and a pomegranate,*
> *upon the hem of the robe round*
> *about. . . .*

He uttered a cry of joy, his hand raised to the river . . . then everything happened very quickly. The door to the room burst open and men were shouting and rushing forward. Joe turned in the open doors to the veranda and looked back, smiling, a mysterious joy lighting his face.

The first shots ripped into his side and fluttered his jacket, spinning him around so that he was facing the room when the next bullets hit him, before a submachine gun roared and exploded into the middle of him, ending it all and nearly cutting him in half, collapsing his small thin body and sending it flying back through the doors to the edge of the river . . . a twisted heap of old clothes on the wooden slats of the little veranda, one hand trailing in the water.

The men went quickly about their business. They gathered up the

370

body in a canvas sack and in another moment there was no one in the airy sunroom but the two tiny ancient women, alone once more with the haunting wicker shapes of memory.

Little Alice quietly sobbing in the stillness. . . . Big Belle gazing steadfastly at the shattered glass doors and the silent river, at the huge empty vista where Joe had been . . . desolate now and passing.

20

A Gift of Faces,
a Gift of Tongues

Early evening, the day after Stern had been killed.

The Major stood behind his desk in the Third Circle of the Irrigation Works, the headquarters of the intelligence unit referred to as the Waterboys. He had just returned from a meeting in the Colonel's office, where the two of them had discussed the information acquired that afternoon in a Cairo slum by one of their better local agents, code name Jameson, an Egyptian blackmarketeer with yellowish teeth and a bad liver.

From conversations with the Arab owner of the bar where Stern had been killed, Jameson had been able to elicit a surprising amount of information on the behavior of Stern and his unidentified companion, prior to the explosion of the hand grenade at midnight. This information, in turn, had led the Colonel to make a number of intriguing suppositions about the case. And since the Colonel had known Stern personally and had worked with him in the past, it was only to be expected that his questions would follow certain lines.

Why had the Monastery been running an operation against Stern?

What had been the nature of the operation?

Bletchley had given the agent working against Stern a Purple Seven designation, the most sensitive of all the categories. Why the need for this extraordinary secrecy? What made the case so important it had required a Purple Seven agent?

Further, the agent in question had been brought in by Bletchley from the outside, although a Purple Seven designation was so sensitive it was almost never assigned to someone from the outside. Why had it been done in this case? How had Bletchley been able to convince London that it was necessary?

Was it true, as the Colonel suspected, that this Purple Seven agent had to be someone who had known Stern well in the past? Again, that he must be someone who had also once been closely involved with an employee of the Waterboys who had been a longtime friend of Stern, the American woman Maud?

And finally and most intriguing of all to the Colonel, what events from the past lay behind the unlikely connections that had existed among these three people?

For the connections did seem unlikely.

Maud. An American who had lived in Greece and Turkey before the war. A likable hardworking woman, trusted and thoroughly commonplace to all appearances, a translator in the Third Circle of the Irrigation Works.

Stern. A wizard of languages and Levantine ways. A brilliant agent who had used his vast knowledge of the Middle East to come and go unsuspected for years. A solitary man who had ingeniously used his role as a minor gunrunner to conceal his espionage activities, who had managed through this sordid cover to escape important notice throughout his life.

And lastly, the mysterious Purple Seven. An experienced agent from the outside, identity unknown, history and previous involvements unknown. Evidently a European but referred to by the Colonel as *the Armenian,* because the false papers of his Purple Seven cover carried an Armenian name and an Armenian background.

When the Major thought about it, it wasn't difficult for him to understand why the Colonel's questions took the form they did. The Colonel had spent most of his life in the Middle East and despite his ordinary army manner, he was a scholarly expert in the cultures of the region who couldn't help but be intrigued by the contradictions of Stern's obscure past.

Then too, in Stern's case, it wasn't just a matter of facts and straightforward information. From the way the Colonel and others spoke of Stern, it was apparent Stern had been the kind of man who had invariably had a powerful effect on anyone who knew him. Almost an hypnotic effect, it seemed, as if in the process of uncovering the truth about Stern it was possible to discover a much larger truth. Almost as if some secret meaning lay hidden in Stern's lifelong journey in search of his arcane goals.

It was only a vague notion to the Major, but he knew that was because he had never met Stern and been exposed to his influence. From the way the Colonel spoke of Stern, even from certain references in the files, it was easy enough to imagine the aura that had surrounded Stern, the peculiar mixture of strangeness and recognition men had felt in his presence, a sense of wonder and familiarity and of profound fear as well.

An age-old tragedy, then, Stern's life. A tale of idealism and disaster on the shores of the Aegean that would always be unresolvable in its depths of darkness and light, a fated play of mystery and suffering in the stony deserts where certain men had always wandered. In its yearnings and its abject failures, a tale on the nature of things, its rhythms spun from the soft roll of ancient seas and the hard tides of ancient deserts. And yet a tale so simple it was known to the poorest of beggars and had been for thousands of years . . . its stark cycle always secretly felt in the heart, always secretly passed from heart to heart through the millennia.

Although the Major could appreciate the profound fascination felt by the Colonel for Stern's enigmatic life and death, his own imagination was more deeply provoked by the unidentified figure in the case. The man who had been brought in to uncover the truth about Stern, the elusive Purple Seven agent known as *the Armenian*.

Nor was it difficult for the Major to understand his own particular fascination with this other figure. For the man's Purple Seven identity had been used only once before, and that was by the professional agent who had designed the identity for himself in the 1930s and used it so successfully in Palestine and Ethiopia, the same man who had been the hero of the Major's youth during the First World War, Columbkille O'Sullivan or *Our Colly of Champagne,* the legendary little sergeant who had survived a bullet through the heart in 1914 and been awarded two Victoria Crosses, an impossible feat.

All his life the Major had wondered about *Our Colly.* What kind of man could he have been and how could anyone be expected to follow in his footsteps? Why would anyone, in fact, even dare to presume such a thing?

And yet Bletchley had done just that. Bletchley had gone out of his way to assign *Our Colly*'s Purple Seven identity to this unknown agent who had been tracking Stern for months or years and had even been with Stern, finally, at the moment of his death.

So the circle was complete and the Major was brought back to the puzzle of the unknown Armenian, sketchily described as a small dark man with a deeply lined face and watchful eyes, wearing a torn collarless shirt and an old dark suit that was too big for him, that looked as if it might be secondhand, not even his to begin with. An apparent dealer in Coptic artifacts. An unknown man *in transit,* as *Our Colly* once had been.

The Major kept a clean desk. When he returned from the Colonel's office that evening the only thing on it was his pith helmet, which the Major raised to see if any messages had been left for him underneath it. There was one, a note saying some calls had come in on his private telephone while he was in back with the Colonel. Three rings each time, the note said, the calls repeated every fifteen minutes on the quarter-hour. Since it was his private telephone, no one had taken the calls.

The Major looked at his watch, feeling a sudden rush of excitement. He paced impatiently behind his desk, waiting, and the next call came exactly on time on the quarter-hour. The Major picked up the phone and said hello, and that was all he said. He listened to the voice speaking to him, then when the call ended he hurried back to the Colonel's office, where the Colonel was locking up his files, preparing to leave for the night. The Colonel looked up, surprised.

Well well, what's this? I thought you'd already left.

I just had a telephone call, the Major blurted out. A very curious piece of business.

Oh? What was it?

The Major explained the repeated calls on his private phone and the one he had just taken. The code words used by the caller belonged to Liffy, including the code word *dove,* which was Liffy's mechanism for requesting an emergency meeting, something he had never done before.

But not at any of the places where we usually meet, added the Major. He wants the emergency meeting to be at the Sphinx.

The Colonel looked up again, smiling.

How's that? Liffy at the Sphinx?

But I don't think it was him, said the Major. I think it was somebody else.

Couldn't you tell from his voice?

No, not really. Liffy always disguises his voice on the phone with me. It's a game he plays.

Well whom did he sound like this time?

The voice had an Irish accent.

Child's play for Liffy, said the Colonel.

But I'm quite sure it wasn't him. There's no conceivable reason why he should need an emergency meeting. He's not in that end of things.

Then perhaps he's just lonely and wants you to hold his hand, said the Colonel. It happens.

The Major frowned, an expression of disagreement he had picked up from the Colonel.

At two o'clock in the morning in front of the Sphinx? Tonight? And only calling now to set it up? Normally he couldn't even expect to find me in the office this late in the evening. He knows that.

The Colonel continued to sort through his papers, putting them away in his file cabinet.

He's been drinking a bit, do you suppose?

No, Liffy never gets out of hand that way.

Well who else knows his code words?

No one. Just the two of us.

Then he must have made an exception and gotten drunk, said the Colonel. Probably thinks he's playing a practical joke, mentioning the Sphinx. If I were you I'd get ahold of him in the morning and let him have it. Inexcusable, really, at a time like this.

The Major said nothing, waiting. He understood the reasons for the Colonel's reluctant reaction to the phone call, but he was still determined to get some resolution to the matter. The Colonel, meanwhile, put his last folder in the file cabinet and locked it. He checked the file drawers and walked stiffly on his false leg to the door. He reached for the door, hesitated, spoke in a casual tone of voice.

How are you and Liffy getting on these days?

We get along well, replied the Major. I think if he wanted to help someone, to give them a contact here, he'd think of me.

I see.

The hand-grenade explosion in the bar, Colonel. You said that if it was the work of the Monks, it was probably intended for the Armenian as well as for Stern.

Yes, I believe I did suggest that.

But the Armenian got away, said the Major. He wasn't killed, he escaped.

Yes, so it seems. But the Sphinx, you say? That certainly seems a bizarre place for a meeting with Liffy.

The Colonel smiled to himself.

Unless, he thought, Liffy has finally decided to go all the way and do *that* impersonation.

Yes, quite, he murmured. But if one were to go to such a meeting, how could any backup men be taken along without them being seen?

No backup, said the Major. The caller was specific about that.

Oh he was, was he? That sounds rather arrogant to me.

Or cautious perhaps, out of necessity. He implied it was the Monks he was concerned about.

The Colonel looked shocked.

You mean he mentioned Monks on the phone?

No, not directly. He made an allusion to St Anthony as the founder of monasticism, although he didn't come out and say that directly either, and he said something about fifteen hundred years in the desert being a danger to a man's health. Or to his spiritual balance, as he called it.

The Colonel smiled despite himself.

Erudite fellow, it seems, and rather accustomed to alluding to things. Colly was like that.

He also said he'd call back in fifteen minutes, added the Major, looking at his watch.

The Colonel's smile faded.

What on earth for?

To find out whether I'm coming or not. He said that given the nature of competing bureaucracies, as he put it, not directly again, he imagined I'd have to check with you before I could agree to come.

That's not just arrogance, muttered the Colonel, that's a perverse sense of humor. How could he have known I'd be here?

He said he assumed it. He said that in perilous times, as he put it, the old man tends to work late.

Definitely a perverse sense of humor, muttered the Colonel. He seems to have said quite a lot in his indirect way.

He was speaking quickly.

Yes, I can see that. Tell me, do you ever take walks alone in the desert at night? To clear your head and get things in order a bit?

I have, replied the Major.

Ever go out to the pyramids just to take in the majesty of the place?

I have.

Well these days, said the Colonel, I'd go well-armed if I were you. And other than that all I can say is Bletchley's business belongs to Bletchley, and if I were to interfere he'd have my head in twenty-four hours, and rightly so.

I understand, said the Major.

It was bad enough that I sent Jameson to check into a killing where a Purple Seven was involved. But to do anything more than that is out of the question. I couldn't authorize it and I wouldn't. Moreover, if I knew anything about it I'd have to put a stop to it immediately.

I understand, said the Major.

So I'm sorry I missed you tonight, the Colonel went on, after our discussion earlier on Jameson's findings. I'm leaving to get some rest because I haven't been sleeping well lately. I fall asleep but then some damn worry wakes me up at three in the morning and I can't get back to sleep. I pass the time as best I can but it would certainly be much pleasanter to share a pot of tea with someone then, if someone had some late business and chanced to drop by after it was over.

The Colonel glanced around the office, his hand on the door.

I enjoyed reminiscing about Colly this evening, he added, but we do have to keep in mind that Purple Sevens aren't everyday sorts. . . . Not at all. That's why they have the designation.

And beyond the rumbling chaos of the city it was an eerie night of luminous stars and strange wan moonlight full upon the reaches of the Nile. In the rambling houseboat of the Sisters, in that pale airy sunroom that had once rung with gaiety and laughter and was now filled to overflowing with empty furniture, in that gently familiar place where faded voices and small unbroken melodies came to mingle in the delicate half-light, there in the stillness Big Belle and Little Alice sat gazing at the Nile, at their own restless currents of memory. The night was too bright for candles so they sat with only the moon and the stars as their guides, occasionally one of them stirring, speaking.

Little Alice touched her hair.

There's no end to it, she murmured. They go right on doing the same things, claiming it serves some purpose. I remember Uncle George used to say when things went wrong that it didn't matter, because summer was coming. He so loved summer. But then when he ended his life it wasn't summer at all, it was the dead of winter.

And *cold*, said Alice. Such a cold New Year's Day when they found him, all the people in the village gathered down at the pond. At least it seemed like a great crowd then, everybody standing around with somber faces, not even shuffling their feet the way they did in church. I remember that.

And they made a great show of standing in front of us and holding us back so we wouldn't see. *Poor dears,* they were whispering, *poor little dears.* But I peeked while they were leading us away and I caught a glimpse of him, just the barest glimpse when they were laying him down on the ground, before they covered him up.

Oh I didn't really know what it meant then. All those whispers and those arms around us gently pulling us away, and the solemn staring faces and Mother crying and crying and trying to be so brave, trying to hold back her tears as she squeezed us and pressed us to her.

It was all so confusing and I began crying too, not for Uncle George, because I didn't understand that yet. But for Mother, because she seemed to be in so much pain, and because of the way everybody else was acting, whispering *first their father and now this,* and looking at us with such sad faces I wanted to cry for their sake.

No, I didn't understand it at all, not even the funeral and the words they said under the heavy sky at the cemetery. I don't think I even heard what they said, but I can still see that sky and the hill beyond the cemetery, against it, as if it were yesterday.

And then there's something I remember that happened after that. It was warmer by then so it must have been late spring, not long before we left for good. I was playing out back and I went into the shed where Uncle George had lived, where Mother had forbidden us to go after he died, to protect us so we wouldn't think of him.

I didn't have anything in mind really. I just tried the door without thinking and it opened, so I walked in. And the sun was streaming in the window and the air was warm and dusty and close, and there were cobwebs everywhere, and the room looked so small and empty.

Most of his things had been taken away, but the little tarnished mirror still hung by the window and the pegs were still in the wall by the door where he used to hang his clothes, and his paddle was still up on the rafters where he'd always kept it, the one he'd used when he went fishing. So those things were still there, but they just seemed to make the room look smaller and emptier than ever. . . . So very empty, so terribly empty, I've never forgotten that. It made me sad because it looked as if no one had ever lived there.

Little Alice gazed down at the floor. She touched her hair.

Belle? Why do you think Uncle George did that? He had a place in the world and people liked him, and he had his job and things to do in his free time. Certainly Mother loved him and he always seemed to enjoy having us around. He was always joking with us and showing us how to do things, how to make little things.

I suppose you'd have to say it wasn't a life with any particular surprises to it, for good or for bad, and there weren't going to be any great accomplishments to come from it, I know that. But it was a decent life and he was a good man, and there didn't seem to be any reason why he had to end it like that, all alone down at the pond on a cold night, drowning himself in the darkness.

I've just never understood that kind of thing. Summer would have come again, he was the one who always used to say that. And it's not enough to call him weak because I'm weak, no one has ever been weaker than I am. And I'm foolish too, which Uncle George never was.

I just don't understand it, Belle, I've never understood it. Why did he do it?

Belle looked at her sister. She shook her head.

I don't know, Alice, I truly don't. But why do any of them do what they do? Why did Stern? Why did Joe? Why are there all those tens of thousands of men out in the desert right now doing what they're doing? Doing the same things that were done in the same places a hundred years ago and a thousand years ago and five thousand years ago? How does it help? What does it change? What's the point of it all? How can. . . .

Belle stopped. She turned abruptly in her chair to stare at the shattered French doors, at the narrow veranda beside the water.

What is it, Belle? What did you hear?

Nothing. I was imagining it.

Alice's voice had dropped to a whisper.

Please, Belle, you know I don't hear well. What was it?

It sounded like something scraping. A piece of driftwood must have gotten caught.

Belle gripped the arms of her chair and began to pull herself forward, her mouth set.

Don't you *dare* get up, whispered Alice. Don't you *dare* go over to those doors. That's where it happened.

I have to see what's making that noise.

Don't you *dare*, whispered Alice. I'll go.

But she didn't move. She sat on the edge of her chair, staring at the open shattered doors, her hands clasped tightly together. The sound was louder now and Alice could also hear it, wood bumping against wood.

Alice gasped. An apparition had appeared in the moonlight, a looming chalk-white shadow of a man rising up out of the river and crouching on the small veranda, the ghastly face masklike, the whole pale figure as insubstantial as a spirit risen from the grave. Alice put her hand to her mouth and silently shrieked. Belle stiffened, her gaze unwavering.

Stop, commanded Belle. *Stop* right there. I *refuse* to believe in ghosts.

A smile appeared on the white dusty face.

And so do I, said a soft Irish voice, and not for a moment and not a bit of it. Of course it's also true that on nights such as this I've heard the odd pooka puttering around in the moonlight on occasion, muttering his jokes and his riddles and his scraps of rhymes the way their kind are wont to do. But that's only natural and pookas aren't ghosts anyway, they're just like the rest of us only more so.

The apparition grinned and hopped from one foot to the other, nodding encouragement, but Belle's stare remained defiant.

Leave, she commanded. *Leave,* o shade, and return whence you have come.

Oh I can't do that, said the ghostly figure. There's no going back in this world, as we well know.

Suddenly Alice found her voice.

Did he say he's a pooka, Belle? What's that?

A kind of spirit, replied Belle. One of those odd little creatures the Irish believe in.

Oh, squeaked Alice, one of those? . . . An *odd* little creature, she added shyly, peeking through her fingers.

And I don't have to tell you, continued the spirit, that I'm sorry about climbing in on you like this, just rising up out of the river and all. But the moonlight was right tonight and for once the Nile was going my way, so I borrowed a dinghy and here I am straight from the crypt.

The crypt, shrieked Alice. Odd little creature or not, he's straight from the dead and still wearing his shroud.

The figure took another step and stopped. He looked down at Alice cowering in her chair.

Here now, what's this terrible thing I've done? Why do you look at me like that?

You're *dead,* whispered Alice in horror.

The ghost's smile faded.

Dead, you say? Me?

A puzzled expression came over the dusty masklike face as the ghost stood there with his arms hanging awkwardly at his sides, his dusty jacket too big for him, his dusty baggy trousers gathered in at the waist.

Not that I know of, he said in a quiet voice. I could have been but I'm not . . . I don't think. But don't you recognize me at all? It's me, Joe.

Belle's face was set. She spoke calmly and with complete conviction.

Joe's dead. If you're Joe, you're dead. We saw it happen with our own eyes, right there where you're standing.

Me? Here? . . . I don't understand.

Right there, right on that very spot, we saw it with our own eyes.

They came here right after you did and they burst in and they shot you. It was all over in an instant. Then they carried your body away.

He frowned and wiped at the dust coating his face, forgot what he was doing, held his hand in midair. He turned and looked at the shattered glass of the open French doors, noticing it for the first time. He looked back at the room.

He was moving slowly now, as if in a dream. Some profound emotion was working within him, causing his face to change rapidly. He felt his short dusty beard.

They? Who's *they*?

The ones who came after you, they must have been Bletchley's men. It was all over in an instant.

A kind of wild despair seemed to grip him. They could see him trying to resist it but he had begun to tremble. He pushed at the air with his hand again and again, a pathetic gesture.

The man you thought was me, what did he look like?

Alice was no longer peeking through her fingers. She was straining forward in her chair, her face filled with wonder.

Joe? she murmured. . . . *Joe*, is it you? Have you really come back?

He looked just like you, whispered Belle, shaking her head. He looked just like you and he talked the same way and he dressed the same way and he moved the same way. It's uncanny. The only thing different about him was that he was so distracted he seemed to be in another world.

Joe was losing hold now, they could see that. He had begun to sway back and forth and his hands were opening and closing, grasping at nothing. He seemed to be sinking, his frail body giving way beneath him. Desperately, he whispered.

But what did he say before they shot him? What did he *say*, for the love of God?

He spoke of everyone leaving, answered Belle. And he spoke of the Nile turning to blood and of those who were going to the land of their pilgrimage. . . .

Belle lowered her eyes.

And he named jewels and called them precious, she whispered, and he called them beautiful, twelve jewels in all he named. And he said they were the names of the children of Israel, twelve, according to their number. Every one with his name shall they be, he said, according to the twelve tribes. . . .

Oh forgive us, whispered Belle. It's all so clear now but at the time we thought he was raving and hurt somehow, wounded somehow, and didn't know what he was saying.

Joe sagged as if from a blow. He sank to his knees and raised his hands, pleading.

And what else did he say? What *else*, for the love of God?

He said their lives had been bitter with bondage and he knew their sorrows. And he spoke of a ransom of souls and he said an angel had been sent before thee to keep thee in the way, and to bring them into a good land and large, flowing with milk and honey. . . . And lastly he spoke of a golden bell and a pomegranate. Upon the hem of the robe, he said, a golden bell and a pomegranate round about. . . .

Belle stared down at her lap. Alice half rose in her chair, tears streaming down her face.

I should have recognized the words, whispered Belle, but it all happened so quickly and it was so strange the way he acted, we didn't understand. He seemed a man possessed but he was speaking from the Book of Exodus, wasn't he?

Oh God, shrieked Joe, *why did he do it? Oh God. . . .*

Joe buried his head in his hands. Alice was kneeling beside him now, her arms around him. Belle raised her eyes.

But who was he? We were so sure he was you. Who was he?

A friend, whispered Joe, choking out the words. A man speaking to his people . . . a dream, a beautiful dream, a golden bell. A man with the gift of faces and the gift of tongues who came and went as anyone . . . the wandering Jew in all of us. Liffy was his name. . . .

But why did he come here like that, Joe? Why did he do it? To save you?

Oh no, not me, much more than that. So much more. . . .

Joe broke down completely then, sobbing on the floor as Alice held him in her arms, rocking with him and stroking the dusty scars in his face that ran with tears.

After a time, when Joe had managed to recover a little, the three of them sat talking amidst the pale wicker shapes of that dilapidated mansion moored on the nighttide of the great river, speaking in low voices in the shadowy moonlight.

As best he could, Joe recounting what had happened. Being in the poor Arab bar when the hand grenade had come sailing in through the shabby curtain at midnight, instantly killing Stern. Joe stunned by the explosion and wandering in a daze through the sordid alleys, stopping to telephone Maud and eventually finding himself back beside the Nile, in the dingy public garden where old Menelik's secret crypt lay buried.

Descending the stairs once more and letting himself into the crypt and lying down on one of those hard park benches from another era. Feeling dizzy and exhausted and slipping into a deep sleep that stretched on through an invisible dawn and the invisible day that followed Stern's death, a fugitive from the light fitfully sleeping into the evening of the second night.

Waking up at last on the park bench with his body cramped and aching, the distant roar of Stern's death and a dim cry from the darkness still echoing in his mind . . . *a beggar . . . a beggar. . . .* Joe appalled by the murkiness of his suddenly strange surroundings and not even sure for one brief moment that he was still alive, above all wanting to escape from the gloomy crypt.

Noticing then that Liffy's small battered volume of Buber was lying open on one of the park benches, which wasn't the way he remembered it having been when he and Stern had left the crypt. Noticing also a small pile of clothes neatly folded near the door, beside them an old makeup kit that Liffy had often carried with him.

Joe realizing then that Liffy must have come to the public garden on the previous night and followed him and Stern to the poor Arab bar, where he had witnessed the explosion at midnight and subsequently followed Joe back to the crypt once more, letting himself in while Joe slept and keeping watch through the dangerous night, until daylight had come aboveground and it was time for Liffy to change into the final costume of his final role, while still Joe had gone on sleeping.

And what had that final costume of Liffy's been? What transformation had Liffy chosen for himself in the end?

A mystery to Joe when he had awoken in the crypt, hours after Liffy had left. Joe wanting only to escape, for safety using the emergency exit Stern had showed him, a low narrow tunnel thick with the

dust of the past. Joe emerging chalk-white from the secret passageway and discovering that it was night again, fleeing wildly through
the park in the exhilaration of his escape from death, a ghostly figure
floating beside the river on the mild breezes of that clear Cairo night.

And furtive telephone calls made to the Major, a man Liffy had
known, and stealing a dinghy and paddling downstream to the houseboat, where he had come rising up out of the currents only to find
that Liffy had been there before him, disguising himself as Joe so the
anonymous Monks from the desert would think their work was done
and Joe would have another chance to escape, another chance to
survive. .

Liffy.

Joe still couldn't mention his name without breaking down. It was
different somehow with Stern, because everything having to do with
Stern had always been expected in a way. Stern himself had always
seemed to know what his destiny would be, and it had been impossible to be around him without sensing that sooner or later. Joe had
felt it long ago when he had first met Stern in Jerusalem, as had
others before and since then.

But Liffy? . *. Liffy?*

Joe turned away, too wrenched with pain to dwell on that vast
multitude of faces and voices once conjured up in Liffy's sorrowing
magic, and laughter, lost now to the world. It was too much for Joe
so they talked for awhile of other things, and then Joe rose.

Well I'll be leaving now, he said. There are things I must try to do,
and whatever way it turns out, I'm afraid we won't be meeting again.

Little Alice looked at him tenderly, and Big Belle's sad eyes were
as strong upon him as ever. They watched as he went to stand on the
small veranda one last time, gazing out over the river. Then he came
back into the room to face them.

And where will you go from here? asked Belle.

Joe tried to smile.

To meet a man at the Sphinx, he said. I have no answers for him,
but I might know the questions to ask at least.

And this time he did smile. Thinly, but he managed it.

I have to tell you I've never been able to handle good-byes, he said. I've just never gotten used to leaving people, even though I've done little else in my life. People have a way of slipping into our hearts and staying there, and we treasure them and don't want to let them go, and more than that, we never can let them go.

Once long ago I tried to live differently, but it never really worked. I used to pretend something could be over and done with, a place or a person, and I could move on and nothing was the worse for it. But I learned soon enough that was only a turn of words on the surface of things, mere childish pretending, and it was pain that taught me that, I'm sorry to say. Of course we do move on all right, but we don't forget nor should we, and nothing important is ever left behind, and no one we've loved ever goes out of our lives. They live on in other ways, that's all, in our words and our gestures, changing us and changing with us and even speaking to us in the quiet moments. Sometimes recognized, mostly not, but always a part of us, woven into the stuff of our lives.

And as for what's out there where I'm going now, well, when you look at it one way it's surely not much of a world, is it? We lose and we lose and that's all we ever do from the time we're born. Lose those who brought us into the world and lose the place where that was, the only safe place we ever know, and then we go right on losing other places and other people and the hopes and dreams that go with them, losing those we love and finding others if we're lucky, only to know we'll lose them too with time. Lose is all.

And that's one way to look at it surely, and all of it true and undeniably the way it is. But then there's also that other side to life, those moments that have a kind of grandeur to them, that speak of love so beautiful it takes your breath away. Rare moments that shine in the darkness, rare precious gems in the night, jewels of the soul beautiful and ancient. . . .

Joe nodded, smiling. He leaned down and embraced Belle and then Alice, kissing each of them. At the door he paused.

I've known those moments here with the two of you. I've known them and I'll always know them, and I'll always remember this room one way. The way it was the other night when I came here, one timeless night like all others on the Nile, and I sat in the candlelight looking at the river and listening to your beautiful music. A night unlike any other for me, on the Nile in the shadows at the end of the darkness, listening to your beautiful music. *Yours,* and now mine. . . .

Then all at once he was gone and the two tiny women were alone in the moonlight of their airy sunroom, alone again with their memories. . . . Big Belle sitting stiffly erect, staring straight ahead at the river. Little Alice touching her hair and softly humming a tune against the night.

21

Purple Seven Moonglow

Midnight past in the serenity of the still desert.

The pyramids stately before the stars.

And far away in the moonlight a wisp of sand swirling lightly over the crest of a dune, billowing softly in the wake of a distant horseman who had suddenly come racing into view from out of the pale stony reaches of the night, pounding swiftly down through the wastes in a headlong charge aimed at that huge crouching figure on guard among the pyramids, the calm and graceful Sphinx.

. . . this mysterious solitary charge in the moonlight carefully observed all the while from an unsuspected lookout. From a black hole in the right eye of the Sphinx. . . .

The horse and rider dropped from sight and came flying over a final ridge to gallop wildly down the last hard stretch of desert, the hoofbeats of the animal drumming more loudly as the charge narrowed, the dashing figure on horseback now clearly visible.

The pale rider wore a pith helmet, a safari jacket and jodhpurs. His face was masked by a gleaming white silk scarf tied around his head and flowing on the wind. His eyes were masked by racing goggles that caught the drift of the moon and blankly reflected it back in opaque white discs. The horse reared in front of the Sphinx as the rider broke his gallop, then went charging off to one side and quickly circled the enormous stone figure so tranquilly in repose in the moonlight.

Nothing. The Major had found no one lurking along the sides of the great stone beast. No one crouching in the crevices of antiquity's hindquarters. The Major was quite sure he was alone.

He drew up again in front of the Sphinx and dismounted, removing his carbine from its case on the side of the saddle. He also checked his long-range sniper's rifle nestling on his back, the large automatic pistols strapped to each of his hips, the small automatic in one pocket of his jodhpurs and the even smaller automatic in the other pocket, and the minuscule ivory-handled derringer under his jacket to the side.

Lastly he felt for the hunting knife at his waist, the two smaller slashing knives taped to his back, and the four throwing daggers strapped to his shins. Jingling around on the Major's web belt was a mass of extra ammunition clips, a half-dozen for each of his automatic pistols and a full dozen for his carbine.

In addition to the large supply of shiny brass bullets bristling from bandoliers crisscrossing the Major's chest, deadly fifty-caliber tracers as long as a man's hand and of no use whatsoever without a large water-cooled machine gun to fire them. But although these utterly useless bullets were no more than a kind of brassy display of symbolic mail firepower in the moonlight, they were still undeniably impressive, awesome because of sheer size alone.

Equipped. Armed. Ready.

Rifles, pistols, knives, tracers, daggers.

Automatic bolt actions and slippery blowback loading and well-oiled breechblock plungers. Beady sights and solid safety switches and slithering barrel screws, and but the merest squeeze of a taut trigger needed to make a hammer slam home and balls explode.

Equipped.

And finally, for reserve firepower, the Major had also brought along a monstrous nine-shot Czech revolver, an enormous pistol once claimed by Balkan assassins to be the ultimate all-purpose secret weapon of the future. This crude Czech masterpiece hidden in a saddlebag on the Major's high-spirited Arabian mare, in case the Major suddenly found himself stripped of his other weapons. In case he suddenly had to leap from the Sphinx onto his mare, against all odds, and make a daring escape in the moonlight, blasting away at skulking shadows as he thundered over the dunes.

Armed.

Grimly the masked Major smiled beneath the flowing silk folds of his white scarf, behind the pale white discs of his racing goggles.

Ready.

As prepared as any masked man could ever be for a dangerous nighttime meeting with a Purple Seven fugitive in the shadows of the inscrutable Sphinx.

The Major cocked his pith helmet at an angle and fitted his swagger stick more securely into his left armpit, which was unaccountably wet in the cool night. Then he went striding up toward the impassive stone face of the gigantic beast and planted his feet in a solid position, just below the great stone nose, which was badly bent and mostly missing as a result of having been used for target practice by Napoleon's artillery, nearly a century and a half earlier.

Standing there between the great stone paws with his carbine at the ready, loosely aiming at the immense expanse of open desert with the noble head of the mythical stone creature looming up behind him, the Major momentarily had the sensation of himself being the courageous British lion, the very beast of the Empire, alone in the pale moonlight facing the vastness of the unknown.

And all the while, unbeknown to him, the Major was being carefully observed from above. . . . From the blackest of the black holes of antiquity—the mysterious right eye of the Sphinx. . . .

The Major checked his watch. Two o'clock in the morning and still no sign of the Purple Seven.

The Armenian's late, he thought, fingering his carbine. Late. Not even on time. And not exactly the way for a Purple Seven to maintain his reputation for being dangerous, or even clever for that matter. But out here, how dangerous could one fugitive agent be? Here in bright moonlight, where the Major had a clear field of fire in front of him and a solid mass of mythical stone beast behind him? With the arsenal he was carrying, in fact, the Major thought he could probably have held off a small army of marauding bedouin tribesmen from his superior vantage point under the nose of the Sphinx. Nor was it difficult for the Major to imagine himself doing just that.

With the telescopic sights of his sniper's rifle trained on the distant dunes, picking off the shrieking rebel sheiks the moment they galloped into view. . . . Quickly lowering his sights and picking off the banner-bearer and his cutthroat bodyguards. . . . Throwing aside the now useless sniper's rifle as the hordes kept coming. . . . Seizing his rapid-fire carbine and gunning down whole mobs of howling tribesmen as they came milling around the base of the Sphinx, blazing away from his hip, bravely slamming in new clips until the burning weapon jammed from the incessant explosions. . . . Finally driven back against the throat of the Sphinx itself by the overwhelming numbers of the enemy. Crouching beneath the great stone chin with an automatic pistol in each hand, a knife in his teeth, fearlessly blasting away at the shadows that came sneaking up from the hindquarters of the mythical beast, recklessly blasting away at this native gas from the bowels of antiquity. The automatics jamming and the Major hurling daggers in a last heroic stand for the sake of the Empire and the British lion. . . .

Tinkle.

The ammunition clips dangling around the Major's waist clinked lightly together. Stupid of the Armenian, he thought, to pick a rendezvous as open as this one. The Armenian must have imagined it would save him from being taken by surprise, but obviously he hadn't foreseen the possibility of the Major's quick dash in from the desert on a swift Arabian mare. And now the Armenian must be out there somewhere hiding behind a dune, helplessly watching the Major astride his commanding position in the lap of the Sphinx. Still, the Major was more than a little disappointed by the silence on every side. This was to be his first meeting, after all, with the Purple Seven who was *Our Colly*'s successor, and somehow he had expected a more romantic encounter, a more dramatic confrontation. Especially in view of the unusual setting.

But it wasn't the first time the Major had been disappointed since coming to the Middle East, and all because, early in life, he had fallen so deeply under the spell of the extraordinary explorers who had roamed the region in the nineteenth century . . . Burton and Doughty, Szondi and Burckhardt, and above all the incomparable Strongbow. The startling images of those romantic adventurers had always been the Major's ideal. Ever since childhood he had been haunted by their unconquerable visions in the strange sun-splashed reaches of distant deserts. So perhaps it wasn't surprising that contemporary life in the bazaars and deserts of the Middle East, for the Major, had never been as romantic as he had always dreamed it would be.

Tinkle.

And so it seemed once again in the case of this unknown Purple Seven. Dreams had proved to be false for the Major and life had never been as exciting as it had been for other men in other eras. Not even here in the lap of the Sphinx, under a full moon, in a perilous wartime meeting with an anonymous secret agent.

Tinkle.

Wistfully the Major sighed behind his raffish white silk mask, behind his dashing racing goggles, beneath his weathered pith helmet tipped at a rakish angle, weighted down with arms as he was in the best tradition of a desert brigand. Sighed and listened to his heavy ammunition clips clinking ever so softly in the stillness, tinkling as merrily as the gay little sounds made by goats' bells wafting through the night to the ears of some illiterate goatherd. Sighed and checked his watch and gazed longingly up at the moon.

A goatherd. Soft breezes. A lunatic setting. . . . But how could anyone pretend for long to be a mysterious masked man in the moonlight, when an Armenian couldn't even be on time?

The Major sighed, vastly disappointed by all of it. Thoroughly glum over his first meeting with a man who carried the fabled designation that was the most secret the Secret Service could bestow. Sighed and groaned.

Where in God's name *was* this Purple Seven?

The first warning that something was out of the ordinary came from the Major's Arabian mare. Abruptly the animal stopped poking around in the sand and raised her head. Was it a sound too distant for human ears? A scent from far away drifting in on the clear night air?

The Major peered, seeing nothing. He gripped his carbine, staring intently, and all at once a booming sinister voice broke over him, a hollow inhuman voice which seemed to come echoing up from the very bowels of the earth.

> *Who knows what evil lurks in the*
> *hearts of men?*

The Major whirled. He spun and kept on spinning, turning around once and twice and thrice under the great stone face, his loaded carbine at the ready. But there was nothing new to be seen no matter how hard he stared.

The pyramids in the moonlight.

The calm face of the Sphinx looming up behind him.

And other than that only stars and the empty desert, a full moon and sand rippling distantly.

Again the unearthly voice boomed and echoed briefly, thundering from nowhere and everywhere, hollow and deep and sinister in the night.

Who knows? The Sphinx knows. . .

The hideous voice broke into a cackle, a deluge of mocking laughter which seemed as if it would never end. Only to be followed at once by a clear human voice, a soft Irish voice gently calling out in the moonlight.

Easy with the carbine, Major.
Easy does it now, please.

The Major stood rooted to his spot, struck dumb in the moonlight. He listened to his breathing and to the reassuring tinkle of goats' bells, and some minutes seemed to pass before he heard light trotting footsteps alongside the Sphinx behind him, coming from the direction of the mythical beast's hindquarters. And then a strange figure came trotting around the side of the Sphinx and began scrambling up one of its huge stone paws . . . a small man in an old baggy suit.

The Major stared. The small man climbed nimbly up to the top of the stone paw and stood there with his hands in the air. He was smiling. He took a deep breath and nodded pleasantly.

Nice night, Major. Lovely air out here.

The Major recovered at once from his shock and edged forward, his carbine trained on the man's middle.

Don't move, he shouted.

Not a finger, came the answer.

Not a hair, shouted the Major.

That too, certainly.

Hands over your head.

Right you are. In our lowly way, we all try to reach for the stars.

The man nodded, smiling, and the Major suddenly blushed behind his mask. In his excitement he had been screaming. He stopped for a moment to get a grip on himself.

Tinkle.

The small man in the baggy suit looked surprised. Are there goats around here? he asked.

No, replied the Major, managing a normal tone of voice.

Odd, I thought I heard goats, said the man. Didn't you hear the tinkling sound of goats' bells? I wonder where the goatherd is.

My ammunition clips, said the Major.

Oh.

Who are you? screamed the Major. *No evasions. Speak up.*

Oh. Well the name's Gulbenkian. Gulbenkian, I presume. At least that's what was on my papers the last time I looked at them. They also say I'm a dealer in Coptic artifacts by profession, which may well be true. As for my status in this war zone, that's down as *in transit,* but I suspect it doesn't tell us much because it's probably the status of most of us in this world. Just passing through, don't you know. They're a first-class forgery though, these papers of mine. So good you could even say Ahmad did them. You know that old Cairo saying, don't you? *When in doubt, say Ahmad sent you?*

Don't move.

Right, square one.

The Major again made an effort to control his voice.

Slowly now, he commanded, do exactly as I say. Lower your left hand to your jacket collar, slowly, and pull your jacket off. Slowly, now drop it.

Clunk, said the man, why not. Never was anything very grand about it.

Your shoes next. Don't bend over. Kick them off.

Sure. Been doing it that way for years, actually.

Now, left hand only. Undo your belt buckle.

Ah yes, said the man. Life is trouble, only death is not. To be alive is to undo your belt and look for trouble, as that old Greek saying has it. Ever come across that saying yourself, Major?

Same hand, slowly. Unbutton your trousers.

Ah, slow as slow for the sake of anticipation. And if I'm not mistaken, that's exactly what the old Greek saying had in mind. But I'm not so sure it was meant to apply to a cool night in the desert. More of an idea for lovely summer evenings on a deserted beach, maybe.

Drop them. Kick them to the side.

Right, a gentle kick maybe. My anticipation's waning in the general chilliness.

Left hand, slowly. Unbutton your shirt.

I'm getting there, Major, but it's also getting cold out here.

Slowly. Do exactly as I say.

The man smiled, nodded.

Yes, and do you suppose that could have been an old pharaonic saying? *Do exactly as I say,* I mean. It sounds like it might have been some pharaoh's standing order from on high to the troops who were building the pyramids. Think so?

Left hand only. Pull off your shirt. Drop it. Now raise one leg, slowly.

Oh dear.

Pull off your sock. Now the other one. Left hand only.

Right. And I guess you've assumed all along I'm right-handed, which only goes to show it's a good thing I'm not Colly.

The Major stared.

What's that? Who?

You know, the man who had this Armenian identity before me. The original Gulbenkian of clandestine obscurity, also known at one time as *Our Colly of Champagne.* As long as I can remember, Colly always used his left hand when he was taking a piss over the side of the boat.

What?

Yes. Colly was left-handed, in other words, so he always used his left hand when the time came to be sinister, to do something fast and unexpected.

What? Don't move.

Right. All I meant was that Colly's left hand was his shooting hand and his throwing hand, as well as his pissing hand don't you see, so it wouldn't have been a good idea to have him undressing with it. Fast on the draw, Colly was. But of course that's just by way of being of historical interest and it doesn't matter tonight, because I'm not Colly and I use both hands for things. Born ambidextrous, I don't know why.

Don't move.

Right.

One hand, either hand, slowly. Pull down your underwear and step away from your clothes. Out there, over to the end of the paw.

Right. For another of life's maulings, probably.

Joe smiled and walked to the end of the paw where he stood naked, shivering. The Major kept his carbine pointed at Joe while he knelt beside the pile of clothing and felt his way through it. Other than Joe's papers and a handful of Egyptian coins, the only thing he found was a large wad of money in various currencies, in denominations he had never seen before. The Major backed away, perplexed.

Where are your weapons?

Don't carry any.

What?

That's right. I dropped out of the maiming and killing business a long time ago. It may be necessary sometimes but myself, I'd rather not take part. Personal prejudice.

The Major looked confused.

No weapons?

None but what's in the head, and do you suppose I could get dressed now? Just plain cold is what it is.

The Major nodded. He kept his carbine trained on Joe while he pulled on his clothes, at the same time sneaking glances at the wad of money he had taken from Joe's pocket. A bewildered expression came over the Major's face, hidden by his white silk mask. The money was printed on only one side.

I keep some money on hand because you never know when you might have to take a quick trip when you're in transit, said Joe, watching the Major out of the corner of his eye. Of course it's true those Bulgarian leva and Rumanian bani can't be worth much this year, and the paras have probably also seen better days. None of them could be worth more than half of what they used to be, which is maybe why they were printed that way. In halves, I mean, on one side only. . . . Things are always deteriorating all over, have you ever noticed that?

The Major forgot himself and nodded. Joe pulled on his shoes.

But the real beauty in the pack, said Joe, is that bill on the bottom. See it? One hundred Greek drachmas on one side, ten thousand Albanian leks on the other. Or is it the other way around? The Balkans have always been a confusing concept to me, I've just never been able to make much sense out of them. Know what I mean?

Again the Major nodded dumbly in agreement. He was having

trouble remembering what he was supposed to be doing, so bewildering did he find Joe's manner. This isn't right, thought the Major. Things aren't going the way they're supposed to.

Tinkle.

Joe smiled, pulling on his jacket, as the Major quickly tried to think of another command to deliver. Any command would do.

Sit down there, he said. Feet apart, please.

Sound reasoning in the moonglow, Major. I was just thinking myself we ought to relax a bit. After all, the Sphinx *is* a riddle and we're right in the lap of that riddle, aren't we?

The Major nodded without thinking. He pulled down his white silk mask, absentmindedly, and wiped his mouth. Joe asked for a cigarette and the Major handed him a packet.

Would you care to sit down yourself? Joe asked pleasantly, striking a match.

The Major nodded, confused, and sat down a few yards away from Joe on the paw of the Sphinx. He removed his pith helmet and wiped his brow. Then he realized he couldn't see very well and he removed his goggles.

This is an impossible situation, he muttered.

Joe peered over the end of his burning cigarette and smiled.

Tut tut, Major, *tut and ho.* Impossible, you say? Best to be wary of words like that in the moonglow here, where the secrets of the pharaohs reside all around us. A few minutes ago you might even have been wondering where I was when you first rode up and the Sphinx seemed to be speaking to you. Were you maybe wondering about that?

The Major stared, fascinated. He nodded.

Sure and why not, said Joe, and I was inside the Sphinx, that's all. It's too long a story to go into now but it has to do with tunnels of the past and lookouts people don't know about, and holes in the universe that are so mysterious they seem to be black, and other lives that affect our own even though those other lives seem to be gone and underground and forgotten to all appearances, even lost. But that's appearances only. They're there all right.

Joe looked up at the sky.

Here now, what's this? What moonglow was I referring to? Seems our gentle white goddess has just down and finished her tour for the night, making the black holes less black but leaving us in more darkness until dawn for sure.

What's that? asked the Major.

No more moon, said Joe. And speaking of that, we were talking about appearances and what's hidden and the apparent differences thereof, and Stern used to have a way of describing such things. He borrowed it from the Delphic oracle and it ran something like this. *Summoned or unsummoned, the gods are there.* Inside of us, it means. Calling themselves by all the names we can think up, some of which we recognize when the mirages come into focus at dawn, now and then when they do. Or in the middle of the night when everything's black and we also see things clearly for a change. Sometimes, for a moment anyway.

Joe smiled, gazing up at the head of the Sphinx.

I may be rambling now, Major, but that's only because the thought of Stern always sets my mind wandering and whisks me right off over time's dunes. A piece of personal dizziness, that's all. Fair enough?

The Major nodded, not at all sure what he was agreeing to anymore, his thoughts tumbling in utter confusion.

Right, said Joe. And it is odd how things can come around and come together. But I have another problem now and I'd like to tell you about it, and it's simply this.

Joe paused, turning his head to the side to cough. While the Major waited for Joe to continue he absentmindedly removed the heavy sniper's rifle that had been resting on his back. Then he lifted off the heavy bandoliers that were weighing down his shoulders. He also undid his web belt with its heavy load of ammunition and laid it on the stone, relieving the pressure on his kidneys.

Joe coughed again, his head still to the side. Numbly the Major went on pulling out weapons and laying them down, unencumbering himself. The automatic pistols appeared, small and large, and the various knives and daggers. When the Major was freed at last of all his weapons he stretched languidly, easily, sensuously. Joe glanced down at the small arsenal and cleared his throat.

Right. Now as I was saying, my problem is simply this. Bletchley has some kind of standing order out to kill me and I don't see any need for it, but to get the order changed I have to talk to Bletchley, and I can't arrange that by myself. I can't just give him a ring and ask for a chat, because the way things are now he probably wouldn't get the call and certainly wouldn't show up. The fellows who take his orders would. Those Monks, damn them. See what I mean?

The Major nodded.

Therefore I'd take it ever so kindly, said Joe, if you could arrange a meeting for me with Bletchley. Surely you know I'm not going to go blasting my way out of Egypt these days, couldn't, even if I had a mind to. Bletchley's my star this night and I have to follow his lead. I need his approval to keep my *in transit* status, and I think I could get it if I could talk to him. So what do you think? Could you discuss it with your Colonel before the night's out? The way things are at the moment I'm short on time. Officially dead as a matter of fact, which isn't a promising condition to be in for long. Makes me uneasy, naturally.

The Major found his tongue at last.

What do you mean, you're *officially* dead?

I mean, according to the Monks, said Joe. According to official Monkish reality. So, can you do this and speak to your Colonel for me?

But what if I did? asked the Major. What arguments could I give him for stepping in? Bletchley's operations belong to Bletchley. The Colonel can't interfere for no reason.

True enough, said Joe, but as I see it it's not so much a matter of argument as it is of points of interest, and those interests are Colly for one and Stern for another and me for a third. Your Colonel, like Bletchley, must have respected Stern a great deal, that's a given for anyone who knew the man. And as for Colly, well I wouldn't doubt they both loved Colly, mysterious presence that he always was. And Colly was my brother, which is by way of slipping me into this configuration.

What? Colly was your brother?

Yes, that's who he was. There were a lot of us to begin with and Colly was the next to the last, and I'm the last. But that's an aside. The points of interest here are the Colly and the Stern and only lastly me.

The Major shook his head, completely bewildered.

None of this makes any sense, he muttered.

Joe smiled.

It doesn't?

No. I have no idea what you're talking about most of the time.

Joe smiled more broadly.

You don't?

No. The Delphic oracle and the Sphinx and moonglow, and Colly and Stern and you? What does it all add up to? I just can't seem to get my hands on it.

Joe laughed.

Oh is that all. Well I wouldn't worry too much about that. There seem to be all kinds of things we can't get our hands on in life. What we have to ask ourselves is, does the intangible thing in question have a certain ring to it?

A ring?

Yes. As with a bell mainly, but also as with a circle. Sometimes that seems to be as close as we can get.

I'm lost, muttered the Major.

Joe laughed.

Then just think of everything as being a tentative arrangement for the moment, a set of circumstances that never stops shifting around, confusing only because it *is* just for the moment. Like you and me, say, with our *in transit* status in a universe that's also in transit. Or a meeting with Bletchley, say. That's just another tentative thing. He could always change his mind or he could refuse outright.

And what if he did refuse? asked the Major. What would you do then?

Joe shrugged. He looked down at his hands.

Don't know, do I. Liffy used to talk about sitting in empty railway stations late at night, hungry and tired and never sure when a train might show up. Never sure where it might be going, if it did.

Liffy?

Joe opened his hands and looked at them.

Better we don't talk about him. Some things are just too painful and enormous to get ahold of right away, and Liffy's death is one of them for me.

The Major was stunned.

Liffy? *Dead?*

Yes, God bless him.

But that's terrible. How did it happen?

He was shot and bayoneted and blown up and gassed and knifed and beaten and starved and buried alive and burned to ashes, and the ashes were scattered on the waters of the Nile.

What?

Dead, that's all.

But who killed him?

The war? Hitler? Some army or other? I don't know.

But why?

On the face of it, a case of mistaken identity. But that doesn't tell us much because so many identities are always being mistaken in life. Why then, beneath it all? Simply because of what he was.

I don't understand. What was he?

A sound as clear as a golden bell, whispered Joe. A sound as of a mighty rushing wind. *There* all right, but never something you could get your hands on.

What?

Yes, that was him. And truly, Major, your question is one that ought to be asked here in the lap of the Sphinx, for the answer to it is the very same answer that solved the riddle of the Sphinx three thousand years ago. Remember how the riddle went? What walks on four legs in the morning, on two at midday, and on three in the evening? And the answer then was a man, first as a baby crawling, then strong in his years, then old with his cane. So *a man* is the answer to the ancient riddle, now as then and forever. A human being is the answer, no more and no less, and that's why Liffy was killed. Because he was human and because he was good, and it's as simple as that and just as complex.

Joe gazed down at the crumbling stone at his feet.

Major? I need you to help me. Will you do that?

If I can.

Good. I'll call you at noon. You won't be able to speak freely on the phone, but if you use the word *Sphinx* when we talk, I'll take it to mean there really is a meeting on with Bletchley. And if you don't use the word, no matter what you say, I'll take it to mean there's not going to be any meeting and I'm being set up to be killed. . . . All right? Just between the two of us?

Yes.

Joe talked then about many things, but especially about Stern and himself and Liffy. Finally he rose and put out his hand.

In any case, Major, I appreciate you coming here no matter how it turns out, and I'm glad we had a chance to listen to the Delphic oracle in the moonglow and hear what the Sphinx had to say, and refresh ourselves by recalling Colly and Stern and Liffy. Things do have a way of being passed along, don't they? Despite even adverse winds and sunspots. Well then. . . .

Joe slipped down to the ground and was quickly gone in the darkness, leaving the Major naked of weapons and lost in thought.

. . . Liffy impersonating Joe at the houseboat and his reasons for doing so . . . Joe's mysterious connections with Stern and others over the years . . . Liffy's feelings for Stern and . . .

But what does it all *mean?* wondered the Major, gazing up at the calm and battered face of the Sphinx.

A light burned in the back of the Colonel's bungalow. The Major went in through the gate and walked down the path to the kitchen door, where he rapped lightly. A voice was humming inside. The door opened.

Morning, Harry.

Morning, sir.

Cup of tea?

Thank you.

He sat at the small kitchen table, his head tipped sideways under an overhanging shelf, while the Colonel busied himself at the other end of the room near the stove. Tipsy unpainted cupboards made from packing-case lumber lurched along the crowded walls of the narrow kitchen, products of the Colonel's fondness for carpentry in his off-duty hours. Every shelf in the cluttered kitchen was askew and the cabinet doors all hung ajar, unable to close. The unpainted kitchen table was heaped with the Colonel's customary assortment of scholarly books on early Islamic calligraphy, medieval Jewish mysticism, the Bahai sect, Persian miniatures, Jerusalem at the time of the Second Temple, archeological finds in central Anatolia. A plate of muffins was squeezed in beside the books and the Major pinched one.

Harder than a paw of the Sphinx, he thought. The Colonel, happily banging around in the corner, interrupted his humming to call out over his shoulder.

Piece of cheese to go with your muffin, Harry?

No thank you, sir.

The Colonel came ambling over and cups and saucers clattered down on the table. He wandered off once more and the Major just had time to pluck the wing of a fly out of his cup before the Colonel came ambling back with the teapot, still merrily humming to himself and doing a sort of bearish dance as he slowly shuffled up and down the narrow room on his false leg.

One step forward and a feint to the side, two steps backward and a feint to the side. Feint and shuffle and one and two, the Colonel turning around to make some backward headway and sidling up to the table more or less rumpside first. One step forward and two steps backward.

The Colonel's Bolshie Trot, as it was called, after Lenin's famous description of the backward advance of historical necessity in a world that seemed to care nothing at all about necessity, historical or otherwise, and preferred to do its advancing hindside first, as the Colonel said, both for protection and in order to keep its eye on the past. A dance indulged in by the Colonel only before breakfast and late at night, rarely, when he had drunk too much brandy.

In his hand the Colonel was carrying a chunk of hard white decaying matter, greasy and crumbling. A vague smile drifted across his face as he popped a piece of it into his mouth and stood beside the table, swaying on his false leg, gazing down at his hand.

Cheese, he muttered, chewing thoughtfully. Do you realize that's what we all must have looked like once upon a time, back when the protein molecules were getting started on this bit of stray matter we call the earth? Makes you think all right, doesn't it. Did you say you wanted a piece, Harry?

I think not.

No? Well the truth is breakfast has always been my best meal. Any old thing in the cupboard tastes delicious and the first pipe tastes delicious and I'm ready to take on the world. But then a half-hour later I begin to creak and wheeze and feel as if I weighed a thousand pounds, and that's it for me for the day. Cheese to cheese. Makes you think all right.

The Colonel hadn't gotten around to dressing yet. He was wearing huge baggy underdrawers that hung down to his knees and one khaki sock, on his real foot, with a large hole in the toe. His undershirt was so poorly darned in so many places it gave his upper torso the appearance of a mass of poorly healed wounds. A faded old yachting cap was perched on the side of his head, and even though most of his body was covered, he looked far more naked than any unmutilated man ever could.

Feint and shuffle, one and two. Humming happily, the Colonel sat down at the table.

404

Nice out, Harry?

Clear, cool, no wind.

Lovely, yes. Best time of the day really. People haven't had time to muck up the camp and the air's sweet and everything tastes delicious. Later it's all just one stale pipe. No cheese for you?

Not at the moment, thank you.

No? Well the tea's almost ready. Been out for an early turn in the desert, have you?

The Major nodded, waiting. The Colonel maneuvered his false leg into a more comfortable position and poured tea. After they had added sugar and stirred, and sipped, the Colonel fell to studying the plate of muffins on the table. He pinched one.

Hm. I thought I'd picked those up this week, but it must have been last week.

The Colonel glanced at one of the open books on the table and raised his eyes.

Well now. You've been to consult the Sphinx?

He's Colly's brother, the Major blurted out.

What?

Colly's brother, repeated the Major. *Our Colly's* younger brother.

The Colonel's eyes lit up.

Is that true?

Yes.

What's his name?

Joe. Joe O'Sullivan Beare. He still uses the full family name. From the Aran Islands by way of a dozen years in Palestine and more recently a tour in America as the shaman of an Indian tribe in the Southwest. He seems to know everyone from his days in Palestine. Stern and Maud and all kinds of people Stern used to work with years ago. I haven't heard of most of them but you probably have.

The Colonel's eyes flickered brightly.

Well well well, and here's more than a chapter or two from the past turning up unexpectedly. . . Colly's brother, of all people. What's he like?

Nimble, speaks quickly sometimes, seems to have an odd way of expressing himself. It's hard to describe.

The Colonel beamed.

As if things were a bit off-balance, perhaps? As if you were in a small boat at sea and the sky and the land and the water were all moving around? Up, down, sideways, never quite still?

The Major nodded eagerly.

That's it exactly. As if nothing were ever able to find a safe place for itself.

The Colonel laughed.

Colly, on the nose. His brother must be just like him.

And there's also something strange about the way he views time, continued the Major. It seems to be all of a piece to him with no past and present and future particularly, just one big sea with us upon it. The dead, for example. No one seems to be really dead to him. But it's not as if they were still out there somewhere, or off somewhere, it's very different from that. It's much more concrete and seems to do with thinking of them as being within us, a part of us, not dead in that sense. Alive because we've known them and therefore they're a part of us.

Hm. You had that feeling with Colly sometimes, but not as much as with his brother, apparently.

The Colonel smiled.

You were taken with him, weren't you?

I suppose I was.

Yes, well, it's not surprising. Colly was a man of great charm. There was something out of the ordinary to him, another dimension. And if his brother is like him only more so, and meeting him for the first time at the Sphinx as you did, under a full moon . . .

The Colonel broke off, humming happily to himself.

Colly's brother, he murmured. How astonishing.

He gazed down at the crumbling piece of cheese in his hand.

Yes, curious. What does he want?

A meeting with Bletchley.

That's all?

Yes, that's all. He says Bletchley has a standing order out to kill him, so he can't arrange a meeting by himself.

Bletchley? A standing order to kill Colly's brother?

Yes, and Liffy's already dead. Killed because he was mistaken for Joe.

The Colonel was shocked.

What?

Yes.

But that's not *right*. That's not right at all.

It certainly isn't. And Ahmad is also dead. The desk clerk at the Hotel Babylon.

406

Ahmad? But he was a delightful fellow, perfectly harmless. What's going on here?

And a young man named Cohen, said the Major. David Cohen.

Of the Cairo Cohens? Cohen's Optiks?

Yes. He was a Zionist agent apparently, and a close friend of Stern.

Well of course he was a friend of Stern, all the Cohens were. That goes way back to Stern's father's time. But what in God's name *is* going on here? Has Bletchley lost his mind? How could his men have mistaken Liffy for Joe?

It seems Liffy was passing himself off as Joe. On purpose.

Why?

To give Joe time to recover after the hand-grenade explosion and Stern's death. To give Joe time, a chance, to save himself.

The Colonel frowned.

Why did Liffy do that?

Because Joe knew Stern so well and Liffy felt Stern's life was . . . what shall I say? Of great importance somehow. More important to him, to Liffy, than anything else. Even more important than his own life.

Is that true?

Yes.

And Ahmad and young Cohen? Why were they killed?

Because they'd talked to Joe about something, or at least the Monastery thought they had.

The Colonel frowned deeply and poked at his pipe, his mouth working. The Major had no idea what connections with the past he was making, and he knew it was useless to ask. Finally the Colonel heaved himself forward and planted both elbows on the table.

So Liffy sacrificed himself in order to save Joe, is that it?

Yes.

But why? What's it got to do with Stern? I don't understand what you're trying to tell me.

Well I don't have it too clearly in my own mind yet. But it seems that above and beyond whatever Joe was trying to find out about Stern, above and beyond all that, it seems Liffy felt that Stern, Stern's life . . . Well it's hard to describe without sounding mystical.

The Colonel's tone was suddenly curt, impatient.

Never mind how it sounds, Harry. Just say it.

Well it seems Liffy felt there was some kind of special significance to Stern's life. In his peculiar background and his sufferings and his

407

failures, in the ambiguities and paradoxes of the man. That just all of it, everything having to do with Stern, added up to a different kind of life. Something more than . . .

The Major gazed into his teacup.

. . . It's almost as if to them, to Joe and Liffy and the other people Joe spoke of . . . almost as if Stern's life is a kind of tale of all our hopes and failures. Living and trying as he did, failing and dying as he did. Ideals that may lead to disaster and yet still contain within them . . . Oh I don't know what.

A clock clicked in the stillness. The Colonel reached out and touched the Major's arm, a kindly gesture.

Never be afraid how anything sounds, Harry. A good deal of what's in these books of mine could be called mystical, or could have been once. It's just another word we use for things we don't understand very well, things *we* don't understand. To somebody else those same things might be commonplace, as routine as the most routine matters are to us. People have different realities, as Stern used to say, and there are many of them going on simultaneously for all of us, and the fact that one is true doesn't make any of the others less true. . . . As for Stern, he was a man who had a powerful effect on anyone who knew him. You instinctively felt great affection for him, even love, you couldn't help it. Yet at the same time there was a kind of indefinable fear you knew when you were with him, a fear that seemed to come from being in the presence of emotions so profoundly contradictory they could never be resolved. Something suggestive of the eternal conflicts in man, the mixture of the divine and the profane, holiness crossed with our dark natures and all of it pushed, *pushed* . . . because that's the man Stern was. . . .

The Colonel nodded. He leaned back and went to work on his pipe.

You were saying, Harry?

Well that's all, really. Liffy felt Joe had to live on as a witness to Stern's life. As Liffy himself expressed it to Joe, so that one man at least would *know*, no matter what the war brings . . .

A witness, murmured the Colonel. Yes, I see. And of course at the time Liffy said that, Joe didn't realize what Liffy was telling him? What Liffy intended to do?

No, not at all. He can hardly mention Liffy's name now without breaking down. He just goes to pieces and I'm sure that's not like him. Obviously he's a man of great discipline.

Yes yes, I understand, said the Colonel. It's a terrible burden for Joe and he knows it full well and he knows it will always be that way. But how strange this all is. . . . Stern, Joe, Liffy. . . . The three of them coming from their various corners of the world to have their fates crossed here, in front of us. Yes. . . .

The clock clicked. A match was struck in the stillness. The Major smelled pipe smoke and looked up from his teacup.

Well, what do you think?

The Colonel puffed.

I think I'd like to hear it all from the beginning, everything that happened out there at the Sphinx tonight. So I'll know where I stand when I speak to Bletchley. But also, frankly, for my own reasons.

The grayness of dawn had come to the windows by the time the Major finished his account. Both men looked exhausted as they faced each other across the kitchen table, but in fact neither one of them felt tired at all. Suddenly, the Colonel slammed his fist down on the table.

Whatley, he exclaimed, referring to the officer who was chief of operations at the Monastery, Bletchley's second in command.

Whatley, he repeated angrily. It's his doing, I'm sure of it. Bletchley must have turned the case over to him and gone on to other things, and Whatley's had his gunmen out running around pushing people off roofs and pushing them in front of lorries and shooting up houseboats. *Damn* Whatley. *Damnable* little snit. Bletchley has always spent most of his time in the field trying to know his agents, almost compulsively conscientious about it, and what does Whatley do out there at the Monastery when he's left in charge? What does he *do,* I ask you?

The Major lowered his eyes. He had heard others speak of Whatley with disgust, but never the Colonel. Normally the Colonel was much too circumspect to speak openly of the defects of a fellow field grade officer.

Dress-ups, hissed the Colonel. That's Whatley's infernal game. Leave him alone for a minute out there in the desert and he slips into a cowl and habit and ties an old piece of rope around his waist

409

and pretends he's a militant monk from the Dark Ages, or worse, some sort of fourth-century abbot doing battle over doctrinal disputes in the early days of Christianity. Pretends he's plotting his way through the intricacies of the Arian controversy, or some such nonsense. Actually keeps a map on the wall showing which parts of Europe and North Africa are on the side of the angels, his side, and which parts are on the side of Arius and the devil. Lucifer and the heresiarchs in one camp, the true defenders of the faith in the other.

Arianism and the Arian heresy today? God and His Son are the same substance? Are not the same substance? What rubbish. Go back far enough and we're all the same substance, just so much cheese. And how did Whatley ever arrive at these grandiose delusions in the first place? Simply because Arian sounds the same as Aryan? I thought only schizophrenics and poets were supposed to be afflicted with sound-alike fantasies?

Malicious nonsense, muttered the Colonel, all of it. Whatley and his incense and his censers and candles and his organs booming out Bach's Mass in B Minor, and acolytes and terrified novices tiptoeing back and forth and aides passing themselves off as monks-in-waiting. Standing directives from faceless bishops and indulgences handed out in the form of overnight passes to the fleshpots of Cairo, staff rooms disguised as gloomy chapels and orders from the desert to kill. Real orders to kill from the heart of the wasteland, blandly referred to as excommunication with extreme prejudice.

Extreme *what?* Madness is more like it, the vicious madness of dress-ups. What is it about men that makes them do that in wartime, or any time? Weren't they able to get enough of it as children, this strutting and skulking and prancing around in costumes? Make-believe is horrible. War isn't a little boy's dress-up dreams come true. It isn't meant to give grown men the chance to be little boys running riot in the nursery.

The Colonel glared, fuming.

Or at least it shouldn't be. *Damn* that Whatley and his kind. *Damn him* to hell with his parchment maps and his toys and costumes and his incense and organ music, his monks-in-waiting tiptoeing in and out with candles. Yes Your Grace, No Your Grace, Up-my-arse-with-pleasure Your Grace. The truth is that man always wanted to live in the fourth century or whatever it is, and that's exactly what he's doing. Reveling in the obedience and piety and obscurantism of the Dark Ages, righteous as he can be as he piously fasts in some filthy hole beneath the Monastery which he pretends was once St Anthony's cell, joyously having himself flagellated before he issues another righteous order of excommunication, *murder* in the name of the Father and the Son and the Holy Ghost.

Piety and power, muttered the Colonel. Self-righteous murder and that repulsive flagellation that goes with it. All power to the nursery, in our age. All power to the gruesome little boy who dizzily sniffs his forefinger and giggles over his playthings.

The Colonel's face grew even darker.

And the other side's unspeakably worse. At least we don't honor these practices officially and make them into institutions by handing out habits as regular issue, the way the Nazis hand out black uniforms and black jackboots and death's-head insignias. Even Whatley can't begin to compare to that Nazi crowd with their insatiable need for blackness. They just keep lusting backward into the past until they've become so many packs of animals loping around in the primeval gloom. Smell blood and you snap at it. Massacre enough and the beast inside may be able to know peace for a moment or two, with the help of some Bach or Mozart of course. Slaughter enough and you have the illusion of immortality because everybody around you is dying.

A civilized people, the Germans. Some of the finest music in the history of the species served up to soothe the beast in Western culture, a beast the Germans just happen to know a great deal about.

Damn Germans, damn Whatley, *damn*. Nothing's as simple as it used to be, or maybe it's just the opposite. Maybe everything's as simple as it used to be, sadly for us. . . . But the damn problem is, Whatley's a good staff officer when he's not playing his games, which is why Bletchley probably couldn't get rid of him even if he wanted to. Whatley's very diligent and thorough and hardworking, not unlike the Germans. . . .

The Colonel paused.

I wonder why those traits always have to bring the Germans to mind today? *Thorough . . . diligent . . .* those traits seem to have become dangerous somehow in our century. As if there's no room anymore for the wobbly human factor. Automatons seem to be what society wants today. By the numbers, one two three. . . . Whatley will even tell you he's not a very aggressive man by nature. Just competitive. . . .

The Colonel paused again

It's true he used to be a good sportsman before he lost his right arm. . . .

A sudden change came over the Colonel. His chest sank and he groaned, looking more naked than ever in his mended undershirt and his faded yachting cap. He reached down to move his false leg and a look of resignation settled over his face.

Damn, he muttered, that's it for me. I've had my early morning fling at being defiant and ready for anything. From now on I take what comes and deal with it in whatever plodding way I can. Breakfast is over.

The Colonel looked at his watch.

Time to get cleaned up. I'll call Bletchley as soon as I get to the office. I can't imagine there'd be any difficulty about a meeting with Joe. Bletchley was a great fan of Colly's after all, and it must have been Bletchley who came across Joe's name in Stern's file in the first place and decided to get him over here from America. Nor can it be a coincidence that he assigned Colly's old cover to Joe, resurrecting this notion of a Purple Seven Armenian. Bletchley had to know what he was doing, and I can't imagine he'd want to give Joe serious trouble now. Maybe he has to straighten some things out with him, but surely it can't have anything to do with the way Whatley's been going about matters.

The Colonel rummaged around cleaning out his pipe.

Oh by the way, Harry. I assume you had your bad ear turned this way when I was going on about Whatley a moment ago. Fellow officer and so forth.

Didn't hear a word, Colonel.

Yes. Well then. . . .

The Major was ready to leave but he hesitated. He had the impression the Colonel wasn't quite finished.

Was there anything else, sir?

The Colonel fumbled with his pipe.

No not really. I was just . . .

The Colonel glanced at the pipe in his hands and put it down on the table, an emphatic motion. There was an odd mixture of regret and wistfulness in his face, something the Major wasn't used to. In his shapeless underwear and his old yachting cap, the Colonel suddenly looked forlorn.

Silence, the Colonel muttered. . . . Why does there have to be so much silence in our lives?

412

He looked up at the Major.

Did I ever tell you I just missed being given command of the Monastery? It was the plum of course, but . . .

The Major shook his head and waited. Something about the Stern case, he realized, had released a profound surge of emotion in the Colonel.

But I didn't get it, muttered the Colonel. It happened a few years ago. I had the background for it, that wasn't in doubt, and I even had this new false leg as an added qualification. . . .

The Colonel attempted a smile, a sad expression.

But I didn't get it in the end. I wasn't considered *determined* enough, whatever that's supposed to mean. A polite way of saying ruthless, I suppose. So they decided to go with Bletchley even though this wasn't the area he knew, and they gave him Whatley as a deputy because Whatley's so thorough, and I was given the Water-boys instead. More your line, they said. Pretty much the traditional kind of operations and a much larger staff and all the ancillary services, which you can handle. . . . Not that Bletchley didn't deserve the job, he did. He's good and no one would deny he's conscientious, and they might have been right about me when it comes to the sort of work the Monastery does. But still. . . .

The Colonel's voice trailed off. He gazed down at the table and shook his head.

Anyway, Bletchley got the Monastery and he saw a lot more of Stern after that than I did. And he also saw a good deal more of Colly, whom he seemed to take a particular liking to, and so . . .

The Colonel's hand slowly went out to the chunk of cheese on the table. He picked up a small piece, toying with it, the crumbs spilling through his fingers.

Enigma, he thought all at once, the idea coming to him from nowhere. That's what's behind all of this. Somehow Stern found out about *Enigma*. . . . Of course, that was his Polish story. And Bletchley found out Stern knew and he dug Joe's name out of Stern's files, Colly's brother, of course, and he got Joe over here and gave him Colly's old identity and . . . But how did Bletchley find out about Stern? There's no one here who . . .

Unless Stern had told someone, thought the Colonel . . . and that someone had spoken to Bletchley.

The Colonel stared at the table. If that was what had happened and Joe knew the truth, there was simply no way Bletchley could let him go now. Joe could never leave Cairo, it was out of the question. Bletchley had no choice in the matter. He would agree to a meeting and then he would have to . . . Well maybe they were right to have given him the job, thought the Colonel. Maybe he is better fitted for it than I am, more determined or whatever. After all, Colly's brother. . . .

The Major was still standing beside the kitchen table. The Colonel glanced up at him and smiled sadly. He shrugged.

Just my mind wandering, he said, it has nothing to do with this. Anyway, I'll call Bletchley as soon as I get to the office and explain the situation. I'm sure he'll agree to a meeting.

The Major nodded eagerly.

Very good, sir.

Yes, well. . . .

The Colonel groaned and heaved himself up from the table. For a moment he stood there tottering on his false leg, getting his balance, gazing down at his books.

Well that's it for now, Harry, it's time to get on with the day. And I hate to say it but I already feel as if I weighed a thousand pounds. Somehow the good things in life always seem to be over almost before we knew they were there. . . .

The Major was at his desk when his private telephone rang exactly at noon. He picked it up and said hello.

A wandering minstrel here, Major. Any news of a meeting with the local pharaoh before the sun sets?

The Major gave Joe a time and a place.

After the sun sets, you say? Well that's all right with me. Most of my business seems to have been conducted at night since I've been in Cairo. Nature of the business maybe, wouldn't you say?

The Major laughed, adding that he was sorry the location of the meeting wouldn't be as dramatic as the Sphinx had been the night before.

No, well, we can't always have such sweeping views of the night-tide sky, now can we, Major? Life has to go on in its little ways and the Sphinx is just too big a concept for any of us to be visiting it every night. Too big and then some, too hard to understand too. An inscrutable notion after all, like life and a lot of things. Until the appointed time and place then. . . .

The line went dead. The Major hung up the phone and looked across the room at the Colonel, who was sitting in the corner watching him. The Colonel nodded, rose.

That's it, said the Colonel. We've done what we could and it's up to Bletchley now.

The Colonel went limping back to his office.

Shameless, he thought, Harry using a private code like that right in front of me. *The Sphinx,* indeed. It's easy enough to understand how he was taken with Joe, but all the same charm isn't really what's wanted in wartime. It turns heads. . . .

And abruptly an image came to the Colonel from before the war, during the Arab revolt in Palestine. An image of Colly arriving at night at a Jewish outpost manned by settlers above Galilee, near the Lebanese border, Colly turning up in one of his disguises to train the settlers and to organize what would later become the Special Night Squads of the Palmach.

A taxi with its headlights off, its taillights on the front of the car to confuse the enemy. And Colly's two young future deputies, Dayan and Allon, approaching the mysterious taxi and seeing a small lean figure come jumping out of the car with two rifles and a Bible and a drum, an English-Hebrew dictionary and five gallons of New England rum.

Flair, thought the Colonel, there's no other word for it. Colly had flair. . . .

He smiled at the memory, then thought of Joe and lost his smile, recalling a saying Stern had once been fond of repeating.

The Panorama Has Moved.

Finished, he thought. What a shame. It's all over for Joe and Liffy died for nothing, but of course there can't be any other resolution to the Stern case. With the secret of *Enigma* at the heart of it, there's no other way. None. Bletchley can only do what has to be done. End the case and close the file with those terrible words, *No surviving witnesses.* But still. . . .

The Colonel closed his door and leaned against it, recalling the strange account of a voice that had come booming out of the Sphinx under a full moon.

> ... *Who knows what evil lurks in the*
> *hearts of men?*

Well the Sphinx surely, thought the Colonel. The Sphinx finally, but which one out of all of them was really the Sphinx in the end? Or is everyone, finally. . . ?

22

Bernini's Bag

They sat on the narrow shaded balcony that opened off Maud's living room, on the far side of the building away from the fierce sinking sun, a promise of twilight gathering in the corners of the alley below.

. . and when the Major let me know there was truly a meeting on with Bletchley, said Joe, I couldn't stop myself from doing a little dance in place for about five minutes. I tried to call you here but there was no answer, so I made my way back to the public garden where old Menelik's crypt lies buried, and I found a sheltered little spot to sit in the shade by the river, and that's what I did. Just sat and watched the currents and let my mind drift.

Joe's hair was wet from the shower he had just taken. His left ear was newly bandaged.

But it wasn't just anyplace by the Nile, he went on. It was the very same spot where Strongbow and old Menelik had once spent a silent afternoon together toward the end of their long lives, just before the First World War, the place where there had once been a cheap open-air restaurant with beautiful trellises and vines and hanging flowers, with a pool where ducks paddled and a cage where peacocks squawked, that very same rendezvous where Strongbow and old Menelik and Crazy Cohen had met for their dreaming and drinking bouts on Sunday afternoons so long ago, when they were three young men starting out. A place for forty-year conversations and then some, the same spot where a famous sign had stood years later in the midst of emptiness, all by itself in a vacant lot . . . THE PANORAMA HAS MOVED. And I guess I got to thinking about that sign and its worlds

417

within worlds, and before I knew it I'd just dozed off to the murmuring spell of the river.

There hasn't been much sleep for me lately, he added, despite my being officially dead. . . . A case of the restless dead, I guess you'd have to call it.

Maud smiled.

Was that really where the sign used to be?

Oh that was the spot all right. Stern pointed it out to me when we were leaving the crypt that night. So I dozed off without meaning to, and by the time I woke up it was late afternoon, so I came straight here.

The Colonel told me I might have a visitor waiting for me at home. Oh Joe, I was so excited. I was sure it meant things were going to turn out all right for you.

And was that all he said?

Yes, but it was enough. I knew what it meant.

Well I'm glad you did, but it was still cryptic of him and that's the trouble with this business. Nobody says more than he has to and you miss a lot that way. Me, I just wanted to shout because I was alive again.

Maud laughed.

Can I get you something to eat? she asked. You must be starved.

I must be, but I don't feel it. I think I might have a drink though.

Have it then. Do you want me to get it?

No, don't bother yourself, I can manage. Where do you keep it?

In the kitchen. In the cabinet over the broom closet.

Swept away, said Joe, and disappeared inside.

Maud heard the cabinet door bang in the kitchen. It swelled and stuck sometimes in the heat, and then flew back against the wall unless you were expecting it. She heard Joe muttering to himself. Glass clinked and there was the sound of ice being broken out of an ice tray.

I forgot to mention the cabinet door, she said when he came back.

Joe smiled.

It makes a racket all right when there's somebody as clumsy as me around. It just goes to show I'm not cut out for this kind of work. The moment I feel a little safe I go crashing around as if I didn't have a care in the world.

He took a long drink from his glass and sat down on the low wall of the balcony. Maud was bent over her knitting. She spoke without looking up.

You seem to drink a lot.

I do, yes.

Does it help?

Yes, I'm afraid it does.

Well that's good then, I guess.

No it isn't, Maudie, it's a kind of weakness surely, but it eases things. So often the world seems such a dark and unyielding place that anything that stills the whispers inside seems to have its uses, even when you know it's a false quiet.

Could you stop, do you think?

If I had to. Human beings seem to be able to do about anything if they have to. Even those things they're doing right now out in the desert.

Maud bent her head, a sudden uneasiness coming over her. She was trying not to let him see her concern, but he felt it anyway.

Are you really sure Bletchley's going to let you leave?

Not sure, no, but it seems likely. If it were going to be otherwise I don't think he'd be handling it like this, giving me the afternoon off and telling your Colonel to give you the afternoon off, too.

But you said he's having you followed again.

Just company, Maudie. I suppose Bletchley doesn't want anything to happen to me between now and tonight. Besides, I was the one who gave him the opportunity by going back near Menelik's crypt, which I knew he'd be having watched. I didn't have to do that.

Why did you then?

So he'd know where I was today and know there was nothing to worry about.

But why didn't you just stay out of sight until tonight?

Well for one thing, I wouldn't have been able to see you then. And anyway, it seemed like the time had come to get some things out in the open. After the way the Major went on last night about Stern and Colly, Colly in particular, it just didn't seem that Bletchley would have gone to all the trouble it must have taken to get me over here, just to do me in in the end.

But does the Major's opinion count? Does it really matter that he happens to have such a high regard for Colly's memory? Bletchley may feel very differently about it. About everything.

He may, but I doubt it.

But how can you be sure?

I can't.

Well I don't like it, Joe. It frightens me. Bletchley has a reputation for being very single-minded.

As well he should be, in a job like that.

But people say he'll stop at nothing to get what he wants.

I know, he told me so himself once. He said he'd do anything to defeat the Germans. *Anything,* and he meant it.

But couldn't that mean you're still in danger?

I don't think so. Bletchley has always treated me in a certain way, which I can respect, and besides, there comes a time when you have to trust somebody. You play it alone as best you can for as long as you can, and then finally you have to come out and say, Look, this is all there is. This is all I am and I can't do anymore. Eventually that time comes, and I know it and Bletchley knows it and it's just that simple in the end.

It doesn't sound simple, said Maud in a low voice. Nothing about it sounds simple to me.

Joe watched her affectionately as she bent over her knitting needles. It was the second or third time she had brought it up. . . . Was it going to be all right? Was he going to be able to leave Cairo? Why would Bletchley let him go after all the things that had happened?

And of course Joe understood her concern. He knew she couldn't share the relief he felt, because she hadn't been through what he had experienced since his arrival in Cairo. For him, something was coming to an end and there was a finality about it, and the inevitable calm that brought. But not so for Maud. Stern was dead and that was final, but the other parts of her life were still the same. It was all just as precarious for her as it had been a day or a month or a year ago, and their son Bernini was still in America and none of that had changed, and there was no finality, no ending. It looked now as if Joe would be able to escape and that was wonderful, a blessing, but everything else was still the same for her.

Except that the British might not be able to hold the line at El Alamein, which would mean packing up and leaving for Palestine and leaving the little place she had made for herself here . . . moving again, returning to Palestine again after all these years. After all, she had only gone there once in her life and that was long ago when she had first met Joe in the crypt of the Church of the Holy Sepulchre. So long ago now, when her dreams had still been young. . . .

Her hands came to rest in her lap, her head bowed. All at once she felt utterly exhausted. To move again? Couldn't anything ever stay the way it was for just a little while? . . . But then all at once Joe was standing behind her and she felt his hands on her shoulders, and even now, despite the years . . .

Joe? There's one thing you don't have to worry about, at least. The Major's feelings are every bit as strong as you think they are. I've heard him talk about Colly and all the rest and . . . well you see the Major, Harry and I, we're . . . close.

Are you? Well that's *good*, Maudie, I'm glad to hear it. It makes it so much better when there's someone to share with. . . . And I liked him too, for what that's worth.

He's not just the way he appears sometimes, she said. There are other sides to him. It's just that he's young and sometimes he romanticizes things and . . . well, he's young.

Joe smiled warmly.

And a good thing, too, for a man to be. As I recall, I moved along those lines once myself.

He nodded, smiling, then turned serious.

So you mustn't worry, my love. It's going to be all right, I know it. . . . And what were you thinking about just now, I wonder? Besides this good piece of news about Harry?

Oh. Oh I was thinking about Jerusalem. A friend there has written, asking if he can help in any way. He doesn't know what I do here, what I really do, but he said he could always find me a place in Jerusalem if I needed one.

Ah and that's just fine, Maudie. You have some very good friends who think of you.

I'm fortunate.

You are, but it's not by chance, you know that. People do such things because they know how much you've always cared, because you've taken the time to show them and it means a lot to them. It helps them. To them you're a still point, a touch of sureness and certainty in all the flux and turmoil.

She frowned.

A still point? I don't feel that way at all. I don't feel there's anything certain about my life. It's all been just one wrenching experience after another, and I haven't handled any of them very well.

Oh yes you have, Maudie, better than most of us ever do. You've worked hard to understand people and it shows. Just look at that little table inside the door. There are letters from all over the world there, people you've befriended through the years in one place or another, people who remember and want to stay in touch, because it helps them to do that.

People are so terribly uprooted in wartime, she said. They're scattered and frightened and they have to survive dreadful things.

Yes they are and yes they do, but in a way that's not just wartime. In a way that's what there always is, and you've been helping in your quiet way for a long time now. Stern mentioned it once in a letter he sent to Arizona. *All those people who write to Maud from their little corners of the world,* he said. *Could they ever manage half as well without her?*

Well it was kind of him to say that but of course they could manage, and perfectly well.

No, not quite so well, and I suspect you know that. You do something special for them, Maudie. You honor the memories they have of whole parts of their lives, and in doing that you honor them. It's trust you give them and faith, the good things. They look to you for it and you give it to them, and that means a lot. The one truly dreadful thing is when people no longer have the faith to go on, when it seems to no longer matter whether they survive or not because nothing they can do is worthwhile and no one cares. And that's when the smallest thing can make all the difference. *I owe Maud a letter, she must be expecting a letter. She hasn't heard from me in months.* When you're off somewhere and everything seems black and hopeless, even a thought as small as that one can be something to hold on to. Maybe even the difference between living and dying.

Pride, Maudie. When we have it it's no more than the air we breathe and the sun overhead. But when we don't have it, God have mercy. To give it to even one person is a beautiful thing, because what is it after all but the laying on of hands, *the* human act. What can be done when we learn to think about more than just ourselves. And you do that, Maudie, and people know it and feel it deep down.

How you do go on, she said.

Joe laughed.

And that's true too, talk's always been my affliction. Long thoughts standing around like pilgrims outside an oasis, leaning on their staves and restlessly waiting to be spoken to life. *Talk*, the poor man's gold. The thirsty man's water.

She looked up at him, her face suddenly serious.

Then tell me something, Joe? Why are the letters always from so far away? Why are they always from some distant place?

Ah well, because your life has been like that, I suppose. Because you've looked so hard for your place, and that's led to moving and to wandering.

Too much, she murmured. Too much, it seems. Sometimes I wonder if I'll ever find a place of my own, yet it's not something so special I want, not something unusual. . . . Well, someday maybe.

Of course someday, Maudie. After the war. There's no question you'll find it, no question at all.

She pushed back her hair.

Yes, she whispered. After the war. . . .

Joe felt her uneasiness. He was sitting on the low wall of the balcony again, looking out at the little buildings and the rooftops and the laundry hanging out to dry, not far from the little square with its neighborhood restaurant and its neighborhood café and its everyday people with their everyday concerns, that little place so far from the war where he had seen Stern sitting in the dust not too long ago. In rags then, a beggar, a solemn quiet man sitting in the dust at the end of the day.

In the alley below, a little farther along, some children were playing. They had scratched figures on the hard baked earth of the alley, circles and squares, and they were following some complicated set of rules to advance from figure to figure, hopping on one leg. When one of the children reached the end he had to start again at the beginning. They were shouting and laughing as they played, but they also seemed to be going about it very intently.

I hope it's not some kind of war game, said Joe.

What's that?

The children playing down there.

Maud leaned forward and looked over the balcony. She smiled.

Don't you recognize it? It's Greek hopscotch.

Is it now? And how could they have learned that, I wonder?

Maud laughed.

I can't imagine. Some old Greek spinster must have taught them.

More likely a younger woman than that, given the leaping and hopping going on. But do you know them well then?

Yes, I know the family. Most of them are from the same family. That doorstep down there where the cat sleeps is the door to their kitchen. Is he there?

The cat? Yes indeed, soundly asleep. What's his name?

Homer. That's his place before dinner. The grandfather of the family lived in Turkey once and he likes to talk about it, and the children are fascinated by descriptions of any foreign place. I'm afraid I spend more time at their kitchen table than I should, they've practically adopted me. Sometimes the wife sneaks over here in the afternoon when I'm home and has a cigarette. She looks at my little mementos and imagines all sorts of grand things, having no idea how tattered my life has been. But then before long she has to leave again because of all the things she has to do . . . all the people who are waiting for her and need her.

Maud looked into the distance.

Sometimes when I leave their kitchen in the evening I take the long way around, strolling through the alleys and just listening to the sounds of the night, people talking in low voices and getting ready to go to bed. The soft yellow glow in the little windows always looks so inviting. I know the people inside may not be content with what they have, but that's never the feeling I have when I walk by.

She was silent for a moment.

I've been to see Anna, she said. It's very difficult for her because she and David were so close, just the two of them for so many years. And Stern going at the same time makes everything worse. But she's a strong person and I'm sure she'll manage. We've talked about some things that might make a difference.

Maud paused.

I'm not supposed to mention this, Anna wasn't supposed to say anything about it. . . . It seems Bletchley is being very helpful and doing a great deal for her, papers and money and so forth. It rather surprised me when she told me. It's not the kind of reputation he has at all.

No I guess it isn't, said Joe, but I'm certainly glad to hear it. Have you known her long?

No. I met the two of them once with Stern three or four months

424

ago. At the time it seemed like an accidental meeting, but later I realized it wasn't. Stern had planned it of course, without telling either them or me. Anna and I figured that out.

Yes.

And I also intend to follow your suggestion about looking up Belle and Alice. I've already sent them a note explaining who I am and asking if I could come to call some evening. If there's time. If I'm still here.

That was thoughtful of you, Maudie. They haven't had many visitors in recent years and I know they'd appreciate it. They'll like you, and it would mean a lot to them because you knew Stern so well.

Good, she said, and fell to studying her knitting.

It's in the silences, he thought. When you're close to someone they speak to you in the silences and the feelings just tumble out.

But there was still one presence softly echoing through all their thoughts, a man who had to be spoken to life between them before they parted. And so as the darkness gathered, Joe told her about his last evening with Stern.

. . . and I realize, he concluded, there's no way for us to know, ever, whether that peace I saw in Stern's eyes in the end was because he *was* at peace with himself, finally, or simply because he saw the hand grenade coming . . . death. But we do know the last word he said before he spoke my name and struck me and saved my life.

Maud sat very still.

Yes, she whispered. *Love.* . . .

Joe muttered something about his glass. He walked inside and a light went on behind Maud. She heard him rattling around in the kitchen and then the light went off and he was back again, resting his hand on her shoulder before he moved away to sit on the low wall of the balcony.

Once Stern repeated something to me, she said, that I've never quite forgotten. It was an ancient Chinese account of caravans in the

425

Gobi desert, of all things. He'd come across it in some obscure book he was reading, and I suppose the description has stayed with me because the images seemed so haunting. It was written about two thousand years ago, he said. Anyway, it went something like this.

A region of sudden sandstorms and terrifying visions. Rivers disappear overnight, landmarks go with the wind, the sun sinks at midday. A timeless nonexistent land meant to plague the mind with its mirages.

But the most dangerous thing that must be mentioned is the caravans that appear at any moment on the horizon, there to drift uncertainly for minutes or days or years. Now they are near, now far, now just as assuredly they are gone. The camel drivers are aloof and silent, undistinguishable, men of some distant race. But the men they serve, the leaders of the caravans, are truly frightening. They wear odd costumes, their eyes gleam, they come from every corner of the world. These men, in sum, are the secret agents who have always given the authorities so much to fear. They represent the princes and despots of a thousand lawless regions.

Or is it perhaps that they represent no one at all? Is that why their aspects make us tremble? In any case we know only that this is their meeting place, the unmarked crossroads where they mingle and separate and wander on their way.

As for where they go and why, we cannot be sure of such things. There are no tracks in such a barren waste. The sandstorms blow, the sun sinks, rivers disappear, and their camels are lost in darkness. Therefore the truth must be that the routes of such men are untraceable, their missions unknowable, their ultimate destinations as invisible as the wind.

If the Son of Heaven is to continue to rule with integrity, we must defend our borders at all costs from such men.

Maud turned to Joe.

Thus an ancient Chinese description of the Gobi desert . the unknown . . . written two thousand years ago.

She smiled sadly.

But that's enough of that. Let's not talk about Stern anymore. Life is always a gift of faces and a gift of tongues, and I don't mean just those of others. I mean our own. . . . All the faces we're given in

426

the course of a lifetime . . . and all the many tongues we learn to speak in.

It's curious you should use those words to describe life, said Joe. I used them myself just last night when I was talking about Liffy. What an odd coincidence.

Maud looked thoughtful, searching her memory. Suddenly she smiled.

It's a coincidence, but I don't know how odd it is. We were together when we first heard those words.

We were?

Maud beamed, she was so pleased she had remembered. She laughed.

Yes. It was in Jerusalem but we never knew who said it. We'd just come back from the Sinai and it was our first evening in Jerusalem and we went for a walk in the Old City. And it was crowded and noisy and so confusing after the desert, overwhelming even. Then all at once there was a great commotion in front of us and we couldn't move. Don't you remember?

Joe was smiling.

Yes, I do now.

It had something to do with a donkey, said Maud. Either a donkey had pitched his load or kicked someone or was just braying at the sky and wouldn't move, something like that, and right away everybody was pressing in and shouting and waving their arms and yelling in all their different languages, every conceivable kind of person, the way it is in the Old City. All those milling throngs of people who look as if they might have lived a thousand years ago or two or three thousand years ago, all of them shouting and waving their arms and yelling as if the world were coming to an end. Remember?

Joe nodded, smiling.

Yes.

And that was when it happened, said Maud. It was just a voice near us, just another voice in the crowd, but there was a yearning and a reverence in the words that rose above everything else and carried to us, part prayer, part anguish, part hope. And *clear* somehow, so very clear. . . . *O Jerusalem. O gift of faces, o gift of tongues* . . . remember?

Ah yes. Laughter and shouts and a donkey braying to the heavens and the chaos of life on every side, and a clear voice in the midst of the chaos which *we* could hear, the two of us just rejoicing in all of it. It was one of those beautiful moments all right, one of those rare precious moments that make it all worthwhile and should never be lost, should always be passed on. . . . *Must* always be passed on.

So you know what I intend to do someday, Maudie? Someday I'm going to tell Bernini all about this, every last detail of it. Liffy with his miraculous disguises and Ahmad with his secret closet, and me with them in the Hanging Gardens of Babylon. And going back, Strongbow with his magnifying glass for seeing through the ages and old Menelik with his underground musicales and Crazy Cohen with his back-to-back dreams in sevens, the three of them feasting away the last century in an oasis called the Panorama. And later on, Half-Crazy Cohen and Ahmad *père* out on the Nile with the Sisters drinking champagne from cups of pure moonlight, and later still, Big Belle and Little Alice playing their bassoon and harpsichord in a timeless shadowy moonroom while keeping watch on the river. And David and Anna dreaming their way to Jerusalem beneath a motionless clock in the dusty back room of Cohen's Optiks. And before them, another Cohen and another Ahmad and Stern striding down the amazing sidewalks of life, three kings of the Orient of old, the one with his oboe and the other with his dented trombone and above all Stern, *that one* . . . alone with his violin in the eye of the Sphinx in the last darkness before dawn, soaring with all our tales of tragedy and yearning.

Rich music, Maudie, the whole of it circular and unchronicled and calmly contradictory, suggesting infinity, and the tales themselves no less preposterous than true things always are. So why not a grand collection of them for that old white canvas bag Bernini always seems to have with him over there in New York? A little of this and a little of that always carefully tucked away in that shapeless old white canvas thing, like a shopping bag of life. But maybe Bernini's kingdom too in a way, at least that seems to be how he thinks of it. Nothing in it really, just his treasures, as he calls them. . . . So yes, I'd like to think of him roaming around over there in the New World someday with this legacy of tales from the Old, rich music to carry with him always, now that he's just starting out on his journey.

Things he can understand straightaway, after all. Jokes and riddles and scraps of rhymes a lad can take to heart and make his own.

Joe laughed in the darkness.

Yes Maudie, I do like it. . . . It has a ring to it, *Bernini's bag.* A sound that can't be mistaken. . . .

They talked of other things, the time drifting and softly slipping away in the night. They talked and fell silent and finally Joe rose and she followed him inside, where he stood looking down at her little mementos.

You'll take care, Joe, won't you? You're very precious to me.

I know, I feel the same way, Maudie. I always have. So you take care too and someday there'll be another time, someday after the war. I do know it, Maudie. . . .

He picked up her seashell, the one she had saved from the oasis on the Gulf of Aqaba where they had gone when they were young, long ago in the beginning of love. He put the seashell to his ear and listened, his eyes closed, listening and listening, then replaced it. And held her and kissed her and looked into her eyes, and was gone.

Maud stood watching the door for a time, as if it might open again. Then she wandered back to the balcony and sat in the darkness with the seashell in her hands, gazing out at the little lights in the night and thinking of many things, a world of faces and voices welling up before her under the stars. And every so often she put the seashell to her ear and listened as Joe had done, hearing once more the soft familiar roar of the sea, the quiet murmur of waves forever caressing the worn sands of memory . . . breaking and washing smooth the sands . . . bare the shores.

Tides echoing in the turnings of the all-healing sea. As Stern had once said, the closest we ever come to the sounds of infinity. . . . Echoing now from the tiny universe in her hand, these soft tides and these ancient waves of all that was and would be. .

Bernini's bag, she thought much later, still cradling the seashell in her hands, still cherishing the shadowy whiteness of its memories against the night.

Yes, Joe's right, she thought. Bernini *would* love it if only Joe could have a chance someday to pass on those worlds he's known. Jokes and riddles and scraps of rhymes . . . rich music on the shores and tales suggesting infinity. . . . Oh yes, Bernini would love every single whisper of it, every last whisper from a beginning that never was, to an end that will never be. If only Joe could have the chance. *If only.* . . .

For of course the Colonel had said more that afternoon than she had told Joe. The Colonel had called her into his office as she was leaving and closed the door and taken her hands in his, holding them tightly, something he had never done before. And when he had quietly spoken his few words, trying to help as best he could, she had heard the sorrow in his voice and had understood what he was telling her about Joe, and about Bletchley and what would happen now.

> *. . . maybe tonight, Maud, we ought to think of something Liffy used to say. He used to say miracles happen all the time, it's just that we don't raise our eyes to look for them. Well you and I know words are easy and life never is, but Liffy knew that too and he knew it as well as anyone, but still he went on trying to look for the miracles. He always tried to see more and feel more, and so for him, miracles* did *happen all the time. They did. . . .*

In the darkness of her balcony, Maud suddenly pushed away her tears and held up her seashell to the stars, whispering.

It's yours. It's a part of you too and so is Bernini, and so is Joe. And how I wish . . .

23

Nile Echoes

An empty street corner with a single streetlamp casting a small circle of weak light. A distant clock striking the hour.

Five minutes passed.

A rickety old-fashioned delivery van came rattling out of the darkness, so old it might once have served as an ambulance in the First World War, so dilapidated it might once have been on permanent tour through the rutted back streets of greater Cairo, its bell clanging pied-piperly, its large awkward owner wistfully offering freshly cooked fish and chips at modest and movable prices.

The small van came sputtering in from the night, its cream-colored side panels recently painted to obliterate any hint of that bright green lettering that had once announced the approach of the fabled Ahmadmobile. The van shuddered and heaved to a stop in the shadows beyond the corner, near a darkened colonnade that ran the length of a block of shops. A small man, no more than a shadow himself, came ducking out of the colonnade and quickly slipped into the van beside the driver.

Bletchley nodded, keeping both hands on the steering wheel.

Evening, he said.

Evening, said Joe.

A match suddenly flared, illuminating the interior of the driver's cab. Joe lighting a cigarette.

There's no one in back, murmured Bletchley, still staring straight ahead.

I can see that, said Joe, but I was doing it more for the sake of your posse scattered up and down the street. Who in God's name do they think I am anyway? Some desperado from Tombstone out to hijack the Suez Canal? I've never seen such elaborate precautions.

Perilous times, murmured Bletchley.

And I believe it, and that's why I lit the match. So your cavalry could see I'm empty-handed and not holding a sword over your head, heaven help us. Sword of justice, I guess they'd call it in Tombstone.

Bletchley snorted noisily and threw back his head, breaking into a braying sound. . . . Bletchley's laughter, Joe reminded himself. Bletchley's infernal laughter.

What do you call that, Joe? Monastery humor?

Joe stared at him.

Well I never have before but now might be the time to start. In fact I should've thought of that when Liffy was still alive, *ho ho ho*. . . . Gallows humor, you say, Liffy? No I was referring to something much blacker than that, so black it's the very heart of blackness. I mean *Monastery* humor, Liffy, the pitiless kind. . . .

So what do you think, Bletchley? Would it sell in the Christian provinces or would good Christians like the Germans rather not hear about it? Would they rather ignore it and pretend it doesn't exist except as an aberration, yours and mine, I mean? But maybe we could get a laugh or two if we worked up a song-and-dance routine to go with it? A gaggle of jokes we could put together in the empty railway waiting rooms where we pass our lives deep in the night? Or in a concentration camp, maybe? . . . *Liffy jokes*, we could call them. Yes? No? Too black altogether for good Christians? Or only when Nazis are massacring Jews, maybe? Or only if you and I are Jews, maybe?

Bletchley was suddenly angry.

You must know none of this has turned out the way I planned.

No? Well I'm certainly glad to hear it, Bletchley. I certainly wouldn't like to think any of this had been planned. Because if it had been, it could only mean God's been off in a different part of the universe these last ten or twenty thousand years, which could only mean He doesn't spend all His time mulling over the grand sweep of human affairs on our little planet, unlike the rest of us.

We'll talk about it later, Bletchley said angrily.

He shifted gears and the van lurched forward.

They pulled up beside the Nile in the moonlight, near a small pier thrusting out into the river. It seemed to be a warehouse district, an area of deserted streets and squat windowless buildings, all of them dark. Bletchley switched off the engine and began wiping the skin around his bulky black eye patch, folding and refolding his handkerchief.

I'll just be a moment, he murmured, his face averted. Joe watched him. He shook his head.

It must be next to impossible driving with only one eye.

It is.

But how do you manage it at all?

Bletchley glanced at him, then turned away.

Like anybody else with what they have to live with. Not very well and as best I can. You just keep trying to make some sense out of the flat picture you're given, which is too flat and never enough, especially when it comes to people suddenly appearing in front of you. You can memorize a street with its buildings, but you can't memorize people. There are too many of them. And anyway, they're always changing their sizes and shapes.

Bletchley finished cleaning around his empty eye socket and put his handkerchief away. He looked at Joe, averted his gaze.

Let's step outside for a minute.

Bletchley climbed out of the van and walked a few feet on the sandy gravel. He stopped, waiting for Joe, gazing out at the Nile. Joe noticed that Bletchley had closed the door very quietly behind him. Once they were out in the night the two of them strolled forward in a natural way toward the river. They crossed onto the pier and strolled out to its end, where they stood side by side looking down at the water. Joe nudged a pebble over the edge with his foot.

You barely make a sound when you close a door. Why is that?

Bletchley stirred.

What? Oh habit, I suppose.

Joe nodded. He looked back at the dark buildings and the empty streets and whistled softly.

What's that? asked Bletchley.

Just me whistling in the dark, said Joe. This looks like the kind of place where a man might be taken to walk the plank, but of course you didn't bring me out here for that, at least I don't think so. . . . Are we going to be here for a bit, do you suppose? I'd like to sit down. I'm exhausted.

Of course.

Joe sighed wearily and sat down on the end of the pier with his legs dangling over the edge. Bletchley sat down beside him and took a flask from his pocket. He drank, swallowed, wiped the corner of his mouth with his hand. He held out the flask to Joe.

Brandy.

Thanks.

Joe took a drink, coughed, took a longer one.

Not only brandy but the real stuff for a change. Not that I'm complaining about the Arab variety, you understand. Any oasis in a sandstorm, as we bedouin say. But the real stuff does have a way of not slashing your throat on the way down. Smooth is what it is, like a trackless path in the desert. Or like a felucca coming around in the wind on a clear night on the Nile. A reassuring motion after all. See that one out there?

He drank again and handed the flask back to Bletchley, who put it down on the worn boards between them.

And it is a clear night too, said Joe. Ahmad used to find it amusing the way I mention the weather. It's always the same here, he used to say.

Bletchley stared straight ahead. Abruptly, he passed his hand over the side of his face, as if brushing something away.

I'll give you the important details first, he said.

Joe nodded, then all at once sagged forward.

Are you all right? asked Bletchley.

Yes. Exhausted, that's all. Tired deep down.

Bletchley looked at him again, quickly, a nervous motion. He spoke in a low voice.

You'll be leaving by plane tonight for England. You won't stop there. You'll be put on another plane for Canada and when you get to Canada you'll disappear. But there's a proviso.

Only to be expected, said Joe. If there weren't, we'd be in a better world. What's the proviso?

Bletchley stared straight ahead. You're dead, he said in a quiet voice. A. O. Gulbenkian is dead, which means the agent who was using that cover is dead.

Joe fumbled for a cigarette.

Forever, added Bletchley, officially and unofficially. So far as the Waterboys and the Monastery are concerned, so far as London is concerned, so far as everybody is concerned.

Joe's hands were trembling. He gripped his knees and looked down at the water.

How'd I die, did you say?

In a fire. There's been a fire.

Oh.

Bletchley reached inside his jacket and pulled out several sheets of folded paper. He handed them to Joe, who leaned over to peer at them. With the moon and the reflections off the water, there was just enough light to make out the typed words.

At the top of the first sheet of paper there was a printed heading, the name and address of a Cairo news agency. The typed copy was in the form of a news story, marked for immediate release.

A fire had broken out in the Coptic Quarter of Old Cairo, destroying a small run-down hotel, the Hotel Babylon. The fire was thought to have started in the tiny cluttered courtyard behind the hotel, where the desk clerk, neighbors reported, had recently been in the habit of sitting up late at night beside a small campfire, along with the only guest who had been staying in the hotel during recent weeks.

The courtyard had been strewn with old newspapers and other inflammable debris. It was assumed a spark had settled into the debris and caused it to smolder until after the desk clerk and his guest had retired for the night, when a fire had broken out and ignited the decaying old structure just before dawn, quickly raging out of control and burning the hotel to the ground.

Fortunately, no other buildings had been damaged due to the alarm sounded by an alert neighbor, a retired belly dancer up the street who for the last thirty years or so had risen every morning before dawn to go in search of fresh chickens, which she roasted and sold locally to support herself.

Two men had perished in the fire, the desk clerk and his solitary guest, both of whose bodies had been recovered.

The desk clerk, a longtime employee of the hotel and an astute observer of the Cairo social scene, had been known as Ahmad the Poet on his little street, itself known colloquially as the rue Clapsius, a mere shadowy byway of an alley and a short stroll to nowhere. Yet although it led nowhere, it was also the place where a good part of nineteenth-century Cairo was said to have acquired an incurable dose of nostalgia during the long lazy siesta hours of yesteryear. This desk clerk's finely tuned social sense was the result of a thoughtful scrutiny of the Cairo scene over the years, particularly on Saturday evenings, which Ahmad the Poet was known to have devoted to undisturbed meditations on the roof of the Hotel Babylon. There in the darkness he had studied the city through a spyglass, aided by melancholy surges of music conjured up on an ancient dented trombone.

It was further recalled that the poet, Ahmad *fils*, had been a fiercely loyal supporter of Ahmad *père*'s idealistic nineteenth-century political cause, *the Movement*, a loosely spun Old World organization which had fearlessly advocated social progress from the there and the then, defying all opposition, in the general direction of the here and the now.

And although Ahmad *fils* had been in seclusion for decades, maintaining his privacy over bouts of solitaire and infusions of opera, he had once enjoyed a stunning reputation as a wildly charismatic figure in Cairo society, both in his professional duties as an interior decorator and in his more unpredictable role as an all-around boulevardier and dandy.

In particular, the poet was remembered for having served as the powerful stroke, and captain, of a racing crew of Cairo dragomen who had triumphantly swamped a racing shell rivered by the British naval establishment back before the First World War, the only time that astounding feat had ever been accomplished by an all-Egyptian crew, in what had been known in those days as the Annual Battle for the Fleshpots of the Nile.

In addition, Ahmad the Poet had once been famous for having introduced the racing tricycle to Cairo, around the turn of the century.

Sadly, it was Ahmad the Poet's fondness for recalling the remarkable exploits of his past glories, in the form of old newspaper stories, that had probably caused the hotel to ignite so quickly. Reference was made to a large closet just off the hotel lobby, a small room really, which had been heaped from floor to ceiling with dusty yellowing newspapers, none of them less than thirty years out of date.

This closet had become a brilliant torch when the fire reached it, causing the hotel to consume itself instantly in a towering pillar of the purest white smoke.

Little was known about the other victim, the lone guest in the hotel at the time of the fire. Through information routinely filed on all foreigners at local police stations, he was identified as a commercial traveler of Armenian extraction, a dealer in Coptic artifacts by the name of A. O. Gulbenkian, who had worn false teeth.

There was no further mention of the commercial traveler. But it was noted that an anonymous group of public-spirited Cairenes, calling themselves the *Friends of Ahmad,* had taken up a subscription to provide their once-renowned social leader with a proper funeral and full memorial services.

The former belly dancer up the street was acting as director general, coordinator, and secretary-treasurer of this anonymous ad hoc group.

Addresses and dates were given.

Joe took a deep breath. For several minutes he sat with the sheets of paper in his lap, gazing down at the river. Finally he handed them back to Bletchley and took a roll of money out of his pocket. He found the bill he was looking for and gave it to Bletchley.

For the *Friends of Ahmad,* he said.

Bletchley looked down at the bill—one hundred Greek drachmas. He turned it over without thinking—ten thousand Albanian leks. He glanced up at Joe.

I know, said Joe, it's not much but it's all I have at the moment. And anyway, Ahmad would appreciate it. Behind that dour exterior of his, if you could find the secret panel in his wall of defenses, there was always a droll sense of humor lurking inside.

Suddenly, Joe shuddered. His voice sank to a whisper.

Was there really a second body in the ruins?

Yes.

Liffy wore false teeth.

Yes.

And no service for Gulbenkian, I suppose.

He wasn't that kind of man, said Bletchley. Gulbenkian was in transit here, just passing through. No one knew him.

No.

And if no one knew him, there can't be anyone to provide him with a service.

No, murmured Joe, it would only look strange, suspicious. He was just passing through after all.

Joe turned away from Bletchley and wiped his eyes, his head sinking lower.

Well if that's it for Gulbenkian's remains, he whispered, could you tell me what happened to that man Liffingsford-Ivy who used to work around here? A movable prop, he called himself. The local illusionist.

Bletchley stared straight ahead.

He's been reported missing while on assignment in the desert, said Bletchley. We've lost a great many of our intelligence agents like that, it's absolute chaos out there. Whole battalions just disappear. Back here, for convenience, we call it a line, a front, but it's not like that at all. Everybody's mixed up with everybody else and it's shifting all the time, a unit here and stragglers there, ours and theirs, back and forth and God knows where. There aren't even any sides out there. Just thirsty exhausted men covered with burns from their own weapons, fighting in any direction they can with no idea where they are, just men fighting desperately and going nowhere. Or wounded and dying in the terrible sun, lying where a shell or a mine went off, one of our shells or one of theirs, one of our mines or one of theirs. . . . The sand blows all night and buries everything except the burning tanks by morning, and the twisted skeletons of the other vehicles. It even covers open eyes by morning, but the one thing it can never cover is the smell, the stench. Radios sit all alone crackling, speaking to no one. . . . *This is Coventry, come in please.* . . . You can be in a place so desolate it might as well be the end of the earth and suddenly there's a whine shrieking across the sky and the ground shakes and the intolerable silence descends as you wait, as you count, *one two three. . .* . You drive over a ridge and all at once there are hands reaching out of the sand, out of nothing, hands grasping and reaching . . . just hands. Rigid hands. The fingers fallen and broken, too weak, too frail, and it's horrible. . . . It's just *horrible.*

438

I knew him, whispered Joe, hunched over and sobbing as Bletchley stared straight ahead at the river.

The felucca in the distance came around into the wind. Bletchley stirred.

Shall I finish with the details?

Yes, said Joe, I guess you'd better. . . . I'm dead. What comes after that?

Once you leave here there won't be any stopovers, as I mentioned. You'll be traveling under a temporary cover that's only good for the trip. When you get to Canada you'll disappear, and then you'll have to begin working out a new identity for yourself. A new history and a new background, everything.

Yes.

I could help you but it wouldn't be as safe as doing it on your own. And anyway, I can't imagine you'd need my help with that.

No, I'll make do.

But understand, Joe, I mean a new *real* name and a new *real* history and background to go with it. The *real* Joseph O'Sullivan Beare, born in the Aran Islands on April 15, 1900, died in a fire in Cairo in June 1942.

Joe nodded.

And so he did . . . and so he did.

Our records will show that, continued Bletchley, and that's what the report to London will say, and the reports London will send to Washington and Ottawa. The Stern case is closed and everybody who was connected with it in any knowledgeable way has been accounted for. The case is closed and there are no surviving witnesses.

Yes, I can see that.

So this has to be an absolute agreement between the two of us, Joe. No one else inside will know the truth but me, and therefore I have to be able to count on you completely. . . .

Bletchley paused.

Completely, he repeated.

Joe looked at him.

How can I assure you of that?

By telling me, said Bletchley. If you know you can do it, you'll tell me so. If you have any doubts, you'll tell me that.

Joe shook his head.

No, no doubts. I can do it and you can count on me.

All right, I will count on you then.

Joe nodded. He waited but Bletchley seemed to have finished. Let it go, thought Joe, for God's sake let it be. He's going way out of his way and doing an enormous amount to make this possible, so just let it be and don't push him. . . . But Joe couldn't let it be. He moved his legs and let his feet swing, gazing down at the water.

You said there would be . . . there are, no surviving witnesses to the Stern case. What about the Sisters?

The Sisters weren't connected to the Stern case, said Bletchley. The two of them are half as old as time and they live on the Nile and maybe they *are* the Nile, and for all I know they haven't spoken to anyone but the Sphinx in decades. And for all anybody knows they'll outlive your grandchildren and Stern's grandchildren and they'll still be around when the Sphinx is turning to dust. They knew Stern over the years, I imagine, but over the years they've known just about everybody on every side of any war, so that doesn't connect them specifically to the Stern case. Their concerns aren't the same as mine, or as yours and Stern's used to be.

Yes, whispered Joe. I can see that.

Joe hesitated. Damn, he thought. Why can't we ever let good enough alone? Why do we have this incurable need for answers?

Again Joe swung his feet, gazing down at the water.

You said no one else inside would know the truth. Does that include Maud? I wasn't sure whether you consider her inside or not.

I don't, said Bletchley. Not really, but I was going to mention that. I intend to speak to Maud privately, after you leave. I feel she has to know the truth, that you're not dead, I mean. I don't think it could work otherwise. But even so, you mustn't try to contact her or anyone else you know out here, after you get back. It has to be all or nothing, Joe, and that still holds no matter what identity you adopt for yourself and no matter how plausible it might be for the man in that new identity to get in touch with Maud in one way or another, or with anyone else. There are people who might be interested and I don't want them to have the least justification for being interested.

Private suspicions and private conjectures are one thing. But a cause for suspicion is something else.

Yes.

I'm thinking now of people who are on the inside and have access to files. People who became involved in this and shouldn't have been, or people who simply might be curious for their own reasons. I'm referring to the Major from the Waterboys whom you met, and to his superior the Colonel, and I'm also referring to Whatley. They're all professionals, and good ones, but they should be allowed to forget these incidents so they can move on to other things.

Yes, I can see that.

And I'm not being sentimental when I say Maud has to know you're alive or it wouldn't work. I feel she has to know for security reasons. Because if she didn't, I don't see how she could keep from trying to find it out somehow, and that could cause trouble. Not because of where she is in her job exactly, but because of connections she has.

Yes. I know how close she and the Major are, by the way. She told me.

I wasn't going to mention that, said Bletchley. There didn't seem to be any reason to.

There wasn't, not for you. I only mentioned it so you'd know I really do understand what it means in terms of security, and the agreement between you and me.

Joe hesitated.

This isn't your concern, I know, but what about Bernini in New York?

Bletchley shook his head. He looked out at the river and shook his head again.

I've thought about that, Joe, and I don't know what to say. Out here, tonight, New York seems very far away from the war, and Bernini isn't involved with the war and he's never going to become involved. So on the face of it there wouldn't seem to be any reason why you and Bernini . . . But damn it, look at it the other way, Joe. We have to consider everything and Harry knows about Bernini, and we don't know what might become of that, Harry and Maud, I mean, so there again, it's just too dangerous now. Your death and all the rest of it has to be absolutely secure and certain with not a shred of evidence to the contrary. After all, we're talking about something that comes before everything else. Before *everything* else. So perhaps someday, after the war's over . . . if it ever is. . . .

Bletchley shook his head, perplexed, saddened.

Anyway, I don't see what you could say to Bernini now, how you could explain anything to him. I mean . . . well forgive me, but from what I understand he's not the kind of boy, young man, who could take this in. How could he even begin to make any sense out of Monks and Waterboys in Egypt, or a mysterious houseboat on the Nile, or the Sphinx speaking to Harry on a clear night and what that means. Forgive me, Joe, but I don't see how Bernini could even begin to make any sense out of any of it.

Joe smiled.

Either that or he'd make better sense out of it than we do.

Joe?

No, it's all right. I do understand and you're right of course, and it'll be as you say. Maud will have to let him know I died in a fire. . . .

Only he won't believe it, thought Joe. Not him, not for a moment. But that's all right. The two of us will have a chance to straighten out matters someday. After the war. Someday. . . .

Bletchley glanced at his watch. He picked up the flask of brandy.

We still have a little time, he said, uncomfortable all at once, an uneasy tone in his voice.

He took a drink from the flask and passed it to Joe.

I don't know, he said, I don't know whether . . . you want to talk about any other things.

What happened, you mean?

Yes.

Well maybe just in passing. Maybe there are a couple of things.

As you like, Joe. I'll tell you what I can, and what I can't tell you, I won't.

Joe touched Bletchley on the arm and Bletchley turned away from the river to face him.

There's one thing that's been troubling me, said Joe. It has to do with Stern. I was wondering if there was any way he could have known where that hand grenade was going to go off? And when?

Deep lines appeared in Bletchley's forehead and he smiled in an arrogant manner, his good eye bulging, a twisted smirking expression.

Surprise, Joe reminded himself. Bletchley's face of surprise.

What do you mean? asked Bletchley. I don't think I understand. How could Stern have known that?

Someone might have told him, said Joe.

Who?

You.

Bletchley's one eyebrow slipped lower and the lines in his forehead disappeared. His expression became one of cunning. Devious, cruel, scheming.

Regret, Joe reminded himself. Bletchley's face of sadness and regret.

Bletchley found it so difficult to answer he almost stuttered.

. . . me?

Yes, you. You admired him and you might have done that for him. He was finished after all and he knew that, and you did, so you might have helped him out by telling him where and when. So he wouldn't have to think about it and could go on to other things, and settle his affairs in a way.

I don't understand. What affairs did he s-s-s-settle?

Oh, with Maud, say. He was with her the night before he was killed and he told her a great many things he never had before, and it was a summing up of sorts and a final parting, he made that clear enough. They sat up together by the pyramids and then he took a photograph of her at dawn. Maud robust and smiling for him on his final day, framed between the Sphinx and the pyramids, a photograph she'd always have, taken by Stern on his final day. Because he did say that, he did tell her it was the last dawn he'd ever see. And he did seem to know all right. He didn't seem to be just guessing.

Bletchley looked down at his hands, the normal one and the crippled misshapen one with its tight grafted skin.

I didn't know about that, Joe. I didn't know what he'd told Maud. But if that's what happened, then he did seem to know. You're right.

And so?

Bletchley covered his bad hand with his good one. He gripped his bad hand, holding it tightly.

You have to understand some things, Joe. Ahmad and Cohen and Liffy, those things were done. It was wrong and it shouldn't have happened, but it did. But the hand grenade in the bar . that *was* pure chance, that *was* an accident. Some soldiers were out drinking and brawling and one of them, in his drunkenness, tossed a hand grenade through an open door as a joke, a door to a poor Arab bar that none of them had ever seen before, as a joke. . . . Well I don't have to tell you how funny the world is, but no one ordered it and no one knew anything about it. The Monastery had nothing to do with it and no one else did, just the soldier who threw the grenade. No one knew anything about that bar or who was in it. No one had ever heard of it. It was all pure chance.

Bletchley gripped his bad hand more tightly, as if to hide its ugliness.

I had it looked into and I was able to have the soldiers traced. They were Australians who'd been in Crete when the island fell and somehow they managed not to be captured. They spent months hiding in the mountains and it was only this spring that they escaped from Crete, by paddling a rowboat across the Libyan Sea. There were five of them who escaped together and they were out drinking that night, having a last celebration. They'd all been reassigned and their unit was moving up to the front the next day. And it did, and of the five, two are dead and one is missing and presumed dead, and another one is wounded. . . . Their new unit took it very heavily. There was nothing much left of it after a few hours. The man who threw the hand grenade is one of those who's dead. Known dead. None of the five was over twenty.

Bletchley fell silent. He rocked, gripping his hand.

That's all, he added in a whisper. That's all. . . .

Joe looked out at the river.

And so that's how it was, he said. And what we call Stern's fate turns out to be some lads roaming in the nighttime and having a last round of fun before their own turn comes, and the playfulness was playful, but not really. And destiny's hand belongs to a twenty-year-old kid from Australia, now dead, who maybe wanted to sing *Waltzing Matilda* while marching across the sands of the Middle East the way his father did the last time around, in the last war. He didn't get much of a chance, that kid, too young by far. And will they send a medal for him to his people back home, because he survived in the mountains of Crete and escaped across the sea and was blown apart at a place called El Alamein, somewhere in the desert in his twentieth year? Will they do that for an Australian kid who had a song in mind?

I imagine, whispered Bletchley, rocking, gripping his bad hand.

Sure, said Joe. His unit took it heavily and so did he, and that's the way it works. And history has a way of dealing with its grand events not very grandly, doesn't it? Here Stern dies in a sordid little place without a conspiracy in sight, without the great powers or the lesser powers taking any notice whatsoever, and what's to mark it? What's to mark Stern's death?

Joe pushed a pebble into the river.

Nothing of course. Nothing reaching that sordid little place but the usual cries of the night, the usual meaningless cries to echo in Stern's ears at the end. Just some yells and drunken shouts and *bloody wogs* and that's it for Stern, and it's as you say. No one knew that bar and no one had any idea who was in it, and no one gave an order and no one knew anything about anything. The whole thing just a case of the night coming around again. . . . Just the night, as Stern said.

Ah well, I guess I had it figured that way, the hand grenade being chance, I mean. I just wanted to make sure I had it right. Stern always was one for knowing his particular patch of the desert, and after all these years of living in a certain way . . . Well I guess you learn to sense things, that's all, and Stern sensed the when, and as for the where, well what can you say about that bar except that it was Stern's kind of place? . . . A poor barren room with bare walls and a bare floor and all of it halfway to darkness, a desolate place and unkind, dreadfully so, but also the sort of place Stern understood. Knew that bare floor and those bare walls, he did, although they'd never been fit for living, as he said. . . . Barren, that's what. Just bare as bare and a cracked grainy mirror for a view of the kingdom and a shabby curtain as the gates to the kingdom, a sordid unkind place. And shouts outside in the darkness and laughter and scuffling and a hand grenade sailing in from nowhere, the darkness coming to meet Stern at last in a roar of blinding light. . . . *Light*. Stern gone. Yes. . . .

Joe sighed.

All right, so that's the way it was then. But what if those Australian lads hadn't staggered down that particular alley on their way to die in the desert? And what if they hadn't been quite so drunk and so playful and hadn't tossed a grenade at the bloody wogs for the fun of it? What then? Would there have been some other kind of accident for Stern before the night was out?

Bletchley shook his head, his round eye blank and bulging, empty.

No good, Joe, no good at all. That's not a question and it doesn't deserve an answer and you know it. There are no *what ifs* in this business, only *what is* and nothing else. *What if* is playing with things and you don't do that, and I don't, and Stern didn't. . . . Or are you asking me whether I would have ordered Stern killed sometime, somewhere, if it had been necessary? Well the answer to that is anytime, anywhere. And I'd have you killed and I'd kill myself for the same reason, if it were necessary. I detest the Nazis and I'd do *anything* to see them defeated.

Bletchley's eye was huge, bulging, overwhelming in its nakedness.

Do you hear me, Joe? *Anything.* I believe in life and the Nazis wear the death's-head and they *are* death. So don't play with things here. It's not a game we're in.

Joe nodded.

You're right and I deserved that. The question was out of line. I'm sorry. . . . So that barren cave of a bar and a man named Stern and a stray grenade in the night aside, some things got out of hand during the last few days, I take it? A matter of somebody, Whatley say, pursuing his righteous course in the name of God and goodness? Is that why there were those other killings?

There was a serious misunderstanding, said Bletchley. Mistakes were made but I'm in command at the Monastery, so the responsibility is mine. Nobody else's.

True enough, said Joe. It always does work that way when you're in charge, and Stern could manage that and you can, but I never could. Well, there's nothing more to say about that I guess, but do you think you could tell me what you *did* have in mind when you decided to get me over here?

Of course, that's easy enough. Some new information had turned up about Stern and it worried me.

By new information, you mean some facts having to do with Stern's Polish story?

Yes.

Can you tell me how that new information happened to turn up?

Bletchley looked at him.

No I can't. And anyway, Joe, the man who came to Cairo to find out about Stern died in a fire in the Hotel Babylon, and his interest died with him.

And so it did, said Joe. A fire decided it in the end. . . . And so this new information came your way and then what?

446

And it worried me, said Bletchley. I knew Stern wasn't well and I was afraid he was beginning to say things to those who were close to him. I didn't know what might happen and I thought someone from the outside might be able to help, someone who had known Stern in another context, from the past. So I went through his file and your name turned up.

Bletchley looked down at the river and a sad, empty expression came over his face.

If I'd told you more in the beginning it might not have turned out the way it did. But that . . . well, that's not how it was.

How it was, murmured Joe. How it was. . . .

Joe squinted, gazing out over the river.

Bletchley?

Yes.

Listen to me. Don't take so much of this on yourself. You came into this in the middle of things, just like the rest of us. Like me, like Liffy, like David and Ahmad and everybody else. You didn't start it and you did the best you could with what was in front of you, so let up on yourself a little. . . .

Joe paused.

Anyway, he added, I know who told you Stern's Polish story.

Bletchley's head jerked back and he raised his hands, stopping Joe almost pleading with him.

No names, he whispered. For God's sake, Joe, no names. We haven't spoken of this.

Joe nodded.

No, we haven't spoken of it and there'll be no names. I'm merely referring to persons unknown and to their haunting elegy that's half as old as time, an allusive recitation to the stars and a hymn as anonymous as the night. So no names, then, but I want you to know you're not alone here, because I know who told you, and I know why they told you.

Bletchley sat perfectly still, unable to look at Joe. Again Joe paused, looking out at the water. He spoke in a very quiet voice.

Yes, they loved him, and they loved him too much to see him coming apart like that. They just couldn't bear to see it happen because Stern was special for them. You could see it in his eyes, they said, and you could hear it in his laughter. . . . *Hope,* they said. For he was a man who stood by the river and saw great things, and his eyes shone at the splendor of the gift, like a hungry man brought to a great table. *Precious,* they said. *Always to be so,* they said.

But then they saw him coming apart like the world itself, and he was too precious to them to be destroyed like that, too beautiful by far, so they took his burden from him and spoke to you. . . . *We would do anything for him,* they said to me. *But there's nothing we can do for him now but weep, and so we do that . . . for Stern our son.*

Joe felt Bletchley move beside him. He looked down and saw that Bletchley had taken something out of his pocket and was holding it in his good hand, slowly turning it over and over.

That looks like an old Morse-code key, said Joe. Worn and smooth with a soft sheen to it, the way things get with a lot of handling. . . . Tell me, what happens to old Menelik's crypt now?

Nothing, said Bletchley. It will stay the way it is . . . locked. The way it was left.

Good. That's something at least.

Slowly, Bletchley turned the worn Morse-code key over and over in his good hand.

I also ought to mention, he said, that someone checked through your room before the fire. All that was found were some clothes and your small valise. The valise had a faded red wool hat in it and a khaki blanket from the Crimean War. Was there anything else?

No, that was it, said Joe. They went the way of the fire, did they?

Bletchley nodded. Joe shook his head.

That must be *Liffy's Third Law,* said Joe. I guess he didn't have time to mention it. *Only the things you care about go up in smoke.*

He took another drink from the flask and they both fell silent, gazing out at the river.

What were you thinking about just now? asked Joe.
The front. El Alamein.

448

Will it hold, the way you see it?

I hope so. In any case it has to. The tide has to turn and it has to turn now or people will lose hope.

Yes. And in the meantime, what will you be doing with that good-luck charm in your hand, do you think?

I'll carry it with me for a while, said Bletchley, and someday, if things work out that way, I'll give it to someone.

Who?

Bletchley glanced at him and looked away.

Did you know there was a child, Joe?

Whose child? What do you mean?

Eleni and Stern. Did you know they had a child?

Joe was stunned.

What? Is that true?

Yes.

Are you sure?

Yes. Stern told me about her. She's a young woman now.

Joe whistled softly.

But that's just astonishing. Who is she? Where is she? Oh my God.

She's Greek, said Bletchley. She was born in Smyrna but later on she grew up in Crete. Eleni's uncle, Sivi, had relatives in Crete. His father came from there, from a little village up in the mountains.

I know that.

Well that's where she grew up when Eleni could no longer manage. Stern took her there as a child.

Joe whistled very softly.

That's just astounding. What else do you know about her?

Very little, that's all really. It came up in an odd way about a year ago, just after Crete fell. Stern said he had an agent there who could do certain things by posing as a collaborator with the Germans. But I thought the agent, as he described her to me, was much too young to do what he had in mind. I didn't think we could trust someone like that in such a sensitive role, and that's when Stern told me she could be trusted because she was his daughter. I was as surprised as you are. Of course, she doesn't carry his name. She uses the Greek name of Sivi's relatives.

That's just amazing, said Joe.

Something crossed his mind and he thought for a moment.

Here now. Don't I recall that it was from an agent posing as a collaborator that Stern found out how Colly died in Crete? That time Stern made a special trip there, after Colly was killed?

Yes. She was the one.

Joe smiled.

What a wonder of a trickster Stern was, always another surprise yet to come. Do you realize I never even knew about Eleni until that last night we were together in the bar? And now it turns out there's a child. Absolutely astonishing, that's what. Does anybody else here know about her?

I doubt it. In fact I'm quite sure no one does. It seemed to be one thing he wanted to keep very close to himself. He asked me never to tell anyone.

Why? Did he say?

Not directly, but it was obvious it had to do with his work. That and the fact that he didn't want to endanger her in any way.

Yet she could have left Crete before it fell, said Joe, or probably even after it did. Stern could have arranged that. Why didn't he?

I had the impression she didn't want to leave.

Oh.

Joe shook his head.

And despite all the things he told me that last night, he never even hinted at this. Why, I wonder? *Why?*

For the same reasons he never told anyone else? Not even Maud?

Yes, I suppose. Still, it does seem strange. . . . But don't you know anything else about her?

No, I truly don't. He really wouldn't say much of anything, other than who she was and where she was.

Joe was silent for some moments. All at once he touched Bletchley's arm, startling him.

But Stern also asked you not to tell anyone about her. Why did you?

Bletchley moved around where he was sitting. He seemed uncomfortable.

Because you're leaving. And since no one else knows but me, and since something could always happen out here, well, I felt . . .

Bletchley's voice trailed off. He glanced at his watch.

The time's getting on. We should be starting for the airport soon.

In a moment, said Joe. I think there's something we haven't quite covered yet.

That's not so, I've told you what I can. There are certain matters . . .

I know, but I wasn't referring to certain matters. I mean something between you and me.

It's getting on, said Bletchley. We ought to . . .

Bletchley moved as if to rise but Joe put his hand on Bletchley's arm, stopping him.

It's just this. What was the *real* reason you picked my name out of Stern's file?

I told you. Because you'd known Stern well in the past, and because you cared for him, and because you seemed to have the experience and the temperament that were needed for the assignment.

Yes. Go on.

But that's all.

Joe smiled.

No it's not.

It's not?

Joe shook his head, still smiling.

No, of course it's not. That's what got put down on paper and that's what London understood, but that's not all of it.

I've told you the truth, said Bletchley, his voice defiant.

Yes, and you've always done that, and I appreciate it. It's just that you've also left things out here and there, bits and pieces along the path. And we both know that's the cleverest way to hide things, from others or from ourselves. But now that I am leaving, why don't you go on for once and say those things to yourself? Not hide them anymore? . . . So then. You studied Stern's file and chose me. Why? What's the rest of it?

Suddenly Bletchley pulled away from Joe, freeing his arm. He seemed both angry and hurt as he stared out at the river, an empty expression on his scarred face, his eye wide and bulging. When he spoke his voice was harsh with resentment.

The rest of it? . . . I don't know what you mean.

Oh yes, said Joe softly, and what does it matter here and now between the two of us? And why does it ever matter anyway? I'm leaving and what's more I'm disappearing, and I'll never be able to talk about any of this . . . so then. Why not the rest of it?

Bletchley looked confused, even frightened. His resentment was gone and his voice was little more than a whisper.

Do you mean . . . Colly?

Yes, said Joe. . . . *Colly.* I mean him.

Bletchley gripped his bad hand again, covering it.

Well I knew him. I knew him, of course. I'd worked with him.

Much?

No, not really. Just since the war started, before he was killed. And I didn't know him well the way some of the others did, the Colonel at the Waterboys, say, Harry's superior. He'd worked with Colly all through the thirties, so he knew him very well. But I wasn't around here much then, I was mostly in India. So I never really saw that much of Colly, although I'd always known about him, by reputation.

And admired him?

Well naturally. Everybody admired him. He was such a talented man and he always seemed to do things with so much dash.

And more than that, said Joe softly, you envied him, didn't you?

Bletchley glanced at Joe and looked back at the river, his eye round and empty, confused.

I suppose I did, he said in a low voice.

Joe strained forward.

Because he seemed to be everything you never could be, wasn't that it?

In a way, perhaps. But I don't see how any of this . . .

Just everything, said Joe. A hero in the last war and a grand one, a hero who survived it intact and all of a piece, in his body and his mind, without a ripped-up face and a crippled hand and maybe crippled other things. Who was so famous as a young man he could afford to go and enlist in the Imperial Camel Corps as just plain Private Gulbenkian. Who was so sure of himself and who he was he never had to worry about ranks and titles and positions, or even about his own name, just imagine that. Who could even be an A. O. Gulbenkian on camelback, anonymous to all appearances, and still be famous wherever it counted because beyond and beneath it all, no matter what name he used and what disguise he put on and no matter where he went, he would always be *Our Colly.*

That's right. Always. *The Sergeant of the Empire, Our Colly of*

452

Champagne, a legend no matter what. You remember what they used to say about him when we were young. There was just no stopping *Our Colly,* not ever. He was a class apart and a man apart and they just don't make them like that anymore, that's what they used to say. . . . *Our Colly?* He was the man who defied the law of averages a hundred times and got away with it. No man could ever do what he did, but *Our Colly* did it all the same. . . . That's what they used to say, wasn't it?

Yes, whispered Bletchley. . . . *Oh yes.*

Sure. *Oh yes* is what it was, and I remember it and so do you. But did you ever know that way back then in the beginning, when the last war started, Colly tried to enlist first in the royal marines?

No, I've never heard that, said Bletchley. Is that true?

Yes, they wouldn't take him. Undersized, Colly was, too scrawny altogether. So next he tried the navy and they wouldn't have anything to do with him either. Not only undersized but his English was still pretty limited then. *Yes. No. Thank you. Please pass the potatoes.* A stunted childhood, you see. He'd always been handy in a fishing boat as a boy, but the cold winds had kept him low to the deck and they'd also kept him from putting on any weight. Cold winds can do that. The weight goes to keeping the wind out and keeping the body halfway warm. So after that, Colly went around to the army, and they weren't about to be particular if a body was halfway warm, so they took him. One scrawny undersized kid who couldn't speak very well. That was Colly and that was how it all began for him.

I never knew that, said Bletchley.

No, most people don't. A hero's a hero, after all, and we like to have them in troubled times. So Colly managed to get into the army by lying about his age and by drinking a couple of quarts of water before they weighed him in, and then he took a big piss and went to France and did what he did there, and pretty soon he was known as *Our* Colly, everybody's, the man who could defy the law of averages and get away with it. And then later he went on to do the same kinds of things out here, on camelback, a mysterious Gulbenkian in disguise pulling off all sorts of wild tricks in Ethiopia and Palestine and Spain.

So that was Colly's way and Colly's path, the way of the *Our,* and once we talked about it in Jerusalem when I was still playing poker there, just before I left. Colly came to call and we put up our feet and talked about it. And the worst part about being an *Our*, he said, is living up to what people expect of you. You have to keep giving more and more of yourself, he said, until . . .

Not that he didn't like what he was doing, he did like it. In fact he loved it. But still . . . and yet . . . as he said. *But still. And yet.*

Sure. You remember all the things they used to say about *Our Colly* when we were young. I heard them often enough and you must have heard them in whatever hospital you were lying around in then, feeling useless with your dreams of a career in the army as shot up as you were, as shattered as the left side of your own face. And maybe you thought about Colly more than once as those next years came along and you were still lying around in hospital beds, waiting while they performed one useless operation after another and tried to get the rest of those glass and metal fragments out of your eye socket, just waiting and waiting while they reconstructed the bridge of your nose a little and kept breaking your hand and trying things a different way so you might be able to move it a little.

Waiting, you were. Waiting. Waiting and hoping they could put a glass eye in. But the bones and the muscles weren't there anymore, and the glass eye looked like a colored bead off in the side of your face somewhere, so you had to settle for an eye patch and wiping around it and being stared at.

And maybe *Our Colly* came to mind again when more years went by and you decided to settle for this, because it was the closest you could ever come to being in the regular army, which was all you'd ever wanted in life because you came from an army family and you'd grown up thinking that someday, someday, you might even have your own regiment. Maybe even the regiment your father commanded and his father before him, because it was a career and a calling that was in your blood and just a natural part of fathers and sons, a natural part of the scheme of things. . . . Nothing to wonder about. Just the way it was.

Or rather, the way it had been back then in the beginning, before it turned out otherwise. Before you went to the front as a young man and put a spyglass to your eye and a bullet shattered the spyglass and shattered your face, shattering everything in sight, all that was and all that would be, shattering every dream you ever had and leaving you with a face that terrifies children and terrifies just about everybody, if the truth be known.

The evil eye, Bletchley. Anybody would be secretly frightened by it and you know why that is. We look at you and we see something that could happen to us, that *is* us, and it terrifies us. So we try not to look at you and we try to ignore you because we're not like you after all, of course we're not, we're nothing like you.

Just consider it. Now, when there's a great war going on and everybody's killing everybody for the sake of . . . just consider the matter rationally for a moment. Children look at you and scream. Children look at you and run away. But don't the rest of us say nice things to little children? Don't we smile at them and don't they smile back? Of course, and we're not like you, we're not ugly. That's not why the whole human race is killing somebody or other. There's no evil in us. . . .

And so we like to scorn you a bit because that's the easier way. Because you're not really human, because you're not like the rest of us. Because we're not ugly, you are, and we don't want to face that face of yours. Our own face . . . adjusted a little by circumstances. . . .

Bletchley was moving around uneasily as he sat there on the end of the little pier beside Joe. He was gripping his bad hand with his good hand and staring out at the river, not sure what to make of Joe's sudden rush of words, so demanding and insistent, so unlike any side of Joe he had seen before.

Joe, I think that . . .

I know it. We have to be leaving and I'm almost finished, and I will be by the time that felucca comes around into the wind again. It's working its way up the river all right and it's due to come around, so just give it another few seconds tacking on its present course.

Joe smiled. He touched Bletchley's arm.

There's a point to all this. Could you just turn and look at me?

Slowly, Bletchley did so. Slowly, he turned and looked at Joe, who was smiling.

Good. It's just this, said Joe. You're not very different from Colly. You're not very different at all.

A peculiar expression came over Bletchley's face, disbelief followed by sadness and resignation, and then by a terrible uncertainty. He was about to say something when Joe tightened his grip on Bletchley's arm.

Wait, whispered Joe. I'm not making fun here and I'm not taking matters lightly and I'm not saying that spyglass didn't do its unkind work years ago, because it did. We both know it did. But I *knew* Colly, you have to remember that. Not only *Our* Colly but the one behind that. When we were young we worked our days together with fishing nets, and there were also long nights when we lay in bed and talked of what was to come for us, the wind howling and the rain beating down as if it would never stop, back before he became *Ours,* everybody's. Just him back then, scrawny and undersized, the way it was, that's all. And when I see what's behind that mask of yours, I know the two of you have a lot in common deep down where it counts. The little things on the surface aside.

I wear a beard so I scratch it sometimes. And you wear an eye patch so you carry on as you do sometimes. But that's on the surface of things and it's not important. Founding the *Friends of Ahmad,* as you did, that's important. And doing for Anna what I gather you're doing on the quiet, from what Maud says, that's important. And as for Liffy, well, it's not even necessary for us to talk about him. His voice will always be inside us and his sorrowing smile will always be there, and all we have to do with him is just listen, *listen,* and get to know him a little better as time goes on.

So those things are important, and maybe the most important thing of all is that worn old key you're holding in your hand. Just holding and turning it and quietly polishing it with the oils of your skin. That little thing you intend to pass on someday . . . if it works out that way.

Meant for sending messages in code. Once upon a time anyway, seemingly so. Meant for tapping out secret messages in all the codes of the race. But not so secret in the end, and not so hard to understand either. Strongbow came across it once in his travels and he took it along with him, and then Stern had it for a time, and now you do. And although its messages may seem complicated in the speaking of them, they're cryptic only at first glance, only on the face of it, for there's a flow to all of this as sure as a river flowing away to the sea. Things sensed in the heart and always known, and I'm glad you have that key now. I'm glad it's in your hand and you're keeping it and taking it with you . . . for a time. Until someday, if things work out. . . .

Joe nodded at Bletchley. He smiled and stretched, raising his hands to the sky.

So that's all I wanted to say, and there's a finish to our moment by the river and an end of sorts. That felucca out there is coming around into the wind now and we can be leaving for the airport if it's time, a few things resolved but mostly not. The Nile still doing what it's always been doing and that felucca trying to make its way as we do, and a terrible war upon the world and too many of those we love gone now, not here with us where they should be. . . . But here with us too in a way. Echoes within us, always to be so. . . . Like Colly, who came along and turned up in your heart tonight to save my life. He never knew he was going to do that, did he? But he has, and he did it just by being what he was. Because what he was got inside you a long time ago and gave a cast to your mind and your feelings over the years, and not only him but all the others who are here with us as well. Just here in the shadows in the strong quiet sounds of their being. . . . Nile shadows after all, the shadows of a world raging. But those strong quiet echoes of the river are within us too, thank God, going right on and never to be still. . . .

They stood. Joe smiled and picked up a pebble.

Three weeks I've been in Cairo, he said, just think of that. It only goes to show there's no shape to time at all but what we give it. . . .

He turned and scaled the pebble out over the water and for an instant they saw it glitter, a reflection from the river set free in the moonlight.

Neither of them spoke more than a few words on the way to the airport. Bletchley was concentrating on the driving and Joe gazed out the window trying to absorb it all, filling himself with the sights and sounds and smells he was leaving, the vastness of the desert and the even greater vastness of the desert sky.

At the airport Bletchley led Joe through a few quiet offices and then they were standing together on the runway, off by themselves under the stars. A wind had come and was blowing strongly. Bletchley handed Joe an envelope with some documents and money, and Joe put it away.

That's your plane over there, said Bletchley, pointing.

He turned to Joe and reached out, stiffly shaking Joe's hand. Then he stood with his arms hanging awkwardly by his sides, the wind fluttering his shapeless old khakis, his eye immensely large and round, waiting.

Joe laughed.

Here now, that's not going to make it at all.

What?

What, you say? Just a shake of the hand, is it, after what's gone on here?

Joe threw back his head and laughed again. He took a step forward and put his hand on Bletchley's shoulder, smiling.

Don't you *know* it yet, man? Don't you know we're on the same side in this world? And I don't mean just the British side or the Allied side with their Whatleys.

Joe leaned forward into the wind, his eyes bright, shadows darkening the deep lines in his face.

Listen to me. I mean the only side there is. And you've been in the Mediterranean long enough to know you have to press flesh when the important moments come, because it's all we have in the end, all we can ever give someone we care for. And anyway, you're not a regimental commander out in front of your troops on parade. You were never that and now you're just another anonymous member of that motley crowd known as the *Friends of Ahmad,* a scarred and tattered little band of irregulars that carries on behind the lines with nothing much in the way of success, and nothing at all in the way of dash. Just passing through, we are, in transit. So open your arms and give me a hug, man. Just give me a hug to help keep out the cold when those nights come, as they surely will. It's not much and it lasts but a moment, but on the other hand, good hand or bad, it's everything and it's all we'll ever really *know.*

Bletchley laughed and they embraced, warmly.

There that's better, said Joe. And now it is time, and as a man we both know used to say at moments like this, *God bless.* Mysterious presence that he always was, so much so I could never even figure out in the end whether he was a Moslem or a Christian or a Jew.

Curious man, really. Just large and awkward and there and no shape to him particularly, yet reassuring somehow, strangely so. And an odd smile on his face and a certain clumsiness about him sometimes, last seen in these parts as a beggar, a dignified man and poor, surveying his limitless kingdom in the deep of the night. . . . *Stern.* I

458

wonder how he ever got a name like that? Because he was always anything but that. Everything else probably, but not that.

Yes. God bless now. . . .

Joe turned and waved and began walking across the runway, a slight figure in a collarless shirt and shabby clothes that looked too big for him, his head down as he bent forward against the wind . . . a small man.

An Editorial Relationship

Many years ago when I was a young assistant editor at a New York publishing house, a stroke of fortune led me into an editorial relationship that was to last a long time, until after the writer's death. Our entanglement, like many between writers and editors, was muddied by friendship on the one hand and by the desire to publish on the other.

The relationship began when the editor-in-chief, Tom Wallace, who was leaving the house for another, handed me the file of an author named Edward P. Whittemore.

He was called Ted. He had gone to school with Tom in the 1950s, they were old buddies from Yale, and there the resemblance ended. Tom was a classic Yale type—sentimental yet incapable of expressing emotion, good-hearted and highly principled, and completely stuck in his ways. Ted, by contrast, was completely out of the loop. He defied the loop. Ted had lived all around the world, been in the CIA (in fact, nobody knew for sure if he was really *out* of the CIA), written several crazy novels that were sort of about espionage and sort of about the mammoth course of history, its large brutish atrocities and the small moments of goodness, books that were compared to Fuentes and Pynchon and Nabokov.

Tom described the books by saying they were really all about poker.

Ted was famous to about six thousand people who thought he was a genius; nobody else had ever heard of him at all. He had two marriages that hadn't worked out, and a girlfriend he was breaking up with, and a strong Maine accent. He was a recovering alcoholic who once had been the kind of drinker who wanted to crawl inside the fifth to lick it completely clean, and a chain-smoker, and he lived on the East side of town.

As it turned out, of all the places he *could* have lived in the city of New York, he lived on Third Avenue and 24th Street, while I lived on 24th Street and Sixth Avenue. This is the kind of magical coincidence that populates the novels of Edward Whittemore and it seemed strangely appropriate that our domestic routines were performed in locations that were exactly parallel, yet existed a precise and unbreachable distance apart, as though we were two matching magnets with the contrary ends facing one another.

In 1981, I was handed the manuscript of *Nile Shadows*, which was third in a projected quartet of Jerusalem novels. This quartet followed his first, and possibly his splashiest novel, *Quin's Shanghai Circus*, which we had published seven years earlier.

Ted had also written several that we did *not* publish. I was told both that Ted was a genius *and* that it was possible that the manuscript was not publishable or needed a great deal of cutting. I knew almost nothing about editing fiction; I had never worked on anything remotely this serious, which meant that I was going to have to concentrate very hard. Once I opened it and began there was no question but that this was what they call the real thing. For me, how terrifying and how thrilling.

The first time I read it slowly, almost without thinking, submitting to it, letting it sink in. The book was both domestic and fantastic, its settings shabby and arcane, and doom was everywhere. Ted understood the big and how it depended on the little. Centuries of conspiracy pivoted on a chance encounter. Friendship was everything, and utterly ephemeral. A shaft of light illuminated horror, then a sweet timeless calm, then slapstick. Words kept it going, words and talk and more talk: chatter, letters writ in stone, a scream in an emergency, a late afternoon's long slow story, a coded telegram.

The editor's job was to be inside it and yet float above it, to see where it wasn't true to its own internal logic, to love the characters and expect them to be themselves, to applaud every song—but to mark the slightly flat note—to be sure the plot had

462

all its small signals straight. The second time I read it I tried to remember every word, every gesture, every motion.

My editorial letter advised—but most of all it paid attention. It is not so much the comments made by a careful editor that help a writer revise, I think, but the simpler fact that these comments show the writer that he is being watched. He is being watched intently by someone who tells him, in as many ways as possible, that this *matters*. And so he thinks harder, he reaches in all directions – plot, character, gesture, sequence, tone, echo – and, so doing, activates the deeper and shadowed part of the brain where music and feeling are stashed. The place where stories begin.

Ted lived in a tiny apartment very high up above Third Avenue. He had a big window and a dark-floored single room, a small kitchen—the refrigerator contained only a pint container of milk and a plastic tub of tofu—and a bathroom with a towel. In his room were a double bed, a desk, a writing chair, a second chair, a television, and an ashtray. Just the setting for a former spy.

I went over there on my way home from the office several times, to drop off the edited manuscript, to look at his changes, to explain the copy editing. I gave Ted more personal attention because the novel demanded it, and also, although without saying a word, somehow Ted expected it. The desk was occupied by his typewriter and a few completely neat stacks of typing paper and previous drafts, so instead of interrupting his work space, I laid the box of manuscript on the bed, cracking it open and leafing through the pages, tracing the progress of one detail or another, the intricate traces of his threads. We bent over the manuscript together.

The revisions took place in the winter, so when I stopped by it was always dark out. I was working long hours, partly to get over a disappointment with a man that had happened at the time; work was a secure place for me in the middle of this unhappiness. One night it snowed and we went to the window to marvel. The snow flew in specks outside the window, tiny furry points of light in the darkness, cold dusty sisters to the lights flickering on Third Avenue below and the many apartments winking on the other side of the canyon. We stood next to the glass and watched the snow swirl, high in the heavens of New York, so far away, it seemed, from the rest of my life.

As we stood there looking at the snow in that night sky, that winter night in New York, Ted Whittemore, quite unexpectedly, ran his hand lightly down my back. Tentatively. I did not move, and he did not touch me a second time.

We went back to being an editor and a writer.

Ted left the country after the manuscript went through copy-editing, but before we published the book. He took a freighter to Jerusalem. Ted said that it was a bad idea to fly to the Middle East, because you were traveling through so much time that it should take a long time to make the journey. Also a freighter was cheaper than flying, and Ted never had any money.

He read his galleys in Jerusalem, where he lived in an apartment in the courtyard of the Ethiopian Church. In the early mornings, on one side of the courtyard wall, a flock of French Nuns sang their devotions. All day, around the circular Ethiopian Church, a school of monks walked and murmured their prayers. And Ted read his galleys in July and we published in the Fall.

When I pitched the book at sales conference, I got applause, which usually doesn't happen at a sales conference, certainly not for a novel that will advance fewer than seven thousand copies. But the sales reps, those cynical hard eggs, put their hands together, not so much for my performance as for what Ted meant to the house as a whole. His books were the books we published that proved to us that publishing could be about good writing and fearless imagination and vision.

Before he moved from New York, Ted sent me a note. "I'm glad you're part of the Quartet," he wrote. And so I became connected to Ted Whittemore, connected forever.

*

The book, as it turned out, did not sell well. It had some good reviews, but the machine of publishing did not kick in for Whittemore. The reps applauded at sales conference, but the machine did not kick in.

Great fiction is hard to sell. What happens to a person who reads a book—if it's any good—is a profoundly private and irrational process, and the more distinctive the novel, the more private and irrational the process. That's where the trouble with publishing begins.

*

Two and a half years later, I left the industry. I was frustrated by the limitations of the business end and I had fallen in love, this time, I thought, for keeps, to a man who lived in Western Massachusetts who had three kids and joint custody and who was very persuasive. Love to me was more important than work, so I moved to Massachusetts and married. But I discovered that I was not as nice, not as accommodating, as I had thought I was. Even though I had always believed that I was able to make anything succeed if I just worked hard enough at it, I was not able to respond to my husband's demands, and he was very far from being able to help me mend my unhappiness. We were soon miserable.

After two years we divorced. Although the marriage had been horrible, still divorce was like suddenly falling into nothing.

The summer after, I got a call from Ted. I had heard from him from time to time. He had heard about my romance and my departure from New York, and now he'd heard about my divorce.

At my end, over the years, I'd also had reports of Ted back from Tom, who visited Ted in Jerusalem. Ted was with a wonderful woman, a painter named Helen, Tom reported. A year or two after that news, Tom told me that Ted had broken up with Helen, abruptly. Without so much as a day's notice, said Tom, Ted had packed up and left Helen and left Jerusalem. Tom said Helen was heart-broken. Tom disapproved and so did I.

Although I disapproved I was still glad to hear Ted's voice. He was back in the country and writing, up at the family home in Dorset, Vermont for the season. Would I come up to see him?

I did, twice. Dorset is beautiful in the summer, green and leafy and a good ten degrees cooler than Western Massachusetts. Ted showed me everything and how much he loved it and how much he wanted me to love it, too. We talked a little about the book he was working on, but mostly we didn't. The Whittemore family home was big and rambling; late afternoon we sat on white Adirondack chairs on the great lawn, sloping into a meadow, and watched the young girls from the dancing school down the road mince like birds into the middle of town, to buy their sweets. Beyond, the mountains misted with blue, and flowers of all shapes and colors and sizes waved in the breeze.

We swam in the Dorset Quarry. The Dorset Quarry is a writer's dream, because when you swim in the Dorset Quarry you are swimming in the space left by the stone that now is the New York Public Library, the great lion library at 42nd Street. The quarry's stone walls rise high and flat, gray streaked with white. Boys in baggy bathing suits jump off the high walls screaming. Women paddle quietly. Children sit on low ledges and dip in their feet. At the far end is an island of stone; birch trees rise skinny and white from its nooks.

After we had spent some time in the water, Ted got out, but I stayed in. He threw me my swimming goggles and I went exploring around the shallower end of the quarry. Looking for what kind of gunk grew down there, where the New York Public Library used to be.

I saw something green. I went to the surface, got a big gasp of air, dove down and swam, down and down and down. I reached for the green and headed back up.

It was a twenty-dollar bill. I swam over to Ted and gave it to him. We were both amazed. "Are you coming out?" he asked.

"In a little," I replied. I went back to see what else was down there. Again, I took a big gasp of air, dove down and swam, down and down and down. Something green. I grabbed it and headed back up.

"Ted," I said. I waved the bill. Ten dollars.

The next time down, I found a five. And that was it. I looked, but nothing else was down there. I shook the water out of my hair and we spent the money on dinner.

It was not surprising to me that magic like this would happen around Ted. It seemed almost predictable. Ted Whittemore was a magician, not only of words, but of moments. He marveled, and any sensation, of light or sound or character or scent, was ratcheted up another notch. We walked past swaying meadows and through the graveyard where all the Whittemores are buried. We drove down roads, looked at the cows, stopped the car near a stream and took off our shoes and hopped from rock to rock and stood in the running water, listening to the leaves rustle and the water bubble, smelling the good air.

Ted put his arms around me and kissed me. I kissed him back, but then I said no.

He could not imagine why I would not grasp this good thing. He could see it so clearly, something between the two of us, he could see it and he wanted it. *The world is full of possibilities*, he said. I could see it, too, when he talked about it, because Ted always made me see whatever he saw, but I still said no.

I came back, however, the next weekend, and I told him I would sleep with him, but only one time, and then it would be over and he had to understand that this was the only way it would happen.

I told myself this was because I was a woman who recently had been hurt, and that Ted was, after all, the man who had left Helen, but my true motives weren't so attractive. Ted's proposal appealed to me a lot—I had a particular weakness for writers (the man who had broken my heart that long-ago winter and the ex-husband were both writers)—but I had no intention of getting tangled up with Whittemore. Like a spoiled child, I wanted to play out this flattering scenario but without accepting responsibility for what would follow. Crazily enough, Ted agreed to my counter-proposition, and so, only once it was.

Afterwards, back in Massachusetts, I spoke to Ted occasionally, but finally, I stopped returning his calls, his persistent, baffled, loving, persuasive, tempting calls.

*

That was 1988. In February of 1994, I was planning on visiting friends in New York (from Washington, DC, where I had moved four years earlier), and so I called Tom Wallace to see if he wanted to have lunch. Tom had become a literary agent, but he was the same Tom, solid as a rock. He gave you a sense that the important things still mattered and that history counted for something. It was a good thing I had called.

"By the way," he said, "I meant to phone you and ask—have you talked to Ted Whittemore lately? You might want to give him a ring. He's back in New York. Ted's had some tough times, I'm afraid, and now there's bad news. He's very sick."

Ted had been diagnosed with a very lethal, inoperable prostate cancer. He was working on a new book and living with a woman named Annie, who had a brownstone on the upper West side, right off the park in the 90's.

Whittemore was completely happy to hear my voice. Yes, he was well; how was I doing? We arranged to meet at Tom's office at 2:30 on Friday, if I could manage to get Tom back by then. We agreed that Tom could talk a person's ear off and lunch was bound to go on forever.

I hadn't seen Ted for so long. Tom's receptionist buzzed him in and he walked into the reception area and took off his knit cap, holding it in both hands, twisting it slightly. His face was puffier than before, but his smile was the same, a smile of such colossal affection that I practically fell down looking at him. He turned his head slightly to the side when he smiled, and the edges of his thin, wide mouth turned up in delighted mystification and complete charm.

He put out his arms; I fell into them. We hugged, hard.

It was snowy and cold. Ted and I walked through Central Park, ice crunching beneath our feet, the same way we had walked down the dusty roads of Vermont, talking, talking, talking. We stopped at a food stand for tea and sat on a patio, in a corner protected from the wind, looking out across an oval frozen pond. Although his attention seemed to be entirely on the beauty of the day, the moment, and the happiness of being together again, Ted still managed to read the notes and overhear the conversation of the man sitting next to him. Once a spook, always a spook. As we headed up the hill away from the tea shop, he told me the man had been writing poetry. Bad poetry, he said, but not as bad as it might be.

That first long walk, he never mentioned his illness. I saw him again the next afternoon and we walked in the blistering cold wind over by the Hudson. He still didn't talk about it. We just walked, often with our arms around one another, to be close and to keep from slipping on the ice, trooping down the streets that became Ted's because of what he saw. "See that fellow at the corner, in front of the shop?" he'd say, giving a friendly salute to a rangy, beaten-up, leather-faced man. "Been here for years. Turkish, you know." And then he'd explain how the junk in the guy's store told you everything you needed to know to understand some invasion in the seventeenth century, and it would all make perfect sense.

He didn't talk about his illness, but we did agree that I would read his novel when it was done. He was very pleased. And so we fell back into the role of editor and writer, but of course we were something else, too, after all of this time. Time makes friendship in a way that no single action possibly can. That, after all, is what Ted's novels are about—time, friendship, and history, the real history.

At one point, but only once, Ted asked me about the events in Dorset, and afterwards, and how I had stopped being in touch. I didn't have much to say about it.

"Bad timing," I said. He nodded.

That summer Ted and Annie went to Italy, and I saw Ted again in the Fall. I had dinner with him and Annie, but before, he and I took a walk. That's when he told me.

He sat me down on a park bench, over by the wading pool where children sail their boats. It was November and getting cold. We were warm enough, though, in hats and scarves and gloves. He had something to tell me, and spoke very clearly and simply and straight. He had cancer and it could not be cured or permanently halted. He was in remission thanks to heavy doses of hormones; they had left him impotent, but that was better than being dead.

"The trouble is, that I can go out of remission at any time," Ted told me. "And the docs say that if that happens, I can go in as fast as three weeks." He paused. "It changes how you view things. Some things, like politics and what's in the newspaper, become utterly unimportant. And things like friends, family, especially friends, become the most important things in the world."

Ted looked at me. He reached for my hand, and held it fast. "So you see, having you come back into my life, now, all of a sudden, well it couldn't make me happier."

I wrapped myself around him. My arms and also one leg hooked over his lap – actually we probably looked fairly ludicrous there on the bench—but it was a moment where it didn't matter how we looked or what we were doing with our bodies. Ted held on tight. Nothing could change what was, the bad or the good. I said I loved him and then we said no more, just held on.

As we walked back to the house, and Annie, and dinner, we talked. He wanted very much to finish the draft of the novel, the last book he would ever write. I wanted very much to read it.

*

When Ted was still in remission, it seemed to me there were some things going on that were suspicious. Ted had always had a bad back, but it had gotten worse, why he wasn't sure. My assumption was that this was the cancer, he just didn't want to dignify it with the name. That would be giving it too much ground.

I called him one Sunday, from my apartment in Washington. Annie said he was out and she didn't know why he hadn't returned. Several hours later, Ted called and told me the story.

"The most amazing thing happened," he said.

He had gone to a hotel to meet a man who was going to do his taxes; the place was way over west on 58th Street, practically in the river. He walked down the hall to meet the man and heard some music coming out from behind a door; the hotel rented larger halls as well as rooms for people who had business to transact. After getting the tax stuff taken care of, he passed by the door again.

This time it was open. And he could hear the music more clearly. It was gospel. There was plenty of gospel, Ted had explained to me, in the book he was working on, but he had never actually been to a live service. A woman standing by the door saw his interest, and pulled him in. He sat in the rear.

"The music was wonderful," he said, "just what I'd imagined. So full of feeling and passion and emotion and all the good things of being human. The sound just rolled over me. Everyone was singing and the sound was immense." It went on for a long time, and then there was quiet. A small woman came to the front of the room Several people stood up, in no apparent pattern.

Ted's back was hurting him, so he stood up, too.

He hadn't understood. All of the people who had stood up were brought to the front of the room.

The woman prayed over them. She prayed for strength and health. Calls of reassurance and encouragement came from all corners of the room. She prayed in front of Ted. And then she knocked him down.

"I could see what was going to happen, because it happened with the other people," Ted told me. "She stood in front of you, and behind you stood this immense black guy, and she knocked you down, and you had to fall right back. Where the man would catch you. You had to trust her, you see. You had to *let yourself go*, just completely."

"And did you?" I asked.

"I did," said Ted. "I can't tell you how marvelous I feel."

*

Ted finished the novel in March 1995. I was working for the federal government at the time. It arrived in my office on Monday and I took the day off on Thursday and edited it and had it back to him on Saturday.

"Don't rush," he had said, wanting not to inconvenience me. "Take your time."

But I knew we had no time. I read it once, all the way through. I could see the shape. The first time through, I began to understand who the people were. I read it again, slowly, and edited it, page by page, I listened to its sounds, word by word.

I was not young, not then. I was no longer a confused and anxious assistant editor at a New York publishing house. I was no longer a damaged woman who did not know her own heart. I had no questions about who Ted Whittemore was to me; I understood in many ways what was important about his work. I concentrated.

This book was not about espionage. It was about a healer. Ted began the book three months before he got his diagnosis, but still the book was about a healer. And, also, for the first time,

Whittemore's main character was female. Her name was Sister Sally and she was unlike any of his other characters; the man with whom she has a brief love affair, Billy the Kid, however, resembled characters in the earlier books and also resembled Ted.

I wrote that I was going to push him very hard. "I think you have a bit further to travel with Sally and Billy. So let's go." I started by telling him that I didn't think the verb in his first sentence was in the right tense. This was a brutal and ridiculous way to start an editorial letter, but I had no choice. I had to be thorough. I told my dear friend what my thoughts were as I read. I tried to remember where everything was and to see when things worked together and when they did not. I commented, I queried words, I flirted with him, I reminded him of old successes and other moments we'd both loved in other Whittemore books, I cheered, I wondered out loud about the characters so he would see how they appeared to someone else, I suggested, I doubted, I applauded, I reflected, I pushed and pushed and pushed.

Ted told me the letter was helpful. Very helpful. He was excited about getting back to work. I sent a copy of the editorial letter to Tom, who had become Ted's agent. Tom called me up. He thought my comments were good.

And, in his old-fashioned manner, Tom said, "You know, the letter you wrote—it's a *love* letter, in a way."

A real writer puts his heart and soul and all his intelligence on the page. Any book can be the last one. Every one of the writer's words, every small motive, counts. The editor must attend as though *nothing* else matters.

*

Ted went out of remission a few weeks after he completed the draft. Although his levels of pain increased and increased in the weeks and months that followed, he was able to do some revisions.

I told him that his revisions were more than I could have hoped for. I came to New York from Washington several times, working on the pages and leaving notes with him, telling him every doubt, but most of all I told him how wonderful the book was, and how each revision made me more convinced that the book was complete and perfect inside of him and our only task was to ask the right questions and bring it all to light.

I called Ted every other day, sometimes every day, until that became too difficult. He told me things about himself, so that in those last months I was allowed to understand more about him and how he'd lived his life.

Combined with my love for Ted was a certain brutality which I tried to keep in check. I tried not to push him too hard. I tried not to let my disappointment show on the phone when he said he was just too tired from the pain, too sick from the drugs, to be able to write.

There was one section in the book that I really wanted him to revise. It was the scene where Sally and Billy fall in love. The woman in this novel was nothing like the women he'd written about before, who quite frankly had always struck me as a little pale. Sally was a real powerhouse, a force, a tragic mess. One day he called me at the office and told me he'd spent three hours writing the day before, and he felt like hell but he'd revised that scene, which was central to the love story, the scene I was sure he had inside him. He told me—but I did not see the pages. I did not see the fix.

Of course, it is dangerous when an editor has a favorite fix. It's not your book.

Because there was so little time, however, I let myself want it. In part, I just wanted what I wanted, and used the drama of death to cover up my presumptuousness and greed—but in part, I felt unconsciously that my desire for the fix would encourage Ted to fight harder, to slow down the illness for the sake of the writing.

Underneath this I must have believed that writing was more important to Ted than everything else, that he had no more powerful motive for staying alive. Was I crazy?

Meanwhile, he was in and out of the hospital. Annie left to go to Italy, alone, to get some time away from cancer, on a holiday Ted told her she needed to take. Carol came to take care of Ted.

Years back, Carol had been with Ted, longer than anyone else. She had ridden motorcycles all around Crete with Ted. She had been with him the day when, discouraged about ever writing anything worthwhile, he spotted a scarab in a dusty British glass case in the British Museum and the whole idea of the Quartet was born. Carol showed up when things took a turn for the worse. From early until late, she moved hospital beds and nurses in and out of Annie's house, not sleeping much if at all.

One night, when I hadn't been able to talk to Ted for ten days—I had been out of the country—I called him from my younger brother's house, where I was visiting.

Ted told me that he felt, suddenly, he had enough energy to really finish the book. Carol would read it, too, and Ted would mark places to cut, which I would then execute, leaving him the time to write the revisions he wanted to do.

My brother came into his bedroom where I was using the phone. So did my sister-in-law, so I moved out to the unfinished porch out their bedroom, carrying the portable phone, which was taped together with gaffer's tape from the results of abuse by children. As my brother and his wife lay together, sleeping, preparing for another day of work and family, I stood on the deck in the black night and schemed with Ted.

"Yes," I said. "Yes you can do it. Yes," I said. "We've had some great breaks already. You finished the draft before you went out of remission. Remember? Now we have another big break."

The night was wide. "This is what you can fix," I said. "With the time left. I'll come to New York. We'll talk about the cuts."

"Isn't it marvelous," said Ted to Carol, "that just when we need her, just like magic, Miss Judy appears. I hadn't heard from her. Wondered where she was. And here she appears. Stage Left. Enter Miss Judy."

"Yes," agreed Carol, wanly. "It's a good sign." I could hear the humoring in her tone, although I did not know, I could not see what she could see.

Instead, I egged him on. One more piece of luck, I said. One more good break. When so much has gone badly, one more piece of good luck. It's a wonder I didn't ask him to sit down at the desk then and there and write me a scene.

I never knew whether I was important to him for anything but the books. And I never knew if he would have been important to me if it weren't for the books. That was where we connected.

Ted had his own brutality. He had his ambition, which resulted in modest living and ruthlessness. He told me once that women were simply more generous than men, that they were better people, and although I never doubted that Ted had deeply loved the women in his life, and made them feel deeply loved, I wondered if that was an excuse for his bad behavior. He had two daughters, who didn't speak to him for years, although they visited him during his final illness. He said he had been a very bad husband, and a very selfish man. He knew what he was and he knew that as a result of how he had behaved, he had lost his daughters. But he had written his books. Ted had two granddaughters; one is named after his sister, as though his family got his children, but he didn't.

*

Six days after I returned from my brother's house to Washington, at 6:20 on a Sunday morning, my phone rang.

"Judy. It's Ted. Listen," he said, speaking urgently, "I'm in terrible trouble and you have to help me."

"Okay," I said. "Tell me what's wrong."

"I don't know where I am. And you have to come and find me."

"Of course," I replied. I paused.

Ted didn't know where he was, but I knew. He was lying in a hospital bed in his bedroom. He was too sick to be anywhere else. He was there, he just didn't know he was there. So I had to get him to bring himself back.

Suddenly my bedroom seemed very big and empty and the telephone cord a slender tie to the voice at the other end.

"Can you tell me where you *might* be, Ted?" I asked. "Can you tell me where you think you are?"

"Certainly," said Ted, practical, sure of himself. "I seem to be somewhere near Annie's. So you can start looking there."

We talked for a while, and got into a conversation about other things that were going on where he was. Some things confused him, like the workmen who were lifting big sections of pipe onto the roof of a nearby building (they might have been there or might not have been there). When we talked about it, he thought of some reasons why they were there and seemed to grow easier in his mind. And so we said goodbye.

One or two minutes later, the phone rang again.

"Judy, it's Ted." He seemed in a hurry. Or anxious. It was hard to tell.

"I just looked at the clock. It's six thirty in the morning. You must think I'm crazy." He sounded a little frightened.

"No," I answered honestly. "I don't think you're crazy. I just think you're on a lot of drugs, Ted. You're probably on a lot of morphine. That can mess you up. Besides," I added, looking out at the pale summer morning sky, "it's already light here. You probably looked out the window and saw how light it was and figured it was okay to call. Is it light where you are?"

Ted was reassured, and again we talked for a few minutes before he became tired and distracted. I couldn't go back to sleep after we hung up the phone, so I made some coffee and tried to read the Sunday papers. But he was much on my mind.

That evening, I came home around nine thirty or ten from a family picnic at the house of one of my older brothers, in Baltimore. I was afraid for the blinking light on my answering machine. My machine tells callers to wait for the famous beep. Ted had waited and left this message. I listened.

"Judy. It's *Ted.*" He spoke very fast, slurring one or two words. "Calling on your famous number that you can't make a call since you're waiting for my beep.

"Judy. I've got some great news from you today. For you today. With you today. And the news is: is that I'm no longer *mad!* And don't you think that it would be nice to know that Ted Whittemore is no longer *mad?* Wouldn't that be fun! I hope it would be! Nice for a change anyway.

"Your number is still the change. Change. Still hasn't changed. My number hasn't either. What changed is that I'm no longer crazy!

"So listen. If you could call me sometime. At that number you know *all* about. And we could talk on *that* number.

"There are a lot of things . . . that are going to become clear – which never were!"

At this moment, Ted's voice, rising in excitement and joy, is abruptly cut off As though he simply went *spinning* off the face of the world. I think I knew then that I would never talk to him again, never hear his voice again.

Of course he did not go, spinning. It was not that simple, that easy, or that much fun. He continued for another month, increasingly disoriented, consumed by pain, pumped with drugs. He soon had nurses around the clock at home, he went in and out of the hospital, and finally went into a hospice. Several years earlier, I had helped to care for someone through the end of a terminal illness, so when my phone calls to New York were not returned by family and by the two women who, at different times, had shared his life and now had the honor and burden of seeing him through his final passage, I knew what this meant. They had too much on their hands to bother calling back concerned but peripheral friends. They were doing the hard work, and the least I could do was stay out of the way.

When it was all over, I knew, I would be handed the manuscript, for Tom was one of the literary executors and he would vouch for me. I would see if Ted had revised that love scene. I would make sure that all the changes in his hand were faithfully entered. I would see if any of the cuts we'd discussed were possible, but be cautious in my acts, just cleaning things up.

Then I would pass the pages to Tom and he would try to sell the story. Tom, however, never was able to make that sale. The novel felt unfinished.

*

The family held a memorial service in Dorset on August 12th. I flew to Hartford, rented a car, and drove north.

The day alternated between brilliant sun and showers. Dorset, in rain or shine, was as beautiful as ever. Tom spoke at the service. He said that Ted had *compartmentalized* his life, that different parts of Ted's life didn't touch. The parts that were represented in Dorset—his family, his true and good friends from Yale, who had supported him during his illness, who spoke of the powerful love they had felt from Ted during that time—were strangers to me.

After the service we were all invited back to the house. It had been renovated, but some parts of it were as I remembered. It was strange to stand there and see those same rooms. Time passed and the house emptied of visitors. Even the family disappeared, for a family meeting that may or may not have had to do with Ted; maybe they were burying him in the old graveyard with the other family members. The house was empty, except for a woman who went from room to room, clearing away food and drink.

I sat in a rocker on the back veranda and had a glass of wine. The rain came and went, yet again, spattering the tall meadow grasses behind the house. And then the sun shone bright. I took my empty glass to the kitchen and then I went to an upstairs bathroom, put on my bathing suit, and headed to the Dorset Quarry.

It was as ever. Young men went screaming over the high cliffs, cannon balling into the water. Two women paddled at the shallower end, near where I had found all the money. Children dabbled their feet, sitting on the ledge.

The water was cool. The birches tossed their leafy arms in the sky. Life contains these perfect afternoons. I swam from one end of the quarry to the other. And then I put on my goggles and dove down, deep.

The rain had left the depths murky, however, so there was nothing I could see.

Judy Karasik
Silver Spring, Maryland and Vitolini, Italy, 2002

478

Edward Whittemore (1933-1995) attended Yale University before serving as a Marine officer in Japan and spending ten years as a CIA operative in the Far East, Europe, and the Middle East. Among his other occupations, he managed a newspaper in Greece, was employed by a shoe company in Italy, and worked in New York City's narcotics control office during the Lindsay administration.